Diary of a Lonely Girl, or
The Battle against Free Love

Judaic Traditions in Literature, Music, and Art
Harold Bloom and Ken Frieden, *Series Editors*

Cover art for Miriam Karpilove's *Diary of a Lonely Girl,
or The Battle against Free Love*, published in book form
by S. Kantrowitz in 1918.

DIARY OF A LONELY GIRL,
OR THE BATTLE AGAINST FREE LOVE

MIRIAM KARPILOVE

*Translated from the Yiddish and with
an Introduction by Jessica Kirzane*

Syracuse University Press

The support of the AJS Women's Caucus is gratefully acknowledged.

This book was originally published in Yiddish as *Tage-bukh fun a elende meydel oder der kampf gegen fraye liebe* (New York: S. Kantrowitz, 1918).

For a listing of books published and distributed by Syracuse University Press, visit https://press.syr.edu.

ISBN: 978-0-8156-1116-5 (paperback)   978-0-8156-5490-2 (e-book)

Library of Congress Cataloging-in-Publication Data
Names: Karpilove, Miriam, 1888–1956, author. | Kirzane, Jessica, translator, writer of
    introduction.
Title: Diary of a lonely girl, or the battle against free love / Miriam Karpilove, translated from the
    Yiddish and with an introduction by Jessica Kirzane.
Other titles: Tagebukh fun a elende meydl, oder der kampf gegen fraye liebe. English
Description: First edition. | Syracuse, New York : Syracuse University Press, 2020. | Series: Judaic
    traditions in literature, music, and art | Harold Bloom and Ken Frieden, Series Editors | A
    Yiddish Book Center Translation. | Summary: "Karpilove's Diary of a Lonely Girl was first
    published serially in the Yiddish daily "di Varhayt" in 1916–1918 and appeared in book form in
    1918. The novel, told from the perspective of a diarist writing about her own love life, offers
    a raw personal criticism of radical leftist immigrant youth culture in early twentieth century
    New York. It boldly discusses issues of consent, body autonomy, women's empowerment and
    disempowerment around sexuality, courtship and politics"— Provided by publisher.
Identifiers: LCCN 2019042333 (print) | LCCN 2019042334 (ebook) | ISBN 9780815611165
    (paperback) | ISBN 9780815654902 (epub)
Subjects: LCSH: Jewish women—New York (State)—New York—Fiction. | Immigrant youth—
    New York (State)—New York—Conduct of life—Fiction. | Free love—New York (State)—
    New York—Fiction.
Classification: LCC PJ5129.K3 T3413 2020 (print) | LCC PJ5129.K3 (ebook) |
    DDC 839/.133—dc23
LC record available at https://lccn.loc.gov/2019042333
LC ebook record available at https://lccn.loc.gov/2019042334

Manufactured in the United States of America

I dedicate this translation to Daniel Kirzane, who keeps me from being a lonely girl. If love is a battlefield, you are my comrade in arms. I also dedicate it to Jeremiah and Esther, who I hope will grow up to be as funny as Karpilove's narrator, but much happier.

Contents

Acknowledgments

A few weeks before I submitted this manuscript, through some clever sleuthing and with Corbin Allardice's help going through Miriam Karpilove's papers, I found myself talking on the phone with Miriam Karpilove's great-niece, Kate Karpilow, and her nephew, David Karpilow, and emailing with her great-niece, Miriam Karpilow (named for the author of this book). I was so delighted to find her family, to talk with them about her work and mine, and to hear their memories and family stories of their aunt. Hearing David talk about his aunt—who lived with her brother in Bridgeport—making him French toast and regaling him with stories of her adventurous life brought her to life for me beyond the world of this novel I've come to know so well. I was moved to tears when, several days after my phone call with David, I received a package in the mail containing photographs of Miriam that David had entrusted to me. What a blessing to see so many images of Miriam, glamorous, studious, confident, and beautiful, looking out at me from picture postcards. Thank you.

I am grateful to the Yiddish Book Center for supporting this translation through the 2017 Translation Fellowship, and to the instructors from the fellowship, whose criticism and encouragement greatly improved this translation. Many thanks to my translation mentors, Ken Frieden and Corine Tachtiris, for their expert advice and gentle criticism, and to Eitan Kensky and Sebastian Schulman for believing in and supporting the project. The enthusiasm and helpful feedback this manuscript received from my cohort of translation fellows at the Yiddish Book Center, as well as the supportive community we shared, was immeasurably helpful: Ze'ev Duckworth, Saul Hankin, Jordan Finkin, Allison Schachter, Beata Kasiarz, Anastasiya Lyubas, James Nadel, Sean Sidky, Andrew Sunshine, and Rachel Field—thank you all. I'd also like to thank Ayelet Brinn, who shares my love for Yiddish newspapers and generously offered to peek into Karpilove's archives for me. Thanks also to Ellen Cassedy for her advice and support, and to Asya Schulman, Rose Waldman, Daniel Kennedy, Sholem Berger, Joel Berkowitz, Yelena Shmuelenson, and Judith Thissen for their help with sticky translation issues. I owe enormous, heartfelt gratitude to Allison Shachter, whose encouragement has meant so much to me at every stage of this project, and who taught a draft version of this translation and attested to its teachability. I can't wait to add it to my own syllabi. I am also blessed to be a part of the Yiddish Book Group of Oak Park, Illinois, who, even before I met them, were the ideal readers I had in mind for this book. Their careful copyediting and lively discussion of my manuscript was extraordinarily helpful and brought me joy.

I am also indebted to the editors at *In geveb: A Journal of Yiddish Studies*, specifically Madeleine Cohen and Saul Noam Zaritt, who published my earliest translations of the first chapters of this novel before I had even decided to translate it in full. Excerpts of this translation have previously appeared in *In geveb: A Journal of Yiddish Studies*, *Queen Mob's Teahouse*, and *Your Impossible Voice*.

I am grateful to the peer reviewers of this manuscript for their helpful advice, and to Deborah Manion and the production team at Syracuse University Press for guiding this work to publication. I presented an early version of the introduction to this book at the 2017 Association for Jewish Studies conference, and I am grateful to the Hadassah-Brandeis Institute for awarding me the Rosalie Katchen Travel Grant that made it possible for me to attend. The 2018 Cashmere Subvention Grant, awarded by the Association for Jewish Studies Women's Caucus, helped defray some of the costs of publishing. I am grateful to the selection committee for their faith in this project.

I would be remiss if I did not also thank the many teachers who, over the years, helped me to learn and love Yiddish language and literature, especially my PhD advisor, Jeremy Dauber. I am also grateful to my colleagues at the University of Chicago, who have received me so warmly into their scholarly community, including but not limited to David Wellbery, Catherine Baumann, Eric Santner, Anna Elena Torres, Na'ama Rokem, Sophie Salvo, Arthur Salvo, Matthew Johnson, and Nicole Burgoyne. I am also wholeheartedly indebted to my friends and colleagues at *In geveb*—Madeleine Cohen, Daniel Kennedy, Diana Clarke, Miranda Cooper, Saul Noam Zaritt, Sunny Yudkoff, Jonah Lubin, Eitan Kensky, LeiAnna Xenia Hamel, and Cassandra Euphrat Weston—for expanding the horizons of my Yiddish world, for believing in the work we do together, for all the times we've laughed together over Google Hangouts, and for their support of this project. And, of course, thanks to my parents, Sam and Debbie Kirzner, and my sister, Rebecca Kirzner, for encouraging my love of reading, believing in me, and never trying to dissuade me from pursuing an unconventional and deeply rewarding passion and career built around little-known Yiddish writers.

I especially want to thank Sonia Gollance, Rachel Beth Gross, and Daniel Kirzane for reading drafts of this manuscript and for enthusing with me over juicy bits of dialogue. When I think back on the translation process for this book, I think I will cherish most of all those late-night chats over Gmail in which I sent Rachel quotes from the text and she responded echoing the narrator's exasperation and then urging me in all caps to finish the translation because it's what the world needs today, and those cozy evenings after the kids were in bed when Daniel and I settled beside each other on the couch and he read my translation out loud to me. This is in no way a project that I accomplished alone, and I am profoundly grateful to have done it in the company of so many cherished friends.

Translator's Note

I discovered Karpilove's *Diary of a Lonely Girl, or The Battle against Free Love* several years ago while researching a footnote on "free love" for my dissertation at Columbia University. I typed *"fraye libe"* (free love) into the search box on the website of the Yiddish Book Center, found a novel I had never heard of before, and started reading. I was instantly drawn in by the intimacy and immediacy of the text, and as I laughed out loud at the sharp and sassy dialogue I knew that this was a translation project I had to take on. This translation emerges at a moment in political and social discourse in which women's stories of disempowerment are coming to light and women are mobilizing around them with new vigor. I have been energized by the startling relevance of Karpilove's text to our own day. I hope readers struggling with experiences of men abusing their social power for sexual gain may find comfort in Karpilove's narrator's self-assurance and humor. As I have gotten to know her through the translation process, I have found her to be a plucky friend, and I sometimes hear her sarcastic voice in my ear as I go about my life as a woman in a world still dominated by men.

In my translation I have tried to do justice to the way that the narrator's economy of words empowers her with men who are annoyingly verbose, and who use "mansplaining" profuseness as a means of asserting their own dominance. I have tried to convey the narrator's fears for her personal safety and her reputation even as she makes light of the situations in which she finds herself, and I have tried to stay true to her own ambivalent relationship with her lovers, whom she enjoys, fears, and loves to hate.

The most difficult word for me to translate in the entire text has been the titular term *meydl*, and I want to draw attention here to the problem of translating *meydl* and how this issue sheds light on the ways that societal attitudes toward women are embedded in the basic terms that we use. It was a hard choice for me to decide to title this translation "Diary of a Lonely *Girl*." I wanted to stay close to the original, but I wasn't sure if "girl" means the same thing to English readers today as *meydl* meant to Karpilove: Will we read the diarist as younger than Karpilove's readers would, simply because I call her a girl? Referring to a grown independent woman as a girl can imply intimacy but can also diminish her status and power. I was tempted to give the narrator the dignity of the more mature-sounding "woman," but I also wanted to indicate that the novel was about a single woman dating, and in the 1910s as well as today "girl" can often be used as shorthand for "single woman." Moreover, I wanted to convey the way that, because of her status as an unmarried woman, the narrator is devalued even in the basic details of the language that she and others use to describe her. There are also moments in the novel in which the narrator's suitor, Charles Cheek (C.), explicitly refers to the narrator as a "girl" not simply in light of her marital status but for a more pointed, and accusatory, indication of her virginity; in order to make these moments work I felt that I needed to use a consistent term to encapsulate both marital status and sexual experience. So, with a sigh, I settled on "girl" in most cases, and, despite this choice, I hope the narrator will accept my apologies and profession of respect.

Another difficulty in this translation was that the narrator's suitors, B. and C., insist on addressing the narrator with the informal, intimate second-person pronoun *du* in place of the more formal *ir*. At several points in the novel the narrator corrects them and they ignore her. In order to convey this nonconsensual linguistic intimacy that does not readily map onto English grammar, I have opted to insert endearments such as "darling" into the text and to have the narrator comment upon them.

I have attempted to highlight the multiple languages present in the text, and the social status attributed to various languages. Where possible, I have tried to retain some of the linguistic diversity of the original. One example of this is when the intellectual landlords display their self-importance and snobbery by using Russian terminology. Likewise, the narrator's female acquaintance Katya uses Russian in her speech in order to signal her leftist political and cultural affiliations. In both cases I left some of the Russian in place, sometimes with English translations embedded in the translated text, though translations into Yiddish were missing from the original. Other characters—such as the landlords' children and occasionally C.—employ English as a status symbol, showing off, sometimes comically, how modern and Americanized they are. German also enters this text in the figure of the German landlady; Karpilove demonstrates the cultural distance between her narrator and the landlady through the narrator's use of German in describing the landlady and through the landlady's use of the language, and at times there is an element of disdain in the way the narrator represents the German woman's speech. German also enters the narrative with Mr. Eshkin, who courts the narrator with a stilted foreignness and formality born of his German education. I have tried to use awkward sentence structures as well as scattered German words to maintain the multilingual sensibility of this courtship. Lastly, it is not always clear in the original when the narrator and her lovers are meant to be speaking in Yiddish or in English. C. offers to instruct the narrator in English, suggesting that most conversations are imagined to take place in Yiddish, but not all. It was not easy to decide when to leave in signals of this multilayered linguistic complexity and when these would be disruptive or excessive for English readers of the text who are not steeped in the social status the narrator would have attributed to these languages. My aim was to create the feeling of multiple languages existing in the same space without overwhelming today's reader in English. Because I wanted to retain this multilingual sensibility, I have left several words untranslated and included a glossary at the back of this volume to aid in reading non-English terms and interjections.

Aside from these artistic and linguistic choices, I have made one very significant intervention in my translation. Karpilove's novel appeared in segments of differing length and frequency during its serialization. The early segments were longer, less frequent, and titled. The later segments appeared more frequently and were shorter, without titles. In its book form, the novel appeared exactly as it did in the pages of the newspaper, including these inconsistencies. The first third of the book is separated into chapters with chapter titles, and the rest of the book has no chapter breaks or chapter titles. In my translation I have separated the novel into chapters and added titles of my own that I felt were consistent with the tone of the titles in the earlier portion of the novel.

Many quotations from other texts appear in this novel. Where possible, I have found these quotations in English translations and replicated the famous quotations as they appear elsewhere, so that they might be searchable or familiar to English-language readers. At one point, the narrator lists quotations she found in a text by Lillian Kisliuk. Lillian Kisliuk (Dinowitzer) was a Washington, DC–based anarchist and schoolteacher. Karpilove's narrator excerpts an article, perhaps translated into Yiddish by Kisliuk, that was originally written by Austrian freethinker, author, painter, musician and feminist Rosa Mayreder.[1] I have reproduced the quotations in the novel as they appear in an English translation of Mayreder's article. Karpilove's reuse of this material with incomplete citations illustrates the way ideas, political rhetoric, and even entire pieces of writing moved between languages and publishing venues to reach new audiences.

At the end of this translation I have also appended my translation of a short story, "The Agitator," which Karpilove published in the literary journal *Di tsukunft* in 1915. The story served as a model for the suitor Charles Cheek (or C.) in Karpilove's *Diary*, and Karpilove slyly

---

1. The original piece can be found in English translation here: Rosa Obermayer Mayreder, "Outlines," in *A Survey of the Woman Problem*, trans. Herman Scheffauer (New York: George H. Doran, 1913), 1–36.

references this earlier story several times during the novel. When C. first encounters the narrator, he asks if her name is Alta, in reference to the protagonist of "The Agitator," and later when she laughs at him for falling down a flight of stairs he huffily recounts the episode with Alta.

Diary of a Lonely Girl, or
The Battle against Free Love

Introduction

JESSICA KIRZANE

onday, April 24, 1916. Boldly stretched across the front page of the socialist and nationalist New York Yiddish daily newspaper *Di varhayt* is a story about the conflict between the United States and Germany over Germany's methods of warfare against passenger- and freight-carrying vessels.[1] Inside the newspaper, among editorials, memoirs, and poetry, is the third installment of Miriam Karpilove's novel *Tage-bukh fun a elende meydel* (*Diary of a Lonely Girl*), entitled "It's Spring Again."

On the face of it, the excerpt has nothing to do with the current events that fill the front page of the newspaper—war, diplomatic relations, labor disputes. In this installment, a lovelorn woman laments that her lover has left her. She goes to his apartment to see him and spies through his window the silhouette of a man and woman embracing. Such a narrative may even appear to be intentionally apolitical,

---

1. At the time of the publication of Karpilove's novel, *Di varhayt* was published by Louis Miller, who had broken from the more widely known socialist Yiddish newspaper *Forverts*. This break was not only due to his personal conflict with its editor, Abraham Cahan, but also because of Miller's agenda of promoting Jewish nationalism within the context of radical leftist politics at a time when Cahan and the *Forverts* insisted that there was no such thing as a "Jewish nation." Ehud Manor, *Louis Miller and Di Warheit ("The Truth"): Yiddishism, Zionism, and Socialism in New York, 1905–1915* (Brighton: Sussex Academic Press, 2012), 3.

providing an escape from the realm of world events into the personal, intimate, and emotional experience of a woman's desires and despair. But Karpilove's irreverent and melodramatic work of entertainment fiction is, at moments, intensely political from within the limits of its form as a romantic serial diary novel.

Indeed, Karpilove's melancholic "lonely girl" offers a political critique in this very moment of desperate longing. She argues that the romantic aphorism that "the youth of the woman is the springtime of her life" is true only for the youth of a wealthy woman, but not for that of the poor, lonely girl who lacks the resources that would make her desirable for social-climbing young men. The narrator is an object of sexual desire lacking in social capital, and politically radical men repeatedly take advantage of her, indulging their own hedonistic springtimes at her expense. These men claim that an ideology of free love goes hand in hand with their liberatory agenda, but when they jilt her and move on, she is left powerless on the sidelines of their political concerns. The moment when Karpilove's narrator is depicted as a spurned lover is not only a timeless motif of the romance genre, but also a sharp commentary on the political and social context of the novel, shedding light on how modern politics entered into, transformed, and disrupted intimate gender relations in turn-of-the-twentieth-century urban America in ways that were often harmful to women.

The author of this deceptively political text was Miriam Karpilove (1888–1956), a prolific Yiddish writer and editor whose work has received little scholarly attention. She was born in Minsk, in what is now Belarus and was then in the Russian Empire, and immigrated to America in 1905, settling first in Harlem in New York City; later in the Seagate neighborhood of Brooklyn; and then in Bridgeport, Connecticut, where several of her brothers lived. She was among the very few women who made their living as Yiddish writers, and she supplemented her income working as a retoucher, hand coloring photographs. Karpilove wrote hundreds of short stories, belles-lettres, plays, and novels and served as a staff writer for the *Forward* in the

1930s.[2] Family lore and photographs depict her as a colorful character with a sharp tongue who "brought us stories from a world of travel and famous people."[3]

Dozens of photographs and picture postcards of Miriam Karpilove show her as alternately romantic, flamboyant, and studious. At times she appears with her hair tidily pulled back in a bun, pearls around her neck, and a pince-nez perched on her nose, looking pensively past the camera. Some images show a glowering, tight-lipped young Karpilove, her hair long, straight, and parted down the middle; another shows her wearing a gauzy veil, her face softly turned to the side; an undated family photograph from the 1920s features Karpilove playing guitar for a circle of female friends. Each of these images shows her deliberately fashioning herself as artistic and rebellious—the kind of self-portraiture that she accomplishes in her narrative *Diary* as well.

In one stunning portrait, Karpilove, draped in a luxurious robe, lounges on a divan, her long hair laying loose across her back. Through

2. Her writing has never been collected. She lists a sampling of titles at the end of her novel *A provints tsaytung* (1926), with a note stating that she has published over three hundred stories and novels in journals and newspapers and is considering publishing them in book form but would like input from her readers about which pieces they would like to see in print. A handwritten bibliography of her printed works can be found in her archive at the YIVO Institute of Jewish Research. See Miriam Karpilove, *A provints tsaytung* (New York: s.n., 1926); and "*Gedrukte verk*" (manuscript), Miriam Karpilow Papers, RG 383, Box 5, YIVO, New York.

3. Little has been written about Karpilove's life or writing. Those wishing to learn more about her work may consult the following encyclopedia entries: Ellen Kellman, "Miriam Karpilove," in *Jewish Women: A Comprehensive Historical Encyclopedia*, Jewish Women's Archive, March 1, 2009, https://jwa.org/encyclopedia /article/Karpilove-miriam (accessed March 8, 2018); and Zalmen Reyzin, "Miriam Karpilove," *Leksikon fun der yidisher literatur, prese un filologye* 3 (1929): 575–76. I am also grateful to Karpilove's nephew, David Karpilow, for sharing his recollections of Miriam as well as pages from a book of Karpilow family history compiled by his cousin, Arno Karlen.

her glasses, she peers into a book as though too engrossed to notice the photographer. Here, Karpilove displays herself as a woman with the room of her own in which to pursue her intellectual interests without interference from prying neighbors or demanding suitors and away from the poverty her readership experienced. Unlike the working-class narrator of the *Diary*, in the photograph Karpilove enjoys fine furniture and clothing; her raiment suggests the kind of figure who would have soaringly passionate love stories to tell. Posed seductively, she directs her attention away from any potential admirer, defiantly turning it toward books and reminding the onlooker to consider her mind as well as her body. The photograph celebrates women's sexual and intellectual freedom—freedom that the narrator of the *Diary* strives to attain with great difficulty.[4]

Diary of a Lonely Girl was one of Karpilove's most popular novels. It was serialized in *Di varhayt* in 1916–18 and published in book form by S. Kantrowitz in 1918. A novel of love and passion, intimate feelings and scandalous behaviors, Karpilove's novel slyly attacks the economic and political inequities that women face. In doing so, it reveals the hypocrisies of the societal expectations that the narrator be at once sexually available to freethinking young men and maintain her respectability according to the mores of nosy landladies. The novel offers a raw, intimate, and personal critique of radical urban Jewish society's complicity in a young woman's vulnerable circumstances: the narrator is struggling to figure out whether and how she can participate in a culture of free love in which she is undervalued, used, and discarded. The novel's insight and wit expose and comment upon the precarious status of women in radical American Yiddish youth culture during World War I.

---

4. For a further discussion of author photographs that captivate by bending gender conventions or posing a challenge to readers, see Briallen Hopper, "Pandora in Blue Jeans," in *Hard to Love: Essays and Confessions* (New York: Bloomsbury, 2019), 59–66.

Miriam Karpilove ca. 1920. From the Archives of the YIVO Institute for Jewish Research, New York.

Though the tone of Karpilove's novel is typical of the wry, re-moved stance and social criticism of the Greenwich Village authors of the *New Yorker* in the same period—the dialogue-heavy novel is reminiscent of the work of Dorothy Parker—it is unusual within the realm of American Yiddish literature, especially in writings that have received critical attention. While women wrote in Yiddish in signifi-cant numbers, their stories were often dismissed, received little atten-tion, or were assumed to be the work of male authors. As Faith Jones explains, newspapers reviewing or advertising writing by women "preferred women in traditional roles," celebrating cookbooks and books of beauty advice rather than literary writing.[5] Women writ-ing from within Yiddish radical secular politics and society were rarely treated as equals to their male counterparts. Women often

5. Faith Jones, "Criticizing Women," *Bridges* 13, no. 1 (Spring 2008): 76–81, 79.

experienced intellectual and social isolation, in contrast to the friendships and community that male writers enjoyed as part of a male-dominated literary and café culture.[6] Karpilove's narrator, though herself not a professional writer, experiences a similar loneliness as an avid reader and intellectual without peers.

As Norma Fain Pratt has noted, Yiddish newspapers sometimes demonstrated how modern and forward-thinking they were by publishing writing by women.[7] Therefore, *Diary of a Lonely Girl* would have been understood as an emblematically modern piece of writing simply because it was a woman's novel in print. The novel seemed even more shocking because the subject matter of the sexually liberated young woman was so controversial, exemplifying the changing roles and expectations for women in a dangerously modern era. However, Karpilove's novel is more than a scandalous or lighthearted romance; the few scholars who have referenced it have noted that it is radical *because* of its courtship plot, for which it might otherwise be dismissed as mere entertainment. Irena Klepfisz explains that women writers in Yiddish leftist circles such as Fradl Shtok, Yente Serdatsky, and Miriam Karpilove wrote with deeply personal awareness of "the unfulfilled promises of secular liberation" in which women were expected to perform domestic roles and obligations even as they fought alongside men for a theoretical world of egalitarianism and freedom.[8] As Jones has described, Karpilove "exploited social anxiety about women's liberation in the modern era, and her own status as a young woman, by writing about young women in sexually fraught situations," and in so

6. Norma Fain Pratt, "Culture and Radical Politics: Yiddish Women Writers, 1890–1940," *American Jewish History* 70, no. 1 (September 1, 1980): 68–91, 82. See also Shachar Pinsker, *A Rich Brew: How Cafes Created Modern Jewish Culture* (New York: New York Univ. Press, 2018).

7. Pratt, "Culture and Radical Politics," 77.

8. Irena Klepfisz, "Queens of Contradiction: A Feminist Introduction to Yiddish Women Writers," in *Found Treasures: Stories by Yiddish Women Writers*, ed. Frieda Forman et al. (Toronto: Second Story, 1994), 21–64, 51.

doing she used the current conventions and expectations of women's writing to participate in the culture of radical leftism.[9]

Karpilove's confidence in shedding light on the challenges facing single women in the courtship scene of Yiddish New York was particularly significant, given the broader, changing sexual culture of America during this period. Scholars recognize the 1910s as a pivotal moment in American gender relations. At the close of the suffrage movement, women moved into professional roles that popular culture decried as unfeminine and feared would disrupt American masculinity and a proper gender balance. In an age the cultural journal *Current Opinion* declared to be "Sex O'Clock in America," a revolutionary shift was underway in American sexual mores, and immigrants took part in and shaped that culture.[10] Due to changes in labor and consumer markets, the growth of leisure time, and rapid urbanization, young men and women also experienced a growing autonomy that was alarming to many of their parents' generation. Participating in a "heterosocial leisure world geared toward youth and vitality," young men and women argued against what they felt were the strictures and double standards of Victorian sexual morality. They saw themselves as participating in revolutionarily new and rebellious behavior in their sexual lives.[11] As historian Kathy Peiss explains, East European Jewish immigrants, along with other working-class immigrant populations, participated in this culture of leisure and social and sexual experimentation as part of their efforts to become American.[12]

9. Faith Jones, "Everybody Comes to the Store: People's Book Store as Third Place, 1910–1920," *Canadian Jewish Studies* 18, no. 19 (January 2010): 95–119, 106.

10. "Sex O'Clock in America," *Current Opinion* 55 (August 1913): 113–14; Kevin White, *The First Sexual Revolution: The Emergence of Male Heterosexuality in Modern America* (New York: New York Univ. Press, 1993), 13.

11. White, *The First Sexual Revolution*, 2.

12. Kathy Peiss, *Cheap Amusements: Working Women and Leisure in Turn-of-the-Century New York* (Philadelphia: Temple Univ. Pres, 1986); Nina Warnke, "Immigrant Popular Culture as Contested Sphere: Yiddish Music Halls, the Yiddish Press,

Yet, as Karpilove's narrator reveals, concomitant with this loosening of sexual mores came an increased danger of nonconsensual sexual contact. Karpilove's narrator finds herself particularly vulnerable to young men's sexual advances because she is a young woman alone, an ocean away from her family. By necessity she lives by herself in furnished rooms, which had become a cultural symbol for the sexual permissiveness of the era. Rented rooms were a space away from parental authority, where sexual experimentation seemed newly possible.[13] Without parental supervision, she associates freely with young men, and her only protection against their unwanted advances is her own quick thinking. Karpilove's novel reflects the excitement, anxieties, and intergenerational conflicts of the moment. Rather than reveling in their newfound freedoms, the book exposes the not-so-hidden dangers of women participating in a sexually permissive youth culture that had emerged from the more restrictive environment of the sexual propriety of the past. Karpilove demonstrates the double standards to which women are held even as they desire the status and economic stability of marriage while trying to navigate the uncharted dating scene that included extramarital and premarital affairs.

Karpilove's *Diary* is surprising for its rejection of free love, an ideology that radical leftists touted as relieving women from the slavery of subservience to a husband in marriage. The famous anarchist activist Emma Goldman, whose fiery political rhetoric earned her fame within and far beyond the American Yiddish scene, was an outspoken opponent of state- and religion-sanctioned marriage and a proponent of free love. She insisted that marriage, like capitalism, is a bourgeois "paternal arrangement" in which women are forced to sell their sexual

---

and the Processes of Americanization, 1900–1910," *Theatre Journal* 48, no. 3 (1996): 321–35.

13. Joanne Meyerowitz, "Sexual Geography and Gender Economy: The Furnished-Room Districts of Chicago, 1890–1930," in *Unequal Sisters: A Multicultural Reader in US Women's History*, ed. Ellen Carol DuBois and Vicki Ruiz (New York: Routledge, 1990), 307–23.

and economic freedom in exchange for financial security and social position.[14] Goldman called for a radical rethinking of love, demanding that women be free to claim the full range of their economic and social independence, including love and motherhood outside the patriarchal structure of marriage. Goldman's discussions of the subject were widely publicized and read by the Yiddish public, and Yiddish newspapers were replete with articles and advice columns that took up the question of free love.

However, even Emma Goldman recognized women's potential vulnerability within a free love value system, acknowledging that true equality requires systemic economic and social reform and cannot be accomplished by a handful of enlightened individuals acting in isolation.[15] Karpilove's *Diary* takes this caveat as a starting point, offering a cynical vantage point from which to view the enterprise of free love: until such systemic reform is accomplished, Karpilove argues, free love is just another way for men to exploit women's bodies and leave them emotionally, economically, and physically vulnerable. For all that Karpilove's narrator radically centers women's experiences and writes frankly about racy subjects for the newspaper-reading public, her conclusions appear to be—perhaps counterintuitively—aligned with traditional values. She rejects the assertions of radical thinkers with regard to free love, arguing that such love is in fact harmful to women, given the realities of the society in which they live. Karpilove's

14. Emma Goldman, *Marriage and Love* (New York: Mother Earth, 1911), 11.

15. For Goldman, free love will be part of a revolution that will upend the political and social status quo. She writes, "Some day, some day men and women will rise . . . they will meet big and strong and free, ready to receive, to partake, and to bask in the golden rays of love." In the meantime, however, she acknowledges that "if . . . woman is free and big enough to learn the mystery of sex without the sanction of State or Church, she will stand condemned as utterly unfit to become the wife of a 'good' man." Here she recognizes that practicing free love could be detrimental to women in a society that relies on patriarchal state-sanctioned marriage and thereby ensures women's economic vulnerability, forcing women to submit their sexual and domestic labor strictly to conventional marriage. See Goldman, *Marriage and Love*, 15, 7.

work identifies a truth lurking in Goldman's own lived experience of radical politics: that the men who professed commitment to absolute freedom for the individual could not release themselves from sexist ideas about women.[16] In light of these inequities, Karpilove suggests that free love becomes a socially manipulative tool that activist men use against women to deprive them of the economic and social protections of marriage.

The novel accomplishes its relevant and important social task through the conventions of its genre; the work is a characteristic example of the diary novel in which a woman confesses her feelings, sets up and measures herself against goals for self-improvement, and offers readers a peek into a "real-time" unfolding of the most personal aspects of her life. Since Samuel Richardson's iconic eighteenth-century epistolary novel *Pamela* and Sei Shōnagon's medieval Japanese court musings in *The Pillow Book*, diary novels have long been received as a venue for women's perspectives on anxiety about sex and gender roles. The genre was a staple of popular literature at the turn of the century, providing Karpilove an attractive medium with which to engage her audience. For example, the sensational German bestseller *Tagebuch einer Verlorenen* (*Diary of a Lost Girl*) by Margarete Böhme (1867–1939), first published in 1905, sold more than 1,200,000 copies by the end of the 1920s. The novel, about a young woman's descent into prostitution, was translated into fourteen languages and was adapted into a stage play and made into a silent film, and, due to its popularity, it is likely that Karpilove was aware of and perhaps drew upon its fame in composing her own work.[17] The genre continues to

16. See Candace Falk, *Love, Anarchy, and Emma Goldman: A Biography* (New Brunswick: Rutgers Univ. Press, 1990), 20.

17. Early twentieth-century Viennese bestseller *Eine für Viele: aus dem Tagebuch eines Mädchens* (One for Many: From a Girl's Diary) likewise generated public debate about prostitution and sexual morality, and inspired several parodies. See Margaret McCarthy, "The Representation of Prostitutes in Literature and Film: Margarete Böhme and G. W. Pabst," in *Commodities of Desire: The Prostitute in Modern German*

play a significant role in popular culture today. Karpilove's *Diary* is a forerunner to Helen Fielding's *Bridget Jones's Diary* (1996) and to the hit romantic comedy television series *Sex and the City* (1998–2004), in which protagonist Carrie Bradshaw narrates her friends' sexual escapades through a confessional, diary-style newspaper sex column.

In *Diary of a Lonely Girl*, the narrator describes the emotional exhaustion and longing of a young woman who falls victim to the promises of free love. In the opening chapters the narrative voice of the novel is heavy with the raw emotion of a lovestruck, desperate, needy young woman. But Karpilove soon thwarts the genre's typical tone and the expectations that the novel sets up at the beginning. As the novel develops, so too does the narrative voice, which is at times distanced and wry, at times self-consciously modern, and at times punctuated with assertive, clipped, fast-paced, cinema-style dialogue to match the narrator's growing defiance and confidence.

Writing within the limits of a serialized novel, focused on courtship, that readers might have predicted to be lowbrow entertainment fiction, Karpilove challenges the reader with an educated, sophisticated female narrator who uses her wit to joust with and fend off her male suitors, even as they exert power over her. She participates in what Lauren Berlant has deemed the essence of "female complaint" literature, lamenting, testifying to, judging, and expressing women's disappointment in "the tenuous relation of romantic fantasy to lived intimacy" and blaming "flawed men and bad ideologies for women's intimate suffering."[18] In this way, Karpilove's writing echoes better known English-language women writers of the period, such as Edna Ferber, Dorothy Parker, and Anzia Yezierska, who lodged similar

---

Literature, ed. Christiane Schönfeld (Columbia, SC: Camden House, 2000), 77–98; and Charlotte Woodford, *Women, Emancipation, and the German Novel* (London: Routledge, 2017).

18. Lauren Berlant, *The Female Complaint: The Unfinished Business of Sentimentality in American Culture* (Durham, NC: Duke Univ. Press, 2008), 1.

complaints about the unstable and vulnerable place of women in the changing sexual norms of urban American life.[19]

Like all serial fiction, Karpilove's *Diary of a Lonely Girl* also plays with the line between fiction and reality through its use of the present tense and the expectations and experiences of readers who are encouraged to understand the story as unfolding in real time, and by its very appearance in a newspaper alongside the day's news.[20] Likewise, its presentation as a diary, told in the first person, increases the apparent urgency and believability of the narrative.[21] Many times readers wrote to the editorial pages of the newspaper to comment on Karpilove's novel. In a letter dated September 11, 1916, a reader writes in praise of the novel and thanks Karpilove for writing on behalf of "us young people." Several months later, on February 13, 1917, a reader writes in praise of Karpilove's "very interesting series of articles," referring to the *Diary*, demonstrating the way genres bleed into one another in readers' minds. He explains, "Such a demonstration of the danger and absurdity of our so-called free-love-niks is long overdue. . . . [T]he writer of this remarkable diary deserves praise and thanks for her logical arguments and beautiful writing." He goes on to assert that the ideology of free love has "ruined" many a Yiddish working girl and says he will be grateful "if this *Diary* helps our sisters come to see the absurdity of the 'free-love-niks.'" In a letter dated March 2, 1917, a reader praises Karpilove's "true to life" characters: "What woman has

19. For more on Edna Ferber, see Eliza McGraw, *Edna Ferber's America* (Baton Rouge: Louisiana State Univ. Press, 2014). Berlant's *The Female Complaint* provides a compelling analysis of Parker's relationship to the aesthetic conventions of "female complaint" literature.

20. See Jennifer Hayward, *Consuming Pleasures: Active Audiences and Serial Fictions from Dickens to Soap Opera* (Lexington: Univ. Press of Kentucky, 1997), 26, in which she writes about the serialized fiction in newspapers and the disruption of boundaries between fiction and real life.

21. Trevor Fried, *Form and Function in the Diary Novel* (Basingstoke, UK: Palgrave Macmillan, 1989), 54.

not experienced such things?"[22] In each of these cases, readers interact with the text, offering opinions of the novel as it unfolds and asserting its relevance not only as entertainment but also as a document that exposes social problems of the day. Karpilove writes for what Berlant has termed an "intimate public" of women's literature, a commodified genre of intimacy sometimes characterized by complaint and sentimentality, which provides "frames for encountering the impacts of living as a woman in the world."[23] Contemporaneous readers acknowledged the novel as doing important social and political work, exposing disparities and dangers in gender relations in the Jewish youth culture. They are also likely to have experienced it, in Berlant's terms, as "juxtapolitical" literature that validates "the expression of emotional response and conceptual recalibration as achievement enough," talking back to a male dominant culture that devalues these modes.[24]

Through her narrator, Karpilove exposes readers to an intimate and immediate women's perspective on topics of relevance to contemporaneous newspaper readers. Readers receive social commentary in the voice of a marginalized, lonely, yet observant and articulate diarist. The remainder of this introduction focuses on three key issues that appear throughout the novel: World War I, birth control and free love, and women's vulnerability under the law.

World War I

Particularly because of its publication in a newspaper, in its serialized version the novel asserts itself as more than escapism. Rather, it is subtly a form of editorial writing about events reported on in the newspaper itself. Appearing alongside pieces such as Y. Podruzhnik's "War Diary (*Togbukh fun der milkhome*)"—a firsthand account of a Belgian resident at the outbreak of World War I—the *Diary* is a

22. "*Editorials fun folk: vos di leyzer zogn,*" *Di varhayt*, September 11, 1916, 5; March 2, 1917, 5; February 13, 1917, 5.

23. Berlant, *The Female Complaint*, x.

24. Berlant, 10, x.

personal commentary on life on the home front. It offers reportage from another kind of battlefield, distant but not disconnected from the theater of war. Introducing readers to the perspective of a woman in the heat of romantic battle—the published version of the novel is subtitled *Der kampf gegen fraye liebe* (*The Battle against Free Love*)—the novel brings readers into single female life in the city to experience its dangers firsthand.

Although the narrator rarely mentions World War I itself or the devastation of Jewish communities caught in the midst of war, hers is very much a wartime novel, written with an underlying acknowledgment of the turmoil of its time. In one key moment, the plight of Jewish communities in Europe is called to mind as the narrator abruptly shifts to thinking about the Old Country in its present upheaval:

> "I can see the sky from here," I answered. "And I love to watch people walking in the street after midnight. They look so mysterious, each like he's going to a secret meeting. It reminds me of my old home where nowadays people must walk around like this, like shadows, even in the daytime."
>
> He begged me to stop. "My dear, don't think of your old home. The Old Country isn't a home anymore. Our home is here, where we are. We are citizens of the whole world. The Poland that I once passionately championed no longer belongs to us. Right under my own eyes they turned me into a German. Fine, so let me be a German, a Frenchman, a Turk, even an Eskimo, as long as I can be alive. Life, in the fullest sense of the word, is the most beautiful and precious thing that we have. Looking at you now, I see how beautiful you are. The pale glimmer of electric streetlamps falls on you and lights up your eyes as they gaze upon me, warming my soul. I feel as though my soul will sprout wings and fly to the highest heavens leaving me here, at your feet."
>
> "My feet would trample a man without a soul."
>
> "Let them!" he cried out passionately. "Go on and take a step! Step, step, step! I myself will place your foot on my neck, on my

head! Don't you see, my love, I lay myself at your feet! I give myself over to you. You can do with me *what you will*."[25]

In this passage, the narrator fleetingly turns her thoughts to the violence facing Jewish communities in Europe, but she is quickly and frantically discouraged from these thoughts. For her lover, C., the role of a young woman is not to even think of the war, or destruction, or the affairs of the world. She exists for him only as a sex object. C. forcefully insists on the limits of the narrator's thoughts and of the novel itself; as a male, he polices the boundaries of the female mind and relegates it to the body, love, sex, and entertainment. This explains and even excuses why the novel has so little to say about the events on the front page of the newspaper—such events are outside the scope of what is acceptable for the genre, and for women's concerns. In this moment, Karpilove briefly rebels against these strictures and then demonstrates through C.'s voice how such rebellions are quelled by the force of male desire and women's immediate need to fend off these advances rather than to focus on distant events.

Moreover, when the narrator *does* turn her mind to the violence facing Jews in Europe, it is to consider that Jews must now walk around as though they are concealing secrets, because they are in danger. Although she ascribes such behavior to Jews in Europe, this is precisely the kind of activity that the narrator herself engages in throughout her novel: trying to avoid the prying eyes of landladies and other people in positions of authority who might endanger her well-being if they knew that, for instance, she was alone in her room with a man. By suggesting parallels in the experiences of young women battling free love in New York and Jews battling antisemitism in Europe, Karpilove draws the sympathies of her audience toward her narrator. She equates the urgency and importance of women's inequality and lack of agency in their romantic relationships with the situation of individuals in war-torn Europe, elevating these issues from the realm of private,

25. Karpilove, *Tagebukh*, 148; pp. 149–50 in this translation.

emotional, frivolous fiction to the realm of world politics, violence, and injustice.

Although the novel rarely directly mentions the war, Karpilove fills her discussion of love with metaphors of war, insisting on the urgency and relevance of women's disempowerment in sexual relationships even in a time when men are dying by the thousands on battlefields. Over and again, the narrator insists that she is engaged in a battle of the sexes to preserve her own dignity and her virginity in the face of lovers who believe in free love and who demand it from her. When C. decides to stop listening to her refusals or trying to reason with her and insists on kissing her instead of debating, the narrator refers to this behavior as a new "tactic" in his efforts to awaken her desires. When she is unresponsive to his kisses, he tells her that she is either made of wood or is a "skilled diplomat" who knows how to fend off his advances by feigning indifference. Nevertheless, he refuses to be discouraged in his new "strategy" that he's taken on in their love war.[26] When the narrator at last runs into the street to escape being alone in her room with C., she thinks to herself that "in love, as in war, it's very nice to win."[27] In this way, Karpilove accentuates the precariousness of her narrator's situation and demonstrates its relevance to the broader newspaper-reading audience. Here and elsewhere Karpilove further enlists her narrator in a battle against free love through military imagery, and in a larger battle to preserve the dignity of all women that takes place bedroom by bedroom. This aligns with the heightened attention during World War I to women's sexual morality as a requisite for preserving the moral fabric of the society on the home front that men were fighting to defend on the battlefield, where civility was shattered by bombs and bullets.[28]

26. Karpilove, 236–38; pp. 223–24 in this translation.

27. Karpilove, 282; p. 258 in this translation.

28. Susan R. Grayzel, *Women's Identities at War: Gender, Motherhood, and Politics in Britain and France during the First World War* (Chapel Hill: Univ. of North Carolina Press, 1999), 122.

Birth Control and Free Love

In the years that *Diary of a Lonely Girl* was serialized, birth control was a subject discussed with frequency in *Di varhayt* in editorials and news articles, sometimes on pages adjacent to the novel itself. In April 1916, *Di varhayt* conducted a contest in which it offered readers prizes for the best answer to the "birth control question," or the question of whether contraception should be legally available and if individuals should use it. The announcement for the contest called the debate around birth control "one of the most important social problems of our time," offering the winner of the contest two volumes of the Yiddish playwright Dovid Pinski's work. Readers wrote from conflicting perspectives. Some argued that birth control is a crime against humanity that prevents it from multiplying in its natural way while others advocated for birth control on social grounds; they saw it as a form of social protection for the poor, who suffer from too many children and whose children are the cannon fodder for wars that benefit only the rich.[29] The newspaper also printed a review of the representation of the birth control debate in moving pictures, with a tagline: "If the 'movies' can agitate for or against the war, why shouldn't they do the same with the question of birth control?"[30] Above all, the newspaper was filled with articles about the exploits of Emma Goldman, a proponent of free love and of birth control, including advertisements for her collected writings; reporting on her arrest and trial; descriptions of dinners given in her honor; and frequent letters to the editor, expressing opinions about Goldman's political stances.[31] The

29. See "*Der kontrol fun gebort: a debate far di lezer fun der varhayt*," *Di varhayt*, April 7, 14, and 26, 1916, 5.

30. "*Milkhome un geburth kontrol in di moving piktshurs*," *Di varhayt*, April 8, 1917, 12.

31. For a few examples, see "*Froyen protestirn farn aynloden Emma Goldman tsu redden far zey*," *Di varhayt*, January 10, 1916, 5; "*Emma Goldman lektshurt haynt*," *Di varhayt*, February 8, 1916, 2; "*Haynt der miting in karnegi hall*," *Di varhayt*, March 1, 1916, 2; and "*Geburt-kontrol onheynger giben a diner Emma Goldman*," *Di varhayt*, April 19, 1916, 8.

newspaper had a veritable love affair with the shocking and politically salient ideas of this public figure.

Characters in Karpilove's *Diary* interact with the issue of birth control in multiple ways. In one scene, in which C. is (again) trying to convince the narrator to have sex, he argues that women are only really concerned about the "results" of sex and aren't scared of sex itself. He reassures the narrator that he has a "way" of preventing those "results" (i.e., birth control) and she needn't be concerned.[32] The narrator is not reassured by this declaration, as pregnancy was not the only danger for a young, unmarried woman having sex in early twentieth-century New York. She is keenly aware that such a misstep could have serious social as well as physical consequences.

C. frequently expresses disdain for the idea of having children, claiming that modern people should not desire procreation and should save childbearing for the unenlightened. In the following passage he explains this as a cornerstone of his definition of the modern woman:

> "Does the modern woman have children?" I asked hurriedly, seeing that he'd paused to catch his breath.
>
> "Children?"
>
> "Yes, children. You know, regular old children."
>
> "What do they need children for?"
>
> "So they can have pride and pleasure from them, for instance."
>
> "They have no use for children! Leave childbearing to women who don't know how to avoid having children. Women who know how to get out of it can be happy without children. And if a woman decides that she wants to have a child, then let her have one! Who cares? I'm all for a matriarchy: let her have the kid if she wants it, and let it be her choice. His responsibility goes no farther than whatever he agrees to. If he wants to have a child, then he can care for it. Right?"
>
> "Sure, sure. I hardly know how it could be any other way. If a man wants a child, he should care for it. That's only right."

32. Karpilove, 230; p. 217 in this translation.

C. didn't notice my sarcasm, or at least he pretended not to. He just squeezed and kissed my hand as though to thank me for agreeing with him at least on one point, when it came to children.[33]

In this passage, C. defines the modern woman in a remarkably antifeminist way—her modernity is predicated on men's freedom from social responsibility. C.'s despicable attitudes about sex, which repeatedly force the narrator into situations in which she is uncomfortable, rely on the idea of sex without consequences for men. Birth control is an avenue toward that goal rather than social reform for women and families burdened by too many children they are unable to care for. Karpilove uses his reprehensible behavior to argue against birth control, showing it to be a tool that empowers attitudes harmful to women.

Characters in Karpilove's *Diary* also interact with birth control as part of their consumption of popular culture. In one installment of the novel, published on February 3, 1917, the narrator and her friend Rae propose to their lovers an outing to see *Where Are My Children?*, an anti–birth control film.[34] This suggestion places them in the center of

33. Karpilove, 188; p. 184 in this translation.

34. See p. 248 of this translation. *Where Are My Children?* (Universal Films, 1916) is a silent film directed by Philips Smalley and Lois Weber. Based on the obscenity trial of Margaret Sanger, it tells the story of an attorney prosecuting a doctor for illegal abortions who learns that women he knows, including his own wife, procured abortions from the doctor. At the start of the film a doctor makes a convincing case for legalizing contraception to prevent unwanted births in poor families, but as the film progresses it makes a case against wealthy women having abortions on a "whim." As one woman dies from complications from a botched abortion and the attorney and his wife resign themselves to being childless as a result of numerous previous abortions, the antiabortion message of the film becomes absolutely clear. The film was widely viewed throughout the United States. See Grace Kim, "*Where are My Children?*," *The Embryo Project Encyclopedia*, May 26, 2017, https://embryo.asu.edu/pages/where-are-my-children-1916 (accessed September 10, 2019); and Richard Brody, "Lois Weber's Vital Films of the Early Silent Era," *New Yorker*, July 19, 2018, https://www.newyorker.com/culture/the-front-row/lois-webers-vital-films-of-the-early-silent-era (accessed September 9, 2019).

trendy popular culture as well as indicates their position on the birth control debate to the reader who has been paying attention to the newspaper as a whole. Elsewhere in the newspaper, this film received critical attention.[35] Characters desiring to see this film position their personal decisions about sex and birth control as part of the national conversation.

The most sustained treatment in the novel of the political and social scene of the birth control debate occurs when the narrator attends C.'s public lecture about free love and birth control, in which he is explicitly compared to Emma Goldman; an audience member boasts that C. is such a superior speaker that he "could fit Emma Goldman in his back pocket."[36] In the scene, the boisterous audience eagerly listens to and cheers at C.'s repetitive calls for free love, using the language of science and politics as he publically argues for the narrator, who is in attendance, to privately oblige his so-called political desires for sex.[37] His arguments against marriage as a tether for *men* fall short of the analysis of Emma Goldman's *Marriage and Love*, in which she argues for free love as a replacement for the unequal, exploitative structure of economic and sexual relations between men and women in marriage. Instead of arguing for freedom of *love* outside the bounds of the law, C. argues specifically for freedom of *sex*, debasing Goldman's elevated claims and expressing that lawless love may be just as dangerous for

---

35. "*Milkhome un geburth kontrol in di moving piktshurs*," *Di varhayt*, April 8, 1917, 12.

36. See p. 191 of this translation.

37. In its political dimensions, free love is a cultural component of anarchism, motivated by a desire to separate the state and other forms of social authority and control from sexual matters. In the social environment of secular Yiddish-speaking immigrants, many of whom were engaged in radical political movements, and for whom the language of radical politics trickled into popular culture, the term "free love" also became a euphemism for sexual permissiveness without these theoretical and political underpinnings. While C. claims ideological commitment to radical politics through free love, Karpilove suggests that his interests lie primarily in the sex act itself.

women as lawful marriage in a society in which women enjoy less power and respect than men.[38]

In the scene, Karpilove skewers C. as a self-righteous political activist whose vapid, unsophisticated ideas about sex and sexuality are couched in educated language, and who uses his radicalism in order to ruin a woman who knows that her ability to rent rooms in reputable households, to be viewed as respectable among friends and neighbors and in society, and perhaps one day to marry are all dependent on her virginity. Certainly his advances—forcing the narrator into precarious situations and insisting that she have sex—are as much "love by force" as the marriage he decries. By placing his arguments in this public world of politics, and positioning them in a newspaper next to descriptions of and advertisements for lectures, Karpilove offers a cynical feminist lens through which to view the broader political landscape of the radical Yiddish world. She argues through her novel that Jewish men's politics overlook women's experiences and that Jewish men with radical politics exploit women's bodies, and she implicates free love as a tool for this exploitation rather than a liberation from women's subservient status within traditional marriage. While a political theorist like Emma Goldman might imagine free love to be a solution to women's subjugation, Karpilove's wry, realist novel about the lived experience of radical Jewish youth culture reveals the genuine risks women face in a culture of free love.

Women's Vulnerability under the Law

In an installment that takes place shortly after the narrator has moved to new rooms after being caught by her landlords in a compromising position alone with C., the narrator contemplates her own vulnerability. Rather than expressing this through reflection or speculation about the ways in which she is alone and powerless, she does so by reflecting on news items that are discussed elsewhere in the newspaper. She writes:

38. Goldman, *Marriage and Love.*

I read in the newspaper today that respectable women are being sentenced for street prostitution. A report from a women's prison association demonstrates that many respectable women and girls are arrested illegally on charges of immorality, simply because policemen, or whoever else, feels like it. The policeman or detective is always believed over the person he's sending to jail, even if the woman accused of immorality is the picture of respectability. . . .

I'd started reading the newspaper to dispel my instinctive fear of my surroundings, but now I only felt more frightened. I was even more afraid than I had been before to make any noise in my room, to open the door, or to go out into the street. I was afraid someone might approach me and ask why I left the other rooms so quickly.[39]

The narrator refers to the effects of the activities of the Committee of Fifteen, a vice commission created by the New York Chamber of Commerce, who turned their attention to the problem of prostitution in tenement houses and apartment buildings. Among the stipulations of their Tenement House Act of 1901 was that a woman caught in the act of prostitution in a tenement house could be arrested and imprisoned for up to six months. In this passage, the narrator reads the newspaper, much like the readers of her own novel, and relates it to her life, speculating on how she is vulnerable to the changing law and social climate of moral panic over changes in American sexual culture.[40] C. later references this when the narrator threatens to protest against his

---

39. Karpilove, 166; pp. 162–63 in this translation.

40. One of the major reforms of the Progressive Era, the New York State Tenement House Act of 1901 is best known for banning the construction of dark, poorly ventilated tenement buildings in the state of New York. The legislation also included penalties for prostitution in tenement houses. Enforcement of this legislation involved a policy of vice districting, as judges sentenced vice offenders more harshly in tenement houses than in regular houses of prostitution. Mara Laura Keire, *For Business and Pleasure: Red-Light Districts and the Regulation of Vice in the United States, 1890–1933* (Baltimore: Johns Hopkins Univ. Press, 2010), 10; Jennifer Fronc, *New York Undercover: Private Surveillance in the Progressive Era* (Chicago: Univ. of Chicago Press, 2009), 43.

unwanted advances. "Oh, so you want to be famous, do you? You want your name in all the newspapers?" He laughed out loud. "Or maybe you want to spend the night in a police station?"[41] C. makes this bold statement as he and the narrator are outside together in the evening, when she tries to escape him by fleeing her room. His attitude demonstrates his awareness of the narrator's precarious position under the law as a victim who will be perceived as a prostitute, a criminal, and a social outcast in an environment of increasing surveillance of women's private and public conduct.[42] By foregrounding the sympathetic narrator's profound worry and distress, despite her proven and hard-fought virginal innocence, that she will be arrested for untoward behavior, Karpilove makes the theoretical problem of vice policing much more real for her readership, allowing them to experience as though firsthand the narrator's fears relating to her vulnerability under the law. She offers through entertainment fiction an editorial on the legal status of the single woman living alone in a tenement apartment in the early twentieth century.

Despite its political agenda and social awareness, for today's readers Karpilove's novel may at times feel narrow and restricted in scope: we never read of the narrator's work, though we know that she is an independent, wage-earning woman. We learn little about the labor conditions, family relationships, leisure activities, or Jewish communal organizations that readers of American Yiddish literature may be accustomed to reading about in more widely anthologized and translated works and expect to see depicted here. Instead, we find ourselves confined within the narrator's relationships to at-times-insufferable men speaking at a whisper in her tiny rooms so as not to be overheard

41. Karpilove, 282; p. 258 in this translation.

42. Under New York City's prohibition against "disorderly conduct," police were charged with the responsibility to keep prostitutes from loitering in public places for the purpose of prostitution. C. is threatening here to inform a nearby police officer that the narrator is a prostitute soliciting him as a customer. See Willoughby Cyrus Waterman, *Prostitution and Its Repression in New York City: 1900–1931* (New York: Columbia Univ. Press, 1932), 12–13.

by her landlords or other residents. Nonetheless, Karpilove's *Diary* displays the political nature of women's intimate lives and relationships, demonstrating that young women's lives, like novels themselves, should not be dismissed as frivolous.

This English translation is offered to bring a new sense of the urgency and importance of the gender anxieties of the period as part of the political landscape of early twentieth-century urban American life, in addition to entertaining readers with its humor and suspense. It should inspire the reader to view historical and contemporary representations of women's struggles within and beyond romantic relationships as an important topic for political and literary study.

Bibliography

Berlant, Lauren. *The Female Complaint: The Unfinished Business of Sentimentality in American Culture.* Durham, NC: Duke Univ. Press, 2008.

Brody, Richard. "Lois Weber's Vital Films of the Early Silent Era." *New Yorker,* July 19, 2018, https://www.newyorker.com/culture/the-front-row/lois-webers-vital-films-of-the-early-silent-era (accessed September 9, 2019).

"Der kontrol fun gebort: a debate far di lezer fun der varhayt." *Di varhayt,* April 7, 14, and 26, 1916, 5.

"Editorials fun folk: vos di leyzer zogn." *Di varhayt,* September 11, 1916, 5; March 2, 1917, 5; February 13, 1917, 5.

"Emma Goldman lektshurt haynt." *Di varhayt,* February 8, 1916, 2.

Falk, Candace. *Love, Anarchy, and Emma Goldman: A Biography.* New Brunswick, NJ: Rutgers Univ. Press, 1990.

Fried, Trevor. *Form and Function in the Diary Novel.* Basingstoke, UK: Palgrave Macmillan, 1989, 54.

Fronc, Jennifer. *New York Undercover: Private Surveillance in the Progressive Era.* Chicago: Univ. of Chicago Press, 2009.

"Froyen protestirn farn aynloden Emma Goldman tsu redden far zey." *Di varhayt,* January 10, 1916, 5.

"Geburt-kontrol onheynger giben a diner Emma Goldman." *Di varhayt,* April 19, 1916, 8.

Goldman, Emma. *Marriage and Love.* New York: Mother Earth, 1911.

Grayzel, Susan R. *Women's Identities at War: Gender, Motherhood, and Politics in Britain and France during the First World War.* Chapel Hill: Univ. of North Carolina Press, 1999.

"*Haynt der miting in karnegi hall.*" *Di varhayt,* March 1, 1916, 2.

Hayward, Jennifer. *Consuming Pleasures: Active Audiences and Serial Fictions from Dickens to Soap Opera.* Lexington: Univ. Press of Kentucky, 1997.

Hopper, Briallen. "Pandora in Blue Jeans." In *Hard to Love: Essays and Confessions,* 59–66. New York: Bloomsbury, 2019.

Horowitz, Rosemary, ed. *Women Writers of Yiddish Literature: Critical Essays.* Jefferson, NC: McFarland, 2015.

Jones, Faith. "Criticizing Women." *Bridges* 13, no. 1 (Spring 2008): 76–81.

———. "Everybody Comes to the Store: People's Book Store as Third Place, 1910–1920." *Canadian Jewish Studies* 18, no. 19 (January 2010): 95–119.

Karpilove, Miriam. *A provints tsaytung.* New York, 1926.

———. *Tage-bukh fun a elende meydel oder der kampf gegen fraye liebe.* New York: S. Kantrowitz, 1918.

Kellman, Ellen. "Miriam Karpilove." In *Jewish Women: A Comprehensive Historical Encyclopedia,* Jewish Women's Archive, March 2009, https://jwa.org/encyclopedia/article/Karpilove-miriam (accessed March 8, 2018).

Keire, Mara Laura. *For Business and Pleasure: Red-Light Districts and the Regulation of Vice in the United States, 1890–1933.* Baltimore: Johns Hopkins Univ. Press, 2010.

Kim, Grace. "*Where Are My Children?*" *The Embryo Project Encyclopedia,* May 26, 2017, https://embryo.asu.edu/pages/where-are-my-children-1916 (accessed September 10, 2019).

Klepfisz, Irena. "Queens of Contradiction: A Feminist Introduction to Yiddish Women Writers." In *Found Treasures: Stories by Yiddish Women Writers,* edited by Frieda Forman, Ethel Raicus, Sarah Silberstein Swartz, and Margie Wolfe, 21–64. Toronto: Second Story, 1994.

Manor, Ehud. *Louis Miller and Di Warheit ("The Truth"): Yiddishism, Zionism, and Socialism in New York, 1905–1915.* Brighton, UK: Sussex Academic Press, 2012.

McCarthy, Margaret. "The Representation of Prostitutes in Literature and Film: Margarete Böhme and G. W. Pabst." In *Commodities of Desire: The Prostitute in Modern German Literature,* edited by Christiane Schönfeld, 77–97. Columbia, SC: Camden House, 2000.

McGraw, Eliza. *Edna Ferber's America*. Baton Rouge: Louisiana State Univ. Press, 2014.

Meyerowitz, Joanne. "Sexual Geography and Gender Economy: The Furnished-Room Districts of Chicago, 1890–1930." In *Unequal Sisters: A Multicultural Reader in U.S. Women's History*, edited by Ellen Carol DuBois and Vicki Ruiz, 307–23. New York: Routledge, 1990.

"*Milkhome un geburth kontrol in di moving piktshurs*." *Di varhayt*, April 8, 1917, 12.

Peiss, Kathy. *Cheap Amusements: Working Women and Leisure in Turn-of-the-Century New York*. Philadelphia: Temple Univ. Press, 1986.

Pinsker, Shachar. *A Rich Brew: How Cafés Created Modern Jewish Culture*. New York: New York Univ. Press, 2018.

Pratt, Norma Fain. "Culture and Radical Politics: Yiddish Women Writers, 1890–1940." *American Jewish History* 70, no. 1 (September 1, 1980): 68–91, 82.

Reyzin, Zalmen, "Miriam Karpilove." *Leksikon fun der yidisher literatur, prese un filologye* 3 (1929): 575–76.

"Sex O'Clock in America." *Current Opinion* 55 (August 1913): 113–14.

Warnke, Nina. "Immigrant Popular Culture as Contested Sphere: Yiddish Music Halls, the Yiddish Press, and the Processes of Americanization, 1900–1910." *Theatre Journal* 48, no. 3 (1996): 321–35.

Waterman, Willoughby Cyrus. *Prostitution and Its Repression in New York City: 1900–1931*. New York: Columbia Univ. Press, 1932.

White, Kevin. *The First Sexual Revolution: The Emergence of Male Heterosexuality in Modern America*. New York: New York Univ. Press, 1993.

Woodford, Charlotte. *Women, Emancipation, and the German Novel*. London: Routledge, 2017.

*Diary of a Lonely Girl, or
The Battle against Free Love*

1

Loneliness

A. came to my home yesterday. As he held me in his arms I felt small and lonesome. He didn't come to bring me happiness; he only came to take some of it from me. No, that's not quite right. He calculated carefully how much love he should give so that he wouldn't owe me anything.

I wanted to tell him that I won't make any demands, that he can leave me to my loneliness if he doesn't love me anymore, that I'll settle for a bit of happiness now even if it means I'll be unhappy later. But I couldn't bring myself to say this. I was embarrassed and afraid that he wouldn't believe in the selfless love I was offering him. In the face of his superficial love, his insipid tenderness, my tongue was paralyzed. He made sure to make it absolutely clear to me that there could never be anything between us, flippantly dismissing me for taking too seriously something he saw as a childish flirtation.

Maybe it isn't good or practical to forget yourself. But it's much worse to remember yourself, to only think about yourself, like he does. His cold, matter-of-fact soul can't understand this, and I can't explain it to him.

After he left I contemplated myself in the mirror for a while and counted the impressions that his kisses left on me. I didn't smile at this, instead I felt hurt.

My soul was soaking in a sea of heartfelt feelings and I wanted to release them in tears. I tried to sink my thoughts like stones into that sea.

I resolved that next time he comes I'll behave badly. I'll laugh in his face audaciously, mockingly. Here's what I'll do: I'll go along with him as he flirts within limits, indulge his careful, almost calculated behavior. And then, when he already has one hand on the doorknob to leave me alone again until he has time to come back, only *then* will I tell him there's no reason to be afraid of taking me once and for all. I'm not at all what he thinks. I know I have no right to expect him to feel obligated to me. Then he'll realize that it's his own sincerity that makes him so laughable. I'll ask: Don't you understand why I'm laughing? I'm laughing at you! At your fear, even when there's nothing to be afraid of.

How bewildered and embarrassed he'll be, standing there! Maybe he'll suddenly try to grab me, but I'll stand firm and show him to the door. That will be my payback for his *love*.

No, I don't know if I'll be able to do that.

Alone, I wander the noisy streets of New York. With autumnal feelings I greet the summer. My soul is encircled by a wintery coldness. While everything around me lives, I feel as though something in me is dying. I know what it is—it's hope. It extinguishes within me.

My room feels small to me. Everything there reminds me of him. I try not to think about A. He's dead to me. He loves other women. He can parcel out his love among many. But I can't; I can love only *one*.

Never mind. Now, I don't love him anymore. I only hate my loneliness. He can go wherever he wants.

When he's with me, I only feel the distance that separates us more profoundly. When he's not here, I think about being with him; but when he *is* here, all I can think about is how he's going to leave me again . . .

❧

I couldn't sit there in my room anymore and wait, knowing it was for nothing. He won't come. So I decided to go back out amid the hustle and bustle. I hoped he'd come to my room looking for me and find that I wasn't there. I decided to get on a streetcar headed far, far away. I wanted it to carry me, and my heavy thoughts, away. That would be easier than walking around, burdened with them.

I traveled far away on a streetcar that was packed with people, until it stopped. All of the passengers left, and so did I. The conductor started to change the sign to drive back and turned to look at me. I was standing and holding onto the car with one hand, as though I was trying to keep it from driving away from me. "There's another one coming after this one," I told myself, and I decided to walk around a little and plant my thoughts in the green field, and see where I found myself.

Suddenly I found I was in a cemetery. I'd wandered into the cemetery without knowing it. The others who traveled with me knew where they were going. They all walked among the graves, and aside from them there were others who came, holding flowers. Why do the dead need flowers, if they can't see them or smell them?

I approached a headstone, began to read the name of the deceased engraved in gold letters and thought about the dead woman, when I suddenly noticed a man standing beside me. He looked at me with puzzled curiosity. I quietly stepped away, and he stepped closer to his—what was she to him?

Now I avoided the graves that others were approaching. I quickly passed those where others were standing. It seemed to me that my presence disturbed the conversations between the living and the dead. And the dead, waiting for their living visitors, were offended by my dull, indifferent glances at their graves. Who was I to them, a stranger, that I should come here and disturb their peace? I was embarrassed in front of them. If I had someone there, if *he* had been there, how different I'd have felt. Not *so* superfluous, not *so* alone . . .

Alone among the living and the dead.

2

Despair

A letter from A. My heart stopped beating. I opened it: he wants to see me, to come to me.

A ray of hope shone through the cloud of my despair like a flash of lightning. Everything swayed before my eyes like it was going to crash at my feet and bring me along with it. I held onto my bed frame. My bed in its spotless whiteness looked up at me as though reproaching me for my desire for him to come.

His handwriting breathes with such calm! His writing evidences such careful economy! He writes so that anyone might read his letter, but leaves space between the narrow lines for me to read into them. He's not afraid to do this; he can be sure that I won't tell anyone what I read there.

If only I could manage to refuse to let him come over, perhaps that would be better for me in the end, but . . . no, *I* want to see *him*! I . . . yes, I'll answer him. I'll write to him in cold, calculated words that anyone can read, and while he arrives, stays, and goes away again I'll pretend to be indifferent to him.

A. just left. I feel that everything between us is over now, and I'm overtaken by a passionate desire *not to exist*.

When you can't stand someone anymore, you tell them to go away or you go away yourself. But what do you do about yourself? I'm tired of myself, and I can't get away from myself.

I watched him leave for a long time, thought about his leaving for a long time, and sent after him the words I wanted to say to him but did not say. My tongue froze in my mouth because of his stern silence and his casual conversation about other, general things. It was hard to think about one thing and talk about another. I wanted to speak to him with familiarity, but had to reply formally in order to stress the difference between detachment and intimacy. Waiting for him, I unwillingly almost wished he wouldn't come. It would have been better for me to remain with my longing, rather than allow for the continuation of *nothing*.

For a while it seemed to me that if he only knew how I suffer he would give everything else up for me, even his love for the other, unknown woman who peeks at him from among his grandiose plans for the future.

I hate his love. I don't want it anymore. A love that has no future is not worth anything in the present. Distant relationships are only good when they are followed by closer ones. You can be a freethinker about everything else, but not about love. Love requires fanatics. A. is not one. He's a casual gambler who risks exactly as much as he doesn't mind losing.

I cried. I cried until I couldn't cry anymore. The tears washed away the last bitter feeling of disappointment over my foolish hope for a miracle—that his love would become like mine.

Because I wanted to feel indifferent to A. and wasn't able to (because I got lost in my love, which is greater than me), I told him in no uncertain terms that it would be better for both of us not to see each other anymore. He was silent, and so was I. Without words we squeezed each other's hands, looked away from each other, and departed.

My love is dead. I will not make any effort to save it. It's dead, if you try to resuscitate it may limp along, but it won't truly come back to life.

3

~

It's Spring Again

I t's spring again.

"The holiday of love is here again, the awakening of nature with its soft, smooth, satiny breezes, its newly awakened longings and hopes of joy." So say many who write, describe, and praise the spring.

I don't say so. I feel differently. When I see the spring, the thought comes to me, "Soon it will be winter again."

Looking at the closed flower buds, I see flowers already withering. When the trees put on their new green clothes I already see how the yellowed, thin leaves fall to the ground in the silent cries of the angry wind.

I see the death of things when they're barely born.

~

For whole evenings, I sit by myself and know that no one will come to see me. I also don't want to go out and see anyone. For hours at a time I stare out my window, which looks out forlornly over many other windows, like my own, that cut lines through the large tenement buildings. They gaze with longing and sigh over the emptiness that fills the poor lives behind them.

In one of the windows I see her, a woman who has not yet begun to live for herself, but who through long years of hard work has helped him to graduate. Now he looks at her condescendingly. Fear shines from her tired eyes with the thought that soon he will no longer want to look at her at all.

I see her as one already run over by the wheels of the car he drives in his pursuit of success.

How sad she looks! How depressed, how discouraged, waiting for him when he doesn't come! And when he does come, she seems to want to become someone else for his sake—a younger, prettier, more pleasing woman. He can tell, and that only makes her misfortune greater. Love is a game in which you must not show your cards.

The youth of the woman is the springtime of her life. That is the youth of the *wealthy* woman. The lonely, poor girl has no spring, for her it's always autumn and winter.

∽

The man always wants to appear stronger than the woman. And if he becomes strong on account of her weakness, then he becomes her enemy.

Nietzsche says, "If you give someone the opportunity to show how great he is and he doesn't use it, he will never forgive you for it."

∽

I look at my hand and kiss the kiss that *he* left on it the last time he was with me, before he left. I love A. He does not know how much I love him and I won't, I can't, tell him. His not loving me while not knowing how passionately I love him wounds my heart. But if he didn't love me even knowing how I love him, that would wound my pride. Everyone would be able to see my wounded pride, but my ailing heart they cannot see. I can hide my suffering. I can keep it well, *well* hidden.

My suffering is dear to me. I bolster it by imagining his love for other women and feel a painful pleasure in torturing myself, in suffering for him.

∽

He insists that I come to him! He says that it's quiet and nice where he lives. There are no other people, no strangers to disturb our lovemaking. He pretends not to be bothered by public opinion, and yet he's looking for a way to hide from it. If his love is truly from his heart, his soul, his conscience, why should he keep it a secret, like it's a sin?

If he wants to be the conqueror, I refuse to be the conquered. My victory will be that I'll refuse to let him win. I must be the ruler of my own will. If I don't wish to make him a slave to his conscience, why bring him to that, so that he'll suffer later on my account?

No. I won't go to him, and I don't care if he never comes to me again!

∽

I just wanted to see the house where he lives. The window to his room.

The room was half-lit. No one could be seen through the thick curtain. I stood in a dark corner on the side of the street across from it, and my heart pounded: "His window. The light is on . . . If I were to go right now to him I wouldn't be alone anymore. I'd just go in and then come right back out. I'd bring with me the touch of his hand, a kiss, a glance, a word—"

But no. I couldn't do such a thing. What would he, even he himself, think of me? No, I must not go to him. Let him come to me if he wants. And if my white room with its thin walls and people close by bothers him, then what he wants to do should never happen anyway.

That's his window, I thought. He's probably sitting in a corner in his solitary room, reading. Or laying on his bed and thinking—perhaps thinking of me. What would he do if he knew I was standing so close to him? He would run and call to me, invite me in.

His curtain opened. From behind it a womanly figure appeared. She stuck her head out of the window and looked at the sky. Behind her, he appeared. It was *him*, him! She turned her face toward him and offered her lips for a kiss. His head bent toward hers. They sank down so that they were hidden behind the back of a chair. Two long, naked, snowy-white arms fluttered above the back of the chair.

Then the arms disappeared. The room darkened. Maybe it only seemed darker to me because of the dark cloud that sneaked into my soul and pressed down on my heart, making me feel as though I'd been banished from the world.

How I fled from there! As though evil spirits were chasing me! But now, now I am calm, calm as a corpse.

A soft wind cools my feverish brow. Someone sings about spring, about happiness, about love.

4

Shabes Night

The ticktock of the clock, the pulse of time taps, taps, like the beat of my heart, steadily, monotonously. Suddenly it skips, dies out, and then pounds again.

I try to think about faraway things, to cast my thoughts on the entire world, and they come right back to focus on me, on me alone. Like an empty thing, like an unattended ship, my little world sails on the great sea of life.

It doesn't matter how much I want to engage with the woes of the whole world, with the suffering of all of humankind. It's hopeless. My ego doesn't want to, can't be indifferent to itself. My pessimism, instead of leading me to thoughts of suicide, makes me not even care whether I live.

❧

I feel lonesome, painfully, horribly lonesome on nights like these, more than any other night of the week. I know exactly what causes it. Tonight is the end of *shabes*.

I've felt the loneliness of *shabes* night since childhood. It has grown into a chronic sadness, a kind of religious melancholy.

In my thoughts I return to my childhood; I close my eyes and see myself on a Friday evening among my own family in that old, faraway world. How beautifully we would welcome *shabes*! My strict father would become gentle as *shabes* approached. My quiet mother would grow calm and soulful. Everyone in our house looked refreshed, especially my *bobe*, my grandmother. She would dress in her finest clothes and would say something kind to everyone with a childlike smile and pious lips. And my grandfather, my perpetually worried *zeyde*, whose mind always dwelt on the long *goles*, would sing *"Sholem aleykhem"* to the angels of peace with such a heartfelt and soulful melody!

We never did weekday work on *shabes*. The adults spent the day resting and the young people spent it having fun; young men would get together with my brothers, young women with my sisters, to read, sing, play at forfeits and take walks.

Shabes—that was the loveliest, best, greatest, most beloved day of the week!

Therefore when *shabes* day turned to evening, a strange burden, a heavy feeling, weighed down my heart. When it came time to make *havdole*, to separate the holy from the workaday, the light from the darkness, my soul would cry out: it did not want to separate with the other soul, the extra soul that only came for *shabes*!

In that same place, where on Friday night so many happy lights burned, on *shabes* night the *havdole* candle sorrowfully sputtered until it was suddenly extinguished by red wine poured over the cleared table.

My mother's bright face displayed a quiet sadness. She helped my father prepare for his journey into the forest, where he was the only Jew among many non-Jewish peasants. She followed him and called after him to watch where he was going. Then she watched the wagon until she could no longer see it.

A feeling of workaday loneliness filled every corner of our darkened home. We could hear my *bobe* singing *"Got fun Avrom."* She purposefully delayed and elongated her *hamavdil* in order to keep the sinners in *gan eydn* a little while longer, so they wouldn't have to return so soon to *gehenem*.

My good *bobe*, she was always so good to everyone, even to the wicked ones in *yener velt*!

She had a very high opinion of the afterlife, the true life. This world, she would say, was only created to test people and see how many good deeds they can perform. And woe to anyone who arrives *there* with empty hands, having accomplished nothing! A man who makes nothing of his life is not worth his death. He doesn't deserve to be taken in by the ground. The earth itself should spit him out.

Almost every *shabes* night she would launch into a speech about death. *Zeyde* would say to her, "Again? Already? We've just blessed the new week . . ." He didn't imagine he'd find much of an improvement in the afterlife. You *have* to go there, he'd say, because you must. No one can escape death. But it's better to be a living dog than a dead lion. If she, my *bobe*, wanted to spend her life getting ready to die, that was fine, she could do what she liked. But he would excuse himself from that pleasure; while you're living you should see what you can do to better your life, not worry about your death. Whether you want to or not, in the end everyone has no choice but to die. As soon as you're born, you're already destined to die. You're destined to return to where you came from. So you dance as much as you can at this foolish wedding, you live your life to its end. Old people must make room for the new, that's how it goes.

That's usually how they talked on *shabes* night as the holy day came to a close, but never on Friday night as the holiday began, or on *shabes* itself. They were careful not to disturb the sacred holy day with sad words. On *shabes* they would thank God for the pleasure and pride they took in their children and their grandchildren and yearned to live to see their great-grandchildren and hoped to experience great-great-grandchildren. *Shabes* brought them rest and peace, it brought more desires and hope to their old-young souls.

My *zeyde* is no more, my *bobe* is no more. My parents are somewhere far away, old and weak, and my sisters and brothers are scattered far and wide. The Friday evening joy no longer exists, all that remains is the loneliness and sadness of *shabes* night.

5

Fighting with Myself

The silent walls of my pale room look at me, reproaching me for not admitting within them even a ray of happiness. My damp eyes look resentfully back at me through the mirror, rebuking me for not allowing them to see the bright world. Is it my fault that I can't force myself to be happy? Do I hate myself for not allowing myself to love? Why do I let my thoughts go against the feelings that are like sisters to my desires? Why, oh why? Perhaps I hate myself. I am my own enemy. I hate myself and I can't escape myself. I'll be stuck with myself until the day I die.

❧

I tell myself to stop thinking about myself, try to lose myself among thoughts of the millions of other people in the wide world and simply *stop existing*, be nothing. I am not here. But then whose arms are these, reaching out for *him*? Whose lips are calling *his* name?

❧

I'm seized by a sudden fear. I'm afraid of going crazy. I want to gather my tired thoughts toward one purpose—not to think at all. I will suppress my feelings. I want to be indifferent toward myself and toward everything around me. I want to call him back and say to him: you love me, I hate myself. I don't care what the end will be; whether I, like thousands of others, will be lost, whether I'll find myself insulted, lost, rejected until some later date. I no longer want to be what I am: lonely and alone. I don't want to be so ensnared in my sadness for my dead life.

To think that I could even consider calling A. back after he's already come and gone, perhaps having already decided never to return! Why did I act as though I didn't see him when he was here, sitting right next to me? He looked at my half-closed eyes, said that I was very pale, that I seemed tired, sick, asked what was wrong with me and I answered—*nothing*.

If my silence communicated nothing, then my passion was a complete waste. Whoever does not understand the language of silence—the language of eyes, hands, and voices—is not in love. He doesn't love me.

But if he doesn't love me, why did he come? Just out of curiosity, to see whether *I* love *him*? Did he want to compare me with other women?

I looked at A.'s neck and pictured the two arms that had wrapped around it while I stood in a dark corner in front of his window like someone banished from the world. At the thought, a gnawing pain pierced my heart like the point of a spear. I freed my fingers from his and suppressed the pain so that a sigh wouldn't give it away.

Why is he to blame if he loves me the same way he loves others? He wants to live the way *he* wants. He wants to exchange the grand feeling of one great love for many smaller ones. If I asked him why he carried on with another woman in his room, he would answer that it was because I had not come to see him. I gave away my place to the other woman; I withdrew myself from him of my own accord.

There's so much I could say to such an answer! But I was silent, silent like all the other times I've had so much to say. I was silent and only retreated further when he tried to draw closer to me. He finally went away bearing his wounded pride.

Men have a different sort of pride than women do. Women are proud of their virtue, and men are proud of their sins. While women yearn to love, men long to *live*. But loving and living are two different things, even if they often go together. Love is what makes life beautiful, while *living*, the way he means it, is the death of love.

∽

I'm trying to wrest control of my feelings from my rational mind. It tells me to rid myself of this crazy desire for fanatical love if I don't want to betray myself, if I don't want to lose not only my self-love, but also my self-respect. It seems to me that there is no struggle more difficult for women than the struggle between love and self-respect.

Will I win this fight?

Fighting oneself is the greatest fight; vanquishing oneself is the most beautiful victory.

6

Sadness

There's a subtle feeling in the soul so delicate, so tender, that words can never fully describe it. That's why I was silent for so long when he wanted me to speak. Captured in the grip of my anxiety, I waited for him to understand me without words.

In my imagination I lay down like a carpet before his feet and invited him to step on me. If I was left alone after he'd walked all over me, I'd still silently kiss the footprints he'd left behind. I didn't show any of this, I hid myself and my suffering, so that I wouldn't be in his way—in the way of his dreams of a more expansive life for himself.

"What are you thinking?" he wanted to know.

"About life—"

"Life is—loss . . ."

"If what they say is true, a woman's life is for loving."

"What is a man's life for?"

"For—living."

My thoughts and feelings, heart and soul, once again struggled against this life, protested against his indifference and indecisiveness. I was seized by a desperate desire to wrench myself away from myself: to be free once and for all from my own instinctive defensiveness, to separate myself from my reservations and to throw myself wholeheartedly into the arms of *life*!

My hands, my fingers, grasping at him whenever he wanted to leave, silently told of my longing, my desire, my decision to sacrifice my love so he can have his life.

"Strange, mysterious hands!" he admired. "See how they reach for me with such desire! How wonderful it would be to have your hands to myself forever, to always be under the magnetic force of those passionate fingers!"

"It would be easier to pry me away from myself than to take away my hands. That's how tightly they're bound to me," I laughed sadly.

"How long would you allow yourself to be taken away from yourself?"

"As long as someone loved me," I responded, trying to still my pounding heart.

"Then what?"

"Then . . . nothing."

"What would become of you then?"

"What do you think would become of me?"

He looked at me in silence. I bit my lips as though they were to blame for my speaking those words that I'd kept so carefully hidden inside myself for so long. My gaze fell to the ground, as though searching for a grave in which to bury myself alive. I had spoken, bared my feminine soul for someone who did not understand it. Even worse, who *misunderstood* it. I felt that he viewed me as someone who pretended to be submissive in order to be able to dominate him later. He thought I only wanted to fool him, to trap him!

I tried to take my hands away from his, hoping to hide my soul's desires from him again. But he wouldn't let me go. He wanted to be good to me, like a tyrant who only wants to protect his foolish subject so he can continue to have someone to torture.

He searched for an answer: he told me that he didn't know what to say, that he was afraid he'd disappoint me. He didn't know if he'd be able to live with just one love, for one person. Especially for *such* a person, the kind of person he'd have to give his whole life over to. He'd despise himself if he betrayed the trust of such a faithful, pure, good, and lovely girl. I'm much better than he is, so much better!

∽

I told him to leave me and never come back.

I hate my love. It forced me to offer myself to someone who did not want me. And he wasn't acting out of goodness; he was only being selfish. He was afraid that my love would be too much of a duty.

It must be true what someone once told me: "There are no good men, there are only selfish ones."

I feel like I could devour myself, tearing through my own skin with my fingernails; I could beat myself to death, rip out my heart and trample it under my own feet . . .

I can't look at myself anymore. I don't want to see myself. I cover my mirror with a black cloth. Now my room looks like a desolate corner in a house of mourning.

I'm in mourning. And I'm also the deceased. My chance at happiness, my last hope, has died and I'm a mourner returning from the funeral. I'm sunken in sadness, in a deep and boundless sadness.

7

The Letters

After not seeing A. for a long time, I met him again unexpectedly. I was terrified by the burst of joy that erupted like a flame in my soul. Such joy, I knew, could only end in sadness.

A. was happy too, and, like me, he tried to hide his joy. I didn't want him to see my foolish desire for happiness that wouldn't last. He hid his excitement out of his selfish desire that later, when his fleeting romantic feelings gave way to his practical view of life, he would not have to regret the words he'd spoken out loud.

I decided to lock up my feelings, not to let him see into the depths of my soul. I still remembered all too well what happened last time I voiced my feelings. And now, through feigned indifference, I wanted to smooth over the openhearted declaration I made last time. No matter how fiercely my heart pounded, like it was trying to applaud for love itself, my lips did not let one word pass that would give me away.

"You look very nice," A. said. "You've gotten even prettier since last time we saw each other."

"I'm well," I answered curtly.

"It's been such a long time since we've seen each other," he said after a short pause. "I wanted to see you, but I've been so busy!"

"Me too."

"You have too? With what?"

"This and that."

"I thought you always just kept to yourself."

"That's how it used to be."

"And now?"

"Now I'm busy with other—things."

"Have you made any new friends?"

"Yes . . ."

"Interesting people?"

"A few, very interesting."

"You see, that's good. New people make your life more interesting. You used to avoid new people."

"I got too used to the old ones."

"And now? Have you gotten used to these new ones?"

"I've made it a habit not to get used to anything."

"That's good."

Why did he seem so unhappy when he said "that's good"? It seems what's good for one person is not so good for another.

"Would you like to go to the park with me?" he suggested uncertainly.

"Sure, how about the park? The weather's so nice. But only for a little while."

"As long as you like."

"That's good."

"What, are you busy today?"

I nodded.

"Is *he* coming to see you today?" he asked with a faltering smile.

"I have to be . . . I promised to be in a certain place at a certain time," I responded firmly.

"Is it very important?"

"Yes, it's important."

"If so, then I won't keep you long. I'll let you go."

"Whether you let me or not, I do have to go."

"You've changed so much."

"This is how I am."

He was quiet and seemed sad. His displeasure pleased me. I felt easy, almost carefree. I thought, "It's so easy to make someone believe a lie. And it can feel so good, sometimes, to make someone else feel bad!"

Neither of us spoke. We walked to the park together like we were in pursuit of something. He kept sneaking glances at me. We ambled toward the setting sun, and for a time we stood and admired it.

"What a beautiful sunset!" he cried. "It would be so nice to sit here until sunrise!"

My heart quivered. Did he really want to sit there with me all night, or was he just testing me?

"Would you sit with me till morning?"

"Not today."

"Why not?" he asked.

"You know. I already told you."

"Ah, yes."

He bit his lip. He broke off a twig from a branch and hit it against the nearby trees. The thwarted lover protested. This woman who he was so sure he could always have at his side had refused his invitation to stay longer with him!

"Do you have to talk about it?" he asked contemplatively. "That's how words are. They can ruin a few hours—they can ruin your whole life."

We were quiet for a while. It was so hard to pay attention to the silence when there was so much we could be saying! How many kind, gentle words I could have spoken! I could have told him how I longed for him the whole time we were apart. But I sat next to him silently. My heart had drowned and died within me, yet it still longed for the time when I'd part from him and be alone with myself and my horrible loneliness.

A painful accusation took hold of me: A. was the one to blame for my suffering. I wanted to cause him pain, to take away some of his contentedness, his confidence in everything. I wanted to make him doubt whether my feelings for him had been true, and in doing so I wanted to bury his faith in others too.

"Do you really need to leave so soon?"

It seemed like he'd been thinking about it.

"Yes, I do, I'm sorry to say." I started to walk down the path that led out of the park. As I went, I was hounded by questions: "Who am

I running from, and who am I running to? From him to myself. And what should I do now? Where can I run to escape myself?"

He walked alongside me and looked unabashedly at the faces of girls heading toward us, into the park. They responded flirtatiously, and his silent glances seemed to promise them something as soon as I left.

"You're walking too fast," he said. "Why don't you take a streetcar, if you're in such a hurry?"

"A streetcar? Good idea. I will. Goodbye."

"I'll go with you to the streetcar," he said, grabbing hold of my arm as I was waving goodbye.

It was all the same to me whether he went with me or not. Either way, it would only be a few minutes until I'd be alone.

With a sharp pain, my heart shattered. I felt like gasping out loud. I looked at him with hidden horror, trying to see if he could tell what was happening inside of me.

"Do you want to say something?" he asked, catching my glance.

"Say something?" (Yes. I wanted to say something that he would remember.) "Yes, I do. Do you still have my letters?"

"Yes."

"You certainly don't need them."

"Do you want them?"

"I . . . yes. I'd like them back."

He looked at me strangely, bit his lips and, after a long pause, said, "Do you want me to bring them to you?"

"You can send them to me, if you'd rather."

Another long pause, and then a quiet, stubborn, "Alright."

The letters that belonged to A. are now laying here in front of me. They silently ask how I could take them away, how he could give them up. He does not love me.

I did it to myself. By taking the letters back, I broke the last thread of memory that connected me to our past. I want to tear up the letters, these tangible signs of my love. I want to burn them. But I can't. My heart begins to pound; my hands fall powerlessly to my side.

A spark of hope, like lightning amid dark clouds, shines through my desperation. Perhaps he'll come for them. Maybe he'll ask me for them back. After all, they're his!

8

Dreams

I heard a rumor that A. was sick and this gave me some solace. Right away, I resolved that I'd visit him.

I could almost see it: I'd knock softly on his door, enter, and stand by his bed contritely, knowing that his illness was caused by pining away for me. Holding my breath as I looked at him lying there, his face pale and his eyes closed, I'd order my heart to beat more softly so as not to wake him. He'd half-open his eyes, sensing my presence, and a pained smile would appear on his lips. He'd reach out his hot, dry hand toward me.

I'd lower myself onto my knees in front of his bed and press his hand to my lips. He'd gaze at me with a weak but contented smile and say, "You came. I knew that you'd come. You angel—don't leave me! Sit right here. Lay your hand on my forehead. How I love your touch! Why, oh, why did you ask me to return my letters? I gave them back to you, I did, but it hurt me so!"

"I was jealous of them," I'd say with a sad smile. "You kept them by your side, but you left me."

"Will you give them back to me? You haven't torn them up, have you?"

"Torn up your letters? After all, they're yours! I'll bring them back to you, all of them, and I'll write you more letters besides."

"I'll save you the trouble of writing. Everything that you want to say, you can say to me out loud. Will you?"

"I will."

But we wouldn't speak. Our eyes, our silence, would speak for us. We'd understand each other without words. We love each other. Love! Love!

This is how I fantasized about him as I was on my way to visit him. When I neared the house where he lived I was gripped by an instinctive fear of reality. My legs buckled as my hands hesitantly reached out to knock on the door.

Did I knock? I think I almost did, but the door opened right away and there he was, with someone else. They looked happy, like they were about to go out and have a good time. I wanted to run for it and jump down the stairs but it was too late. He'd already seen me. Affecting a formal tone to mask his astonishment, he asked what I wanted.

"Nothing! I made a mistake. I knocked on the wrong door. Excuse me." Having said this, I climbed sheepishly up the stairs. It was obvious that there was no one there I intended to see.

He watched me leave, stunned. He would have gone after me, no doubt, but the woman he was with urged him to hurry, they were running late. As for me, I hid in a corner like a thief, waiting to hear the gate close behind them, and only then I went home, utterly humiliated.

∼

For a while I lay awake in bed and thought about my dream and about what really happened. I went on thinking until the thoughts and memories blended together. I closed my eyes and I felt as though I were being lifted higher and higher, all the way to heaven, to God.

"State your request!" demanded an angel as he flew toward me.

"I want—to leave this world. I want to be in heaven."

"Your time to leave this world has not yet come. Pray for something that you need."

"Pray? What should I ask for? Perhaps weights and balances to measure my love."

"That's something you shouldn't ask for," the angel scolded. "It's not right. Too cheap, too small. You should give love without measure, even until you give all you have. Woe to anyone who measures and weighs love. Now come a little higher; soon they will pronounce a judgment for a man whose heart of stone could not be penetrated by the God of Love's arrows. Come!"

Clasped under the angel's white wing, I flew higher. I sat on the heights of a snow-white cloud.

"The judgment is coming!" the angel whispered in my ear. With bated breath I strained so I wouldn't miss a single word.

"This man," said one of the older angels, gesturing toward a young man, "as handsome as an angel, was preoccupied with measuring, calculating, whatever he gave to others. He was stingy, he kept everything for himself, and as a result others suffered terribly. Now let's hear what he has to say in his own defense."

A hush fell over the angels. There was a frightful expression in their heavenly eyes. Out of this silence the voice of the accused sounded like a broken reed.

"I calculated every last thing because I didn't know how long I'd live. I couldn't give my love to just one person because I had a big heart and wanted to give it to many people."

"Your heart is large enough for many people but too small for the one who gave you everything, who gave up her whole life for you!" cried out an angel. "Enough! We will deliberate on this sinner's punishment!"

All of the angels flew away but did not tarry long. Soon they returned with the ruling: "This man who weighs and balances everything will be punished with his own weights and balances. He will see plentiful goodness here in heaven but will not get any more than he was capable of giving. He may reside in *gan eydn*, but his palace there will be so sparse that it will be *gehenem* for him."

I looked at the defendant and I thought of A. He was young and handsome too, and he was also miserly with his love. I prayed to God, "Forgive him, for it was You who gave him the weights and balances, and You who did not soften his heart. If You had wanted, You could have enriched his soul, You could have made him a better man!"

"That is no argument," came the answer to my request from on high. "A man is given many things, but what he does with them depends on him. He must decide for himself."

"All by himself?"

"Yes, alone."

"And is he given enough wisdom to make such choices?"

"Yes, he is given wisdom."

"And a heart too?"

"And a heart."

"And also a soul?"

"And a soul."

"And a will?"

"And a will! Yes!" The voice was growing angry.

"Did You also give all of this to the man that I love?"

God was silent.

"Give it to him!" I begged.

"You, Daughter of Israel, should not bother the Eternal One with requests for another," my angel told me.

"But my happiness depends on another."

"He must make a petition for himself."

"He, himself?"

My angel left me. Heavy clouds drifted above me and pressed me back to the ground. Everything swam before my eyes and I collapsed with a shudder. I woke up.

9

Alone and with Others

I went to the park and thought about A. The bench where we once sat together had now sunk deep into the ground. Large, clear dewdrops hung on the grass next to the bench. It was as if they were tears I'd once silently shed in the darkness that had never dried.

There was a stone next to the bench. It looked to me like a gravestone for my dead love. I wanted to tie my love to the stone and let it drown. I can't bear to hate him. I wanted to let my feelings pour out of me in tears.

But no, I told myself, I must not cry! I shouldn't waste so much love on someone who wants only to *live*. I must forget him in the hustle and bustle of the life around me.

I went to a friend's house, and I saw A. there. I wanted to leave right away, but I composed myself and decided to stay. I wouldn't let him or the others see what I was feeling. I'd pretend to be happy.

The popular B. and his wife were among the guests. She's beautiful. Everyone thinks of her as pretty and foolish and considers her husband likeable and very smart.

A. eyed Mrs. B. She's nice to look at. She's beautiful. Her jet black hair is the perfect contrast to her snow white face. When she laughs she displays her beautiful teeth. Maybe that's why she laughs so often.

I started to feel restless. I didn't know what to do with myself. If I'd been alone, I probably would have cried, but I was with others so I decided to laugh.

Other than A., B. was the only interesting person there. So I invited him to sit next to me and talk about whatever he wanted. He told me that he wanted to talk about something he'd been thinking for a long time. It was something close to his heart. He simply had to say it.

"Well . . . ?" I asked.

"Didn't I tell you once, a year ago, that I like you very much? Do you remember?" He asked, looking right at me with his bright gray eyes.

"I remember something . . ."

"Good. But you didn't believe me. That's just my luck. I say something serious and people take it as a joke. Now, let me say that I still like you, even more than before. There's something about you that draws me to you. Something about your eyes, your whole being—your lips call to me, though your words push me away."

"Now I remember," I laughed. "You said the same exact words last time."

"Even better. That shows my constancy. I don't change my opinions as quickly as others. I'll say to you now what I wanted to say to you then—shall I? Will you permit me?"

"I don't know what you want to say," I smiled coyly.

"Do you think you could love me?"

"That wasn't a statement, it was a question."

"Alright, fine, let it be a question. Let's have a love affair. It will last as long as we love each other. What do you say? Say yes."

"That's a request."

"Alright, then let it be a request. So, listen to my request. You won't regret it. I'll love you so well! Why won't you let yourself love, like others do? Try to *live* a little and you'll see how you'll love it. Your little world will become wide and large, and you'll understand what life is."

"Now you're speaking as though it's already decided."

"Who cares what form I use to express myself? My point is the thing itself, this feeling we're talking about. I'm making you a proposition. Let's decide on a period of maybe two or three months that we'll love each other. Why are you laughing? How long do you think people can love one another? How long do you think you could love someone like me?"

"Someone like you? Forever."

"Don't joke with me. I'm serious. How long do you think you could keep up a passionate love?"

"Until it cooled off."

He moved in toward me and whispered, "I could love you much longer than other women. There's a quiet goodness about you that draws me to you. It would be a sin to leave you before you stopped loving me. You are one of those who would suffer silently, you wouldn't show your frustrations or your pain."

He spoke and I barely listened. His wife was chatting with A. She laughed and *he* laughed too. He avoided my eyes; he glanced at me when he thought I wasn't looking. Was he trying, like I was, to cover up his inner turmoil with forced cheer? Or was he simply enjoying himself with a pretty woman, even if she wasn't a very clever one?

The woman's husband wouldn't leave my side. He insisted that I answer his question. I knew that the socially acceptable response to such questions was to be insulted, to protest, to appear shocked, and so on. I didn't do that. I felt such indifference toward myself that I didn't want to defend myself. It didn't bother me that he was taking such liberties. The best I could do was to give an answer that made it seem like I thought he was only joking.

"I see that you're stubborn and I like it. You have spunk. The fiercer the battle, the sweeter the victory. So what do you say, should we have a love affair?"

I turned a blunt gaze on his sharp, fiery eyes and casually asked the banal question that any girl would ask, "What would your wife say?"

"My wife?" he exclaimed. "Nothing. Why would she need to know about it? If she carried on with a good-looking young man, would I forbid it? She's younger and prettier than I am."

"And it wouldn't bother you?"

"No. Jealousy's not my line. She's not someone who'd try to trick her husband. And if she did, that wouldn't bother me either."

"Don't you love her?"

"Love? How should I know? Maybe I did once. You know how it is. She's my wife!"

"No, how should *I* know how it is?" I laughed.

"If you don't know now, you'll know when you're married."

"I doubt I'll ever get married."

"It's better not to."

"What do you mean it's better not to?"

"Because I love you. I like you very much. Don't you see?"

"And what difference would it make if I were married? Who would care?"

"Who? Your husband! But maybe it would be better if we went behind his back . . ."

"Could we?"

"There's nothing we couldn't do if we wanted to. That's a law of nature."

"That must be a new law."

"Whether it's a new law or an old one, it's a good one. So, will you love me?"

"I can't say."

"Won't you let yourself love me? I'll come to see you. Do you live in a private room? I want to see you in your room, alone, without all these other people. Just with me. The two of us, alone."

I jumped up and said it was time for me to leave.

B. insisted on escorting me. His wife, seeing that her husband wanted to leave, also got up. A., after a moment's hesitation, stood up and followed her. They all accompanied me to the house where I board.

I said goodbye to all of them and caught my breath in the dark hall, behind the heavy door.

B. furtively glanced behind at my door. A. didn't turn around to look.

⌒

For a long time I've been staring at A.'s picture and I see myself in him. Me, with my stubborn need to hide what's going on inside my head.

Maybe he was trying to run into me on purpose, just to make me suffer. Maybe he wants to wait it out until I finally talk to him so he can repair our broken "friendship."

Which one of us will give in? Who, and when? He can take as long as he wants, but *I* will never be the first one to approach him. Not me.

10

〜

Let's Make Up

Sunday. I was sitting by my window watching the life passing by and imagining my future alone when Rae, a friend who's as lonely as I am—but with less patience for it—came to ask me to go to a picnic with her.

"It's no use waiting for some man to swoop in and take you out," she said with a cynical smirk. "You just have to go out alone. It's good to go out and meet people. If you don't, you'll never make new friends. If you end up running into people you know, that's fine, and if not, you meet new people."

"You want me to go out and meet people on my own?"

"Well, why not? Why shouldn't you go out alone? Can't we act like people too, even though we're girls? How come they can do everything, while we can't do anything?"

"That's a timeless question."

"Yes, it's an old one, and it should've been answered a long time ago. It's getting tiresome acting like old fashioned, well-mannered girls just waiting to receive a declaration of love and a marriage proposal. The whole notion is absurd. If you want something, if you have something to say and you know how—you should just say it!"

"Nevertheless, would *you* really be the first to approach a man you didn't know?"

"I wouldn't approach him the way a man would go up to a woman, but I would do something to make him approach me."

I laughed. She realized that I'd caught her out and said angrily, "This isn't a joke! Let's get to the point. Would you like to go to the picnic with me? Come on, let's go, if you want to. If not . . ."

"If not?"

"I'll go by myself!"

"Alone?"

"Yes, alone. I'm not going to shut myself up in my room and wait for nothing. I want to get away from my own company, I want to be with people, I want to—be happy!"

"I'll go too. I also want to be happy," I answered.

It occurred to me that maybe I'd see A. there with some other woman, young and pretty as an angel. If that happened I'd have to pretend to "be happy."

☙

When we got to the park the picnic was already underway. Large and small groups of people sat and lay in the grass. I felt a familiar, instinctive fear that I'd see *him* with someone like the woman I kept picturing in spite of myself. I noticed a secluded spot where I'd be able to see everything but wouldn't be noticed, so I asked Rae to sit there with me and help me think about how to begin to be happy.

"Wait a second! Just look who's sitting over there!," she said, squinting her near-sighted eyes at one of the larger groups. "Isn't that the famous B.—surrounded by two, four, six, seven women?"

"Yes, that's B.," I acknowledged, my heart pounding as I strained to see who else was with him.

"Do you see? Seven women around one man!" Rae laughed mockingly.

"Either the Messiah has come or they're at war."

"His wife's there too. Tell me, is she really such a beauty?"

"Yes, she's beautiful."

"But what a fool!"

"You might say that a woman who's that pretty can afford to be a fool."

"Maybe. See how they all laugh whenever B. says something witty? He's so lively and cheerful, certainly no fool. But there's someone else behind the tree. I can't see who it is. Can you?"

I looked and felt as though the park and all of the people lurched before my eyes. *He* was there. *He* was with them, next to Mrs. B. I wished that I hadn't come, but—could I really run away now? No. There was only one thing I could do: appear to "be happy."

Rae wanted to go over to them but I refused, saying, "Did we come here to add two more people to the seven already hovering around B.? *They* should come looking for *us.* Let's go where people are singing and playing guitar instead."

We went over to the singing group and found some acquaintances. They welcomed us warmly and invited us to sit with them and sing. We sat down. I sat a little further away from the group than Rae did. Rae protested against their Russian songs and started to sing her favorite Yiddish folk songs. People gathered around, which made her want to sing even more. Suddenly, I felt a hand on my head. I looked up and saw B. bending over me. He knelt in the grass and quietly asked me how I was, what I meant by running away from him, and why I was avoiding people.

"Because I like them better from a distance," I said, smiling.

"Do you also prefer *me* from a distance?"

"Aren't you a person?"

"But I like you when you're close."

"Thank you!"

"It would be better to say: if you like it, it's yours."

"I have no reason to say that."

He laughed and squeezed my hand, and I let out a quiet yelp. The others from B.'s entourage came and joined us. A. kept his distance. We barely greeted each other, nodding.

"I want to see you at your place, alone," B. whispered in my ear. "I'll come to visit you one of these days. Tomorrow, or the day after."

Mrs. B. sat down next to her husband, resting her hand on his shoulder. A. searched for a place to sit and found one between me and Mrs. B.

"Why aren't you singing?" he asked.

"When I hear others who sing better than I do, I prefer to stay quiet," I replied.

"I don't like these folk songs. They're too primitive."

"If you sing them with feeling they're beautiful, precisely because they're primitive. She sings them very well," I commented, gesturing toward Rae.

He shrugged his shoulders indifferently and looked away, annoyed. Rae finished singing "*Afn pripetshik*" and started singing a popular song with lyrics by Sholem Aleichem called "*Lomir zikh iberbetn*":

Let's make up
Have pity on me
Let's make up
I love you dangerously
Let's make up
I beg you to forgive me
Let's make up
Give me a smile
Let's make up
Quickly don't be scared
Let's make up
It's wrong to take too long.

"This is a nice song!" he exclaimed. "I like this one! 'Let's make up, it's wrong to take too long!'" He sang along and asked Rae to repeat it for him until he'd learned the song himself. In his enthusiasm for the song he clasped my hand.

"Let's make up! Let's make up!" he sang and looked at me until my whole attitude toward him, all of the anger that I felt for him, vanished. In my mind I sang out, "Let's make up, let's make up!" It was as though everyone was singing it just for us. "Let's make up, let's make up!"

11

Making Up

He was so handsome and looked so inspired singing "*Lomir zikh iberbetn*," and he held my hand with such warmth that all my resentment vanished. In that moment, I felt I could forgive him everything! Goethe knew what he was talking about when he said, "True love is that which remains forever the same whether all that it asks is granted or refused."

As it grew darker, many eyes began to shine. The picnic continued as it had begun, large groups separated out into small ones.

Rae, tired from forcing herself to "be happy," and not as sure of herself as the others, stopped singing and lay next to me in the grass with one arm flung around my waist and the other above her head. She called out, gazing vaguely into the distant darkness, "This is the life!"

"Could it get any better than this?" A. asked. It seemed to me that he was quietly laughing at us, two lonely girls who were trying to act joyful but not succeeding.

I withdrew my hand from his. His hand lay alone in the grass as though it had been snubbed.

B. must have thought that the hand was mine as it lay there in the grass looking so pale and quiet. He bowed his head sneakily so his wife would not see and . . . kissed it! A. startled, threw a surprised glance at me, and, seeing that I was choking back laughter, understood B.'s blunder. He yanked his hand out of the grass and scowled.

In the meantime, A. decided to get back at me. He drew closer to Mrs. B. and gave her his full attention. He removed his jacket and handed it to her so she wouldn't be cold. He offered to spread it out underneath her because "the grass is damp" and he didn't want her to "catch a chill." And was she comfortable sitting there like that? Perhaps she'd like to lean on him? He gave her his shoulder, so that she could get a little more comfortable.

"Oh, how nice," sighed Mrs. B. happily. "It's so nice to have a friend, isn't it?" she asked her husband.

"I think so too," her husband answered, and he inched closer to me until his head leaned on my shoulder.

I felt like crying so I started to giggle and act playfully instead, pulling out fistfuls of grass and throwing them at B. He pretended to nip at my fingers and I called him a cannibal and tattled to Rae that he was biting me.

"Watch out for rabies!" Rae laughed.

B. turned to Rae, joking, "What am I, a dog? What nerve!" He'd give us girls such a spanking we wouldn't soon forget it.

Mrs. B. acted startled, like she'd just woken up from a sweet dream, and watched with astonishment as her husband flirted with us girls.

A. avoided my gaze. In the middle of all this gaiety, against my will, I let out a deep sigh.

"She's in love!" B. cried out.

"Do you think so?" Rae asked. "Who's the man?"

Mrs. B. answered pointedly, "These days you may never find out, because it usually turns out that the man has a wife."

"The poor lover!" Rae cried, feigning a sigh, "I don't envy him."

"It's the woman who loves him that you should worry about."

"Hardly! After all, it's possible to divorce a wife."

"Would you like to sing something?" A. asked Rae, trying to change the subject.

"Sing? No. I much prefer to talk with clever people. And, if you must know, this topic is very interesting to me because I'm also on my way toward falling in love with a married man."

"You could just fall in love with a bachelor instead," said Mrs. B.

"A bachelor? There's the rub. All the bachelors today are in love with married women."

"Why?"

"Why? Why not? Probably it's more convenient for them."

I suggested we go for a walk. We'd been sitting in one spot for long enough. As I tried to stand up, B. pulled me back toward him. Finally I tore myself out of his hands and tried to get away from him, almost running. He chased after me.

The others joined us and we all left together, each of us preoccupied with our own thoughts.

∾

"Can I tell you something?" I heard A.'s voice saying to me when the others had gone off ahead.

My heart pounded as I answered, "Go ahead . . ."

"I want to give you some advice."

"Oh, thanks. What is it about?"

"You should keep your distance from B."

"Why?"

"He's a married man, you know."

"I know."

"He knows the art of love."

"Is love really an art, then? I thought it was a kind of feeling."

"It depends on who you're talking to. For him, it is an art. A girl should be cautious with such a man. I'm telling you this as a—good friend."

"As a good friend . . ." How noble of him, and how condescending. A *good* friend. Apparently there's such a thing as a bad friend too. He came to me to tell me to be wary of—someone else. Not to be wary of *him*, no, but to be wary of someone else! And he only came to warn me as a "good friend." How fine, how gracious of him!

"Is that everything you have to say to me?" I asked with unconcealed sarcasm.

"That's all. No—there's something else. I wanted to ask you something else. May I?"

"Ask away."

"Let's be friends, like we used to be," he suggested with a guilty smile. "Let's make up! Let's be friends!"

"That's all?"

At the thought of being friends, my heart filled up with a strange emptiness. How can you be friends, especially good friends, with the man you love?

12

Friendship

He walked me home from the picnic as a *friend* and was silent almost the whole time. He used to get silent that way in my room, sullen in the face of my own silence when I refused his advances. In a way, he's more transparent than those who lie out loud. He even lies with his silence.

"There's no love without desire, but there *can* be desire without love." That's how I used to chide him when he made passionate advances toward me without showing that he cared for me. Now, through his silence he wordlessly communicated his desire, even as he claimed to want only friendship. I refused to reciprocate this desire. I resolved not to show him anything but friendship as long as he continued to try to conceal his love. I'd lock up my feelings of love inside myself, beat my thoughts and emotions down with stones. I'd only be a friend to him and nothing more.

His calm, measured steps as he walked me to my apartment echoed in my mind and hammered out my resolve not to let him get past my front door.

I wouldn't allow him to sit at the foot of my bed like he used to, weaving threads of love into a beautiful lie to wrap around my soul, only to have him unravel it someday. No longer would I be like an orphaned child begging to be held in a stepmother's arms. I wouldn't let myself be silenced anymore. From now on, it would be all or nothing, love or friendship.

"Why don't you say anything?" he asked me suddenly. He, the man whose silence I'd tried so often to decipher.

"Why?" I said, surprised. It seemed to me that *he* was the one who'd been quiet this whole time.

"Yes, why? Your silence is so strange."

"Is it different from yours?"

"Yes, it's different. You want to say something, but won't."

"And you?"

"There's nothing for me to say."

"Oh, you have nothing to say. That already says a lot."

"Even if I did say something, you'd misinterpret it."

"For example?"

"I'm sure that you just took my words about B. the wrong way."

"What was there to understand?"

"A lot. You shouldn't let him think about you."

"It is hard enough to control my own thoughts, let alone someone else's."

"He's a married man and he has no right to fall in love with a girl like you."

I didn't say anything.

"Tell me," he said pensively, "why did you ask me to return your letters? I didn't understand it then, and I still don't. What did you need them for? And that time when you came to my door and then disappeared right away, after showing up so unexpectedly—what was that supposed to mean?"

"I heard that you were sick and I wanted to know more."

He looked at me warmly and pressed my hand in thanks. We walked together for a while, hand in hand, saying nothing.

I wanted to go past my door, but he stopped in front of it. He opened the door, took my arm and pushed me through, following me inside just like he used to do when there was no talk of friendship.

My heart started to pound. Suddenly I was left without resolve. I struggled with the thought: "Should I let him follow me, and there, in the quiet darkness, forget all about friendship? Or, should I leave him here, show him only friendship and refuse to let him get any further with me?"

Before, I had accepted his offer of friendship out of pride. I was afraid he might interpret a rejection as a confirmation that I still wanted his love. Now, my pride insisted that I shouldn't let things go any further than this friendship. I gave him my hand to say goodbye.

"I wanted to say goodnight to you upstairs."

"You can say it here."

"But it isn't even late yet. We could spend some time together upstairs. I want to talk to you a little longer."

"Then let's walk some more," I said.

"I'm tired of walking. I want to sit somewhere."

"But it's too late."

"Didn't we used to stay up together until much later?"

"If you were already up there and you wanted to stay longer, that would be one thing. But you can't come up so late."

"Are you afraid of what others will say?"

"Well—"

"But can't friends—"

"What do they know about friendship? All they care about is love affairs. They're always on the prowl for something naughty."

"So you mean to say that in order to stay late in your rooms, I need to arrive early? If that's how it is, then—"

"Good night!" I cut him off.

"Yes, good night! Though I don't want to go to sleep yet."

"Ah, but by the time you get home, you'll be tired enough."

"Are you going right to sleep?"

"I'll read for a while first. That's what I usually do."

"I will come see you again."

"Fine, come again. But if you want to see me in my room, it'll have to be at some other time of day."

"I'll write to you. Alright?"

"Alright."

❧

He left unwillingly and I went upstairs alone regretfully, thinking about him and his friendship, which stood like an iron wall between me and love. You can be friends before you fall in love or after your love is over, but you can't be friends while you're in love.

13

Nothing at All

He was here and now he's gone. He came and he left. We can't love each other. We can't be friends.

"You've changed," he said. "You're acting like someone else." He was unhappy that I didn't let him in, with his talk of friendship, so that he could kiss and cuddle.

"I want to protect our friendship."

"But can't friends—"

"Can't friends what?"

"Spend time together?"

"No, only lovers can do that."

"Don't you love me?"

I didn't say anything.

"I asked you something."

"What's the point? Why should you care if I love you or not? The only important thing is that *you* don't love *me*."

"How do you know?"

"Because you only want to be *friends*."

"What do *you* want to be?"

"Nothing at all."

❧

Rae came to see me and asked me to go for a walk with her. I went. She spoke about B.

"Everybody's talking about B.," she said. "He's the most well-liked man of all our friends because he's successful with women. He's interesting, you have to give that to him. It's never boring to spend time with him. Whatever he talks about, whether he's being funny or serious, it's always good to hear him talk."

Rae spoke about B. and I thought only of A. I thought about him and the "nothing at all" that I let come between us. What did he think I meant by it? Would he come to see me again?

I tried to catch the tail end of what Rae was saying, and to guess at the rest that I'd missed while my thoughts were elsewhere.

Suddenly she blushed and said, "Why are you looking at me that way? You don't think I'm in love with him, do you?" She scoffed, "You're all the same! You can think what you will of me, I don't care! I can fall in love with him if I want to, just to spite all of those married women. If men can have love affairs with married women, then I can have an affair with one of their husbands."

"That'll show them!"

"One way or the other."

"More one way than the other."

"But, my God!" Rae cried out dramatically. "Life is so boring! What are you supposed to fill it with? What about you, for example? What do you do with your time? Who do you spend it with? With books and books. All you do is read, read, read! You won't find life's answers in a book. Don't you want to have a friend?"

"I have friends."

"A *good friend*, I mean."

"I have good friends."

"What do they do for you?"

"The same thing I do for them."

"And what do you give them?"

"Nothing at all."

"Nothing! Nothing!" Rae exclaimed. "That's what's wrong with us! We give and we get nothing at all! We wilt before we bloom, we die before we've ever lived!"

I rushed home with the thought that I might have a letter from *him* waiting there for me. Rae didn't hold me back. She gladly offered to accompany me for a while. A few times she looked back as she walked with me, lost in thought.

"Wait up!" A voice suddenly called out from behind us. We both stopped short, startled. It was B.

"Speak of the devil," Rae laughed.

"Is that so? What were you saying about me?" B. asked, grabbing both of our hands.

"We won't tell!" Rae teased.

"And you?" he asked, turning to me. "How are you? What are you doing today?"

"Nothing at all."

"Well, nothing for you is something for other people. Are you the same naughty girl you were before?"

"The same as always."

B. took out his watch, glanced at it, and asked if we'd help him kill an hour or so, walking with him.

"Why should we want to go walking with a married man?" asked Rae.

"Should I divorce my wife so I can take a walk with you?"

Rae burst into laughter. He went on showing off his clever repartee. He gave her a few compliments and watched me to see my reaction. I said goodbye to them and went home alone.

I opened my mailbox. Inside it was nothing at all.

☙

B. came to see me. He came bearing many fresh flowers. They smelled so good!

"I've come," he proclaimed jokingly, "to set the time for our love affair. So now it's begun."

"It's started already?"

"Sure, it started at the picnic, didn't it? Okay, maybe it didn't. All the better. We can start it right now. It'll go from now until, let me check my calendar . . . what is today? The first? Let's make it until the end of next month. Is that enough time?"

"It's a little too long," I responded, smiling.

"If you knew how well I can love, you'd say it's not enough. Let's decide on the last day," he said, taking out his fountain pen and thinking out loud. "What should we write in here? Well . . . let's call it just what you said it was: 'Nothing at all.'" And he wrote in his calendar: "Nothing at all."

"Now we can start loving each other," he said, sitting next to me.

"But . . . no touching," I stipulated.

"No hands? What am I, a cripple?"

"A moral cripple, maybe, if you try anything with your hands. You'd do better to impress me with the power of your spirit."

"I need to get to know *your* spirit better first. Where is it, that soul of yours? Show it to me!"

"Find out for yourself."

"Alright. I'll find it soon enough. It can't hide from me. I've seen souls before!"

We went from joking to serious conversation. He told me beautiful stories about his childhood. We hardly noticed as the whole evening passed.

ᔕ

Maybe while B. was with me, A. was with Mrs. B. Why did I agree to let B. come back to see me again tomorrow? What can come of it?

I don't have to look far for an answer. All I have to do is lift my calendar's page to see: "Nothing at all."

14

Something

A kiss from an unmarried man seems to have a future. A kiss from a married man can instantly be written off as belonging only to the past.

B. doesn't believe in the future and doesn't concern himself with the past. All he cares about is the present.

"You think so much about the future that it robs you of every pleasure in the present. That's a shame, if not a crime," B. said to me today. "Take, for example, Schopenhauer. He says, 'Each day is a little life; every waking and rising a little birth, every morning a little youth, every going to rest and sleep a little death.' It's like Börne says, 'Happiness is the best life preserver in the current of life.' And even your Gorky says, 'You must bear yourself with indifference toward everything, not spoiling your life with philosophy, and not putting questions.'"

"The same Gorky, my Gorky, as you call him, also says that 'every minute of our lives must be dedicated to its highest purpose.'"

"Well?"

"What's the purpose of a love with an end we've already settled on, a love that we are calling 'nothing at all'?"

"There is *something*, though, between the beginning and the end."

"Oh, you mean *that* something!"

"Better something than nothing."

"Better nothing than the something you're after."

"I don't agree with you."

"I accept that you don't agree," I pontificated. "I mean, from *your* point of view. For someone who wants to stave off his boredom in the intermission between the acts of a humdrum family life, this *something* would be a good distraction. But for someone like me, for whom the *something* is not just a small episode, but an important event in her life, maybe that person should avoid it."

"I look at you"—B. wrinkled his brow and spoke after a long silence—"but I can't understand you. Does your platonic temperance come from a romantic perspective, or does it come from a pragmatic approach to life? What are you, really?"

"It's your job to figure it out."

"I can't! We've been carrying on a love affair for three weeks already and you are more of a riddle to me than ever. You're like the moon: the closer I get to you, the farther away you are. Instead of going forward with you, I'm going backward. What can be the end of such a path? I don't know! I'm so confused!"

"You won't get to the end of it, and you won't come here either. You'll go back to your own home."

"But when I go home, I take the thought of you with me there too. I think about you very much."

"But not too much."

"Very much. I am afraid I'll actually fall in love with you."

"Are you capable of that?"

"More than you might think. And what would become of me then?"

"Why do you need to think about that now? But if you're really so scared of what might happen later, you can tear yourself away now."

"Do you want me to go?"

"No. What's the alternative? After all, being with you is not as boring as being without you."

"Thank you!"

"Thank you for saying thank you!"

⁓

There's something about B. that makes me think about him and makes me want to see him again. I'm afraid I'll start to love him because I hate being lonely.

If the man I love with my whole heart won't come to see me, I'll let the man who loves me come, the man who speaks words of love to me, beautiful and carefully chosen words of love. Yes, maybe I'll start loving B. because he helps me forget A. for a while. If only B. were able to drive him from my soul forever.

But he won't be able to do that. No one can extinguish the death he left me with when he tore himself away from me to pursue his "life": a better, more comfortable, more certain life, from which I am excluded.

∽

A letter from A. Just a few words: "I wanted to write and to visit you but I didn't have time. I've been very busy." He said he might come by one day when he's in my neighborhood.

Very good. Next time he's passing by he'll come up to visit, find me with my "friend," B., and take in the scent of the fresh flowers that B. brings to my room. Although I love A. when he isn't around, when he's here I'll act as though I'm thinking about B. instead. When A. asks me what I'm thinking about I'll tell him it's B. That will be my revenge. A. is so ungenerous and calculating that he doesn't want to give me his love. So I'll take my revenge instead.

15

Loneliness

I sat alone in my room for three evenings, waiting by my door, and A. didn't come. I resolved not to wait for him anymore. I would respond to the other man's advances.

"If he comes he'll find nothing but a locked door, and he'll never know how long I waited for him!" I thought on the way to see B.

"I'm so glad you came!" B. exclaimed. "I was afraid you'd just look at my letter with one those melancholy smiles of yours and lay it to the side, or tear it up."

"Maybe that's what I should have done."

"Why would you do that? Darling, why? Isn't it better for us to spend the evening together instead of sitting alone, longing for each other? It's been five days since we've seen each other!"

"How awful!"

"It *is* awful. Wanting to see someone you love and not being able to is a horrible thing. But I couldn't come to see you." He paused. "Aren't you going to ask me why?"

"I'm sure you're going to tell me anyway."

"You're so cold!"

"No, I'm just waiting for you to tell me."

"You have a little too much patience. But I'll tell you anyway. Last time I left you and came home late, I found my wife in tears. She cried so much, you should have seen how she was crying! She knows I can't bear it when she cries, and that's why she does it."

"The poor woman!"

"Don't you mean 'the poor, unlucky man'?"

"Never mind that *you're* the one who made her cry."

"Yes, but when you're at fault it only makes it harder to bear."

"I see. Then what did you do to get rid of your discomfort?"

"That's why I wanted to see you and tell you about my situation. I want to hear what *you* would do about it if you were in my shoes."

"Me? I'd promise her never to come home late again, or never to leave at all. I'd try to show her that what I do with others means— nothing at all. It isn't worth crying over. I'd tell her that she's the only one, the best woman, the most beloved, and when I look at others from time to time, it's only to compare them to her and see once again how much lovelier she is. I'd say, 'You must understand that *you* are my wife, and I love *you*!'"

"But that would be a lie. She *is* my wife, according to the law, but I don't love her. I love—"

"Yourself."

"It's possible to love myself and also to love you," B. responded. "In the past, I've handled myself with others the way you act toward me. But you've taken away my sense of irony. I've lost myself to you, just like others lost themselves to me. You've vanquished me by not trying to win. But let's return to the subject of my wife. She and I are two very different people."

"Naturally."

"I mean we are strangers to one another. Strangers in spirit. They say that marriage is a graveyard for happiness, and it's true. If I could be free, I would—"

"Get married again."

"Yes. To you."

"It seems that one graveyard for happiness isn't enough for you."

"With you, my whole life would be a pleasure until its end. Why shouldn't we take what we can out of life, even in these circumstances? If we want to, we can take everything!"

"You're so modest."

"'Only fools are modest,'" B. countered with Goethe's famous quote.

As we bantered we came to a park. We sat, almost in silence, on a bench in a dark alley between thick trees, until it grew late.

～

When I opened my book the words I read there seemed to echo my own thoughts:

"No one can be indifferent to kindness and affection from someone else. When someone you love (or, I should say, like) kisses you, you feel happy, proud, and . . . required to respond."

"A young man came by and knocked on the door," my landlady told me. "A tall, handsome man. That's how it is. You can sit and wait all evening long and no one comes to call, but as soon as you go out, someone comes."

"Yes, that's how it is," I agreed. "It happens almost every time." I went into my room, where my angry thoughts held a meeting in my mind.

I wasn't well rested but I couldn't sleep. I kept tossing and turning. I'm so tired. Playing at love so late when I have to get up early to make a living is a luxury I can't afford. But . . . the loneliness!

～

B. paid me another visit today. He claimed he would only stay for a little while, just to see me and find out how I'm doing. But, like every other time, when he stood up as though to go, he sat back down.

"I missed you so! Yesterday more than ever," he told me. "You're becoming dear to me." Lost in these sad thoughts he sat for a long time, holding my hand.

"Go home, B.," I prodded him. "It's getting late."

"I won't go home. I want to be here with you."

"You have a wife," I reminded him, "and you don't want to make her cry again."

"Why should you worry about my wife? Do you think she cares about you?"

"*She* worry about *me*? What a joke! Go, go to her."

"She's not going anywhere."

"But she'll suffer. For no reason. For *nothing at all*."

"You suffer too. Don't you . . . also suffer? Do you really not love me at all?"

"I hate loneliness."

16

A Night with B.

B. just left. By the time he went, day was already breaking. There's no use in trying to go to sleep now, when I'm going to have to get up again so soon.

Now that he's gone I can breathe more freely. Now I don't have to worry about whether the people on the other side of the wall are awake to hear us. I can leave my door wide open. Let them come in to check on me! They'll find me alone.

For a man it's certainly nice to be in a young woman's room until dawn, speaking of love, urging her to *live* a little, and stealing kisses. But for the young woman, it is very, very uncomfortable. She can't give herself over to passion; she must also be governed by her cautionary thoughts. Restrained by her modesty, she must be vigilant, lest she become a "fallen" woman. She must always be wary of what others will think. What would her respectable landlady say if she found out that one of "her" girls was alone with a man, and not only that, but, of all things, a married man! Wouldn't that just make the heavens crash down! It might be better for the young woman to find a grave and bury herself alive in it. No wonder, then, that in such circumstances romance becomes laughable. Even the most earnest feelings must be buried in jokes.

He, for instance, out of passion for her, throws himself upon his knees and cries out, "My love! Dearest! Angel!" and seals his profession of love with a passionate, noisy kiss upon her lips. She, rather than throwing her head onto his shoulder, as would befit such a moment of passion, tears herself away, presses her finger to her lips to shush him, and looks this way and that, listening for a sign that someone might have heard them.

"What's the matter?" he asks, worried that his passionate kiss might have injured her teeth. "What happened?"

"How reckless can you be?"

"For God's sake!" he cries, looking into her mouth with concern.

"Don't you realize that you're not in the middle of a forest? People are sleeping right on the other side of this wall!"

"So? They're asleep . . ."

"They're asleep! Who even knows if they're really sleeping? What if they can hear us? They could throw me out and smear my reputation in front of everyone because of a kiss like that!"

"Slander you because of a kiss?" But this frustrated thought runs through the kisser's mind: "I can't believe she's thinking about the people sleeping on the other side of the wall at a time like this!"

Something like this happened between me and B. last night. Every time he tried to express his passion for me in noisy kisses I covered his mouth with my hand. He felt insulted. "Who are you afraid of?" he asked earnestly. "If you want, I won't hide my love for you from anyone. I'll tell your nighttime eavesdroppers who I am and why I'm here. I'll even tell my wife, if you want me to. She already knows I'm indifferent to her, that I love someone else, and if she knew how much I love you she wouldn't want to stay in the same house with me. She'd leave me and then we could—take your hand off my mouth and let me speak!"

"Shhh . . ."

"Be quiet? You ask me to be quiet when I feel like snatching you up in my arms and running with you, crying out wildly that I love you! I love you!"

"Please! Love me a little quieter . . ." I begged him.

"Why should I be quieter? Tell me, what are you so afraid of? Even *if* what the people on the other side of the wall might think were actually true, how bad would that be? Quite the opposite—I'd think it was a good thing. Imagine, dearest, how nice, how wonderful, how beautiful it would be if you had a baby! Don't you think so?"

"Yes, very nice . . ."

"You can't think that I would abandon you if that were to happen?"

"No, never!"

"I would never leave you alone like that!"

"No, not alone, just with a child."

"I wouldn't leave you with a child."

"If not me with a child, then the child with me."

"I'll show you! You'll see!"

"I don't have time. Show someone else."

Seeing that I turned his serious words into a joke, B. said nothing more. He held his face in his hands and it was hard for me to tell if he was crying or laughing. I knew that he'd hold that pose for a long time if I didn't ask him what was wrong. I took up the same pose: let *him* ask *me*.

Aha, this caused him to break from his pose faster than I expected. I felt his hand on my shoulder, my neck, my head, stroking my hair, trying to remove my hands from my face to see if I had shed tears. I almost fell down laughing, and he thought I was hysterical. He asked me if I was crying. "What's wrong? What is it?" He couldn't see any tears. He pulled my fingers away from my face and I buried him in kisses. With great surprise, he touched my eyes, trying to feel for any dampness, some sign that I had been crying. But his fingers only found that my eyes were dry. Disappointed, he hung his head.

It was funny to me.

My facial expressions betray me. I smile without even meaning to. I would look so different if these circumstances had been different! I would certainly have been more upset.

17

∽

With Rae

I love A., B. loves me, and Rae loves B. Three unrequited loves. It seems that one of us should be willing to make an exchange. But we each love the one who won't allow themselves to love us back.

∽

I saw Rae at the library. She didn't look very good, she was pale and run down. She glared at me with suspicion and I felt guilty.

She was looking for a book someone had recommended to her. "I have to read it," she told me. "It's called *When God Laughs* by Jack London. Help me look for it."

I helped her look, but my help was no help at all. We couldn't find it. She asked the librarian, who handed her paperwork for locating a missing book. "I'll have to wait for it!" Rae said as she followed me out of the library unhappily. Then she hurriedly asked, "Have you read it?"

"Yes, I've read it."

"Did you enjoy it? Did you regret it?"

"Regret it? Why?"

"Because—I'll tell you another time. Now, can you do me a favor and tell me what it's about? I want to know sooner than I'll be able to read it. Will you?"

"Gladly. There are two main characters, of course, a man and a woman. They are very much in love. To keep their love from dying out they decide to keep their distance from one another, even after they are married. They avoid embracing or kissing because they don't want to cheapen their love. They were both made for love, but they're devoted to their belief that everything is better before it's attained. They say that satisfaction is death. They live this way for months and years, and no one understands why. Women ask her why she doesn't have any children yet, since no one knows their secret. The two lovers live this way for some time, pious and chaste, when suddenly, one morning, while looking into one another's eyes, they realize that something has gone away. Their desire for each other has ended. Their love is dead. They look at each other with cold indifference. Shortly afterward he dies, and she writes in her diary, 'No hour passed when we did not want to kiss one another, but we did not kiss.'"

"Oh, how ironic!" Rae cried out furiously.

"Yes, they allowed their love to die because they wanted so badly to keep it alive! Instead of allowing themselves to love one another they followed abstract ideals. Hunger, it turns out, brings about a more certain death than satisfaction."

"Now I understand why he recommended it to me," Rae said to herself. Then, turning to me, she asked eagerly, "When was the last time you saw him?"

"Who?"

"You know who I'm talking about! B.! I *have* to see him. Should I tell you why?"

"If you want to."

"Here's the issue: things got very close between B. and a girl, one of my good friends. You don't know her. Well, he told her that he was prepared to sacrifice everything if she would just—love him as he loves her. He told her he would even marry her."

"How? He's already a married man."

"Well, he'd even divorce his wife for her. But all of a sudden, he stopped seeing her. Entirely. She doesn't know what to think. She feels so humiliated. She just wants to see him and tell him what she thinks of him. What do you think she should do?" Rae asked with a penetrating gaze.

"Nothing."

"Nothing? But she's so upset, despondent—how can you say so coldly that she should do nothing? What would *you* do?"

"I wouldn't say anything."

"What would come of that?"

"The same thing that would come of speaking."

"No! He shouldn't have let her fall in love with him. He shouldn't have spoken to her like that. He shouldn't have made her believe him and then left her with nothing at all."

"She should've expected it."

"Because he has a wife?" Rae laughed ruefully. "But let me tell you: he didn't leave her to go back to his wife. He left her for another girl."

"He'll leave the other girl too. He'll leave many other girls, and he'll always come back to his wife only to leave her again."

"Did he tell you that?" Rae asked, looking at me sharply.

"Did he say so? No. Men don't say such things. You just have to understand them for yourself. To a married man, unmarried girls are like plays, songs, poems, novels. In a word: they are fiction. But a wife is like the Bible. Fiction is interesting, pleasant to read, it is a good way to pass the time. But he won't stay riveted for long. He can be fascinated with it for a while, but as soon as he's done reading it he forgets all about it. And, just like a man of honor, he always returns to his Bible. However dusty and old it may be, however familiar its contents, he'll stay faithful to it. It is chosen and honored above all others!"

"True, that's how it is. But what can you do if your love doesn't want to abide by such logic? Blind feelings don't follow clear thoughts. You can hate someone and still love him anyway—do you know what I mean?"

I thought about A. but didn't say anything.

"Do you think B. will also leave the other girl?" Rae asked, taking my hand.

"Yes, he'll leave her too," I answered firmly.

"That is—good to hear. The girl, my friend, will be happy to know that. She will *not* be convinced by your Bible. He'll never love his wife, he'll only do for her what law and duty and . . . bad habit require!"

She laughed hoarsely, smiled to herself, squeezed my hand, and left. I watched her go and thought for a while about that girl, her good friend, that Rae seemed to understand so well . . .

18

My Name

It's been two whole weeks since B. came to see me. Am I suffering out of injured pride? Or longing? I can tell myself the truth. Why should I hide it from myself?

But no, it's not B. I'm in love with. Not B. I only love his love, and I only love it because I hate being lonely.

Rae spent the night in my room. We talked and talked until we fell asleep. She told me all about the girl who loves B. so much that—who knows if she'll ever love another man again. Rae had tears in her eyes as she spoke of the girl's hurt feelings. Poor—Rae!

In the morning we heard the sound of footsteps creeping up to the door to my room. Someone knocked.

I leapt out of bed, threw on my robe, and opened the door halfway. It was the landlady. "I thought you were still asleep. I came to wake you. You know what they say, 'Work makes life sweet!'" she said.

"'Work makes life miserable' is more like it. But, either way, I do have to get up, so thank you for waking me."

"You didn't sleep long. You were sitting up until late."

"Lying down," I corrected her.

"But—you had company?"

"Yes."

"And—who was it? Oh! I see!" The landlady smiled as she saw Rae through the half-open door. She had been trying to peer through the door the whole time she was talking to me. "I see now. And since everything is in order, I can tell you, just as though I were your own mother, that I'm glad to see it. You know how tongues wag. A girl should be very careful of her reputation. Since we're on the subject, I have to tell you that people have been asking me, 'Who's been coming to visit your girl so late at night?' I tell them that no one needs to worry their head about my girl. She knows how to protect her own good name."

Who knows how long she'd have stayed talking about my good name if she hadn't remembered that she'd left the milk on the gas stove.

❧

A letter from B. His wife had a baby.

B. writes: "I'm in turmoil about the child. It arrived at a time when I wanted so badly to leave, and now I feel twice as tied down. I sit here by my wife and child and I think shameful thoughts: I want to be with *you*. I want to hold you in my arms like a child. I only want to love *you*, for I love you so! I look at my wife and child and a heavy dread fills my heart. Why didn't I find you sooner? I could have been so happy now if only you, and not she, had been the mother of my child!"

He begs me to write to him and tell him how I feel and whether I'm longing for him as he is for me. But I won't write. What would be the point? I'll just congratulate him on the new baby, and nothing more. How could I bind myself to someone who is twice as tied down as ever?

❧

How strange. You go around with an impression that someone is like a god, and then you suddenly run into him in the pouring rain with an umbrella turned inside out by the wind, wearing rain boots and with a nasty head cold, and you feel like the whole time someone's been pulling the wool over your eyes.

That's how I felt when I saw A. today on the subway platform.

My heart leapt into my throat and I tried to make myself invisible. But he approached me and stretched out his hand for mine, and I gave it to him.

"Where are you going in such weather?" he asked me.

"Uptown. You?"

"Downtown. How have you been? What have you been doing with yourself?"

"The same as always."

"I stopped by a while ago," A. said, looking me in the eye. "When I saw there was a light in your window I went up, but when I knocked on the door you didn't answer."

"I believe it was already late at night," I said, trying not to blush. I remembered that evening when B. wanted to make the gas flame smaller and then put it out entirely. When I heard a knock on the door I couldn't open it. My reputation—what would people think if they found me alone in the dark with a man?

"Do people have to come to visit you so early?" A. asked.

"Yes, the earlier the better."

"I'll remember that. I'll come to see you next week!" he said, stepping onto his train, and he tipped his hat as he rode away.

When my train arrived I was distraught. Why couldn't mine have come before his? During the whole ride, I couldn't help but think that our lives will always be like our trains, taking us in two different directions.

∾

Another letter from B.

He writes: "You didn't write to me about your feelings like I asked you to, but I understand. I understand your silence. You're suffering and you don't want to show it. You care too much about these two weak creatures I might mistreat out of love for you. Do you know, my love, what I've done? I have given my child your name! Now I won't have to look around to see if anyone has overheard when I call out your name. I can call your name out loud freely. Your name is the most beautiful name I could have given my daughter! I know what you're thinking, 'What if she finds out?' But she'll never know. Now I feel a painful joy over the secret buried in that name. And I will be more affectionate toward the child thanks to your name."

My name . . . My name will make him love his child more. *My* name.

19

⁓

Guests

My heart pounded when I heard his knock at the door. This heart of mine had waited for him for so long! I decided not to hold it back. Let it love as much as it wanted, as much as it can. Let it love so hard that it breaks!

"I hope it's not too late?" he asked, entering with a smirk.

"Just in time," I answered, smiling broadly.

He sat down. He looked around my room and said, "Your walls seem strange, upside down. How dreary."

"Maybe they're angry that you haven't been here in so long."

"Did they hear you complaining about me?"

"A little, but . . . how's life?"

"I'm getting by."

"That's more than I can say."

"What, you're not?"

"No, I'm just—existing."

"You know, your hair has grown much longer since I last saw you," he said, stroking my hair.

"It's thinner than it used to be, so it looks longer."

"You always find a way to be self-critical."

"Let others give me compliments."

"You want others say nice things about you when you can't say anything nice about yourself?"

"Of course. Can you kiss your own lips?"

"Well . . ."

"See, love is like anger. It takes two."

There were footsteps outside the door. A. glanced unhappily at the bright gas lamp. B. would have thought nothing of dimming it until it was completely dark. Then he wouldn't have been able to find a match to light it again. A. didn't do this. Should I have done it instead? But that would have been . . .

∽

A knock on the door. The landlady had a letter for me in B.'s handwriting. I couldn't believe I was going to read a letter from B. in A.'s company!

"Don't worry about me," said A. "Read your letter! I'll peruse your books. I see you have a lot of new ones." I hurriedly read the letter:

"My dear, my love! Can you imagine how desperately I want to see you? It's been three weeks since I was last with you. *Three* weeks! An eternity. Tomorrow or the next day—for certain—I will come to you for the whole evening, or perhaps until morning, as I did that time before. I have so much to say to you, or, if you would prefer it, we can say nothing at all! Yours, B., who may love you more than he loves himself, and that's a remarkable thing! P.S.: Can you hear now, child, how my heart is pounding for you? No, you do not hear. And I can see how your eyes, so soft, and good, and bad, and wise, are smiling, smiling and almost laughing . . . Oh, my love!"

"You're already done reading? What did *he* write?" A. asked teasingly.

"He's well, thank God. The rest is no concern of yours."

"When's he coming to see you?" he prodded.

"Who knows."

"Today?"

"Would you rather tomorrow?"

"Is that what you want?"

"No," I said, looking him right in the eye. And I thought that B. might actually come, as his letter proposed, so I suggested that it might be better for us to go for a stroll. A. said that he would prefer to sit as we were, with my hand in his, listening to me talk. It was so warm and pleasant in my room. Outside the wind was blowing, and there were so many people.

We sat close to each other and both looked at the gaslight with the same thought—if only the light would go out on its own!

"Is the gaslight bothering your eyes?" A. asked quietly.

"Yes. Should I lower it?"

"No, let me—"

My heart was pounding harder, like it was applauding him for his initiative. I imagined the two of us sitting in the dark, clinging tightly to one another. I'd tell him all of my feelings. He would understand and passionately kiss my lips, my eyes, my hand, all of me.

A knock on the door. It jolted us like thunder. A. stood still, his hands poised at the gas lamp. I looked at him, bewildered.

"Well, open it." And he went to look at my books.

Yes, I had no other choice. I opened the door. Rae and another girl with fiery red hair and blood-red lips came in.

"Oh, so it's you!" the fiery girl cried out, and grabbed both of my hands. "I've heard so much about you! Rae says you are the cleverest girl in the world. I'm Katya."

"Oh, Katya—" I remembered that Rae once told me about a Katya, a girl with a passionate soul, a taste for modern literature, who hated men and loved life. A unique girl, an eccentric. I introduced her to A.

"Do you speak Russian?" she asked him.

"No," A. answered.

"But you understand it!"

"Only a little."

"But you're a Russian."

"I'm a Jew."

"All the same, you're from Russia."

"I'm an American citizen."

"A citizen. How banal! And who do you vote for?"

"That's not something I share."

"Are you for women's rights?"

"I'm for . . . the right women."

A knock on the door. I opened it. It was B. Rae grew pale and turned to speak to A. B. looked at everyone curiously, and his gaze rested upon Katya. I introduced her to him: "This is Mr. B."

"And my name is Katya!" she introduced herself.

"Oh, Katya?" B. repeated, laughing. "And how are you, Katya?"

"Fine. I'm alive."

"It's good that you're living. And how are you?" he asked Rae.

"I'm living too."

"So it seems that everyone is alive. Good! And do you know why I've come?" B. asked, turning to me. "I've come to ask you, in my daughter's name, to come to our home for a party. And since you are here," he said to A., "I will save the cost of stamps and invite you in person. It's happening a week from today. Will you come? Good! And you can come too, Katya."

"Will there be a Russian *kruzhok?*"

"A kru-what? Company, certainly. And a Russian *samovar* too."

"Weren't you born in Russia?"

"Of course, where else would I have been born?"

Katya asked questions like a class of kindergarteners. B.'s answers made everyone laugh. He exchanged glances with A. over Katya's logic and smiled. So the evening passed, and as the evening went away, so did my guests.

I stood for a while in the dark and watched as they all went out together into the street. Rae with B. and A. with that girl Katya. Katya took A.'s arm and looked up at him with her vampire lips and, instead of love, my heart was filled with hatred. My soul was choking to death.

My love came looking for roses and found thorns instead.

20

The Party

All week long I fooled myself with the hope that A. would take me to B.'s party. B. came instead and I went with him disappointedly. This way, if A. comes to the party at all, and he shows up with another woman, at least he'll think that I wasn't waiting for him.

At B.'s home I met many guests. Mrs. B.'s friends with their husbands and children. Several more without husbands, and of course without children. Mrs. B. showed off her baby daughter to all of us. "Isn't she beautiful?" she asked in English, excitedly. "And her name is also pretty. My husband picked it out. The first name for a daughter was my choice, but since his idea for a name was prettier than the one I would've given her, I let him have the honor. He promised me he'd let me name our second child whatever I want, even if it's a son."

B. called the child by her name a few times, gave her a couple of kisses, and winked at me slyly. He's such a jokester.

Rae arrived. She was dressed nicely, but she didn't look good. Straining not to appear forced, she flung off her hat and gloves with exaggerated lightheartedness. I thought if I loved B. like she does, I wouldn't have come to his home. I wouldn't have been able to look his wife in the eye. I felt uncomfortable enough as it is. But the knowledge that I don't return his love, and haven't sought it out, left me with a clear conscience. She, Mrs. B., should thank me. It's because of me that he's so good to her and the child, to whom he speaks *my* name so affectionately.

B. bowed politely to Rae and told her to make herself comfortable. But it seemed to me that he, himself, was not very comfortable in his own home. He seemed like a guest among his guests.

Rae sat down next to me. She said that she hadn't wanted to come, but when she came to my room and saw that I wasn't home, she decided to come anyway. "And where's A.?" she asked, looking around. "Didn't you come with him?"

"No."

"Katya must have turned his head. If she sets her mind to it, she can do it. What do *you* think of Katya? Isn't she an extraordinary girl?"

"Perhaps."

"She says that you are the kind of girl who knows how to stay quiet. One can never tell for certain what you're thinking."

"No, you can't."

"She thinks that you're in love with A., and maybe also with B."

"Is that what *she* thinks . . ."

"And what do you say to that?"

Just at that moment, Katya tore into the house like a storm wind and I was saved from having to answer the question. Her copper-red hair and purple-red lips sparked like firecrackers. A. entered behind her with measured steps. B. greeted them with a loud "Hello!" The house and all the people swayed before my eyes and it felt like my heart had stopped beating.

A. was standing in front of me. He took Rae's hand first, and then mine.

"Your hand is so cold!" he said.

"It's a sign of a warm heart," teased Rae.

"Oh, how banal that is," Katya chided. "And you, Rae, could say such a thing? Come, my cavalier, and introduce me to Mrs. B."

"Why don't you ask B.? He's right here," A. answered.

"Oh, how—"

"—banal you are!" B. finished her sentence with a smile.

"How unhelpful, I was going to say." She went away with B. and came back with a full report: "B. has a very pretty wife, and his child's like a cuckoo bird. And they have a lovely home too. What doesn't he have? Such a fortunate man. I like to see happy people. And how are you?" she asked, noticing me. "How've you been? Do you remember when we left you the other night? We walked down the street for a while. Then B. took us to a wine cellar. It was very interesting, isn't that right, B.?"

"Yes, that's right, Katya. But why do you have so many words to say? Wouldn't it be better to put something else in your mouth?" B. led her to the table with wine and food. "Enjoy!" Katya didn't take much convincing and was soon enjoying herself.

"And you?" B. turned to Rae. "Will you sing us one of your pretty folk songs? Maybe *Akh du sheyne meydele*:

Oh you pretty girl
Oh you fine girl
How can you go
So far away?"

Rae shook her head no and rebelliously sang to B., "It is good to have a romance, who would refuse? But with one, not with three!"

Katya began to gesture with her hands. *She* was going to sing. "*Desiat'ia liubila, deviat' razliubila!*"

It was getting loud. I stood apart from the fray, looking out at the street. Clouds covered the dark sky. A lonely star twinkled faintly above me. My star . . .

"Why are you so contemplative?" A. asked, approaching me. "It's so cheerful here but you sit alone with your sorrow."

"Happiness fades quickly, sadness lingers."

"Do you prefer that it doesn't vanish so fast?"

"Yes." A pause.

"May I walk you home?"

"Wouldn't you rather ask the girl you brought here?"

"*I* did not bring *her*. *She* came to *me*. She told me that she didn't know the way, and asked me to show her. Now she can find her own way home. What do you think?"

"I don't know. She's had a lot to drink . . ."

"Then let her spend the night here. B. invited her. She's his guest. Let him take care of her."

I didn't feel so depressed anymore. I laughed out loud. B. squeezed my hand when he thought no one was looking.

B. gave a speech in his daughter's name. I took my necklace off—a little golden charm with my name engraved on it—and put it around the baby's little neck. Mrs. B. was enchanted with the present and A. quietly said to me, "What a lovely and good woman you are, all of a sudden."

"That's because I'm so happy."

"Why are you so happy?"

"I'll tell you on the way home."

"No, when we are in your home. Yes?"

"Yes."

Many people could be very good friends, if only they knew when to leave each other alone. But they don't know. They cling to you just when they're not welcome. When they're *so* unwelcome.

As A. and I left the party, Katya, Rae, and some others followed us. Rae had forgotten the key to her room and she didn't want to ring the doorbell so late at night. She invited herself to spend the night in my room. Katya, who did, in fact, have a key, wanted to stay with Rae because she thought it would be fun. Once Rae decided to stay with me, Katya didn't want to go home alone and so A. had to escort *her* home.

21

The Trial

I went to the theater with B. and afterward we walked in the park for a long time.

He told me he doesn't know what to do with himself. His wife and child aren't at home. They're visiting her mother in a nearby town for a week or two. He finds himself sitting alone in his house missing—me.

We weren't far from his house and he asked me to go in. I refused.

The more I said no, the more he asked, and when he saw that his pleas weren't helping, he grinned and needled me, "You're scared!"

"Fine, so I'm scared!"

"I promise you we'll just spend some time there and then I'll walk you home. Come with me, show me that you trust me."

"I will *not* go."

It seemed like he'd given up on asking me, and then he started all over again. When it was obvious that I'd never give in he cried "Have pity!" so desperately that I acceded.

B. led me to his house quickly before I had time to regret my decision. I followed him with an angry, strong decisiveness. I wanted to show him that I wasn't afraid of him.

"Turn on the lights," I said, standing at the door.

He made it bright. I saw an empty house that was nevertheless full of *her*, his wife, who was present even in her absence. Her spirit was still there.

"Why are you staring like that?" he asked quietly, forcing a smile.

"Everything's looking at me like it's telling me to go away."

"You want to go already?"

"Yes, B. I want to go home."

"You're just like a child. 'I want to go home.' Don't look at anything else, just me! Just see how much I love you!"

"I see."

"Come in a little more. Make yourself comfortable. Do you know what? Let's have some tea. Let's sit for a while, and then you can go to sleep. If you want to, you can sleep in a separate room and keep the door locked, and sleep with the key, alright? But don't go away. I beg you! Be a good girl. You're so clever! With one word you can do with me whatever you will. I'll be as obedient as a child. I'll kiss you before you go to sleep. I'll kiss you so nicely, the way you kiss something pure. The way you used to kiss the *toyre* in *shul* when you were a little girl."

"That was on *simkhes toyre*."

"Let today be our *simkhes toyre*! Let it be what you like! It can be whatever you want, my love. I'll do what you please. I love you. I love you so much and I want you to be my . . . Listen! I love you *so*! I would give up everything for you. You are the meaning of my life. Come—"

He led me to a large bed next to a small child's crib. I tore myself out of B.'s arms and stubbornly stood by the door.

"Come—"

"No!"

"Why not?"

I just looked at the two beds. I looked from them to him. My glances must have conveyed everything I was thinking and feeling, because he lowered his eyes to the floor and softly but clearly admitted, "You're right."

I took his hand and quietly led him out of the room, as though I was trying not to wake someone. In the next room, he sat on a chair and hid his face in his hands. I stroked his hair. My heart beat warmly for him: he understood me. He listened to my feelings over his desires. I felt like kneeling before him, holding him tightly in my arms and— loving him.

"Not here, not here," a voice cried out in me and I jumped up to leave.

He walked me home without saying anything. He led me to my room and stood by the door, his head bowed in shame.

In the darkness I quickly changed my outfit and then held out my arms to him. He held me passionately and we sat together on the edge of my narrow bed.

"You see how much better you have it than I do," he reflected. "There's no one here to bother you. You're free to do what you want."

"And yet—"

"Yes, *and yet*! Who are you so afraid of?"

"Maybe of someone I don't even know yet."

"Perhaps. You are a strange person, but I love you just as before. And maybe even more. Today, because of you, I found myself to be a different man. I never would have believed myself capable of withstanding such a trial. *Me*! You don't know, child, what kind of a man I am. But your eyes, knowing so much and saying so little! You're able to rise above without letting yourself fall. You don't know what kind of spell you cast, or maybe you do know. Yes, you know. You said as much in the way you beckoned me to come!"

∽

Once there was a rabbinic sage who felt that he was not strong enough to withstand a trial. He stood in the door to his tent and cried out with all his might so that people might run to him and keep him from sinning. We both laughed at that great rabbi. We, in silence, without crying out, emerged greater heroes than he ever was, thanks to our own selves.

∽

B. stayed with me. I kissed him with kisses I learned through my romance with A. I gave my kisses to B. instead.

I love A. because of how I love him, and I love B. for the way he loves me. I am to B. what A. is to me. It's hard to stop loving, unrequited love refuses to die. But B. will stop loving me sooner than I'll stop loving A. A man can't love *loving* the way a woman can. He loves the woman herself. It'll only last a little longer, and then my heart tells me that B. will leave me. He'll look for happiness with someone else. And I—I'll long for him in my loneliness.

22

B.'s Letters

Saturday.

My love! I told myself not to go to see you today. It's hard for me to be close to you and yet keep my distance. It's not easy, my dear, to be a hero. My God, to be a hero every time when, after all, I'm really no more than a man!

You won't let me act like an ordinary, human man. Beloved, gentle girl, you force me to kiss your fingertips and grovel at your feet. With you, I must gently bend myself to your unbending will. Your will, which is so steadfastly . . . unwilling.

Maybe you'll think less of me if I tell you that I regret allowing myself to overcome the temptation. But that's how things are. You would already have been mine, and once I'd already *had* you once, you'd be drawn to me again. Yes, I regret very much that you have nothing to regret. Do you understand what I mean?

Yours, B.

Monday.

You say that you understand and you think I should put mind over matter. But, my dear, I don't want anything to do with this "mind." I don't want to let it help me. I want to love and live. And you, my love, if I could give you some advice, it would be to set aside your reason, to leave it behind and give yourself over to what you call my foolishness. Let yourself be fooled, but allow yourself to love!

If you write and tell me to come, I will. I'll love you, my God, I'll love you as I've never loved before! Tell me to come, and I'll know that you understand me completely.

Yours, B.

❧

Friday.

You say that it's better for me to write a letter than to come to you! Thank you very much! I appreciate how much you enjoy my letters. It's true, it's easier to sleep undisturbed with them. It's easier to carry on a platonic love with a letter than with a living man. Here, you have a letter from me. Enjoy. Good night!

B.

❧

Sunday.

Yesterday evening I came to see you and for a while I stood in front of the closed door to your room. Where were you? I wanted so badly to see you! I wandered the busy streets alone and thought: I love you, I love you, I love you.

I searched for your face on every passing woman. I ran into Rae, but I wished I were with you instead. I came to her room, passed the time with her and thought of you. Do you think of me? Do *you* love *me*? You've never told me so.

❧

Tuesday.

You are incapable of love? *You?* You are the embodiment of love. What you really mean is that you *don't want* to love. You are afraid because I'm not free. Do you want me to separate from the woman I'm bound to by law? Tell me. Maybe I will. I love you so much.

❧

Thursday.

Your refusal to allow me to make such a sacrifice on your behalf is very fine. Fine and no more. You are very measured. Your measuredness comes from indifference. Only those who do not love can think so clearly about matters of love. Your concern for my family's interests only shows that you are not interested enough in me.

Your letter was so cold, so stiff, so dry that even my wife could have read it. It was buttoned up from top to bottom. You have an exceptional ability to keep up the boundaries of decorum. You are so careful!

B.

჻

Sunday.

Because you have kept me at a distance, you have thrown me into the arms of another. You, with your strict morals, have forced me to make love to my wife. If only you were the mother of my child—I would never hold another woman. But that's not what you want. You just want to hold on to your high ideals. I cannot reach them.

Today I saw that lively girl, Katya. She was angry at A. for being such a *razocharovaniye*.

She's a foolish girl, that Katya. But what's the use of being wise? She, in her foolishness, lives more than you with your reason. A., it seems, has already gone far with her, but he's a practical, confident man, and he'll be able to get out of it after a while. She's not the kind to get too attached to one person. And, as Rae says, "Good for her!"

I'll come to see you tomorrow evening. I won't beg for an invitation anymore. I will come, and that's final.

Yours, B.

჻

Tuesday.

Today I am not myself. My lips are still trembling from your wild kisses, which were bewildering, I must say. Strange thoughts swirl in my mind. Was it *me* you were kissing, or some other man, through me? Because you *say* that you do not love me, not the way that you should. I wonder: if you can embrace me like *that* when you don't love me, what must you be like when you do love?!

You're not just one woman. You're so much more. I'm losing myself in you.

I'm jealous of whomever it is that you've loved before, if you've loved someone. And maybe you still love him. Who is *he*? I wish I could tell him that I've seen your magnificent body. I left marks from my kisses on you. I want him to know.

If my love for you lasts much longer, it will turn into hate. That's what your aloofness will bring me to. I'll brace myself and give you this ultimatum: all or nothing. You must answer.

Yours, B.

⤮

Thursday.

My love, what can you mean? Why are you so punishing? Why did ask me to stop writing about how I love you? Why? Are you afraid that someone will read my letters? Are you ashamed of *your* love for *me*? Do you only want me to write about my feelings for you so that you can have something to laugh at with your friends? Oh, you! Even after everything, I still love you. I close my eyes and imagine that I can feel your breath, hear your heart beating.

Do you understand, my sweet girl, what it means when you forbid me from writing this way to you?

I'm as open as a postcard.

Yours, B.

⤮

Saturday.

You cruel, lovely girl!

It's been more than a week and you haven't answered my letter. Is it because you don't want me to write?

You're mad at me, and I admit that I deserve it. A strange irritation made me provoke you. I was angry at myself because of your uprightness and character, and I wanted to cause *myself* pain through *you*.

Forgive me, my dear! Please, forgive me! Give me a chance to make it up to you. After all, I'm only a man, and my nerves are not made of steel. The indifference that you showed me in your letter, right after you showed me your feelings so passionately and wordlessly in person, drove me mad.

Tomorrow, I will definitely come to see you, and I hope that you'll understand.

Your B., who no longer understands anything because he loves you so wildly, so hopelessly!

23

The Argument

By now he's become convinced that it isn't worth wasting so much time on me. He has no more patience for wooing. It seems to me that rather than taking it slow because, as the saying goes, "If you want to fall asleep, first you need a pillow," he wants me to hurry: "If you want to love, do it already, I don't have time for this!"

He's exasperated because I won't allow myself to learn from him how to *live* in the world. Not just to live, but to *enjoy* life.

"Do you enjoy life?" he asked, shaking his head in concern.

"I enjoy . . . a head cold." I quipped. He got irritated and called me a tease. He said I was trying to make him feel desires that I know I won't fulfill. And he loves me so very much!

Love!

"And yet I still love myself too! I love you against my will. I beg you, try to understand what I'm saying—"

"I understand."

"Tell me, how can you possibly understand?" he demanded.

"I don't want to argue."

"Are you trying to hurt me?"

"I'm not."

"You're only hurting yourself," he accused me.

I responded stiffly, "If I'm fighting myself, I hope I'll reach a détente soon."

"Will you, really," he asked, jokingly, "be a little girl forever?"

"No one lives forever."

"Will you die a maiden?"

"Once you die, it doesn't matter."

"Yes, it does. Before you died at least you could comfort yourself that you had *lived*. You won't be able to say that, because you aren't alive. Why won't you live?"

"I'm alive."

"Not like you want to be!"

"I don't want to live like I want to."

"You'll suffer instead."

"Who cares?"

"You're as stubborn as a mule! The way you set yourself apart from life will only make everyone else around you upset."

"Why should I care what others think?"

"You don't like others?"

"Who, exactly, are others?" I asked.

"Others are real enough. They force you toward love and push you into marriage. If you were married already, like other women your age, it would be much easier to talk to you about this."

"Oh, because then I would have their approval?"

"Then you would have someone to blame," he retorted.

"Is that so?"

"That's how it is. You're speculating, like in business," he explained.

"This is America, after all!"

"Aren't you a woman? I'm starting to think you're not."

"I also doubt it."

"Then what are you?"

"A girl."

"And do you want to stay one forever?"

"Yes, sir!" I answered in English.

"Enjoy it!"

"Thank you!"

He left in a huff. My landlady entered.

"Tell me," she demanded, "is it true what they say, that the man who just left your room has a wife?"

"Yes, and he has a child too. What's the matter with that?"

"What's his business with you?"

"His business? He was talking to me about a *shidukh*. He's going to find me a marriage partner."

"Is that so? That's very considerate of him."

"Very kind."

"Then I hope it all works out for you."

"Thank you!"

The landlady left, content with this news.

Nevertheless, I'm thinking that I'd better find myself another room.

Now I *have* to find myself another room. The landlady won't stop talking to me about the *shidukh*. She says since she's such a good friend, like a mother to me, she will inquire after the man that B. suggests for me. Because, "these days you have to be ten times as certain before you go and do anything. This is America, and you don't know *who* you're dealing with. Maybe your male acquaintance is familiar with the other man he's proposing as a *shidukh*, but what does it matter if one man knows another? A man knows another man, who knows another man—who cares? It's you who has to spend your life with him. You should find out who he really is. But since it isn't suitable for a girl to ask after a strange man, and since you have no family here and are all alone . . ." My landlady told me she wanted to show me that there are good people in the world, and that's why she was unable to hold back her generosity and burst out saying, "Well, I'll dance at your wedding and I'll take pride in you after all!"

The poor landlady! She won't take pride in me, in the end. Her generosity will only make me move sooner. I could tell her that I don't like the *shidukh* he proposed and keep on living there, but she'd ask why the *shadkhn* kept visiting me when I didn't like the *shidukh*, and what could I say then?

I know he'll come back. We're having an argument, but we haven't split up, and until he breaks it off with me entirely he'll try, a few more times, to be "good friends." He's already invested so much time in this love affair, why would he give it up so quickly?

"When your *shadkhn* comes to call," the landlady directed, "call me. I want to speak with him. I'm a married woman, you know, and I know better than you do about certain things. Making a *shidukh* isn't as easy as eating a bagel." I simply *had* to promise to call her, so that *she* can speak to him.

24

The Breakup

Now I really have to move. A man who used to board with my landlady inquired about staying with her again. She told him, "I'm very sorry," and explained that I'm currently occupying his former room. He told her that he'd be willing to pay a few more dollars than before to have the room, so she agreed to rent it to him.

"So what will you do now?" my landlady asked me.

"Move, I guess. Since he's going to pay you so much more."

"And, what's more, he's a man," she added. "You must understand that a man is not like a girl. He won't be at home as often. He'll go out and we won't see him at all. And he'll be paying a few more dollars. But of course I don't want to make you move, unless you're willing . . ."

I had to reassure her that I'm planning on moving anyway. Besides, she's already promised the room to the man. In three days he'll move in. So now I must move.

I'm worn out from looking for a place to live. And I didn't find one. I returned home to hear a voice coming from my room: "As sure as I live, she's as dear to me as my own child. Once I'm attached to someone, I can't detach myself."

"So it would seem."

"Don't they say I'm a good woman? Look! You, yourself, have a wife, may she be well, and a child too? So you must know what a *shidukh* means for a girl. Where are you from?"

"Where we're all from."

"I mean, where were you born?"

"In a bed."

"Now you're joking with me. It isn't nice to laugh that way."

I opened the door and went in the room. My landlady quickly explained that the man (B.) had come to call and I wasn't home. She let him in to wait for me, since she knew his purpose. In the meantime, she entertained him, but now she had to see what was happening in the kitchen. Something was probably burning.

"Why was she going on with me about a *shidukh*?" B. asked after she'd left, laughing. "What am I, a *shadkhn*?"

"Yes, a *shadkhn*. That's all I could think of to tell her. Why are you here?"

"To see you. I missed you. How tired you look!" He held my head in his hands and looked into my eyes. "Did you miss me? Tell me, please!"

His noticing my tiredness made me feel a strange sort of self-pity. I wanted to cry. I hid my face in my hands so he wouldn't see my tears. In sorrowful moments like these, the touch of gentle hands can be so comforting.

"I am so sorry," he said, softly kissing my hair, "that I caused an argument. You don't know how I've suffered because of it. You are so lovely, so good, how could I cause *you* pain? Can you forgive me?"

I laughed and patted his hands. "B., don't be so good to me. I'll be just as bad to you as I was before. You must know that. I can't be any different."

"Why not? Your whole body seems to say with longing, 'Kiss me, love me, *take* me,' but you . . .'"

How was I supposed to answer such a question? Was I supposed to explain to him that I was using him, expressing through him my love for A.? Or should I tell him that I was only with him to ease and silence the smarting pain of my loneliness? I silently, playfully freed myself from his embrace and buried him in kisses. He stood for a while, his head bowed over me, and stroked my hair. Then he walked away. I opened my eyes and found myself in the dark. He had turned out the lights.

"B.—"

"To be or not to be," he said, grabbing me, "that is the question!"

"B.!" I cried, not knowing what to say. "The landlady will hear!"

"You're moving soon anyway!"

"B.!"

"It will happen sooner or later, if not with me, then with some other man. I won't be made a fool of. Enough already. Be what you are. You are a woman, not a child."

In the darkness, I groped for his face with my fingernails.

"You wild creature! You could have blinded me! Calm down!"

I wanted to be "wild" but he brutally tried to civilize me. He angrily asked me why I wouldn't let myself love him. He threatened never to see me again. He said it would have been better not to get started with someone like me. He'd never get anything out of it, even if he waited his whole life. And, after all, I'm not the only girl in the world, there are others who *understand* more about life. It's just a shame he wasted so much time on me.

The sound of B. slamming the front door had barely died out when the landlady knocked on my door and entered, asking why I was sitting alone in the dark and why he'd gone away so quickly. She wanted to know what was going on with the *shidukh*. I told her that I wasn't happy with it.

"To tell you the truth," my landlady said, "I wasn't happy with the *shadkhn*. He was full of jokes. What's the saying? 'A dog should not be a butcher'? He was always making light of everything. A girl should know to be on guard with men like that. They claim to be interested in you for a reason, a *shidukh*, for example, but they're really after something else . . . Have you found another room?"

"Not yet. I'll try again tomorrow."

"You'll have to hurry. That man is moving in soon. I don't want to return his deposit. I gave him my word. I don't want to deceive a man like him."

Since B. won't be visiting me anymore I might have been able to live comfortably in that room, but I've already agreed to give it up and now I have to move. I'll have to search for some other lonely corner.

So, B. and I broke up. But the certainty of a breakup is better than the doubt I felt before.

25

Among Strangers

"Today I begin a new chapter in the story of my diary. In another part of the city, in a new room, among strangers."

Just now, while I was writing these words, I heard a man's voice in the front room asking, "You rented the room already?"

A woman's voice responded, "I rented it to a girl."

"A pretty girl?"

"Aha! I knew you'd ask!"

"Why shouldn't I ask? It's only natural."

"What's it to *you*?"

"You know I like pretty girls. It's just in my nature."

"That's some nature you have."

"It'd be the same for any man."

"But my future son-in-law shouldn't talk that way. He should only care for my daughter."

"Well, he certainly can't marry the daughter's mother. That's the way it is. Probably that's the way it's meant to be. You fancy the mother, so you marry the daughter."

"Bite your tongue!"

"Consider it bitten. Now, how can I get a peek at the new boarder?"

"You probably won't get a chance to see her today. She said she won't be coming home until evening, because she has a lot of things to buy."

"A shame. I'll have to see her another time. But I will see her eventually."

They walked away from my room. They didn't realize I was here. I'd already been home from my outing for a while. But I didn't want them to know that. I stayed quiet so they wouldn't find me out. I just wanted to ignore everyone. To be a stranger to the strangers, to be alone with my books. Books are so much better than people. They don't try to find out who and what you are. They just tell you a story, and they do it when you want them to.

The voice that had asked about me must belong to the young man who's pursuing the daughter of the house, and the woman's voice is the mother's. She didn't speak more than a few words to me before telling me that her daughter has a *boy*, a *fellow*, a *gentleman friend*. He's a salesman, makes a lot of money, and "cares" for her. "Oh, he's just crazy for me!" she confided to me in English, promising to introduce me. "Mind you, crazy for his future mother-in-law!"

She asked me, "Do you have anyone?" When I told her that I didn't, she said in English, "Too bad," and comforted me with the thought that eventually I'd catch someone. All you need to attract a "gentleman friend" is to know how to dress up to date, in style. Her daughter, who dresses herself "like a doll," would help me with that.

I thanked her for wanting to help me. I was forced to answer her questions in Yiddish peppered with English and Russian to prove her worth, such as: What relatives do I have here? How old am I? Do I have a *steady position*? Do I take *vacations*? Did I attend *gymnasium* in Russia? Am I familiar with the Russian classics? Am I a *paklanitsa*, a devotee, of modern literature? Because she, herself, is a *strastna* reader of anything Russian. She graduated *gymnasium* with a gold medal. She would show it to me, but it's nowhere to be found, it disappeared into thin air. When you come to America and become a mother with many children, medals don't matter to you anymore. You outgrow all that. As the children grow you have to chase after them to make yourself into an American so they won't laugh at you.

There used to be a girl staying with them, she told me, who seemed to be an intellectual. People were good to her the way only intellectual people can be to a lonely girl in possession of some education. But she didn't know how to show her appreciation. She was ungrateful and handled herself poorly.

I didn't want to hear more about that girl. I resolved that I wouldn't let anyone be "good" to me like that. I don't want anyone to pity me or to talk about me in front of other people.

⤙⤚

As I look at the dirty pink walls of my long and narrow room, a heavy unease weighs upon my heart. I miss the room that remains on the other side of this vast city without me in it. Remembering all that I experienced there, I quietly ask *these* walls what will happen to me here. Will I be able to bear the loneliness that I've condemned myself to, foreswearing love after my all my mishaps? Or will I be drawn into—coupledom?

Whomever I end up sharing my loneliness with, it will certainly not be A. or B. It's all over with them. My fantastical love for A. and B.'s stubborn passion for me—let them both lie in the grave of the past. Let all the Katyas of the world pursue their lust for *living*. I wasn't made for such love affairs. My motto will be: one or none, always or never, all or nothing—

My new landlords just interrupted my thoughts, knocking on my door and calling in to ask if I want tea. I thanked them but declined, saying I already had some not long ago. I don't want to get too close to them. It would only make it harder to separate myself from them later on. In any event, they'll have more respect for me if I don't accept their kindness. All of them, especially the mother of the family, love to talk about their intelligence so much that I'm beginning to doubt whether it's true.

Yes, I'll be respectful to them from a distance. I won't have any reason to argue with them, especially not with the girl, because I won't be kind or close to them, so there will be nothing to argue about. I've rented a room from them and I'll pay for it, and that's all.

⤙⤚

Another knock at my door. This time with an invitation to go to the movies.

"No, thank you, I don't want to," I refused politely.

"Are you going to stay at home all evening?"

"Yes, I think so."

"What will you do?"

I felt like saying, "What's it to you?" But I didn't say it. I didn't say anything.

"You'll probably go to sleep?"

"Maybe."

"That's for old people. They need their rest."

"I need mine too."

"Oh, so you're tired."

"I *am* tired."

She, the mother of the bride, left, unhappy with my answers. Apparently, she'd thought she'd make me her friend right from the first day. Maybe I shouldn't be so mean and refuse her friendship. But I'm doing it for her sake. Why should I be good to her now, only to be mean later on? It's better for me to be distant from the beginning, and if I find they're actually kind people, then I can get closer to them.

A knock on the door. The landlord. He wants to know if I know where the landlady went.

"She's at the movies," I wanted to tell him, but I thought better of it, and said instead that I didn't know. It's better if he thinks that I don't know where his wife went, so he doesn't ask me about it anymore.

"She didn't tell you where she was going? What a disgrace to come home to find that she left the house empty and didn't say a word to anyone. Have you gotten settled in already? It's a decent room, isn't it? We rented it to a man for eleven dollars, but for a woman we're renting it for nine. You have to make concessions for a woman. A woman doesn't make as much money, right? When a woman rents a room on her own, she doesn't have much money to spare. Most people rent one room to two girls, even three. You must be a good earner, right?"

"Yes."

"That's good. These days it's hard to make a steady living. Especially if you're the father of grown children, like I am."

"Grown children can earn money of their own."

"Small potatoes, that's what they earn. It seems like they're going to earn something, but all it amounts to is a drop in the ocean. In the old country I had a big role to play. The private police commissioner and I were like two peas in a pod. I ran a *billiardnye* that the governor's son frequented, I hosted soldiers. And what do you think I do here? I'm hired help at a firm, I turn phonographs on and off. And if that's not enough, I also peddle tea, Popov's tea, if you must know. That's America for you! Tell me, don't you have anyone here in New York, even a friend?"

"I have friends."

"Are you a bride-to-be?"

"Not yet."

"Every young woman is a bride-to-be."

"Is that so? But not everyone has a groom-to-be."

"Sooner or later they all get married. Jewish girls don't become old maids. Every girl I've ever known has gotten married eventually."

"I know a lot of girls who haven't."

"They will! Marriage and death are two things you can't avoid. That's just how it is. You can't go against your nature. You know what I mean?"

I told him that I understood so he wouldn't explain any further and would go away. But he wasn't in any hurry. I had to listen to him until his wife came home.

They were both heavy-set and long-winded, both of them prying and tactless, and neither of them let you forget for an instant that they were "intellectuals." I had a strange feeling about them. I didn't hate them so much as I knew that I was going to hate them later on.

26

The Library

In order to avoid my landlords' lack of restraint, I've started staying away from my room every evening until I think they're already asleep. I go to the library and read there until closing, and then I go for a walk before creeping back into my room. I turn on the light so I can read some more, or sometimes I sit in the dark, just thinking.

You can really think when you're in the dark. I can see the workings of my imagination better with my eyes closed. Dipping its paintbrush into various colors, I paint a picture in my mind. My fantasy is filled with *him*, with A., the very man I'm trying to drive out of my thoughts. He comes to me unbidden. He plants himself in my brain and forces me to think about him. If only, over time, I can drive him away, then maybe I'll finally forget him.

No one knows where I am. No one other than Rae, and she won't give my address to anyone. It's not in her interest for B. to be able to find me. She's still in love with him.

I banished myself of my own accord. I brought about my own exile. I must keep to my own room so my landlords won't expect to see me when they're looking for someone to make peace. As a united front they quarrel with their children for bringing up arguments against their fatherland and their intellectualism. "The girl," they say, "is a neutral party, and she will judge everyone equally." I claim not to be objective because I don't want to get involved. So they ask me where I go every evening.

"To the library."

"Do you go with something in mind? What takes you there?"

"My feet," I answer flippantly. Then I continue seriously, so I won't offend them, "I'm learning, if learning means reading for its own sake, for myself, not in order to get a diploma."

"Oh, you mean to say that you read purely for the sake of *obra-zovanie*," says the landlady.

"Yes, that's my goal."

"What can come of that?" the landlord asked. They were both standing in the doorway to their front room. "The more you learn the less you know."

"You mean the more you realize how little you know," I corrected.

Their daughter piped up from behind them, "I think reading too much isn't good. 'specially for girls. They should focus on settling down. No man wants to marry a philosopher. He wants a good house-keeper, a housewife, someone he won't be embarrassed to show off in front of people. A girl has to know how to dress, how to entertain company and how to run a household. Isn't that so, Mother?" she finished pointedly in English.

Mother answered with the terse English response, "That's so." Before the father could add a further thought, his sons came in calling out "Ma" and "Pop" and "Sis" and they all went out the door. I chained the door shut because it didn't lock properly and then . . . nothing. I'd been asking myself what the purpose of life is so inexhaustibly that I'd run out of answers. I decided the best thing I could do would be to lie down and go to sleep.

∽

Several times recently I'd noticed an unfamiliar young man watching me as though he'd picked me out and decided to get to know me. I'd pretended not to see him. These past few evenings, I'd already got-ten used to his watching me, and when he wasn't looking it seemed as though something was missing.

Although I like the idea of someone watching me and thinking that I haven't noticed, his gaze didn't make me feel any particular good feeling. On the contrary, it annoyed me, even made me angry. But even anger, for me, is better than feeling nothing at all. I don't feel good when I can't feel anything. My soul feels trapped in an expanse of emptiness. I must—if I can't have someone to love—have someone to hate. I must have *something* to consume at least some of my feelings. And it seemed to me as though the sole reason the young man had been put on earth was so that I could experience the feeling that I can't stand him. I told myself that if he'd just talk to me a little, then the first thing I'd say to him would be, "Take a long walk off a short pier!"

He has oddly pale skin, but maybe that's just his complexion. He's very tall, and wears thick glasses over his squinty, sleepless eyes. His long, straight, dirty-blond hair is disheveled in an artistic fashion. His upturned nose and pouty lower lip make him seem whimsical, or stubborn. His clothes are old and disheveled.

I noticed that he prefers the art and philosophy sections of the library, while I tend toward literature and fiction. His glassy eyes would gaze at me intently from behind a scholarly book, as though he wanted me to see what he was reading. I pretended not to notice. Then he'd approach *my* shelves, as though he was interested in taking a look at what ordinary people were reading. He's a regular library visitor and he seemed at home there. From time to time he'd chat with the librarians and ask them to help him find a book. He often inserted himself into conversations to give advice to others who didn't know what to read. I could tell that sooner or later he was going to talk to me.

And today was the day!

I was sitting in a corner, reading Tolstoy's *War and Peace*. I'd read it long ago in Russian and I wanted to know how it sounded in the English translation. I was so absorbed in the book that I didn't notice him approaching. Sensing his presence, I looked up from my book.

"Excuse me, Miss," he whispered in a voice that was meant to be soft but came out scratchy. "Can I ask you something?"

I looked at him questioningly.

"Do you know a girl named Altka? Altka, or Anna?"

"No."

"Really?" He seemed surprised. "You look like you could be her sister!"

I waited until his surprise passed, and then I returned to my book. He asked if he could ask something else.

"Yes?"

"Are you from Palestine?"

"From Palestine? No, I've never been there."

"You must be from Poland, or maybe from Lithuania."

"Well, I must come from somewhere, after all."

"You read a lot—but only novels?"

"I don't think you're supposed to talk here. We're in a library! You might bother someone who's trying to read."

"Talking is fine, as long as it's quiet," he said, speaking in a slightly hushed tone. "It's interesting how many people are drawn to reading made-up stories while there is so much truth that they ignore."

"Made-up things must be nicer than real ones. That's why—"

"That's why what? They just prefer not to know the truth? And then when you try to talk to them about anything, there's no common ground. Knowledge—that should be the foundational principle for everything and everyone! Above all a person should try to understand life. To understand it, in the fullest sense of the word. You can only do that by living, not by studying it in a book."

He was now speaking twice as loud, and it seemed like he was only going to get louder. I looked around uncomfortably to see what impression he was making on the people nearby.

"Are you waiting for someone?" he asked me, as though we were already friends. "Lots of people come here for rendezvous, as you call them, and not for reading."

"Is that so? And is that what you call them too?"

"I call them . . . I call them . . . maybe I'd better not tell you what I call them. Unless you promise not to get angry with me. I'm the kind of person who likes to call things what they are. I look at them from a scientific or philosophical perspective."

"Oh," I said. I let him look at them from whatever perspective he wanted, and I stood up to leave.

"You're leaving?"

"What does it look like?"

"May I escort you?" he asked, following me.

"That won't be necessary. I live close by." I gestured to show him how close it was.

"No matter. I'll walk with you just a little while. I'm tired of sitting in the library." He followed me out.

I decided not to let him follow me any further, since I didn't like him at all. But something in the way he followed me made me hold my tongue and walk in front of him, silently. I decided to be as unfriendly to him as I could. I thought that he must be one of those annoying types who are intrigued by the lives of people on the East Side. I'd try to get rid of him as quickly as possible.

"Do you really live here on the East Side?" he asked, trailing after me. "Right here, on the famous Broadway of the East Side?"

I could tell that he was mocking me with his question, so I didn't answer.

"You can say goodbye to me at the next block," I told him.

"Why can't I go any further? You don't want me to know where you live? I'd never come to your place without an invitation, regardless."

"Goodbye," I announced in English when we reached the next block. I wanted to leave, but he ran ahead of me.

"What *frechheit*!" I thought. "He's got a lot of nerve." I looked him up and down. But he thought nothing of it. He just walked next to me with even more certain steps. I was prepared to walk with him all the way to my house, and then let him stand there while I went in without so much as a goodbye.

"You're a very interesting girl," he said. "You don't seem to have any desire for others to like you. I've never met another girl like that. How do you explain it?"

"It's just that I have no interest in attracting someone I don't find attractive."

"You certainly speak your mind! So you don't like me. Why not?"

"You latch on to people."

"I'm sorry if you find that offensive."

"You force the offense on others."

"But, as a lady, you must—"

"A lady is a person, after all."

"A lady is a lady first and foremost. I'd never allow myself to make the acquaintance of anyone who didn't seem intelligent enough to me. I must tell you that I graduated law school and I'm a medical doctor too. I'm in my second year of college and I give scholarly lectures. I'm studying with a full scholarship. That shows you what an exceptional student I am. If I'm interested in you, it's not because I'm interested in whether you like me or not. It's because I like you, and I rarely find women I like. I can't even say what it was about you that drew me to you. It wasn't your looks, because you're not too much to look at. You're pleasant enough. You aren't so young either. Your eyes are full of hidden sadness, and you often press your lips together like you're holding back a sigh so no one will hear it. You're too proud to show how sad you are. I've often noticed you looking at the pages of a book but not reading. Your thoughts take you somewhere far away, and I can see the hatred or bitterness in your eyes. You pretend not to notice other people so they won't notice you, just like a rooster that closes its eyes while it crows so that no one will hear it. I'd love to see what you look like when you laugh. I imagine that you laugh with your mouth and your lips, but your eyes still have the same sadness. Maybe someone close to you died? If so, it must have been someone very dear to you—maybe a lover? Oh, there's no need to look away. I know, even without looking at you, what you must be feeling. I know human psychology like the back of my hand. Your severity doesn't scare me. Your character is really very mild and malleable. You could be as soft as wax. You just haven't met the right sculptor who could make from you the figure that they want. It wouldn't take long for me to win your trust, your friendship, and maybe even your love."

I just gave him a derisive, close-lipped smile. He noticed.

"Really? You don't believe me?"

"How could I believe something so unbelievable?" I answered.

"A while ago, you said goodbye to me, and yet here you are, listening to everything I've said."

That was true. I'd even walked past my building. He had a good point, and I wasn't sure how to counter it.

"You heard me out because I was talking about *you*," he continued, not waiting for my response. "You are very interested in yourself. You're one of those people who never gets tired of plumbing the depths of her own soul. I hit at the truth with something I said. And even if you didn't like it, you won't tell me. You'll just be quiet about it. But you'll think to yourself that what I said is true, and wonder how I knew, how I was able to guess at the truth. Did I get it right? Didn't I hit the mark?"

"You guess like a blind horse in a cave."

"That comparison isn't very pretty, and it's also not fair."

"You talk so much, I guess *something* you said has to be true."

"So you admit that I know the truth! You couldn't guess as much about me."

"I think I could."

"Of course."

"But you'd probably be pretty insulted."

"It doesn't matter. Go ahead."

"You are—audacious. I don't mean that you're daring, just fresh. You're trying to make an impression with your bad manners. You flirt with the truth about someone else—about the person you're speaking to. You want to be original, surprising, exceptional, and so you share your opinions and your company, not caring whether or not they're welcome. Instead of staring so much at other people, you should take a look at yourself. You'd be able to make many more aesthetic judgments. Also, you . . . don't believe in water."

"What do you mean by that?"

"I mean you don't care much for it."

"Are you trying to say that I don't wash myself?"

"Bingo!"

"How can you tell?"

"From your face."

"It's just a tan."

"You've tanned so much that it even got under your nails?"

"Oh, that's nothing," he said, glancing under his nails and then quickly hiding them. "That's nothing, just a little mud."

He was quiet. Though outwardly I was angry, inside I was gloating. I'd managed to get back at him and make him feel like a schoolboy! Now I wanted to hear what he'd say, but he was stubbornly quiet, and that made me uncomfortable. Perhaps my insult about the dirt had gone a little too far? But something compelled me to keep behaving badly, and I told him not to take the dirt to heart. It's not worth it. A little water can wash it away.

"Do you want to know what I'm thinking?" he asked, as though he hadn't heard my comments.

"Yes, I'd like to know."

"You're going to fall in love with me."

"Why?"

"Because you hate me so much right now. Ordinary people start with loving someone and then eventually hate them. But you are no ordinary person. You're unusual. You start out your loving with hate. That is to say, you start from the end. You sense, instinctively, the battle ahead of you, and in order to protect yourself you shield yourself with hate. You're trying to get even with me now for the sadness you'll feel later."

I looked at him while he spoke and, strangely, felt an inevitable danger in his words. How could he talk about this right now? What kind of a subject is this for idle chatter?

"Goodbye," he said suddenly, and before I could say another word, he disappeared. I looked for him to no avail. He was nowhere. I felt powerless. *I* was the one who was supposed to leave *him* behind. If I go to the library again, I'll certainly meet this insult of his with an insult of my own. How dare he act this way toward me?

27

With Rae

Rae came to see me. It was the first time since I moved, and that was, she admitted, forever ago. But she couldn't come sooner. She told me that she's given up on her old friends and went looking for new ones. It's not in her nature, she said, to just put out her hands and wait for God to drop her special someone down from the sky. You can only find someone if you go looking for them. And now she's actually found someone.

"An actual person?" I asked, jokingly feigning surprise.

"Yes, a person, an actual person, although he hasn't graduated yet."

"Oh, and what does he want to be?"

"An engineer. We met each other at a lecture on birth control and it was love at first sight. But, the trouble is, love isn't enough. Eventually you have to get married, and that's where the troll's waiting under the bridge. He doesn't want to marry before he graduates and he won't graduate for another three years. He started his studies older than most. I'd have to wait for three years, supporting his studies. Waiting like that could drive a girl mad! Instead of landing an educated man, I'd have to pay for his education myself."

"Doesn't he want to get married now?"

"Well, if that's what I wanted . . ."

"Do you love him?"

"Oh, what's love got to do with it?" Rae said, brushing the thought aside with a wave of her hand. "We always fall in love with people who are in love with other women. I like him well enough. I think I could get used to him. But the waiting! With my luck I'll wait, and in the end, when he graduates, he'll feel that we're no longer *the same*. He'll wait until that moment to fall for someone else and nothing good can come of it."

"Is he very young?"

"Younger than me. To top it off, I'm not sure if he'll be able to stay committed to a long term love affair like I can."

"Then he certainly can't commit to spending his whole life with someone!"

"Certainly not!" Rae exclaimed. "But, still, you want things, you can't help feeling that you should take what little life you have and try to make something of it. Once you start doubting, you become afraid to love at all."

"Love is stronger than fear." I smiled sadly. "You can't take out an insurance policy on it. You have to take risks."

"Yes, take risks, take risks," Rae said doubtfully. "That's the way it is. When the right one comes along, the risk bothers you less."

She sat with me for a while. She spoke of B. She told me that he'd gotten close to Katya recently. A. gave Katya the boot, so she turned to B. Rae tried to warn her against it. "It's a shame, for her sake. Sometimes you're wrong about someone. That's how he is. He just goes from one to another."

"Then you don't think A. loved her?"

"Loved!? You're such a foolish girl! With you, it's all about love. He saw an opportunity, that's all. Now he's taken up with someone else, a friend of Katya's, also eccentric, but a little quieter."

I felt like my heart had fainted and refused to beat anymore. It was pierced by a sharp, nagging pain. The room swayed. I took hold of myself so I wouldn't give myself away in front of Rae. I felt a need for vengeance. I'll get even with A. by loving someone else. I'll freshen up that library acquaintance who's approached me so many times and make A. believe I love him. Then A.'s ego will suffer. He'll be amazed that I could be so in love with anyone but him. I'll get even with him through that impudent pea brain. I'll use him for revenge and then leave him with nothing. Let A. believe I'm completely in love with him. So there!

I couldn't get to the library today because of Rae. But I'll go there tomorrow and begin to play my role in the farce. My nerves are on edge and I can't just be passive in the face of all this. I have to do *something* so that I can stop thinking so much about him, the eternal A. I love him, but I hate thinking about him. It hurts too much.

I feel like my head is on fire. Rae's words keep ringing in my ears: "But a little quieter." A. hates shrill, vulgar women. He likes the quiet ones. Maybe he'll carry on his affair with this one so long that he'll decide to keep on with her forever. And what about me? What will happen to me?

28

Cheek

I feel as though some great danger is approaching and I'm just waiting for it. Do I want it to come faster? Do I want new troubles to help me forget the old ones? I don't know. I just feel that the worse it gets, the stronger I'll be to fight it.

I met him again in the library. Now I know his name: Cheek. Chaim Chisky, he told me, named for his mother's family. He got rid of the "sky" to make it easier to pronounce, and so that it would sound more American.

"And what was your father's name?" I asked. He must have had a father.

"Yes, I had one, but you're always more certain who your mother is. Did you ever read Strindberg's *The Father*? You can never be sure of your father. I mean, you can never be sure if the child is really his. But you know for sure about your mother. I would be all for living in a matriarchy. Children should follow the mother's line, and take her name. Then we wouldn't need to worry so much about illegitimate children. The word 'illegitimate' would be erased entirely. Every mother would have the right to have a child, without a husband."

"And the man would be freed from the yoke of having to take care of a family."

"Yes, and that's as it should be. Why should a man have to dedicate his whole life to others, with only minutes to spare for himself? It isn't right. A man must be free, free in every regard, so that he can be creative. Women were not made to be free. They were enslaved by nature itself to give themselves over to motherhood."

"So what is your name, using your father's name?" I asked, trying to change the topic.

"It's an ugly name. Mort. It means death in Latin. The god of death. I hate everything that has to do with death. I honor life. As long as you are alive, you have to live."

"But cheekiness is brash."

"Yet a cheek is smooth. Charles Cheek sounds very nice. C.—lots of people say, 'See here!' you know."

"I think that's what they say when they're upset."

"What's the difference? Someone says it. And it's nice to have a name that starts with the same sound as church."

He started talking about God but I didn't pay attention to his conversation. Instead, I thought about him for a while. He wasn't as dirty as he used to be. My words must have had some effect on him. I even noticed a remarkable freshness about his clothing. He wasn't missing any buttons. His collar was starched and bleached, and his face looked like he'd been given a massage, smooth and clean. We stood in the library's entryway, and he graciously made room when others tried to walk by. He seems to have decided to change his tone with me. He wasn't trying to surprise me by making sudden strong pronouncements. He wasn't as full of himself as before, and his demeanor was calmer.

"I don't have much time," he said, looking at his pocket watch. "If you'd be so kind, would you come for a little walk? It isn't very comfortable to stand here, and we're both going to be sitting for a while so it seems right that we should take a walk."

I decided I had nothing better to do. And it wasn't at all unpleasant today to go for a walk on the street with him. He looked very presentable and intelligent.

"Let's go somewhere quieter," he said, going down the steps, "so we can talk."

"Somewhere quieter is fine." We walked for a long time. He seemed to have forgotten that he didn't have much time. His watch lay in his pocket unheeded as he went on talking, displaying that he was well read and an expert in oratory. Maybe I could learn something from him after all. He was good at explaining things. He gave them his full attention.

"Were you insulted when I said goodbye to you so suddenly last time?" he asked before we parted.

"Oh, no!" I demurred. "That was the best thing you could've done!"

"The best, you probably thought, would have been if I'd never approached you in the first place. You were thinking: 'Who's this good-for-nothing who's coming on to me? Maybe I should call the police.' Am I right?"

"You're right."

"Is that what you think of me now?"

"Now, not as much."

"Now I don't bother you as much as I did before?"

"Not as much."

"I'm happy to hear it. I regret the way I behaved to you before, talking to you like that the first time I met you. That must have made a bad impression. Now I hope to redeem myself from making that bad impression with good thoughts. And do you know who they will be about?"

"About humanity?"

"No, about you. I must give you what you need."

"What do I need?"

"English. Good English. Your English is no good. You don't know enough words to express yourself well."

"I don't want to express myself well. And if I wanted to, I could do it in Yiddish."

"Yiddish is not a language. Yiddish is just a mishmosh of a lot of other languages."

"If Yiddish is not a language, so much the better. I'll express myself in a lot of other languages, then."

"You need a teacher."

"Now not only do I need English, but a teacher too?"

"He will systematize your knowledge."

"You want to give me a teacher?"

"I want to be your teacher."

"How much does a lesson cost?"

"For you—nothing."

"Why should I be so fortunate?"

"Just because. Because that's what I want."

"But I don't want it. Time is money, and I won't take money from anybody. Name a price."

"Fifty cents an hour. Will that do? I charge everyone else a dollar."

"And for me it's less by half?"

"Fine, make it seventy-five cents. I'll use the extra money to bring you candy."

"I don't eat candy."

"I'll bring you a flower. I'll give you a little more time. You'll earn dividends from that quarter. You won't lose any invested money on me. You'll get your money's worth."

He haggled with me like a market woman until he ruined the good impression he'd been making. But he soon realized that he was losing his way. He corrected his course, gathered his senses, and, for another half hour, lectured me in front of the door to the building where I lived.

29

Lessons

When I responded to the landlady's inquiry about my visitor by telling her that he was a teacher, she smirked and winked at me.

"I know all about teachers. Why do you need to bother with English?" asked the landlord, who was sitting nearby. This was in the morning, when I came in to wash up. Both of them looked disheveled, but they didn't seem to notice their own appearance. Instead, they looked at me and told me that I look like I don't sleep enough, and that I shouldn't stay up so late.

"How much time is he giving to you?" asked the landlady.

"What's it to you?" asked the landlord. "He'll give as much as he wants. You're not laying anything out for it."

"You must be paying him something for it, or doesn't he ask for money?" she asked, laughing.

I thought about it. If I took her seriously, I'd have to argue with her. But, out of self-respect, I didn't want to do that. I just told her and her husband that we'd negotiated a price.

"Without mediation?"

"That's right."

"That young man is in love with you," she said, "and you're taking lessons from him. You should be giving *him* the lessons!"

"He should marry you," the landlord asserted. "If you want, I'll stick my oar in and arrange the *shidukh*. A girl is like an ox. She has a long tongue, but she can't talk."

I laughed at his witticism, and he liked that. They feel very comfortable with me because I let them speak their minds. Should I feel guilty about that? I'm not doing anything wrong. Maybe I'm already feeling guilty for what will inevitably come later? I can tell that something is bound to happen and it'll take all my strength to keep from having a serious fight. My indifference toward myself sometimes leads me to let myself have a go at people that I can't stand.

He's given me three lessons already. When I think of all that he's taught me about *life*, it's enough to make me completely forget everything that he's taught me about English. As much as I'm skeptical of him, I have to admit that a lot of what he says is true. And it's very hard to hear someone tell you the truth about yourself.

He's dismissive of the way I live my life. He tells me that I should embrace as much life as I possibly can. I can live without being lively if I want to, but he can't see any reason why I should go on this way, living without really *living*.

I watch him while he talks and think, "Did bitter Fate send him to me to tell me the truth and to bring me something of life for a while? Or did he come to ensnare me in his net?"

Who is he? What is he? Why don't I tell him to leave me alone? Am I really so lonely that I'm starting to like someone I hate? Am I my own enemy, fooling myself by searching for meaning in his words? Or do I want to make him believe that I believe everything he's saying to me so he'll keep talking and drive the shadows of loneliness from my bedroom walls? I don't take ninety-nine words out of a hundred seriously, but I still let him go on speaking. I press the pain into my heart, like a mother holds a sick child to her breast. She cries out over her love, though her cries are not meant for anyone to hear.

If only A. had spoken to me this way! My God! How happy I would have been! And here a man wanders into my house with his mouth full of wisdom, spouting his assessment of all that a person, that *two* people could want to do, and I listen to him like I'm made of stone and have no spirit, no soul. And I refuse him.

"I will never tire of explaining to you what we are and what we were created for," said C., "until you understand and come around to my point of view. You'll say: 'Here I am. I live for today. I won't hold anything back for tomorrow. Let anarchy, full anarchy reign here, where until now only dark thoughts ruled. My young body will no longer serve my old spirit. Let me separate from myself, or let my spirit follow my body, as science decrees it must.'"

"That's ridiculous. I'll never say that," I replied skeptically.

"Yes, you will," he said with a certainty that didn't permit me to respond. "You will *have* to say it."

"Why will I have to?"

"Science says so."

"Science can say what she likes. I don't know her, and she can't hurt me."

This is how our lessons began and ended. The landlady, who was often listening at the door, must have heard some of it, and that's why she doesn't feel the need to be tactful with me.

My landlord tries to be friendly with me. He feels obligated to tell me about his life experiences, so that I can learn from them.

I don't like his daughter's "gentleman friend." He says I'm not pretty. He likes a girl to be a "peach," a lively thing, and I'm pale and moody. It's a good thing he doesn't like me, or he'd want me to learn something from him too.

Yesterday the daughter, foaming at the mouth, spoke of long-haired intellectuals. All that they want to do is have love affairs. Let others marry, they say.

༄

I've decided to give up the lessons. I forget more than I learn with them. And why should I to be the talk of the house? They all see the lessons as a pretense hiding a love affair. I would have stood up to all of them if I cared for him. But my heart does not beat for him. No, not for him. I just find him a little interesting, that's all.

I told him that he could stop teaching me, and he told me that he expected I would say so. He doesn't want to be my teacher anymore. He would rather be my guest, my friend.

I accepted his friendship for an hour or two at a time, and not in my room but out in the street.

"That's a cold friendship," he said, looking at me with his glossy, resentful eyes.

"Well, that's all I have."

"No, you have much more. But you don't want to give it. How did you get to be so stingy?"

"I was born this way."

He was silent for a while. Then he tried to explain to me with facts that one is born with neither stinginess nor warmth. He had gathered these facts from himself and from others he knew. You develop stinginess over the course of your life by not giving others what they want. Scientifically speaking, this is absolutely not ingrained. If I just tell myself to act differently, then I will *be* different.

"I've told myself to be different before, but I don't want to listen to myself. What can I do? Should I punish myself? I can't force myself to be worse than I am."

"That's because you call it worse."

"And you'd call it better?" I asked.

"Of course it's better."

"Fine, it's better. Even so, I can't be any better than I am."

"You don't want to be better," he said accusingly.

"Maybe not."

"Why not?"

"Maybe I'm afraid that by being better I'll allow myself to be worse. From all you've said as long as we've known each other (and I must add that you've certainly said your fair share), I gather that you believe a woman must give over her entire self to a man. Her own will must—what? I forget."

"She must give up her own will and desires, and then she will be happy," he supplied.

"You see, and I'm someone who can't get on without her own will. So, for example, I don't want to talk about these things anymore. We've already exhausted them. I just want to rest and be alone with my books, with my own shadow. Why can't I be allowed to do this small thing?"

"How old are you?"

"You're counting up my years again. I've already told you many times."

"Yes, but you look older than you are."

"That's sad, but what can you do? Older is older." I shrugged.

"You have to *live!*" he insisted.

"So I've heard. You're not the only one concerned with my *living.* There are those who want to force me to *live* to death!"

"How much are you paying for your room?"

"Nine dollars. Why do you suddenly want to know?"

"The other girl paid ten. Let me advise you to rent another room. Firstly, this room doesn't have up-to-date improvements. Secondly, the people are *intellectuals.* You won't be able to stand them. They're slaves to fashion. And the stairs and hall are dark and dangerous."

"In that case maybe you'd better not come and see me. And if you do come, don't stay so late, since you're so concerned about the stairs, and the landlords."

"Are you afraid of them?" he asked.

"I'm not afraid. You know what they say, 'The wolf is not afraid of the dog—he just hates his bark.'"

"I'll stand above their gossip. I'll spit on them!" He spat.

"If you don't mind, please stand above them in your own room, and spit there where they can't hear you and make me answer for it."

He spoke louder, saying that I didn't have to answer for him. He could do it himself, and if I'd only let him, he'd make those people lording themselves over me eat dirt. He's a lawyer, and he'll show them that if I'm paying for something they have no right to tell me what I can or can't do with it.

In order to make him stop carrying on that way on my account, I grabbed my hat and coat and headed out to the street. He followed me carefully down the stairs. When I laughed at him for being such a fraidy-cat, he told me that stairs call up bad memories for him and make him feel like he's being set on fire.

It would be easier to free myself from a rope I was already hanging from than to free myself from C. My God, where does he get the stamina to talk so much? Everything is a lecture for him. He talks about everything, and always from a scientific standpoint!

30

We'll See . . .

Rae came to see me today and I introduced her to C. She was crazy about him. He made a very good impression on her!

"How can a person know so much?" she said admiringly after he left. "My God! He's practically an encyclopedia! Whatever I asked, he knew the answer!"

"Do you know if they were the right answers?" I asked.

"No," she admitted. "But if he didn't know the answers, he wouldn't have given them. He did know. I'm sure he knew. And he's so handsome too. Yes, he looks very intelligent. You can see right away that he's educated. And the way he stares so intently—"

"He's nearsighted."

"Oh, that's why. But that's also a good thing," Rae said with a melancholy smile. "I wish my beau had worse eyesight. Maybe then he wouldn't see my flaws and I wouldn't have to hide them. Only just yesterday I wished that my engineer—I said *my*! He's as much mine as I'm his!—I wished that he couldn't see."

"Couldn't see what?"

"He noticed that I had a gray hair and he wanted to pluck it out. What a fool! As if it would solve anything to make me look a little younger by pulling out one hair. Three years from now, when I'm finally through waiting for him, there'll be a lot more gray hairs."

"Does he really expect you to wait for him?"

"Yes. Just wait. Wait for him to graduate before we get married. In the meantime, we'll go on with our affair and see what happens. B. saw him with me and didn't like him."

"And you trust B.'s opinion?"

"Why not? B. is my good friend. I don't know why *you* seem to have fallen out with him."

"It's better to be good friends from a distance."

"That's not the way I see it."

"Then we have a difference of opinion."

"He loved you, didn't he?"

"Who knows."

"I know he did. And what's more, you weren't indifferent to him either. You wouldn't have broken it off with him if it weren't for his wife and child. And, as you know, I'm different than you. If I loved someone, I wouldn't worry about such things. I'd carry on the affair, up to a certain point, of course, for as long as I could. What else is life for? That's why Katya amazes me. She *lives* in a way that you don't."

Rae spent the night in my room. In the morning when we went into the hall and I unlocked the kitchen door and opened it so we could wash up, my landlord's family looked at us very strangely. It seemed like they were puzzling out whether Rae had only just appeared to take someone else's place. Maybe they thought that she was a man dressed as a woman.

It all felt so insulting, and I didn't know how I was supposed to take it.

∽

C. proposed that we have a love affair. As long as I have no marriage prospects ahead of me, I should at least take whatever life offers me. Whatever bit of beauty I now possess will fade over time, and I'll regret that I didn't take everything life gave me.

That's how he spoke to me and I threw him out of my room for it. I didn't even scold him for talking that way. I listened to him and I hated him for it. My hatred gave me an odd sort of strength to hear him out. I didn't even let him see that I hated him. But when he took my silence as assent and wanted to move on from words of propaganda to practical actions, I calmly showed him the door, as though he'd asked me for directions.

"You don't mean it," he said, with a skeptical smile.

"Leave my room."

"But, you know, you can't drive me away like that."

"I'm not driving you away, I'm asking you to leave."

"But why? You listened to me so patiently, all the way to the end. Surely you must be joking!"

"You came here with a bargain in mind, a sale. You wanted to cheapen me in my own eyes, so that you could get me more easily. I listened to you devalue my worth, but I found that it would cost me too much. And so—I'm not for sale. Go look for some other wares."

"You can be so cutting, so severe! I didn't mean it that way."

"No need to say anything. I don't care whether you meant it or not. We won't be making any deals. Go."

He looked at me, biting his lip. He grabbed his hat, reached for the door, and slammed it behind him.

He still thought he was in the right!

৽৵

I see that my landlords are watching me, and I'm embarrassed to show that I can see it. I know how restricted I feel here, but I still can't bring myself to move to another place. Maybe I have it out for myself. It's like I'm my own enemy and I'm trying to get even with myself.

Sometimes I want to go up to those who take themselves for the morality police and ask them, "Can't I just look after myself? Why do you need to keep tabs on me? I'm old enough to watch out for myself. And if I should decide to fall, my dear society, no matter how much you tried to protect me, you wouldn't be able to keep me from it!" But I don't confront anyone. I ask nothing and I say nothing. My self-respect and my higher ideals stay with me.

৽৵

For a whole week, C. pursued me tirelessly in letters and in person, all the while insisting he wouldn't speak to me anymore. I didn't care what he talked about, I didn't want to hear him talk at all. I told him to get it into his head once and for all that I will not cede *my* will to someone else's. He can't force me into his ideal version of "such love affairs." He should look for someone more desperate for such high callings. They're not for me.

He promised to be quiet. He'll wait for me to come to him. Sooner or later I'll realize that free love is the greatest happiness, the holiest ideal, the world has to offer!

I had no argument to make against his waiting for me to reach that conclusion. He can wait as long as he likes!

"You'll be waiting for a long time, though," I warned him.

"As long as it takes!" he agreed. "What do I have to lose? I'm a man. In the meantime, I can live however I want. *You're* the one who doesn't have it good. Retreating from life as you do is bad, even from the standpoint of health. You'll grow old and decrepit before your time."

I told him not to worry about that. He should stop trying to talk me into being sick. I feel very healthy, no thanks to his threatening me with my own demise. If I meet someone who wants to share my whole life loyally and earnestly, then perhaps I'll become his life partner, as they call it. I'll make us a clean and comfortable home and trade in poetic love for practical devotion. But to throw myself into the waves of the sea, as he says, to be tossed into the stream of life—that's not what I'm after. You'd have to be either a dumb fish or an accomplished swimmer to want to throw yourself in like that. I am neither of those things. I'm just a person, a girl, who wants to stay out of the mud, who wants to keep herself from crawling into the swamp. Did he understand?

He said that he understood me very well, better than he wanted to, and he felt he should bite his tongue for saying such words to me. He won't talk to me that way again. He'll only come to see me every now and again and talk about general things. We'll read interesting things together, or he'll go with me on a stroll, or to a concert or the theater, or even the opera.

"So now we're good friends," he said, giving me his hand.

"Good acquaintances."

"When you know me better, you'll certainly accept my friendship."

"We'll see."

It was like we were competing with one another, placing bets. Actually, I'm almost curious to see if he'll be able to keep up this role and not resort to any tricks. He's an interesting subject to study, after all. He's certainly planning to study *me*. He'll examine me from a scientific standpoint and I'll approach him from a psychological one.

31

He Cannot Be Silent

It almost feels like I wasn't actually taking part in everything that happened to me this past week. I'm like a fiddle without a musician, apathetic to myself and everything that surrounds me.

My memory won't allow me to forget. I'm like a stranger to myself. I look over my own shoulder and wonder what will become of me. I don't know today what I'll do with myself tomorrow.

All of this watching myself from inside my own room is driving me out into the street. I'm beginning to see myself as a sinner, and it seems to me that I'm going to sin right under my own nose. I want to prove something to everyone, after all the troubles I've had from my unearned insults. I've decided that when C. comes to see me I'll receive him with loud, demonstrative hospitality so that those listening behind the door will hear me greeting him, won't think I'm hiding anything, and will spend the whole evening thinking about how to protect me.

C. stood by his promise. This time he didn't tell me that I'd eventually come around to his way of thinking in spite of myself. He talked about astronomy, psychology, mythology, zoology, and all manner of other subjects, and when they did have something to do with physiology or love-ology, he only talked about it from a scientific standpoint. This, I had to allow. To suppress science would be a sin. It was enough that I asked him to suppress the feelings he'd already declared toward me.

We went together to the theater and to a few other artistic venues. He was sure of himself there, and he believed that I was proud of him because he knew so much about everything and he knew how to explain it so that others would listen. To be honest, I did enjoy it. Often on these excursions, I imagined that we were married. As a couple we'd run into a certain A. As A. got to know C., he'd come to believe I was deeply in love with him because of his breadth of knowledge; there was so much to say about him, and so much to listen to. A. would be overcome with sadness and wish that he, and not an educated man like C., had taken me, when he knew I had loved him so much!

To please me, C. started paying more attention to his appearance, and it did make him much better-looking. I began to seek out and find appealing things in his face, though it was far from handsome. I even joked that it bothered me that he was taller than me because it was a sign: he was continuously growing better. He said he wouldn't stop at the title "doctor." He'd go farther—to "professor." Then he'd be able to marry a rich, beautiful girl. He'd live broadly and in style. And maybe then I'd regret that I hadn't agreed to carry on an affair with him.

∽

In the meantime, I busied myself imagining what might happen. I held these thoughts over myself as an excuse for my suffering, although the source of it was really my continued feelings for A. I tried to fill my emptiness with something else, with the poisonous desire for revenge, but I kept grasping at A. in my thoughts.

The demonstrative familiarity I'd shown in welcoming a young man into my room (my landlords had no way of knowing if it was always the same man) made me act even more brazenly. That evening was the last in an entire week of evenings of taking in visitors. When I heard his footsteps, instead of my usual behavior of drawing attention to myself I didn't wait for him to knock before I opened the door.

He took me in with desiring eyes and held me in his arms. He probably thought I'd just been standing by the door, waiting for him to come.

"How nice!" he cried. "The door seems to open itself for your lover by magic! I didn't even have to knock!"

"Please don't talk so loud," I begged. "It's especially important to speak quietly when you're talking about such things."

"Be quiet? Oh, no! Today, like the world famous Tolstoy, I declare that 'I cannot be silent'! I have decided to speak out today, and so I shall! Here you are, standing by the door waiting for me to arrive. How can you explain this? You love me. And if you love me, why should you put off your life for later? Who knows if we'll even be alive later! Live for the present, and in the future you'll have a past. Time does not stand still. What vanishes today does not come back tomorrow. I want today. See, I don't even ask you what you did before today, I don't try to learn about your past. I don't want to know anything about it. Nothing."

"I want people to want to know *everything* about me."

"Why? So that they will know about your—respectable behavior?"

"Why not?"

"Who cares about that?"

"I do."

"Well, well. That's fine. I don't want to argue with you about it. You can be as respectable as you want. It's fine for you to be refined."

"Isn't it?"

"Yes, it is."

"Thanks!"

"Why the sarcasm? Why the smirk? My dear friend, be good. No, not 'my dear friend'—from now on you are 'my darling.' No need to be so formal. Let me . . ." He lowered himself to his knees. "Let me make you happy!"

"This is the first time in my life I've seen someone begging to give happiness away. And for how long?"

"That's a hard question to answer. It depends how it feels later. One day you're in love, and the next day you're not. Love is like life. One day it's here and the next day it's gone. Who can tell? That's why it's no use asking, 'For how long?' Love is part of life, and life doesn't last forever. And life is meant to be *lived*! Down with the slavery of superstition! We must fight, loud and proud, against the whole world for our right to be human and to *live*. You love me and I love you. It's not our first love. But it might be our last. After all, you're not the kind of woman who can love for a long time, because you don't allow yourself to love, my dear friend. How foolish it is for me to call you 'friend,' when from the first time I saw you, I thought of you as more."

"It's good that you only thought it."

"And who can keep me from saying it? My darling, my love! You're an awfully dear girl! And today I've decided to show you that I love you. I love you so!"

"Why so much?"

"Don't ask. Don't ask why. You can't explain these things. I just know I love you and to me it's so wonderful that I've suddenly stopped being interested in scientific questions. Even if someone else could explain why, it's not something that *I* could ever explain. I love you for the intensity of your longing to be loved and to love. I'm amazed by your strong yet supple will, by your bitter yet sweet smile. I love you because you are as closed-lipped as a diplomat and yet as pure and open-hearted as a child, because of your severe glares and the soft expression hidden in your eyes, beneath that severity. I love you for your Jewish beauty, for your body, for your hair, for your arms, for . . . oh, how can I account for it *all*? Maybe I just love you because—I love you!"

I sat by the window in the blue-violet electric light of the street-lamps, and he knelt at my feet. The flowers on the curtains pressed against the walls and fluttered in the breeze from the open window as though alive. I looked down at him quietly and intensely as he spoke. He seemed so unlike himself. I almost thought I could see in him some similarities to A. There are moments when one person in love looks so similar to another. Love, whether full of elevated longings or base instincts, is always beautiful when it speaks, and especially when, after it speaks, there is silence.

But, although C. speaks beautifully, he cannot be silent. To prevent his hands from acting in place of his tongue, I kept him talking. One word from me prompted a flood of words from him, one question led to endless explanations. He was proud to give me as much information as he could, and he especially wanted to speak about anatomy. He divided human beings into components so that he could put them back together again. He didn't care if this aroused unseemly associations. He was happy to explain that, from a scientific perspective, it does no good to feel uncomfortable about such things. Once you understand the matter thoroughly, the false feeling of shame and discomfort will dissipate.

It seemed to me that he was making me the subject of his lesson.

"What's this?" he asked, for example, pressing my nose, my eye, my cheek, my neck, my arm. Like a child just learning to answer such questions, I smilingly gave the answers.

"In Latin we call this such and such," he explained and pointed to something else, asking, "What do you call this?"

"My heart?" I said, not sure if my heart was exactly where he was pointing. Who knows, maybe it's located somewhere else in Latin. That turned out to be true.

"Not there!" he said, strict as an old professor. "It's much lower. Right down here. This is where it beats."

I already knew all this. He told me that I wasn't missing anything except for a bit more passion. Not just more, I was actually missing passion entirely. Considering that I was so normal, I should really be a bit *more* normal. I should let myself follow my own normal desires; I should make use of God's gift of human happiness and well-being.

I didn't know (and maybe I never will) how to use it. To fully use it, so that, as they say, "the wolf will be satisfied and the goat remain whole." A young man up to his ears in love, overtaken by passion for me, and on his way to being a college graduate, was right in front of me ripe for the taking. He looked at me like I was about to bring redemption to the world, and I just sat there. I sat, and sat, and . . . that's all.

He showed me, from a scientific standpoint, that it was not healthy for me to sit that way, on a chair, as if I were in a public place. I was in my own room, so why shouldn't I make myself comfortable?

"I can see the sky from here," I answered. "And I love to watch people walking in the street after midnight. They look so mysterious, each like he's going to a secret meeting. It reminds me of my old home where nowadays people must walk around like this, like shadows, even in the daytime."

He begged me to stop. "My dear, don't think of your old home. The old country isn't a home anymore. Our home is here, where we are. We are citizens of the whole world. The Poland that I once passionately championed no longer belongs to us. Right under my own eyes they turned me into a German. Fine, so let me be a German, a Frenchman, a Turk, even an Eskimo, as long as I can be alive. Life, in the fullest sense of the word, is the most beautiful and precious thing that we have. Looking at you now, I see how beautiful you are. The pale glimmer of electric streetlamps falls on you and lights up your eyes as they gaze upon me, warming my soul. I feel as though my soul will sprout wings and fly to the highest heavens leaving me here, at your feet."

"My feet would trample a man without a soul."

"Let them!" he cried out passionately. "Go on and take a step! Step, step, step! I myself will place your foot on my neck, on my head! Don't you see, my love, I lay myself at your feet! I give myself over to you. You can do with me *what you will*."

I didn't know what to do with him. His passion did not win me over. My temperament was probably at fault. I was no poem, but a plain paragraph of prose. Instead of being persuaded by his enthusiasm I was preoccupied with thoughts of my intellectual landlords. They must have overheard the quiet ruckus going on in here, and who knows what they were thinking.

"My dear, love is the greatest happiness in life, especially for a woman. A woman's life must be filled to the brim with love. Of all the varieties of love, free love is the only one that can raise up the soul, delight the spirit, and so forth, and so on."

"What kind of a free love can this be, if we have to be so secretive about it? Hidden love is what it should be called," I said, "and if you have to hide it, it must not be as wonderful as you say it is."

"But keeping it secret is what makes it so interesting, so nice, so sweet!"

"Whatever you say," I answered. "But don't say it so loud. The people in the house—"

"—are asleep."

"Then you shouldn't wake them."

"They sleep so soundly that they won't hear anything. Simple people are heavy sleepers."

"They're . . . intellectuals."

"Never!"

"Regardless, you shouldn't wake them."

"They think that we—that *you're* asleep."

"And that I'm talking in my sleep?"

"Alright. I'll be quiet, if you're so afraid. You're as scared of them as if they were your parents, or as if you were dependent on them to make a living. I'll be quiet. But you can't blame me if when I close my mouth I speak with my hands. A man must have some way to express his passion."

"Go away! Go home! Go!" I begged him. Biting my lips to quell my distress, I grabbed his fresh hands and frantically pushed them away with all my strength.

"Oh, my darling!" he said, his passion increasing with my actions. "You beg me to leave, but you are holding my hands. How like a woman! When a woman says no, she means yes. It's a woman's nature. She wants to be taken by force, so she can claim later that she didn't ask for it. Women are complicated. But you, my darling, try too hard to suppress your desires. Why should you fight it? It's for your own happiness as well as mine. Instead of holding a man back, a woman should help him to achieve happiness."

I did not feel like helping him achieve happiness. I felt that I'd feel a lot better if he were on the other side of the door. But perhaps then I'd want him next to me again. That's how it is.

"We'll talk about this some other time," I said. "Now is not the time."

"But now *is* the time for it. Now, now, now!"

"It's almost daytime. People will be getting up soon."

"Who cares if they get up or not? They have nothing to do with us. We love each other and we have a right to live however we want. Soon the sun will rise and look at us with contempt for not making use of the dark, dark night, which was given to us for our brightest moments. We'll regret not trespassing the boundaries between my 'we can' and your 'we mustn't.' Where is the logic in such living? Tell me, where?"

I was utterly spent from not sleeping and from straining to listen to see if others could hear us. I'd had it with his wild gesticulations. I refused to leave my chair, as though I was chained to it, and pushed his hands away. He lay down in front of my feet and swore that he wouldn't get up until I sent for an ambulance to take him away.

"I'm sick, tired, broken, and it's all because of *you!*" he cried. "You are so hard, so cold, that you don't care if a man expires right here at your feet. You have the eyes of a dove and the heart of a tiger. And you have no soul."

"What can I do about that?"

"Let me give you my soul."

"And then what about you?"

"I'll die here at your feet. No, not here. Let's go to your bed. Why are you sitting there on your chair? Are you nailed to it? Did you grow into it? Look, she won't budge!" Now he wasn't even talking to me directly. It was like he was complaining to someone else about me. He chided me this way, talking on and on, until he finally grew silent. He lay still, with his head on my footstool, and I thought he had fallen asleep. A knock on the door sent us scrambling to our feet.

"Who is it?" he asked.

"Who is it?" I called out toward the door.

"Open the door, and you'll see!" a deep, gravelly voice answered from behind the door. "Open up!"

32

Move!

My heart pounded and my hands shook. I didn't touch the doorknob, but instead reached for the key and unlocked the door. In my nervousness, I pulled out the key and flung it under the bed. I wanted to retrieve it, but the knocks on the door grew louder and more impatient.

"Don't open it," C. said. "You have a right not to open your door. And you don't want to open it."

I glared at him to tell him to keep quiet. I opened the door, holding my nightgown closed at the neck, and peered out into the dark hallway. The landlady stood before me in a long large brown bathrobe. With eyes like daggers, she spoke words meant to draw blood. "You may no longer live in our home. Find another room."

"Mrs.—"

"Not in *my* house!"

"You—"

"No shenanigans!"

"But—"

"I don't want to hear it!"

"But—"

"Don't put your finger in my mouth, or I'll bite. I rented the room to one person. If you want others to stay in your room, there are *plenty* of other sorts of houses in New York for that!"

"How can you—"

"It's *alright,*" she scoffed in English, and then continued in Yiddish. "If you can do what you do, then I can say what I have to say. It isn't the first night that you've—that you've had a man in your room. I've stayed quiet up to now. But there's a limit to everything. I have patience of iron, but even that can give way. Enough!"

"That's what I think too!" said the husband's voice suddenly from behind my landlady's back. "This *povedenie* is not suitable for an intellectual girl in an intellectual home living among intellectual people. We can't allow people in our home when we don't know them or who they are. What is he, who is he, your man?"

"Why should you care who he is?" C. butted in. "The room is paid for until the first. No one has the right to change that."

"Say, *mister*, who do you think you're talking to?" said the landlord, edging closer to my door. "Who are you to tell me what my rights are? I wouldn't wish this on my worst enemies. You're an *aferist*, a swindler, a white slave trader! I'll call the police if you don't hear me out."

C. stared at them disgustedly. "I am her fiancé. Don't you know that?"

"Her fiancé!" said the landlord, turning to his wife. "He should be shot. Her fiancé?"

"Her husband, alright?" C. said as though to provoke him. "We got married but haven't been able to get an apartment yet. Until then, we're living in this room together."

"Her husband?" The landlord had begun to believe him, and asked, "Do you have something to prove that you're her husband?"

C. gave him the finger.

"How dare you give *me* the finger!" said my landlord, temper flaring. "Let me at him!" he yelled, tearing himself from his wife's grasp. "I'll give him what's coming to him! Scoundrel! Bastard! *Skatina*! Did you hear how he insulted me?"

"Why, that's the limit!" shouted their daughter in English. "It's a shame! Why, such a shame! Did you ever? Oh, my! I didn't sleep a wink. I heard *everything*."

"Daughter, you'd better stay out of this," said her mother earnestly, prodding her daughter away. "It's not good for you to stand here and hear such things. And as for *you*," she cried, shaking her finger at me. "Move out of this house at once!"

She ushered her husband and daughter into the hall. I sat on the edge of my bed, staring dejectedly at the doorway. In my mind, the word "move" pounded like a hammer. Painfully and frantically, my heart squeezed out pity for myself and for the insult that I, of all people, had to endure. They thought of *me* as a fallen woman! Soon, the rumor would be all over the house, all over the street. Everyone would point their fingers at me and say, "There she is, that girl—" They would look at me with scorn and shoo me away like a pest. Why wasn't I running away from there? Why was I still sitting there? What was I waiting for?

I tried to stand up, but my legs buckled under me and I fell back onto the edge of my untouched bed. I thought to myself that they must have looked at the made-up bed and supposed that when I hesitated to open the door I had been hastily straightening the covers. Yes, they were capable of thinking the worst of me.

"Why are you so upset and helpless?" C. asked, standing next to me and stroking my head. "What happened to make you feel like the world is ending? All that happened is that you discovered the small, ugly nature of those miserable 'intellectuals.' Now you know how they think about other people, whom they cannot judge any higher than their own lowdown, dirty thoughts. Don't worry, be glad that it happened this way. Now you'll leave this place. You'll move. You'll find a better room. You know what, my dear? Why don't you move to my place? I'll rent a pushcart and carry your things to my place, and we'll live together. This is a great idea! At my place you'll feel free as a bird! No one will worry about you, and you can do whatever you want! Come!"

"One insult after another," I thought to myself. Their insulting me had bucked him up.

"Living together will be much cheaper for both of us," he continued. "I'll teach you how to be frugal. You'll see how nicely we'll manage things. And we'll love one another like—no, I can't describe it in words! Come—"

I felt an odd inertia preventing me from opening my mouth to answer him. His words seemed to come from somewhere far away. I strained to connect each word to the next. I felt like I was in the kind of dream where you try to move but you can't because you're paralyzed.

"Why are you looking at me that way?" he asked, annoyed. "Perk up! My God! Take your life into your own hands. Look at me! Look me in the eyes! Say something!"

"Leave me alone."

"How can I leave you alone? What can I do for you? Tell me!"

I stared blankly ahead and said nothing.

"Maybe," he said after a short pause, "we should go to city hall and get a marriage license?"

His question shook me out of my stupor. It made me think differently about him. This is how an honorable man would speak if he wanted to prevent his lover's suffering. I would show *them* the license and leave their intellectual home with pride and scorn. If I wanted to, I could even take them to court for insulting me the way they had. Maybe I'd forgive them, but only after I'd taught them a lesson for the way they'd treated me. I'd refuse to move, and they'd have to call the police. And when the police came to arrest me for indecency, I'd pull out the license. The scandal would be about *them* and their conduct, and not about me.

All of this ran through my thoughts as quick as lightning, and I was grateful for his question. He was a much better man than he seemed. He was able to bend his principles a little to preserve the honor of the woman he loved. No man is entirely good or bad. When it comes to the critical moment when the soul is laid bare, you can see what a man is truly capable of.

"Do you want to go to city hall?" he asked again.

"Maybe. Should we?" Out of instinctual modesty, I returned the question to him.

But he didn't answer. He just looked at me with a smirk that made all the blood rush to my head. I now understood that he'd only asked me to see what kind of reaction he would get—and it was working! I tried to control myself so he wouldn't see the hatred his cynical smile aroused in me. I needed some time to think about how I could hurt him so that he'd know for certain that I was the cause.

"You want to go to city hall?" he asked, gesturing toward the outside. "But why? Is it because you love me so much that you want to belong to me forever?"

"Yes."

"Is that so? And you won't trust my love for you without it?"

"No."

"But you know that legal marriage is against my principles."

"I know."

"And yet you want me to go against them."

"That's what I want."

"And if we don't get a license, then—you won't love me?"

"I won't."

"Where does the love go?"

"Nowhere."

"How can you want to bind yourself, without reason or love, to a man? Is it because he would have to support you?"

"Yes."

"Very practical. You're a very practical woman."

"A girl."

"Oh, I beg your pardon. It's such an honor to be a *girl*! That's something to be proud of! They should give you a medal! But let's be honest. You want to get married because you are afraid. Right?"

"No."

"Your answers are so *laconic*," he responded in his guttural English. "You're boring me to death. But, wait, should we go now and call a rabbi? He would conduct a ceremony and make us legitimate for a bargain price. We would honor our old-fashioned relatives, and laugh at them in secret. Let's go to a rabbi! Come!"

"I don't want a rabbi."

"What do you want?"

"A judge."

"So you want me to make an exception to my rule that a man shouldn't tie himself to anything? You want me to be a slave to the law for the rest of my life?"

I didn't say anything. When he saw that I'd fallen back into apathy and was no longer even responding laconically, he gave up and decided he'd better leave. He could see very well that I didn't care for him. He'd be willing to assume the yoke of the law, to make a man out of himself, by getting a license, if his lover were a different kind of person. But he's not the kind of man you can just lead around by the nose. There was nothing else to say. It's beneath him—a lawyer and soon a doctor to boot—to stoop to begging someone to so much as say a word to him.

His self-esteem was wounded. He was looking for respect, but he didn't get it. He'd lowered himself for my sake, hoping that I'd look up to him, but I hadn't obliged. He even suggested that I'm in love with another man and only want to marry him so that I can do *more* than just love my lover. I didn't refute him. He said that I don't appreciate his greatness, that I think he's out of his mind, that I don't believe in his future. I didn't refute that either. He said that I wanted him to leave, and I agreed.

"And you don't want me to come back?" he asked.

"You can come."

"Today, before nighttime, you mean? In the evening."

"This evening."

"And we'll both go looking for a room today, right?"

"Yes."

"Good! And then we'll decide where to go from there, right?"

"Yes."

"After all, no matter how much we argue, we have to remember our feelings for each other haven't changed. We'll be friends, as we were before. Right?"

"Yes."

"I shouldn't have said what I did. But you won't hold that against me, right?"

"No."

"How good, sweet, and kind you are, my dear! You are so good, you know, that you could make me your eternal slave. There may come a time when I'll beg you to marry me and you won't want that anymore."

I wanted to agree with him and laugh. But if I did that, all my efforts would have been for nothing. I held myself together. I buried myself in my hidden stores of self-composure so that he wouldn't see any sign of helplessness or sorrow.

He must have felt instinctively that I was unusually calm. He turned around at the door to see if I was watching him go.

As soon as he left I started packing my things. I worked with unnatural speed, urged along by my fear that I'd take too long and he'd come back before I had a chance to leave. Soon I was off looking for a new room, prepared to take any room, so long as I didn't have to remain where I was.

I rented a room on a side street on a weekly basis. My landlady was a half-blind, elderly German woman. I found a man and a boy who would carry my little trunk and large satchel to my new room for a dollar. It was faster to have them do it than to take the express train.

33

My New Room

The thought that he might come to my room and I won't be there, that he'll knock and knock and my door won't open for him, makes me feel uncomfortable and uneasy. In better, calmer times it would have had the opposite effect on me. My new room is as certain as a grave. I feel like I've been thrown into a different world. The old darkened walls decorated with *goyish* pictures; the large round dresser; the quilt stitched together with scraps of fabric; all of these and more are unfamiliar to me. I've never been in such a *goyish* space, and no one I know will ever guess that I'm living here. I can hardly believe it myself. When I wake up I have to pinch myself to be sure it's me who's here, and not some other woman.

I've been here for two days and already it seems like forever. I'm not working. For now, I'm free to lock myself in my room and try to withstand the coldness it makes me feel.

I feel hidden, torn from the entire world. Everything here seems foreign to me.

A little cat ran in through the window and I played with her. I petted her and looked into her feline eyes. But she was soon bored of me and just as quickly as she came, she leapt out the door and ran away.

The whole house is quiet. I only hear doors opening and closing. The people who live here only come home to sleep. They are all weekly renters. My landlady, the sickly half-blind German woman, told me that she doesn't rent any rooms here for a whole month at a time.

You can earn more by renting weekly than monthly—you earn an extra half-week's rent every month (that is to say, an extra few dollars). "*Nicht wahr?*"

"*Es ist wahr*," I agreed. I wanted to ask her if she could take down her pictures—secular ones and the holy icons—I couldn't bear to look at them. But I didn't ask. I was so grateful to her for taking me in. And she didn't ask any questions other than where I had moved from, and why. Let her hang whatever she wants on the walls. I won't look at the walls. I'll just look at the ceiling.

The first night I was afraid to sleep in the bed. It was such a wide bed with such stiff, starched old linens. Who knows what kind of person had slept on them the night before? I spread my sheets out over the bed and lay down on the edge, fully dressed with my shoes still on. I thought about the previous evening's events, and the morning when they had insulted me and driven me out. My thoughts led me to my home in the old country. I sobbed, thinking of it.

And then a deep sadness, a heavy feeling of unearned suffering weighed upon my heart. Tears welled up in my eyes and fell on the white pages of my only friend—this diary. I asked myself: Did I do something wrong? Maybe I should have . . . what else could I have done? Cried out to them before they threw me out and told them that I hadn't sinned? Would they have believed me?

It's foolish to cry over such foolish things. I know that. And still the tears won't relent. I let them flow. No one can see them, and maybe they'll lighten the burden that weighs on my heart.

A. and B. are out there, somewhere. If only B. were here with me now! He'd understand me without any need for words. He'd stroke my hair, smile softly, and call me "child."

No, I shouldn't pine after them. They're dead to me now.

I should go and see Rae. She'll try to visit me in my old room and won't know why I left so hastily.

Today I tried to count the hand-stitched patches on my quilt. I lost count in the middle and stared at the icon of the holy mother and son. *Me*, in a room with a picture like *that* on the wall! What would my family in the old country have to say about that?

The wardrobe is made of plain wood and painted dark red, and there's something running around inside of it. I'm afraid to get too close. I don't want whatever it is to jump out into my face. The floor is covered with thin old pieces of oilcloth, splattered with fish stains. The mirror above the corner table is streaked, so it seems like whoever looked into it before left residue from her crying. Maybe the sorrows she lived through took physical form in the mirror. Now, it reflects *my* tears.

I don't want to go back out into the street because I might run into C. I'll avoid him as long as possible, and if we should chance to meet again, he'd better watch out for me!

Actually, it was all my fault. How could I have acted the way I did, bringing about such behavior in him? Probably there's something wrong with me that makes him feel like he should act that way. Maybe it's my pride that ends up causing me so much suffering. I won't let on that I'm insulted, so I'm unable to settle the score.

It would never even occur to him that I'm here, so close and yet so far away. Here I am, in a furnished weekly rental, surrounded by holy pictures, and covered, trapped in sinful silence and shame.

☙

I read in the newspaper today that respectable women are being sentenced for street prostitution. A report from a women's prison association demonstrates that many respectable women and girls are arrested illegally on charges of immorality, simply because policemen, or whoever else, feels like it. The policeman or detective is always believed over the person he's sending to jail, even if the woman accused of immorality is the picture of respectability.

"With the new tenement house law," according to the report, "persecutions of unmarried women accused of leading immoral lives have risen significantly. The law has created a situation such that no woman who lives by herself in a furnished room or tenement house can be certain of her freedom or her reputation. Many women have been sentenced under this law, and women who have worked doggedly to earn a living are being detained by plainclothes police officers who arrest them without cause, warning, or evidence against them. They have been informed on by gossipmongers, spinners of lies, neighbors who like to spread rumors. Many women languish in jail and are forever branded as prostitutes, even if they can prove their innocence. The courts ask no questions and these women are sentenced simply because, according to the law, 'A policeman's word suffices and there's no need for further proof.'"

The arrested women are treated so poorly that from the beginning they think it can get no worse. But their situation will be much worse where they're headed. The report continues, "The police conduct a raid on a brothel. They assume that the madam of such a place is usually not at home so they arrest the housekeeper. In special sessions court, the housekeeper is sentenced to thirty days in the Tombs. She goes gladly, the madam sends her money, and she lives well there, befriending the young women under arrest and forming close relationships with them. There are certainly enough young women under arrest to choose from. She gives them her address and wishes them all luck. When they leave prison, they are good candidates for brothel work, and soon the housekeeper's madam is doing so well that she has opened a second house."

The report says that the Tenement House Act has only brought about a situation in which any reprobate can pay money to bring misfortune upon an unmarried woman who lives alone in a room. If he wants to, all he has to do is claim that she's bringing men home. Whether he's invited or not he can come up to her room while a detective watches, and, nine times out of ten, the detective will see this as grounds for making an accusation. He'll break into her room and arrest her without a warrant.

ↄ∽

I'd started reading the newspaper to dispel my instinctive fear of my surroundings, but now I only felt more frightened. I was even more afraid than I had been before to make any noise in my room, to open the door, or to go out into the street. I was afraid someone might approach me and ask why I left the other rooms so quickly. I had the feeling that that my moralizing, intellectual landlords were looking for me to see what had become of me. To see if my "husband" was with me. My heart pounded at the faintest sound of footsteps in the long, dark corridor or a rustle by my door. Maybe this is just a house set up to attract lonely girls, only to capture them and never let them go? Maybe on the other side of my door is one of *those people* seeking girls like me: lonely and in trouble.

I won't have any way to make a living for a long time. I'm not worried about scraping by, but people look at you so strangely when you don't work. They jump to whatever conclusions they want. They're suspicious and they keep an eye on you, like you're breaking some law.

೦౨

I want to approach the German lady, my half-blind landlady, and explain to her what I'm doing alone in my room in the middle of the day. I want to tell her that I'm about to head out to visit a friend, so she won't think that I'm doing nothing to earn a living or that I'm venturing where I shouldn't. But I manage to hold myself at bay. Going to her of my own accord would only raise her suspicions. And why, in all honesty, should I explain everything to her if she hasn't asked? But think of the "New Law" Tenement House Act! One misunderstanding could send me who knows where . . .

Although at first I appreciated that she didn't ask me any questions when I moved in, now it's made me suspicious of the house. She trusts me without knowing me, and instead of feeling grateful now I mistrust her. I have trouble believing that she could really trust me so much and I keep looking around to see if others are watching me. I actually want someone to be watching. I want them to see that I'm alone, buried here in this tomblike Christian room. Books and newspapers are my only companions.

It seems to me that the holy pictures were hung on the walls to cover up the sins of the house. The mother and her son in those pictures—I have strange thoughts about them. Today, an illegitimate child would never be attributed to God. We require children to have human fathers. If we recognized all illegitimate children as children of God, think of how many more legitimate people we'd have!

೦౨

The German lady came to see me and I paid her in advance for another week, even though the week I'd already paid for begins tomorrow. She took the money, $2.75, and asked me for another quarter. She explained that I have to pay more for gas because I use so much. She doesn't know what I'm doing, but she can see from the door that my light is still burning late at night. The rule is that after ten o'clock you can't burn gas. If I do want to burn it, then I'll have to pay extra. I paid her.

She looked around the room for a while with her old, sickly eyes and asked me if I was cold. "It's almost winter, but it's still warm, *nicht wahr?*"

"Yes, that's right," I said, deciding that I would suffer the cold until I could find myself a regular room, just so she wouldn't light me a fire.

She warned me not to keep my bowl and water pitcher on the chair because I might knock it over with my foot. I did as she said.

"One more thing," she continued. "Don't leave the door to the back entrance through the dark hallway unlocked." I promised that I wouldn't. I'll only let myself in through it. Anyone else who wants to come in, even a tramp, should come in through the parlor. I didn't understand what she was getting at. Although I felt like laughing I reassured her that I had locked the door. Someone else must have left it open.

"Who else could it be, if it wasn't you and it wasn't me?" she asked. Her son? He was at his job all day. He was a carpenter and he certainly knew how to go in and out of a door. Well, whoever it was, I shouldn't let it happen again.

⌒

I need to start seriously looking for another room among my *own* people. This is no place for me. I'm afraid to walk around at night in my nightgown. I'm always looking for the key to my door, checking to make sure it's still hidden under my pillow.

I'm always afraid that there will be some danger, that something out of the ordinary will happen to me. When each day passes without incident, I feel like I've been fooled. I almost want the danger to come.

Let some misfortune happen to me. The fear and anticipation is worse than the misfortune itself. I'm ready for anything. One thing is for certain: there's one way to free myself from everything and everyone. Perhaps my life is not in my own hands, but my death, my death . . .

34

Lacking in Passion

To keep Rae from going to see those intellectual landlords, I went to visit her. But I was too late. She'd already gone to see them, and they'd told her that I wasn't living there anymore. It's a good thing I left so soon, they told her, because if I'd behaved like that one more time, they would've called the police and had me arrested without even hesitating. How could a young woman who appeared to be an intellectual spend a whole night in her room with such a *buyan*, such a ruffian?

Rae told them that she didn't know me well. She'd only come to tell me about a job. So they told her all about me and what I'd done. Rae told me everything she could remember. "Now," she said, "you really have to get even with them. It won't be hard. Mr. Cheek"—she knew very well that's who they were talking about—"is a lawyer, after all. I can bear witness to the fact that they are injuring your reputation."

If she really knew what sort of a man he was, I thought, she would advise me never to see him again. She wouldn't inquire after him as if he were a person from a higher, better class.

"Why do you like him so much?" I asked.

"He's interesting."

"What's interesting about him?"

"His narrow, squinty eyes, his good English, his fair skin, his one and a half diplomas and promising future. I've heard so much about him. I know people who know him and they say that someday he'll be an important figure, he'll have an important place among the greatest in society."

"So they say!"

"They don't ring the church bells unless it's a holiday! After all, they don't say such things about everyone. He is exceptional. If someone like that were interested in me I'd be proud, and I'd try all the harder to make him love me."

"That wouldn't be so difficult."

"Who knows?"

"I can imagine."

"Would you be jealous?" Rae asked, looking at me with one of her rakish smiles.

"No," I shot back. "Definitely not."

"Are you sure you won't regret saying that?"

"*You* should be careful that you don't have regrets. You should think it through before getting involved with someone like that."

"Love and thinking things through—a fine combination. No, you're too practical."

"It's not about what I am, but about what *he* is. He's more than practical. He's mercenary. He's—but it doesn't matter what I say, you'll find out soon enough."

〜

"He speaks very nicely."

"Oh yes, he can talk—"

"And how does he behave?"

"How? All you'd have to do is cut off his hands, and he'd be a perfect gentleman."

"No, I mean, jokes aside. Is he—honorable?"

"Depends what you mean by that."

"What does he want?"

"Free love."

"Aha!"

Rae looked at herself in the mirror, tossed her hair over her shoulders, and, sitting down on a chair, leaned her legs against the wall. She stared ahead with a bitter expression of anger mixed with pain. Then, with resolve, she turned her gaze on me and took all her frustration out on me, saying, "Fine, I accept! Free love, not free love—the devil take it all! It's better than what I've been doing. It's better than thinking and waiting until—death. I want to be myself. I've given up on the idea of saving my happiness for later. Eternal love, a peaceful home, a happy life—it's all made up. I've never met anyone who actually had those things in real life, other than Mrs. B., but she's a cow who doesn't know how to appreciate what she's got. Take Katya—she's daring. She doesn't care what will happen later. She takes things as they come. I want to be like that!"

"Maybe that's what you want, but you won't be able to. Especially with *him*. And what good would it do you?"

"What good does it do me now?"

"At least you have the knowledge that you haven't lost anything."

"Ugh! You with your *knowledge*!" Rae turned to me impatiently, like a man. "You're winning by not letting yourself win. I've heard enough about you. I won't let it bother me if I don't live up to your strength of character. Just one false step and you're lost! And when we lose ourselves, we win. You know what I mean?"

"That's the kind of talk I'd expect to hear from a man." I smiled. "That's how *he* talks . . ."

"Give me his address!" Rae said, with forced brazenness. It would have been fitting for her to discard a cigarette and extinguish it under her shoe right then and there.

"You'll find him at the library, by the art and science sections, to the left of the entrance."

"I mean his address. Of his room."

"I don't know."

"How can you not know? What if you want to see him and find out how he's doing?"

"You force yourself not to want that. You wait until he wants to see how *you* are doing."

"You are so cold!"

"Yes, I'm lacking in passion."

"Is that what he said?"

"He said it. They all say it."

Rae's smile promised that he would not say that about *her*. I listened as she told me some news about B., A., Katya, and the others. I went home, thinking about the man I wanted so badly to forget.

I should have known that I would hear about A. from Rae. So it seems that B.'s taken up with Katya and A.'s thinking of leaving New York. Fine, let him leave . . .

How could A. think of leaving New York without seeing me first? Maybe he doesn't love me, but he can't be indifferent—entirely indifferent—to me? And I still love him so!

I close my eyes and imagine A. coming to see me. This ugly room magically transforms into a beautiful chamber. He looks at me, takes me by the hand, and pulls me closer. He doesn't want to leave here without me. He wants to take me with him because I love him so much. He's afraid that I'll take my own life out of longing for him, and he could never forgive himself for that. I close my eyes, press my lips together, and feel my sorrow dissipating. A deep, gnawing, painful happiness floods my heart. I want to tell him what I'm feeling, but I'm silent. I don't want to explain it in words so I tell him with my silence.

I open my eyes. He's not here. I know he won't come for me. When he hears the rumor that someone else already *had* me, someone other than him, he won't feel the need to take it upon himself to be my first real lover.

Cheek won't be attracted to Rae, precisely because she wants to attract him. Like all men, he wants the chase. I'm sure that he'll speak to her about me. He'll try to find out my address.

༄

If he comes to me, after everything that's happened, talks again about his "holy ideal," and proposes free love, I'll . . . no, maybe I won't be so quick to drive him away. I won't accept his kind of love, instead I'll take up the battle against it! And maybe . . . ?

I think I could probably have married him and been loyal and devoted, even if I don't love him at all. But I ask myself: Why do I hate him so much? Is it possible to hate someone this much if you haven't loved him first?

When I hate A., I know why. It's because I love him so painfully. He causes me to bear unearthly suffering. But C.? He only wounded my self-confidence, my womanly pride, a little bit. He made me believe his promise to marry me and give me his name, and then he cynically laughed at my credulity. Maybe now he regrets it. Maybe my disappearance made him think better of his behavior.

My desire to see him only comes from curiosity, nothing more. If it were a more serious feeling, I would go where I knew I'd be sure to see him. But I won't go there. However long he searches for me, I hope he never finds me!

35

It's Not for You

I've been living here for two weeks and I'll have to stay longer. I'll rent and I'll vent my sorrows. It's so hard to find a good room!

"Tell me," a woman said to me, a doctor's wife, when I came to see the room she had to let. "How could I rent my room to you, a girl I don't know. If my husband saw you . . . You're not a child. Surely you understand that you don't leave cream out in front of a cat!"

I stared back at her, shocked to hear a doctor's wife talking that way.

"Do you have a boyfriend?" the doctor's wife asked, in a thick, conspiratorial voice, like an Americanized yenta. "You're engaged, right?"

"I have no one."

"Wouldn't you be afraid to be alone with a man in the house?"

"Is a man a bear?"

"He's an animal, just the same."

"A civilized animal, in any case. And it depends what we we're talking about."

"What would you say to such an animal, who wanted to persuade you? You'd stay quiet, just like any other girl. You wouldn't even make a peep. Don't worry, I know what I'm talking about. I rented to a girl once before, and now I refuse ten times over to take in any others. She taught me well enough. No matter. I won't let it happen again. I won't let anyone pull the wool over my eyes!"

"Why didn't you say in your advertisement that you won't rent to a girl?" I asked, annoyed.

"No, I wouldn't do that. Let them all come, and I'll refuse them all!"

"Why are they all to blame, just because one girl 'taught' you?"

"*She* taught *me*?! That'll be the day."

"It's what you said."

"Oh, never mind what I said. She taught *herself* a lesson."

"So you say, and you must know," I said, looking at her smooth face, round as though stuffed, with two calf-like eyes peering out. At that moment I wanted to see her husband, compare the two of them, and try to guess: Did he take her on an installment plan that he's paying for until he's done, or did he pay for her in cash, buying her all at once? Surely it was with borrowed money, because she looks like a "hurry-up," up-and-coming social climber.

A thought ran through my mind: that C. would also be a good candidate for such a marriage. He'll carry on many free love affairs until he settles down to his inevitable marriage so that he'll end up like this husband, chasing after a girl boarding in his home whom his wife wants throw out as soon as she's taken her in.

"What do you think?" asked the doctor's wife with a mocking, nervous laugh. "You still want the room?"

"No. Not even if you rented it to me for nothing, not even if you paid me to live here! Living under the same roof as a man whose own wife recommends him so highly would certainly be unpleasant."

"That's your choice, if you don't like it." She chuckled derisively.

I'm sure that the jealous doctor's wife was relieved that I left before another girl came. It seemed that she'd only advertised the room to entertain herself. She was bored, so she was looking for someone she could let into her home, only to throw them out again.

I was also refused at another house because I'm a girl. "Yes, there's a room for rent here," they told me, "but it's only for a man. That is to say, there's already one man here, but he's not enough to pay the rent."

"So you're saying that you're only renting a bed? Or half a bed?"

"Yes, it's just a place to sleep. It's not for you."

Certainly not. So I stay here, with the carpet made out of stitched-together pieces of oilcloth. I cover myself with the patchwork scrap quilt. I look at the picture of the holy mother and child and feel so orphaned and alone.

⁓

Rae came to see me.

She looked around my room with a skeptical smile. "The room is *wunderbar, nicht wahr?*"

I wanted to help her laugh at the room, but she interrupted. She turned to me and quickly, as she tends to do, asked a question.

"Are you lying to me?"

"Why would you ask that all of a sudden?" I looked at her, startled. "What a question."

"I know, either you can't answer the question or you don't want to. Alright. Let's get to the point. Do you want to see Mr. Cheek? He wants to see you. He has something important to say to you. He, well, he loves you. Do you love him?"

"Not yet—for now."

"But maybe you could love him some day."

"Who knows what will happen in the future?"

"Don't be so clever!" she snapped. "Tell me honestly, do you love him or no?"

"No."

"You don't think so."

"Fine, I don't think so."

"I have to know."

"You already know. I don't even like him."

"But he likes you."

"I wonder why."

"What do you want?" Rae asked, laughing angrily. "Do you want me to list all your good qualities so you can understand why he loves you?"

"You can be sure that I won't love him for any of the good qualities that you see in him."

"That's what you say."

"And you can believe me. It's true that I don't say everything I think. If I shared everything I feel for all the world to see I'd have nothing left for myself. But I mean what I say. I do not love C. In any case, I don't love him as he is now. Maybe I could love him for what he might some-day be. For his great future. But he wouldn't share that future with me, nor with you, nor with any girl like us. He thinks that we, the lonely girls, were created for the opposite purpose. He just wants to use us—"

"Maybe *I* will use *him*," Rae said. "Why shouldn't we think of our-selves as his equals?"

"We can't. Our sex sentences us to a—limited life. We're oppo-sites. No matter how much you pretend that we're equals and that you have a right to live life as they live it, eventually you'll think better of it. You'll lose yourself. You want to be someone you aren't, but that's impossible. We can't escape ourselves. We have to be what we are."

"We have to be cautious, reserved, restrained? We have to battle against ourselves to preserve ourselves for some man, just because he'll feed us and let us raise his children? Terrific!"

"The prospect isn't very glamorous, but—"

"No buts about it, I'm tired of it! There's nothing in this life worth living for."

"So you want to die."

A quiet knock on the door startled Rae to her feet. "It's him!" she cried.

"Who?" I asked, walking toward the door.

"You'll see . . ."

It was no "him" but a "her," my landlady. She wanted to know the time. I told her and she left.

"What an old witch she is," Rae commented. "Does she always come to ask about the time when you have company over?"

"Before you came today I hadn't ever had any company here."

"No one? What are you hiding from? My God!" (This was the same "My God!" that B. always said.) "Why am I so dependent, and you so shut up inside yourself? You're trying to hide what I can see with my own eyes!"

"What do you see? What are you talking about?"

"I saw it myself," said Rae, looking straight into my eyes. "I saw B. coming in the door."

"In this door?"

"In the hall door, in the door to the street. What's the difference?"

"There's a big difference. He could have come in the house without coming to this room."

Rae stared hard at me. Poor Rae! Only then did I understand all of her earlier behavior. She's trying to use her affair with C. to confuse or silence her love for B. B. is her ideal, something she could die for, because she knows that nothing can compare to him.

"Didn't he come to see you?"

"No. I give you my word. No one other than you and the sickly old German lady has crossed my doorway. B. has never been here and will not come here because he is not interested in me."

"He was very interested in you."

"He was, until he learned what I really am."

"What are you?"

"Uninteresting," I answered with a sad smile.

"You can make yourself interesting."

"I don't believe in making myself anything. You just have to be yourself, be natural." We spent a while longer together, talked about a few more things. Later, I thought for a long time about what Rae had said about C. Who knows, maybe if I was better at making myself lovable C. would want to share his great future with me. He accuses me of being too pragmatic and practical, and that's the truth. Especially when it comes to him.

36

The New Woman

I've read so many books in my life, and I read myself into each heroine, so that now I don't even know who I am!

C. says that he'll show me who I am. He knows every breath, every nerve in my body. He says he'll need to devote more time to know my soul. He's never encountered a thing in his life as complicated as my soul. And he's met many souls; he's met souls, as he says, "by the bushels." He studies the psychology of every living thing.

He says that I have a very rich psychology. It will take him some time to unlock it. He's going to examine and analyze, taking care to study every corner of my soul, every feature of my body.

Toward that goal—of studying me—he had reversed his collar to the clean, white side and trimmed his fingernails. He lowered himself to the floor next to where I sat on the old, unsteady, unsanitary chair and wrapped his arms around my legs.

He began his examination.

"Why do you need to examine my legs?" I asked. He answered that the most important things always start from the bottom up. Take, for instance, the French Revolution, or the battle that the first American colonists fought for independence from England. In Russia the revolution was led from the top down, from the intelligentsia, and that's what was wrong with it.

"How does starting from the bottom lead to those in power granting rights?" I asked. He answered that it had to do with *my* power to grant what is right. "We have something in us with the power to make us powerless, and we must surrender to the power of that powerlessness."

"We're forced to surrender?"

"No, we do it willingly. We become convinced. All I'm doing is telling you about it, not forcing you."

I'm afraid he wants to do more than tell. He came to see me the morning after Rae was here. He said he'd only come to tell me that he'd asked Rae for my address so he could come to tell me that he wouldn't say a single word about what happened between us at the horrible intellectuals' apartment. But after that he said so much more about it! He told me it was all a misunderstanding. And I left in such a huff! As though the whole world were chasing me! He went back to see me at the time we'd agreed on, knocked on the door, and the land-lady told him that his "wife" had left. He could go look for me if he wanted to—that disgraceful girl, she said. He was so annoyed to have that *nobody* see how he'd knocked on the door and I hadn't answered. "But I found you in the end, darling!" he ended his reproachful speech triumphantly.

"No 'darling,' if you please," I responded in sarcastic English.

"Oh, I beg your pardon!" He matched my English with his own. "Of course I won't use such a familiar term. I'll only say 'darling' when the lights are low."

☙

I decided for myself: *preparedness; watchful waiting.* He can study me, and, while he does, I'll study him.

☙

C. says that I'm conservative. I don't understand the New Woman and her modern strivings. I should get to know her. I could learn something.

I tried to find a way to meet this New Woman. Not personally, of course. I'd learn about her from what great people have to say about her, even if they are men. Sometimes men have more to say about women than women have to say about themselves. And sometimes a woman knows more about a man than he does. But a woman doesn't say everything she knows. She must be circumspect. A man's not afraid of embarrassing himself.

In an article by Lillian Kisliuk I learned many great men's ideas about women. Here are some of the quotes:

Rudolf Virchow says: "Gentleness is part of a woman's character. It goes together with the gentleness of her body."

Havelock Ellis says: "Nervous irritability is women's primary characteristic."

August Ferdinand Möbius says: "Women are very conservative and hate all innovation."

Theodor Gottlieb von Hippel the Elder says: "The spirit of revolution broods over the female sex."

Heinrich Heine says: "The element of freedom is always alive and active in the body of women."

Havelock Ellis (again) says: "Under ordinary circumstances a woman can do as much work as a man, but she cannot work under high pressure."

W. O. von Horn says: "When it is a question of fulfilling very heavy requirements the female is often far superior to the male and shows a tenacity and endurance which put him to shame."

Hermann Lotze says: "The female hates analysis and is therefore incapable of distinguishing falsehood from truth."

Pierre Lafitte argues that the female prefers analysis, but the male prefers the observation of the relations between things.

Cesare Lombroso further claims that in synthesis and abstract reasoning the female intelligence is defective. Its strength lies in acute analysis and in the vivid comprehension of details.

Friedrich Nietzsche says: "Those who know how to discriminate will perceive that women have intelligence and men emotion and passion."

Richard von Krafft-Ebing says, "Certainly the inward tendency of a woman's heart is toward monogamy, whilst a man is inclined toward polygamy."

Laura Marholm holds the opinion that "woman likes change and variety; man thrives in that monotony which drives a woman to desperation."

Cesare Lombroso says: "It is quite certain that when another relationship offers her greater practical advantages she will in the cruelest way leave her first love, and often without the least remorse."

In the past week I've read many other things that have been said about women, and I'm not one step closer to learning what C. wants me to know.

He decided it would be better to conduct an intentional program of propaganda, rather than filling me with everything that everyone has to say on the matter. Anyway, he said, my feelings toward *life* must come from myself, and not from these thinkers. If I don't have it in me, no amount of reading can help.

37

At Odds

I'm not myself; I'm like someone else. Something is beginning in me. Something is ending. My mood changes like the weather. Sound reason compels me to tell C. to go away, since I don't believe anything will happen between us. And yet, when he comes, I invite him to stay. I'm not interested in his scientific speeches and yet I listen to them obediently.

When he wants to, he can speak very nicely. But his voice is so cajoling, almost like a priest, and it's too sweet, embarrassingly sweet. Also, when he wants to, he isn't bad at what he does when he's *not* talking. He's fine in every "circumstance," as he would say. But he needs a reason. Good behavior must be well compensated. He's hoping that over time I'll come to see his merits and I won't make him suffer anymore.

I let him hope.

He awakens and arouses my desire to *live*. When I think of how I've withered, a sort of physical despair settles over me. What am I? What is my purpose on earth? Was I born to die without ever really living?

C. says that I'm terribly backward, not modern at all. I have so many old-fashioned beliefs and I'm suspicious of everything new and progressive. I'm romantic, and at the same time so practical, so careful and calculating. I'm poetic and prosaic, sentimental and cynical. From what he says, I know that I am a lot of different things. I don't know if there's anything I'm not.

Oh, yes, there's one thing. I'm not so young anymore.

When he tells me this I can see that he's trying to provoke me. But I just smile and agree that I'm not only "not so young anymore," I'm quite old. And I don't understand how he, a man who is so *very* young (though he is in fact not so *very* young) could love me, or at least pretend to love me.

He answers, "I love the autumn of life."

C. tells me that many great men, especially learned men, were in love with older women. They not only loved them, they even married them.

"Were they happy?"

"Very happy! They understood each other very well."

"And they were still happy? They must have been truly great men."

"I also want to be a great man," he said with certainty. "You'll see."

"God help you."

"Maybe *you* can help me."

"How?" I asked.

"It's simple. Give me the spirit to accomplish great things."

"For—others?"

"Above all, we'll help each other."

"So that you can climb to the heights of those you value more than me and leave me behind?"

"We won't make any contracts. If you make yourself so important to me that I can't do without you, then maybe we could be happy together forever."

"That seems like small hope for happiness. We aren't great enough for that."

"We can be great."

"Maybe *you* can. You're so small that you have a lot of room for growth," I retorted.

"You are trying to pick a fight with me."

"I'm not trying to do anything with you. Let someone else find the spirit that's already in you. I'd advise you not to waste any more time on me. It will come to nothing."

"You'll get better," he reassured me.

"Not for you!"

"Then for whom?"

"For—someone else. When I'm with you I fight to maintain self-control. If you ever finally convince me that I must, as you call it, *live*, I'll go to him, to someone else."

C. bit his lips in angry silence.

⌒

"Our romance began at the end," laughed C. "Most romances start with the good, and end in anger. We argued in the beginning, but things will be good by the end."

"Perhaps a love like ours might have yet another end," said C. "Maybe it'll end in marriage."

Then he laughed. "Oh, I hate legal marriage! I can't imagine a worse misfortune. What could be worse than taking two separate people and binding them together by law for their entire lives, so that they can never be free?"

"So if you don't like it, don't get married," I said.

"But what do you do if you want to be with someone who thinks that people should marry?"

"Then you shouldn't want her. Want someone else."

"What if you don't like anyone else as much as you like her? What if you only want to love her, and no one else?"

"Then love her from afar."

"But what if you want to love her from nearby? What if you want to be *very* close to her?"

"Then marry her."

"Isn't that wrong?"

"Then don't do it."

"Isn't that worse?"

"Then do it."

"It's just like Sholem Aleichem's 'Advice': 'Divorce, don't divorce; don't divorce, divorce!'"

"Yes, it's like that."

Cheek, exasperated by my "cruel" indifference, had the cheekiness to want to prove to me that I absolutely *cannot* understand what *living* is. No matter how much I've read, I haven't read what I would need to read in order to understand. What I need is a "master": a modern person with a systematic education, a professional who understands me better than I know myself. He enthusiastically explained that with such a man I'd finally open my eyes and see that those naïve, innocent girls of once upon a time whose romances ended in weddings don't exist anymore. "Girls don't think about their holy innocence as a treasured possession like they used to. Girls today like to go from one man to another, not settling with one person for their whole lives so that he can support them. They want to live and to enjoy their lives just like men do. And they don't want to be a burden to a man for his entire life just for a minute of happiness. Today's girls would be ashamed to live under such circumstances! They don't want men to have to pay that kind of a price for them! It's obscene! It's—"

"Does the modern woman have children?" I asked hurriedly, seeing that he'd paused to catch his breath.

"Children?"

"Yes, children. You know, regular old children."

"What do they need children for?"

"So they can have pride and pleasure from them, for instance."

"They have no use for children! Leave childbearing to women who don't know how to avoid having children. Women who know how to get out of it can be happy without children. And if a woman decides that she wants to have a child, then let her have one! Who cares? I'm all for a matriarchy: let her have the kid if she wants it, and let it be her choice. His responsibility goes no farther than whatever he agrees to. If he wants to have a child, then he can care for it. Right?"

"Sure, sure. I hardly know how it could be any other way. If a man wants a child, he should care for it. That's only right."

C. didn't notice my sarcasm, or at least he pretended not to. He just squeezed and kissed my hand as though to thank me for agreeing with him at least on one point, when it came to children.

After speaking about many other things, he returned to the topic. "So, when it comes to children we agree. But about love—"

"We're at odds."

"But why?"

I could easily have told him that it's because I hate him. But I kept my mouth shut about that, and instead I said, "Because I believe in marriage."

∽

"No," C. said after a long pause, "I won't go against my principles. For me marriage would be suicide. I must be free! My darling, you don't understand me. I cannot, I simply cannot, go against myself. My convictions are who I am. My principles are my heart and soul. They're everything."

"Stick with your principles."

"And you?"

"I'll stick with myself."

"By yourself?"

"I'm used to it by now."

"Living like this, just fading away, growing old . . ."

"Everyone wants to live longer and not grow old! But we inevitably grow older until we die."

"Let's not talk about death. We have a long time left to live and to enjoy life. It's true that winter comes after autumn, but before your winter comes I will give you a summer. An Indian summer! Say yes, say *yes!*"

I didn't say yes. I didn't say anything. I just watched as he got down on his knees and begged me to love him. An ugly enjoyment overtook my soul, which was so unhappy with my life. Maybe it isn't kind for me to act this way toward love, whatever it is, but that's just how I am. I'm starting to love the hate he inspires in me when I think of how he wants to hold me in his arms only to toss me aside later.

I'll embrace my hatred for him and that will help me win my battle. I'll bring him to the point where he wants to marry me, and then *I'll* be the one to reject *him.*

He's told me all sorts of horrible, disgusting stories about his life with women. He thinks this is the way to arouse my instincts, which he describes as not yet awakened to *life.* I listen to them as though I were an ignoramus looking up to a wise, all-knowing man whose every word is sealed with the stamp of science. Knowing that I won't fall for his charms helps me keep up my pretense and make it hard for him to tell whether his tricks are working on me.

Love makes you good, soft, generous, and kind. Hatred makes you hard and cruel, but strong. And I have to be strong. I must be strong. I have only myself to take risks for me and protect me from ruin.

The circumstances were good. I was dressed when he arrived and ready to walk in the street, rather than having him in my room until late at night. In the street, his arguments against marriage are weaker. His surroundings limit his thoughts, and he concentrates only on his feelings. His words of propaganda aren't as weighty without his gesticulations. Until he notices that the reason I want to go into the street with him is to keep him from sitting in my room, I'll keep on walking with him.

38

We Study Each Other

Sometimes it's as hard to tear yourself away from pretended love as it is from real love! I'm afraid that we might get so caught up in our pretend-roles that it'll be hard to leave them.

We study each other. C. realizes that there's no use getting angry with me; it's better to be nice to me. I know that getting angry with him won't accomplish anything either. You have to make nice. So our previous anger has turned toward politeness, and I need to be careful that nothing bad will come of all this good behavior. It's so much easier to be good than bad, so much easier to smile than to grind your teeth. It's so hard to hate, when all you want to do is love.

I don't know. Has he really gotten better, or have I just gotten worse? We make choices. Two nights ago we had such a lovely time together. We went on a long walk, we talked and at times we *didn't* talk . . . We stayed in my room in the light of the streetlamps until late at night.

When he wants to, he can be very pleasant and interesting. I told him so, and he said that he *has* to be that way with me. I could turn the greatest sinner into a reformed man. He feels calmer, his angry thoughts are driven away, something inside him forces him to take stock and to help create a chaste environment, to support my aims of modesty. "The more I look at you, my beloved," he said, (apologizing for calling me "beloved," a term he would use in prayer to God), "the more I realize that at first I didn't really see you at all. I wonder at your composure, you're so consistent in the way you hold yourself. Anyone else in your place would get annoyed with me, would hate me, but you are measured with me, the way you should be. You are so good that you don't see the bad in others. You don't even understand what bad is, in the full sense of the word. It's so far from who you are. You only look for the good and when you find a sign of it you are so good that you could forgive the worst man. You create an atmosphere of goodness around yourself, and when I try to stand up against you I feel disarmed." Does this mean that I've played my role extremely well, or just that he's playing his even better than I'm playing mine?

My suspicions fell on him like a searchlight. I could tell that he felt them instinctively because he started energetically reassuring me that he'd never spoken the truth so earnestly before in his life. Everything that he said was true, didn't I believe him?

"I believe—"

"But you don't really believe me, right?"

"A little, not entirely," I admitted.

"Do you think that I'm lying?" he asked, annoyed.

"Maybe." I smiled affably. "Maybe. But even if it's a lie, I like it. It's a nice lie."

"So you like a nice lie?"

"It's better than an ugly truth."

"No, you must sense that I'm telling you the truth. It would be impossible to try to fool you."

"I don't think so."

He seemed upset at the idea (that it's impossible to try to fool me), but he tried not to show it. He kept tactfully silent. Who knows what plans he was concocting for me in his own mind.

The more he improves himself for me, the more careful I have to be. It's hard to tell truth from lies when the lie is nicer. It's dark outside and it's nicer to love than to hate.

C. says that he doubts that anything will come of his relationship with me. He talks and talks and it seems like I don't listen to what he's saying. I'm thinking of something else entirely. "What are you thinking about?" he asked me.

"This and that." I answered.

"What do you think of everything I've said?" he asked.

"I haven't formed an opinion yet. Or maybe I have more than one opinion."

"That's impossible. That can't be true!" he cried, "The matter has two sides—negative or positive, abstract or concrete. Would you like me to explain it to you?"

"Explain away."

"You say that with the same tone that you might say, 'Speak, what do I care? Whatever you say won't convince me. Your words are like peas thrown against a wall—nothing will stick!' I'm afraid that I'm just wasting my breath."

"Then don't talk."

"It's all the same to you."

I was quiet for a while, thinking about how to respond. Finally, when he complained that I didn't pay enough attention to his speeches, I told him that he would be better off renting a hall and lecturing in front of an audience. Why should he waste so much energy on speaking to just one person? What would it matter if that one person should actually become a bit enlightened and acknowledge—

"Oh heavens!" he exclaimed in English. "That's exactly what I want. Acknowledging something means following it to its logical conclusions. Someone once said, I forget who it was, 'If even one person understood my work, it will not have been for naught.' Let me tell you, if someone—especially if *you* were that someone—should acknowledge the truth of my words, then I will have reached my goal."

When he said "my goal" I felt very uncomfortable. I didn't stop feeling that way for a long time. I asked myself why I didn't protest and tell him not to talk like that. I was firmly opposed to his reaching his goal. I pretended not to understand so that he would take more time to explain to me, and I could think about other things while he talked.

His method of convincing me to *live* was propagandizing to me about free love. It is necessary to love freely, he explained, supporting his argument with facts from life. He claimed that everything he said was theoretically grounded and factually supported. Only a great ignoramus could disparage or deny the facts he'd collected. Anyone who failed to acknowledge the truth of what they had to say was only denying themselves!

I didn't want to acknowledge him, nor did I want to deny myself. I begged him to stop trying to convince me, because the whole matter was unappealing to me. He said that it didn't appeal to me because I didn't understand it. As soon as I began to understand, I would know. Then it would certainly appeal to me, and just like all the others that he had convinced before me I would beg him, "Please convince me further! Explain to me, open my eyes more to all the things hiding behind the curtains of *life!*"

His scientific knowledge gave him the right to call things by their true names. And I should hear them, he claimed. But I tapped my feet impatiently and bit my lips and was quiet. I let him say what he wanted to; talking with his mouth was better than explaining with his hands.

I asked myself why I let him go on this way, and I answered, "I want to study him."

39

The Lecture

I've just returned from a lecture C. gave. I ran out of the hall before he finished speaking.

A group of his followers had put together a gathering for him. They arranged a lecture series with an entrance fee to cover the costs, and they advertised it as open to the public. The goal was to inoculate the masses against buttoned-up bourgeois morals, to show them appealing freethinking ideas, etc.

The theme "free love" attracted a large audience. The narrow lecture hall was filled with people, young and old. So many people wanting to find out how to start their first affair, or how to end their last one.

"Do you see, Miss?" said one of the committee members who had seen me enter the lecture hall. "He's a hit! They're hanging onto his every word. He could fit Emma Goldman in his back pocket, he could shake seven of those anarchist speakers out of his own sleeves. That mouth of his! It's like gunpowder! He sure is persuasive. Just listen to how he talks!"

I listened. C. assured the audience that he wasn't pulling their legs. He'd come to persuade them. He'd prove that everything he said was theoretically grounded and proven by facts. If Darwin, the great discoverer of evolutionary biology, were standing here in his place, he would say no different. Every living creature wants to live and to love. They pursue bodily connections. Animals mate at particular seasons but a human can always love, at any time. Because a human is more refined, more sensitive. Yet he keeps himself from reaching his goal by holding himself back with laws. "Forbidden fruit is sweet, they say. But the question is: Who has a right to go against nature? How dare one man make laws for all others to follow?"

The audience applauded in response and someone cried out, "Down with the lawmaker!"

"Quiet! Order!" the floor manager called out at this enthusiastic response. "*Siddown* and *shuddup!*" And then he quietly reprimanded, "Don't make such a ruckus!"

The enthusiast argued, "Don't I have a right to show my feelings?"

"Sure you do!" someone else agreed.

"Yeah, he sure does!" said a third.

"But not to interrupt. He can wait until the speaker is done."

They practically had to restrain the men while C. kept on talking: "Every human organism is compelled by the thirst for—love. A dog expresses it in his bark, a bird in its nest, holy priests, lonely girls, young people of all sorts, even older people, just about everyone dies searching for one thing—to *live* and to *enjoy life*. And if they aren't allowed to do this they are sucked dry. They become horribly fat or sickly thin, their nerves fray, they grow angry, they become degenerate and depraved."

"Bravo!" the enthusiast cried out. And from the back a voice called out, "Louder! Louder!"

The floor manager told the man to quiet down, stop being so deaf, and listen to the speaker.

C. waited for everyone to settle down and then continued. He begged his audience not to just believe him but to judge for themselves whether free love is better than marriage: "Because what is marriage? Love by force!"

"Bravo!!"

"Marriage is no more than a vile institution held together by a sham of a ceremony. It's a bridle holding back an individual, holding back man's free will. It's a scandal in the twentieth century, an insult to civilization, a curse on the youth, a death sentence for *life*! What we need is a revolution! We must lay the cornerstone of a new epoch. We must change the order of things because if we do not things will only get worse. The end will be—"

I didn't wait to hear what the end would be. I stole out of the hall and waited for the lecture to be over. I didn't want to listen to the entire thing just so C. could walk me home at the end, only to hear the same lecture all over again on the walk home, but with some additional illustrations.

By not being in the hall at the end of his talk I'd show him how little of an impression his agitation for free love had made on me. Just let him *try* to convince me!

～

"Just let him *try* to convince me." These words echoed loudly in my ears, filling me with angry pleasure.

I examined myself in the mirror and thought I wasn't so bad-looking when I took an honest look at myself. I was overtaken by a strange indifference to myself, and I tried to defend myself from it. It was like poison in my soul. I wanted nothing more than to defeat my self-loathing, to throw off this horrible feeling that oppressed me.

I felt C.'s hand pressing down on me, though he wasn't there. It was pushing me down to the ground. It was trying to force me to debase myself, to fulfill the desires of a man I don't love, who only loves me as much as his economic, ethical, psychological, and physical ideologies dictate. I'm nothing more to him than a thing to spend some time with. Soon he'll discard me into his past and find someone else to share his future with—his great future, which Rae and so many other girls await so enthusiastically.

"That man and his ridiculous lectures!" I thought as I lay in my cold bed under the patchwork quilt. "I'm glad I left! Very glad! He was speaking to *me*, trying to convince me, in front of everyone. And I, the one who was supposed to act on those words, wasn't there when he came looking for me to walk me home."

In my mind I went to another of his lectures, just so I could walk out again.

I couldn't fall asleep. I was feeling such hatred toward *him*, the man who taught me how to hate. I was so angry at A., the only man I've ever truly loved! *He* was the reason that I hated myself so much, that I felt capable of throwing myself in the way of misfortune, ruining myself, utterly destroying my life!

The harsh light of the streetlamps lit up the icons on the walls, which stared at me with shining eyes. Behind the ugly wall I could hear the old German lady's son snoring through a high window papered over with cardboard boxes. There were scurrying little footsteps and pitiful squeaks coming from my closet. A flirtatious couple whispered in the long, dark corridor.

The couple's silhouette fell over the corridor in front of my door and crept up my curtains. They grew larger and larger, then suddenly disappeared. Somewhere behind them a door quietly closed, and all the noises died down.

The image of A. appeared in my imagination. I begged him to leave, but it was no use. I burst into tears.

In the middle of my muffled, bitter cry, in the lonely silence of that strange house, I heard a low knock on my door.

I shook myself awake and covered my head with a pillow to drown out the noise, but the stubborn knocking did not let up. I was worried that it would wake up my landlady. Barefoot and in my nightshirt, I went to the door.

40

I Said Nothing

Who's there?" I whispered.

"It's me." I recognized C.'s voice as he tried to whisper, though it came out as a squeak. I didn't know what to do.

I couldn't ask what he wanted through the closed door. Someone might hear. Should I open the door? That would be as good as an invitation. I said, "It's too late," and walked away from the door.

He knocked again. I went back to the door angrily and quietly but firmly said, "Go away!"

"Just give me a minute," he begged. "I just have a few words to say to you, no more."

"I can't."

He knocked again.

"What is it?" I said, opening the door an inch. "What do you want?"

"I need to ask you something."

"Come back in the morning! How dare you? I was sleeping!" I lied. I tried to close the door in his face, but he forced it open and came into my room. He closed the door gently behind him.

We stared at each other for a while, each of us gearing up for a fight.

"My God! How beautiful you look like that!" he said, gathering his hands in an almost religious pose. "Darling, I've never seen you like this before."

I realized that I was almost entirely undressed. Although he'd just called me "darling" (which seems to be some kind of rule with him when he's alone in the dark with me), I ignored it, looking around for my robe.

He tore the robe out of my hands and threw it aside. "Why do you need that?" he asked. "Are you embarrassed of your own beauty?"

"I'm cold," I said through clenched teeth. It was true, I really was shivering, though not so much because of the temperature as out of anger at his tearing my robe away from me.

"Cold?" he said, and he grabbed my hand, lay me in my bed, and covered me with the blanket. He sat on the edge of the bed and looked me in the eyes, laying his hands on my head. "Why did you run away from my lecture?" he demanded.

"I wanted to," I answered.

"Was it a bad speech?"

"It was absurd."

"You didn't hear the end."

"I can imagine it."

"You can't. They practically threw me into the air when I was finished. Everyone shook my hand. I looked for you. I was upset that you weren't there to see it. They're going to rent a bigger hall for my next lecture so that everyone can come. So many people were turned away today because there wasn't enough room in the hall."

"Good for them!"

"Do you think so?"

"I think that I think so."

"Why are you so angry?"

"I want to sleep. Go away!" I sighed. "I don't want another scandal like we had last time in the other room. People here don't know who or what I am. They might think—"

"If they hear noise they will certainly think it. Let's be quiet and let them sleep. I hate when people make scenes. People like your old landlords who threw me out, they make me crazy. I hardly know what to do with myself."

"Why do we have to argue in the middle of the night?"

"Is it my fault that it's the middle of the night? I feel like the sun could rise right now, just for me. What does time have to do with me?"

"But I—"

"Darling!"

"Don't call me darling."

"Alright. No more darlings. Although such endearments are made for silence, darkness, for what you're wearing now. And, darling, I love you, do you hear me? I love you with all of your whims, with your childish grudges against that thing that is so essential to your life, and to mine. You're cruel to yourself, you suppress your natural urges. Your soft, velvety body begs to be caressed, to be covered in kisses. Your romantic soul wants love, but you, darling, turn away from it. You're afraid to look the truth in the face . . . Are you sleeping?"

I closed my eyes. I didn't want to see him. When he talked this way, when I closed my eyes I saw B. in him. And as he sat there in silence, holding my hand, I could almost imagine that he was A. instead.

୭

When I kept my eyes closed and didn't answer his questions, C. said, "She's actually asleep." He started to undress.

"What do you think you are doing?" I stared at him.

His plan was a simple one. Why should he sit there if he could lie down instead? And you don't lie down with your clothes on. He only sleeps with his clothes on when he's studying for an exam, he explained. But he'd already passed his examinations when it came to love. He was in no hurry to fall asleep. He could take his time and remove the unnecessary clothing.

It seemed to me that he was suggesting that everything he was wearing was unnecessary.

"No! What do you think you're doing?" I protested, though weakly, since I didn't want anyone to hear. "Where do you think you are, at a bathhouse?"

"Shhh," he said to me. "Enough with these questions! Now's not the time."

I got out of bed, grabbed my robe, and sat in a rocking chair. He could lie down alone if he wanted!

He lay down in my bed and laughed at me. What was I so afraid of? Why was I running away? He wasn't going to lecture me! If I wanted him to, he'd be very quiet, absolutely quiet, quiet as a mouse. He knew that I preferred men not to say anything. At the beginning of our relationship he thought that I needed to be taken by storm like other girls, but he soon realized that he could only persuade with actions, not words. "Won't you come a little closer, so I don't have to speak so loudly?"

"No."

"The landlady will come in, and that won't be pretty."

I didn't say anything. "How can I keep quiet about this?" I thought. "He came to my room in the middle of the night—no, he *broke into* my room in the middle of the night like an intruder, undressed, and got into my bed. My bed! Warmed by my own body! And he's lying there and I'm sitting here covered in a thin robe, shivering in the cold, terrified, angry, and powerless, because—why? Because I'm afraid of making noise! Can he just do whatever he wants, and I'll say nothing?"

"You know," he said conspiratorially, leaning on the edge of the bed with his head resting on his hands, "for a long time I've been picturing this moment, when I'd be with you in this position. I couldn't imagine it any other way. At night, in my dreams, I held you in my arms and kissed you. My God, how I kissed you! And then when I awoke and you weren't beside me, I cried for sleep to return. My God! How bitterly, how pitifully I cried! It was like my soul was flying out of me. Neighbors had to wake me up and—"

"After you woke up someone had to wake you up?"

"What? You see my dear, I made a mistake and you noticed. I was just trying to see if you were paying attention to what I was saying. And now that I know that you're listening, I'll say something more important. Don't be such a child. Come to me. You'll catch such a chill sitting over there in your chair that you'll never warm up. And a chill is a horrible thing that can turn into a serious illness. Come."

I didn't come.

"I swear by all that's holy," he said, raising his right hand, "they can cut off my hands if I touch you at all against your will."

I heard someone talking somewhere, and then steps, a door opening. Two dark shadows grew larger in front of my door and then smaller again until they faded away.

C. lowered his hand.

41

Mutual Consent

How about this?" C. said gleefully, after thinking for a moment. "Come here and I'll go sit in your chair. I don't want you to catch a chill and get sick because of me."

I didn't budge. I knew what he was up to.

"Why aren't you moving? I'll just sit here beside you."

"I won't move until you go away."

"You're afraid I'm trying to trick you. You think I'm going to slip back out of the chair and try to get into bed with you, right?"

"Well . . ."

"No wells! Admit it—you're afraid. Didn't I just tell you that there's no reason to be afraid of me? I would never force you to love me. It's not in my nature to force myself on someone. I only approve of things that happen through mutual consent. I even agreed not to call you darling if you didn't want me to. It's beneath my dignity to resort to such measures when I see that a woman isn't interested."

"Oh!" I cried out in impatience.

"No ohs!" he said. "They are absolutely unnecessary. Come and lie down. I'll just sit next to you for a while and then I'll go away. You should trust me more, out of self-respect. Your fear of me shows how little you believe in yourself. How badly you trust in your ability to control yourself—"

I stifled a yawn with my hand and repositioned myself against the side of the chair, where I was more comfortable. In my imagination I'd already gone looking for another room to live in. I knew I couldn't stay here much longer because of him. If the blind old lady caught this vagabond in my room—

C. got dressed in a huff and made a show of getting ready to leave. His glasses fell off his face and he polished them and put them back on.

"I'm going," he hissed.

I nodded my assent. He wasn't happy with that. He wanted to hear what else I had to say.

"I'm going," he said again, louder this time.

"Alright."

"And I won't be coming back."

"Alright."

"Does that make you happy? You'll only be happy for a minute. Once I've left you'll want me back. It's true. You want to live, but you're too afraid. But soon you'll never have the chance to live, because you'll die. You're already dead."

"How long do you plan to lecture a corpse?"

"As long as a there's a chance I might resurrect it. I want to awaken your slumbering instincts, only once they are awake, I won't be here anymore. Your lonely soul will regret not taking what I wanted to give you. You'll come looking for me. You'll beg me to come back to you but it will be too late."

He stood and waited for me to say something. I didn't say anything. I just looked at my door. Someone was standing behind it, starting to unlock it.

My heart began to pound. I jumped out of my chair.

It was just my next-door neighbor, who had accidentally tried his key in my door. He cursed and went into his own room.

C. laughed at me. "Such a big girl, yet the slightest sound at your door makes you jump! It's a good thing I was here so you didn't have to be afraid. If not—"

He didn't realize that I was afraid of someone coming and seeing *him* in my room. Or at least he pretended not to understand.

"You're too weak to live alone, darling," he said to me, returning once more to that endearment. He took my hand and kissed my fingers. "Don't make me go away. Let me stay here as long as you want me, darling. I'll overcome all the unnatural restrictions you place on love. We'll unite suffering with spirited union, love with joy, friendship with boundless devotion. You'll get to have a man, but you won't have to be his slave. You'll be *free*. Don't you want to be free, my darling?"

"Of you, yes."

"You don't mean that. You're not saying what you really feel. You're trying to be firm because you're so soft, so gentle, so full of longing to be loved! You want someone to love you fiercely. Don't you want that? What do you want, if not to be loved?"

"To love someone."

"Good. Here is a *man*. Love me!"

"Not you. Someone else."

"Someone who doesn't exist?"

"Someone who isn't here."

"Why love someone who isn't here, when you can love someone who is right here, someone who is so full of feeling and who loves you so much? None of the many girls I've known before was able to refuse me. And you—why are you so stubborn? You not only refuse me, but you refuse yourself. You go against your own interests. Do you think you'll find happiness in restraining yourself? You won't."

"I don't want to."

"Stubborn girl. You'll take out your own eye to take two of mine. You're just like other girls who'd sooner give themselves in slavery to a single man than be free with more than one man. You don't know what freedom is."

"If I don't know what it is, I won't miss it."

"You're ignorant. That's what you are!"

"You just noticed!"

"You're nothing more than the same old girl looking for a man. A reliable man who will take care of you, support you, control you."

"That's exactly what I am."

"I can no longer call you my darling."

"Then don't."

"And you consider yourself an intellectual. Let me tell you, you're not."

"What a shame. But I guess that's enough. Go! Why won't you just leave my room already?"

"You're throwing me out!"

"Oh, no! I'm asking you to leave. Please go away."

"I won't go. I once knew a girl like you. She was stubborn for a long time until she drove everyone away and then she was an old maid."

"Is that so? And I knew a man like you who stood so long that they had to throw him down the stairs to get him to leave." I said that for no reason, I didn't expect it to move him.

He got upset and cried, "That's a lie! They didn't throw him down the stairs! He fell down on his own!"

I was starting to be amused by his behavior. I laughed. "He fell down on his own? How can a man just fall down the stairs?"

In response to the question came a whole story that he insisted on telling me so that I would know that whoever told me about throwing the man down the stairs had told me a lie. If he knew where that woman was now, he'd tell me the whole story in front of her so that she wouldn't be able to make up stories about throwing him down a flight of stairs anymore. It was in the same house, with those same miserable intellectuals, just one floor up, if he remembered correctly. The girl, he couldn't remember if her name was Alta or Anna, lived there. He came up to see her. Things were starting to heat up between them and then suddenly, when he almost had her wrapped in his arms, she asked him to leave her alone for a moment. She had to do what people sometimes have to do when they need a little privacy. He was good enough to leave her alone. How was he supposed to know that she was playing a trick on him? He went into the hall looking for her. It was dark and a cat ran between his legs. His shoelaces were untied. He lost his balance and fell down the stairs!

He ended his story indignantly. Can you believe that she would claim to have thrown him down the stairs? There is a big difference between being thrown down the stairs and falling down the stairs yourself, don't you think?

I had to agree that there is a difference. And I had to promise never to listen to anything that woman said. And if I ever saw her again, I should tell her his version of the story.

42

The World Is Large,
and There's Nowhere to Hide

For a long time after C. left I lay in bed, thinking about the evening and night that had just passed. For a little while I was filled with angry pleasure over the way I'd acted toward him. His figure stayed before my eyes like a dream until the morning. I saw A. in my mind's eye and I felt like weeping, weeping, weeping . . .

I always feel that A., above all, is the reason for all the suffering I endure. It's all his fault. If he were with me then no one else would try to come close. No one would have the chance to say a word to me about the kinds of things that C. talks about.

It's possible too, that if I'd been nicer to C. he would've acted differently toward me. I could have kept him from taking such a rude tone with me. I'm just as good as anyone else. I didn't see, I didn't notice the way that *he* felt insulted. I only paid attention to the way that *I'd* been insulted. And even though I knew it wasn't right, I refused to forgive him for it. What I'm trying to say is that the whole thing was really my fault. Who knows, maybe I want to take the blame because it's better to feel guilty than to feel insulted.

C. was very upset when, before he left, I told him that I could never respect someone like him. His whole education seemed like a hoax. He pretended to laugh and said that he would save his methods of persuasion for those who were enlightened enough to understand that he had given himself over to his ideals and principles. He said that the way I talk made him feel sick. I told him that he deserved it. I told him not to dig graves for anyone else, because he might fall in them himself. I told him that I have no desire to, as he calls it, take pleasure from life.

He didn't believe me. Women have an inborn tendency to suppress their desire for pleasure, he told me. Women claim that they want to love. They like to decorate themselves, to make themselves fancy. They try to fool men. They make themselves into goddesses for nothing. They're more interested in worrying about little details and they overlook larger matters. They care more about a beautiful lie than an actual truth.

"If there is any truth in what you say," I told him, "women aren't to blame. If women didn't restrain and discipline men, men would gladly ruin them. A woman who is alone in life must be very patient and clever in order to prevail in the fight. There are so many stumbling blocks that, whether she likes it or not, she has to eschew desire for *living* in favor of logic, a strong will, and control over her own mind."

He listened attentively and said that he had one thing to add, which was that I am very clever. Too clever. That will save me from any foolishness, but it won't make me happy.

I know that. And I also know this: I wouldn't be so clever if I were up against A. Because I love him. It's impossible to be clever when you are in love! Sometimes I think that my love for A. is nothing more than stubbornness. I want his love because I know I can't have it.

Do I know that? How can I be sure? Isn't there still a glimmer of hope that I could ever win his love? Maybe if I did win his love it wouldn't be all that I imagine it to be.

I get lost in myself. My God, how long will I have to keep trying to find *myself*?

∽

I look at C. and I feel like he's turned into someone else. Has he gotten better, or is he just trying a new tactic against me? In any case, it's like magic. Someone should study how he does it.

It's been a week, and he hasn't once tried to force me to accept his holy ideal. He hasn't defended his principle, he hasn't even uttered the words "free love."

If he acted casually toward me, I'd think that it was some kind of trick in order to draw me in by making me doubt his feelings toward me so that I'd try to win him back. But he isn't acting casually at all. He says more now with his quiet glances than he did before with words. His every move is full of devotion. Everything he does is full of honest attention. I look at him and I wonder, "Can this be the same man?" Now he's finally beginning to interest me.

We went to the theater together. When there was a moving scene I had tears in my eyes and he pressed my hand gently, sympathetically. I softly returned the gesture. Sitting with him, among all the lonely people, I didn't feel so lonely. I was so grateful to him for this! A man hardly needs to put in any effort at all to make a lonely girl grateful for his sympathy toward a heroine. The heroine of the drama loved and suffered, and I saw myself in her. And he, whether he understood me or not, tried to comfort me by pressing my hand.

Even during the intermission we sat quietly, not saying a word, still under the influence of the drama. I felt we both must be sharing the same thought. We thought about love: how good it is to love, and to be loved!

Once, we went to the movies together. Rae also came with us, and he was friendly to her because she is my friend. After the movies, we walked for a long time in the street while he talked cleverly. Rae was entranced by him. She conveyed to me through half-spoken words that she was impressed with him. She hurried to leave so she wouldn't bother us.

I invited her to spend the night in my room. Before we fell asleep we talked about many different things, but especially about C. I angrily insisted that a girl should not trust a man's fine behavior. Who knows what he's really thinking, deep down.

"It's impossible to please someone like you," Rae said. "You always see in every situation possibilities that others wouldn't even dream up. C. is a very fine young man. A smart girl with a little more affection could get herself attached to him."

"For how long?"

"Forever!"

"You couldn't attach yourself to him forever unless you chained yourself to him. I mean with the chains of law. But he'd try to break free, even from that. The fact is that he'd try to break free the minute he was attached to you."

"He only wants free love?" Rae asked again.

"Yes."

"Do you love him?"

"No. Not exactly. Not enough that I would admit to it."

"Would it be right to marry him if you don't love him very much?"

We were quiet for a moment, and then we laughed. The laughter ended with a sad, regretful sigh.

Rae told me about how "her" engineer was making plans for the future. Great, grandiose plans. But when he talks about her, he's always speaking about the past. "It's like an epidemic," Rae warned me. "These days everyone is talking about the past, about seizing the moment. And if you remind them about weddings, they look at you like you've brought them a greeting from their grandmother from beyond the grave. Do you know what I feel like saying about them?"

"What?"

"Hang them all!" And, not asking me if I was with her in this, she fell asleep.

꩜

We hadn't had time yet to get dressed when there was a knock on the door. Rae looked at me with surprise. "Who could it be so early?"

I wondered what I would do if someone else, and not Rae, was here in my room? I was in no hurry to open the door.

The knocking stopped, but I didn't hear the sound of someone walking away from the door. Someone was standing there, listening.

I wanted to show that someone a lesson. I tiptoed to the door and tugged it open. The old German lady was standing in the doorway, holding something in both hands. That something seemed to be a flowerpot. There was far more of the pot than there were plants inside of it.

"*Vielleicht*—perhaps you would be willing to keep this here?" she asked. It was very dear to her and since it wasn't as hot in my room as it was in hers, it wouldn't dry out so easily.

I agreed.

"You didn't have to say yes!" Rae opined once the German lady had left.

"Why not?" I asked.

"Because now she has an excuse to come in to your room and see who's here. That's why she came in the first place."

"True! But who, and when, would there be someone else here, other than you?"

"Of course no one else would be here. But it does happen sometimes that things go a way they shouldn't. You're talking, you sit together, and then, all of a sudden—hello little flower plant! I can only imagine how welcome that surprise visit would be! You're busy with love, and suddenly the blind German lady opens the door. She came to see if she needs to water her flower pot!" Rae laughed.

"The door can't just suddenly open, and I can promise her that I'll water the plant myself."

Rae didn't want to talk about it anymore. She told me to wait and see for myself that she knew what she was talking about. She wasn't making things up. She knew from experience. One time she had a landlady who had a habit of keeping things in her room and coming to see them or take them precisely at the moment that Rae had a guest. She was so focused on seeing who was there that she sometimes would forget what she came for and needed to be reminded. "I think, I think . . . No . . ." She would try to remember and when she couldn't she would decide to leave and then come back later, because that's the best way to jog her memory.

"You'll find out soon enough. Oh my! The world is large, but there's nowhere to hide."

"That's true," I thought, looking at the flowerpot like it was an uninvited guest. With its wilting leaves and dry roots, the flowerpot looked guilty and ashamed. It was like a thorn in my eye.

43

Conflicting Opinions

It's not in my nature to hold a grudge. I'm always looking for the reasons why someone behaved badly and when I uncover them I blame the reasons and not the guilty party. I'm always trying to understand and forgive the one who acted wrongly. To understand is to forgive.

I understand C.

I'm beginning to forgive C.

In talking about living and *living* we both discovered that there's nothing that can be said about it. Things like these have to be discussed without words; both people must come to an understanding and express themselves with silent voices. Trying to persuade one another out loud will only ruin it. It can make you suspect that the other person is only trying to do you a favor.

C. admits that when it comes to *living* he thinks more about himself than about anyone else. He justifies this (if such a thing needs justification) by saying that no one else has given the matter as much thought. Since his childhood he's been determined to see the world as a grab bag. Those who don't push their way in and grab what they want come away with nothing. Sure, it's not nice to grab. But why should he try to be any nicer or better than anyone else?

In his life, he's met women who approached their relationships with him like men, businesslike and cynical. They taught him not to take women too seriously. Over time and with experience he came to base his view of women on those who, if they were still able to feel shame, would never have stopped blushing.

And it wasn't only these women who taught him to take women with a grain of salt—he learned the same lesson from many great men as well. He read their atrocious views and tried to remember them and take them to heart. He has a whole collection of such views. He wrote them out by hand in books. In his efforts to educate me he told me to read the collection so that I could see that he was not entirely to blame for his own beliefs about women. Living with books taught him what women are, and that they can be no other way.

This is a part of what I read about women in C.'s horrid list:

Zola: "A woman is the axis around which evil turns."

Heine: "Women have only one way of making us happy and thirty thousand ways of making us unhappy."

Napoleon: "When a woman heads a government, the government will not succeed."

Confucius: "An ordinary woman has as much reason as a hen; an extraordinary woman has as much as two hens."

Urri: "Every woman consists of three parts: a body, a soul, and a dress."

Cervantes: "Between a woman's 'yes' and her 'no' I wouldn't venture to put the point of a pin, for there would be no room for it."

Totsitum: "All women are good, but not in their own homes."

Bodenstedt: "There is no logic to a woman's room."

Axenstern: "The Almighty God is fashionable with the women."

Metelus: "Nature made it so that it is impossible to live with or without women."

Alfred Misa: "A woman is like a shadow—if you chase her she runs away, and if you flee her she chases you."

Propertius: "Beautiful women are always frivolous."

Andreiev: "A woman's room is not a goal, it is a tool for reaching the higher goal."

English proverb: "A woman becomes what a man makes of her."

For a long time I have wondered how to respond to C.'s list of bad opinions about women—and I've come up with an answer!

I will give him a list of other opinions—good opinions—of women also written by great men. This will show him that you always find whatever you are looking for.

Here's what I've found so far:

Lessing: "Nature meant woman to be her masterpiece."

Goethe: "The society of women is the nursery of good manners. Only he who knows how to respect women can earn their pleasure."

Bernardin de Saint-Pierre: "Women are only untrue in lands where men are tyrants."

Because C. collects the opinions of so very many great men that they keep him from forming his own opinion, I gave C. a large number of good opinions by great authors and authorities.

He didn't like it and was annoyed at himself for showing me his disgraceful list (which was grimy, to boot). He took it back. He didn't want me to add good opinions of women to his list.

C. was very candid with me. He told me that he's sad I don't trust him when he's been so good to me.

When a good man is good, he's just doing what comes naturally and doesn't deserve to be thanked. But when a bad man is good, when he forces himself to be good for someone else's sake, then he deserves praise.

C. forces himself to be good for me. He wants to see whether in keeping his distance from me he can be closer to my ideal. He thinks that maybe in time he'll be converted to my religion. He'll begin to believe that goodness is the religion of all religions.

He believes that I'm a very good girl and that by being good to me he might even be able to convince me to be bad. Let him go on thinking this way. There will come a time when he won't believe this anymore and then he will realize that I'm not as good as he thinks I am, that I can be bad too.

For now, I've lost my appetite for hating him. I'm starting to get used to him, I guess.

He's driven by loneliness. Loneliness and a desire to fool other people. People look at you with pity that's almost insulting when they see that you're alone. And they show you respect or even jealousy when they see that you have someone else.

That's how Katya looked at me yesterday when C. and I went with another girl to a concert and ran into her there. She stared at us almost the whole time until C. noticed (he couldn't help noticing) and asked me with a smile, "Who's the redhead who keeps looking at us?"

"A girl. Do you want me to introduce you?"

"No. Why would you?"

"Just because."

"I'm not interested in her."

"Why not?" I asked, because it seemed to me that she did interest him, but he didn't want to admit it.

"She looks sassy."

"She's a daredevil," I corrected him.

He rebuked me loudly. "So she's a daredevil. I hate that type of woman!"

"I think that a fox like that is drawn to honorable men."

"Why?"

"They're easier to fool."

C. smiled and took my hand. He glanced flirtatiously at Katya and blew her a kiss.

"Do you think that I want to fool you?" he asked, considering what I'd said before.

I answered that I might think so. But I'm not worried about it.

"Why not?" he asked, narrowing his eyes at me.

"It takes two to have an argument," I said with a grin. He sighed, then laughed. Katya looked at us again and the concert continued.

Katya told Rae that she saw me at a concert with a young man who looked like an intellectual. A. overheard (this happened at B.'s house) and asked why he hasn't seen me around in a long time. Rae asked him where he could expect to see me, since my intellectual man hardly lets me out of his sight.

"Is he so in love with her?" A. asked.

"He's head over heels!" Rae answered.

Rae says that she takes a strange pleasure in exaggerating every time that she talks about love.

"And she's in love with him?" A. asked.

"She? She doesn't let on."

"She's a quiet one," Katya added, "still waters run deep."

"As long as they're not full of mud," A. retorted.

Mrs. B. added pointedly, "*She* isn't the kind of girl who's interested in inserting herself as a third where there's already a twosome."

Rae said that Mrs. B. knows who's been keeping B. out late at night and she wants to expose Katya to the world. She's only waiting for the right moment, when she's gathered some more facts about her. A. probably won't give her any dirt, but B., who talks in his sleep, might share information unawares. And then she'll have a picnic!

Rae can't wait for the picnic. She hates Katya. And she's jealous about B. Perhaps even more than Mrs. B. is.

A. asked Rae where I'm living now. She told him.

Maybe he'll come to see me?

My God! I'd be glad to make the man I hate love me, if only to make the man I love stop hating me! If only he'd love me, even just a little bit.

No, I'm forgetting myself. My wholehearted love won't be satisfied with a little bit of his love. It has to be as I said before: all or nothing.

A. must be curious to see how C. loves me. He must also want to find out if I love C. Very good. Let him conclude that I love C. That I don't love A., only C.

I'll show him! I'll show the whole world and I'll even convince *myself* that I love the man I hate.

44

❧

Ways

I don't understand why I'm so on edge. Why does my heart jump every time I hear a sound outside my door? I know that A. is definitely not coming. He'd certainly write to tell me he was coming first. And if he came unannounced, what then?

Why do I want to get even with A. by using C.? Would I think it was fair if C., or some other man I didn't love, tried to get even with me like this? Is it my fault that I don't love him? Is it A.'s fault that he doesn't love me?

No, those who don't love are not to blame. It's the fault of those who aren't loved, who don't know how to make themselves lovable!

I look around my ugly room and think about going to look for another one, but I'm afraid I might miss him. A. might still come.

I'm sitting here in my room because of him (when I could just leave), and I can't get him out of my mind. I tell myself that it's only because I want to have an opportunity to show him that I love someone else now. But that's a lie. Before I even say a word, he'll see right through it. You can play a part with anyone except someone you love. True love will ruin the greatest lie, even if told by someone with the greatest self-control.

C. is glad that I've stopped asking him to go out to the streets with me in the evening and now I let him stay in my room. He thinks it's because I've realized that love is better inside than outside. He says I must have come to terms with the fact that I'm basically no different from anyone else. However idealistic I might be, I have to admit that my soul is not so precious. The world is only a world, after all, for sinners and nonsinners alike.

C. says that whether I like it or not, I have to agree with Schiller that "life's youthful May blooms only once" and that to die is nothing, but to live without truly living is a misfortune.

"And Ibsen says—do you want to know what Ibsen says?" he asked, after finishing up with Schiller.

"Yes, I want to know. Why wouldn't I want to know what Ibsen says? I want to know what everyone says, everyone in the world," I answered with a bitter smile, thinking that nothing that anyone says could make A. love me.

"Ibsen says, 'There are men who were born to live and men who were born to die.' Isn't that nicely put?"

"Very nice. A clever man. He knows what to say."

"And a clever girl should know what to do," he nudged.

"That's also true," I responded flatly.

"So—"

"So? Oh, yes, a clever girl. You said a clever girl."

"You're a clever girl."

"Yes? And I didn't know it. I thought to myself—what am I? Clever or foolish? Am I clever or foolish? And I came to the conclusion—I'm a fool."

"You think too much. You're always thinking. Especially these past few days." C. said. "And Sophocles says, 'Thinking about nothing is the best recipe for a happy life.' What do you think of that?" C. prodded.

"He must have thought for a long time, that Sophocles, to have come up with such a phrase," I responded.

For a while C. tried to convince me not to think so much and to just be happy, but it didn't help. I was stubborn. I only want to be unhappy.

"You *are* a fool." C. had to agree, in the end.

༄

I try to stop thinking my thoughts, or to think about something else, but I can't. They take hold of me like pliers, they compress my mind, they squeeze my brain, they force me to beg for release, if leaving this world is indeed an escape.

But without love it would be impossible to live in this world!

Of course, many people do live without love. They live and live. Or they wipe themselves from the face of the earth for the sake of, as C. calls it, an abstract thing. Soon I too will be like someone who burns their house down to rid it of mice.

C. came to see me and asked me why I'm so lost in thought, so confused and nervous and paralyzed. Maybe I'm not feeling well? He could bring me to one of his friends who's a doctor, to figure out what's wrong. Something's wrong, even a blind person could see that something isn't right with me. I wouldn't act this way without a reason— I'm not myself. Why am I so quiet? Why won't I say what is wrong?

"Nothing's wrong," I said several times.

"Maybe you're unwell?"

"I'm perfectly healthy!"

"If that's so," C. decided, "then what's wrong is that you need to *live* a little. You're dying for lack of living. You refuse to live, not because you don't want to live, but because you're afraid. Yes, you're afraid of the *results* of such living. But there's nothing to be afraid of. That is to say, there's nothing to be afraid of if you lose yourself to someone like *me*. I know how to *live* in such a way that it won't result in anything, if you catch my drift. I have ways. I've known a lot of women, I won't even tally them up, but *no* children."

He said this with an odd sense of pride, and I looked at him coldly. He took my hand, like you would take the hand of a sick person to feel their pulse. The door of the German lady's room opened and the German lady came in with a glass of water to water the plant. It wasn't the first time she'd waltzed in to water her plant. But this time it happened while C. was holding my hand, trying to convince me.

If you could die from a look, the German lady would no longer be among the living. C. looked up at her and told her she should be aware that American manners require her to knock before entering. In response to this advice, she cupped her hands around her ears and claimed that she couldn't hear. So, instead, he showed her that the plant's soil was damp and there was no reason to water it so often. She could ruin the plant with so much water. She pointed to her eyes and claimed that she couldn't see what he was talking about.

☙

Once C. realized the old German lady wouldn't overhear us, he started to act sure of himself. "Since she's deaf and blind, we can do whatever our hearts desire!" he said, "and what our hearts desire is *to live*. All living things in the world want to live, but they don't all know how." He explained that I, for example, want to live but don't know how. He wants to live and he knows how to live, so he's obligated to teach me.

He told me that he's lost patience with my insisting that there's no need for him to live up to that obligation with me and with my telling him he can pay his debt to someone else instead. I've strained his nerves so much already that if I pull them any further they'll snap. He's no more than a man, after all.

"Yes, no more," I agreed.

So how can I expect him to be an angel?

I told him that I don't expect him to be an angel. All I want is for him to be a man somewhere else, away from me. But he doesn't want that. He says there's something in me that draws him to me as though by force. Maybe I'm the one nature created specifically for him? Who knows. That is no doubt one of the world's deepest secrets. The only way to find out would be to see if he's ever so attracted to anyone else.

I recalled the scene that occurred between us at the home of the "small-minded intellectuals," as C. calls them. Remembering this, I got angry again and wanted to get back at him. I cold-bloodedly retorted that if he wants to find the answer to the question, all he'll have to do is get married.

"Get married?! Pfui, what a horrible thought!"

"It may be horrible, but everyone does it."

"We are not *everyone*."

"We are not everyone, true, but—"

"But, but, but—you're being a nuisance."

"I may be a nuisance, but nevertheless—"

"And nevertheless," he said, cutting me off, "we won't even consider it. We'll do whatever we want. The only thing holding girls back is the *results*. If it weren't for that, they'd be a thousand times worse than men."

I looked at him askance.

"Yes, worse! A thousand times worse! But usually it's the ignorant girls who are afraid—and it's only natural that a girl should be afraid of something when she doesn't understand it. Take the Christian girl's lead. She isn't afraid, or at least not as much as a Jewish girl. The Jewish girl is so small-minded, so restrained, so limited in her perspective on life. She's only interested in the bottom line. All she wants is a wedding. The 'road to happiness.' The Christian girl also wants a wedding. But she wants to *live* too. And until she marries, she lives. Later, when she can fool someone into marrying her, she fools him, and if not, then she doesn't! The fact is men are more attracted to women with a little experience. They already know what to do. That's why statistics show that so many men fall for widows. I can see from the way you look that you don't understand me. But I'm talking myself hoarse."

"Have a little water, or a sip of milk."

"I don't want any water or milk. I want you to understand me."

I assured him that I understood.

What difference does it make, C. said, that I understand him? It doesn't make anything better for him. I'm still the same stubborn, fearful girl that I was before!

"And why are you still so afraid?" he asked. "Haven't I explained to you over and over again that there's nothing to be afraid of? The trouble with you is that I can tell you the same thing a hundred times and you'll still forget. What are you, anyway?"

"I'm me."

"That doesn't answer my question."

"Well, I *am* a pessimist!"

"Not true. A pessimist wouldn't want to get married. You wouldn't be worried about what tomorrow would hold. Only an optimist would think this way."

"That's right. Then I'm an optimist."

"This is the way things have always been—" he started to explain.

The German lady came in to check if it was time to water her plant. She walked straight to it without looking around, as though there was no one in the room but the plant. C. cursed in Polish. Although she can't hear, he was cautious anyway, despite his anger.

Meanwhile, C. forgot what he'd been doing. Once the German lady left he started trying to convince me again to make myself comfortable. He told me to take off my extra clothes. He told me that he prefers to talk in the dark, amid phantasmal shadows. Saying this, he adjusted the gas lamp so that it wouldn't bother our eyes. Anyway, now the deaf-blind German lady might think I was going to sleep. He'd tell me a story. "Do you want to hear something about my childhood?"

"Yes."

I'd rather hear about his childhood than his adulthood. He looked at me, thought awhile, grew dreamy and started to look a bit like a child. He told me his story. He came to the part when he started to get to know the world and to enjoy life. Then he thought out loud about how good it would have been if he'd never experienced those years. If only he'd never grown up!

He told me about his childhood and all the while I thought that when he came to the part in his story where he grows up, I would tell him that I'm tired and that I have to get up early, and I would ask him to save the rest of the story for later.

But he jumped from childhood to the present moment faster than I anticipated. From getting to know the world personally he went straight to making a personal request of me. He told me that there's no need to sit in such an uncomfortable pose. He suggested that I get up from the chair and lie down in my bed. He was drawn to the bed.

Instead of going to the bed, I moved from my straight-backed chair to the rocking chair. I sat down in silence, letting him know that I would not be convinced by his asking me to lie down.

"Do you plan to sit there all night?" he asked.

"No," I answered. "I think you'll leave soon, and then I'll lie down."

He put both hands on his forehead and lay there thinking.

☙

"No! A thousand times, no!" C. cried out defiantly, flinging his hands from his brow. "It's an impossible thing!"

When I inquired about the "thing" that was so impossible to have that it caused him to hold his head in his hands, he told me that he doesn't think I'm normal. If I was normal, like most people, then I'd feel that I must *live*—like other people do.

"Yes, my dear," he said, looking me in the eye with regret, "you are not as you should be."

"Who cares what I should be?"

"Yes, but if the world were full of people like you, it would have ended long ago."

"Is that so? And how long would men like you, with your pragmatic 'ways' to love without consequence, keep the world from going under?"

He glared at me intently and responded, "I only spoke about the 'ways' in case you wanted—"

"Oh!"

"If you want to *live* like that, without any 'ways,' that's fine with me. I'll go along with it with or without the measures I can offer you. It's up to you."

"Is that so? How nice of you. You're so self-sacrificing, so kind-hearted and generous."

"It *is*. Others wouldn't feel that way. Because if something *comes of it*, the time will come, inevitably, when we'll reach the question of whether I should be recognized. A man can lose his free will that way. Unless there's law that the *results* become a ward of the state. Otherwise, the law is always more concerned with the fallen woman than the man."

"Aha! If only the law worked that way!"

"You think that would be good, do you? But maybe not."

"What does good have to do with it?"

"Then you wouldn't have so much to be afraid of!"

"Never!"

"But since there's no such law, you have to use protection to keep such a thing from happening."

"If everyone protected themselves that way, wouldn't the world end, as you said?"

He started to laugh at me. "What am I, someone who only worries about the fate of the world? What do *I* care about the world? What does the world care about me? I could die right now and the world wouldn't lift a finger. The world doesn't take individuals into account. I'm worth as much as a drop in the ocean, a needle in a haystack."

"It's a rotten world." I said, thinking of how little it cares for me. "A flood should drown it all!"

He told me that he was certain that if a flood were to come, *he'd* be the man I'd choose as a partner to take with me on Noah's ark.

I assured him that wasn't true. It would be better if men like him drowned. Then future generations wouldn't suffer.

"Fine," he said, to make an end of our conversation of drowning. "Who cares if the world ends or not? In the meantime, we're still alive and we have to *live*. Don't you like being alive?"

"No, I hate it."

"But don't you love loving?"

"I hate it as much as death!"

He wanted to get angry with me, to yell at me for being abnormal or narrow-minded, but he reminded himself of our agreement: no personal insults. So he fell into thought, no doubt searching for a way to talk to me without insulting me.

45

Skilled Diplomat

A new tactic: rather than insulting me directly or indirectly through personal insults, he would go about insulting me by embracing me and kissing me.

"Look," he seemed to be saying with his forced kisses, "I don't care much for your soul. It's your body I like to kiss. If I want to kiss you, I kiss; if I want to hold you in my arms, I do. If you try to go against me, you won't succeed. I'll kiss you, I'll pinch you, I'll bite you!"

How disappointed he seemed to be when I didn't resist! He was expecting me to protest, to beg him to stop. But I just acted like this was what I expected and deserved, as if this were no insult to my soul.

"Do you have nothing to say against my kisses?" he said, annoyed.

I was expecting his question and had already formulated an answer: "They don't bother me."

"No? Your soul isn't insulted when I pursue only your body?"

"My soul can't be bothered with it."

"And you?"

"I am with my soul."

"Don't my kisses excite your desire to kiss me back?"

"No!"

"They will. I'll make them arouse you. You'll kiss me back. It's true, you will."

"I will not."

"But why not?"

"I can only kiss a person I love."

"But you'd let anyone kiss you?"

"I'd let someone who loves me kiss me."

"So you believe that I love you?"

"I believe you."

"You don't believe that I love your soul, though."

"Oh, no."

"And that doesn't insult you?"

"I already told you. It doesn't bother me."

"You're either as hard as a block of wood or you're a skilled diplomat. You're saying all this just to get a rise out of me, right? But let me tell you something: *I* never take offense at anything. I'll show you. Even *you* will forget yourself with me. You'll have to love me or hate me. You won't be able to remain indifferent for long."

"Yes, I will."

"You will not. You'll squirm, you'll try to tear yourself out of my arms, you'll fall at my feet and beg for mercy. But there comes a turning point when a woman is being caressed, a moment when every wish can be fulfilled. That's the moment women always deny afterward, claiming that the men were unsuccessful. I just have to be clever to get to that moment. I'll soon reach it, don't worry, you'll hold me and kiss me and nothing else will matter!"

"Is that so!"

"You don't believe me? I'll show you which one of us is stronger."

"In brawn or in spirit?"

"Both."

"Alright."

"I *will* reach that moment, in the end."

"You'll see. You'll never get there."

"You won't be able to slip out of my hands."

"I'll never even slip into them."

"We'll see about that."

"We'll see."

This is his new tactic. A new "strategy," as they call it in other languages, in our love-war. Hmmm . . . Now this *nudnik* is finally becoming interesting.

∽

Now C. is trying every possible way smooth over the impression he made by predicting his own victory. He pretends as though he's forgotten the whole exchange. Nothing can interfere with his success as much as promising his opponent that he will conquer. C. understands this now, and he regrets the way he boasted to me. After all, the war will take place in my room, and I could nip it all in the bud by denying him entry.

I've already done that. After he left last time, the next time he tried to see me I pretended to have forgotten my key. I told him that I'd have to enter my room through the German lady's room, and that she wouldn't allow me to bring a man with me.

"Tell her that I'm your cousin," C. suggested.

"Oh, a cousin! That's some excuse. Everyone claims a man is their cousin when they don't want to say who he is. It won't pass muster."

"Then say I'm your brother."

"My brother? That's even worse. Who's ever heard of a brother coming to visit a sister at night and staying with her until dawn?"

"No one would have to *hear* it."

"But they could. Deaf as she is, she'll be able to hear it. No, I've already learned my lesson, and I don't need to learn it again."

"What if you go through the German lady's door first, and I follow later? You could open your door quietly and—"

"It's no good."

"You're afraid she'll hear? She's as deaf as a doorknob."

"She has a son, and he's not deaf."

"He's probably already asleep, and he sleeps like a log."

"I doubt it. He usually works in the evening, and he also has a cold and wakes himself coughing."

"When he's coughing, he'll hardly be in the mood to pay attention to what we're doing."

I didn't like his implication that we'd be "doing" something. I replied curtly that there was nothing more to talk about, and he'd better go home.

"Say what you like!" he retorted. "Why bother giving all these excuses when the main thing is that you just aren't interested? If I so much as threaten a hair on your head you get flighty."

"There's no need for you to threaten anything."

"You're such a child! Don't you understand that if I really wanted to hurt you, I wouldn't have told you my intentions? I'm not such a fool that I don't know that by telling you them I've given myself a handicap."

"Sometimes it just comes out."

"Not for me. I know what the future looks like."

"Is that so? Then tell me, am I the kind of girl that you can just take if you want her, or am I not?"

"You're not."

"And why not?"

"First of all, no one can ever really force himself on someone else. Second, the more you're convinced that someone wants to take you, the less you're willing to give. The more men beg you, the more you refuse."

"So what can you do about it?"

"Nothing. With you, I just have to take things as they come. I'll have to wait until you figure out what you really want. Am I right?"

"You're right."

"See what a good psychologist I am?"

"Very good. And as a psychologist, you must understand that the more you try to come into my room the longer you'll have to stand here, waiting. So wouldn't you be better off just saying good night?"

He said it grudgingly. What choice did he have?

46

An Accounting

My financial circumstances require that I make an accounting, my life longs for me simply to exist, and my love wants me to hate.

Yesterday I saw A. walking past my window. I was consumed by wild joy mixed with instinctive fear. My heart stopped beating and sat in me silenced, dead. Waiting for him! I threw myself at the door, pressed myself against it, and waited for him to knock.

I don't know how long I stood like that, but it felt like forever. He never knocked.

My legs collapsed under me. I sat myself down and gave myself over to the cold tears that flowed down my face. They hid in the corners of my lips. I swallowed them.

The German lady crept into my room quiet as a shadow, carrying a watering can. As she made her way to her plant she bumped into me. It gave her a fright, and she spilled half the water, almost dropping the watering can entirely.

"*Um Gottes willen!*" she cried, and she swore that she hadn't known there was someone in my room. Since I was there, what was I doing sitting all alone in the dark? The coals had burned out and the oven was cold. "What's wrong with you?" she asked me. "Are you ill?"

"I'm healthy, entirely well," I replied, and, in order to demonstrate, I stood up and started putting on my coat to go outside.

I wanted to wait until she left the room so that I could lock the door behind her. Truth be told, she could just unlock it with a knife, but I wanted her to know that I wanted it locked. If she can be afraid when she runs into me in my own room then certainly I can also be afraid when she comes into my room unannounced. But I only thought these things and didn't say them out loud. What would be the point? "If you don't like this room, find another one," I said to myself, dismissing my thoughts.

But I soon came back to myself and thought that maybe A. forgot my address and was looking around and trying to find me. Or maybe Rae was exaggerating when she told me about A. Maybe she only said all that to see what my reaction would be. She wanted to figure out which man I was in love with.

Or could A. be here to visit some other acquaintance? Maybe the "quiet" girl that he jilted Katya for lives nearby? I started to picture the girl. I imagined her with every advantage a girl could possibly have that would attract A. I added them all up so that I could have even more reason to hate her!

I felt as though my heart, longing for love, was poisoned with hatred. I hated everyone and everything, and above all—myself.

This was the mood C. found me in. He didn't let me turn on the gas lights. He said his words could also reach me in the dark. He would only talk—would I hear him out?

There was nothing to hear. It would just be the same old boring speech about my lonely life and his principles. Why should I live my life in the dark, when a bright world full of joy was spread out before my feet? Would I really try to stamp out any joy? What did I think would happen to me? And so on, and so forth. He had apparently decided to bore me to death.

I did get one thing out of all his speechifying: he'd prefer that I not kill myself.

❧

Tears blemish my face like cracks on an old mirror. I imagine my own death. I see my dead body lying in my bed under the patchwork quilt, and a dull ache pierces my heart.

Last night I could hardly sleep. In a room a floor above mine a woman poisoned herself and died. She must have regretted killing herself because after she took the poison she cried out for someone to save her. The German lady heard her and sprang into action. The police arrived, they called for an ambulance and carried her off to a hospital.

With a long coat covering my nightgown I stood in my doorway and peered into the half-darkened hallway. The suicide victim, a stranger to me, filled my thoughts. The thought of death hovered over my head and covered me in cold fear. I responded to her death in a thousand different ways. She accomplished something huge and difficult. She freed herself from a life that she must have come to hate.

Goethe says, "Great people do not die from natural causes." This must be true. You have to truly be great in order to give up everything, if you are certain you have nothing left to gain from living.

People gathered around to get a peek at the girl. No one was interested in her when she was alive, but they were all clamoring to see her now.

"Poor woman!" bemoaned the German lady, recalling how unfortunate the girl had been. She had toiled to bring her sickly sister over to America. But she was unable to earn enough before the sister died, and she herself became sick. It drained the life out of her, and she did not want to wait until she, like her sister, would die from illness. So she took her own life.

When the activity died down, after they took her away, I sat on the edge of my bed with my coat still on but no shoes, thinking about death. Why had the suicidal woman cried out in such wild doubt? If I, so pained by life, decided to end mine, would I cry out too?

I think I'd be mute. My lips, which I bit so often in life, would not so much as utter a sigh. Once I made the decision to die, my strong will wouldn't let me change my mind.

"Did she die of at her own will?" A. would ask intently.

Rae would answer, "Who knows. She wasn't one to share her thoughts. She was very introspective."

Katya, biting her red lips, would be silent, her eyes narrowed. B. would be racked with guilt for not coming to see me. He would stroke his little daughter's hair, and with hidden tears in his eyes he would call her by my name.

"She loved me," A. would confess to himself, "and I ignored her. Her love was so true and deep. She told me wordlessly in her meaningful silences, but I pretended not to notice. Why, oh, why, did I allow such a good, dear girl to die?"

He would stand before my grave, his head bowed, and his tears would fall one after the other. They would be hot, heavy tears like the ones falling from my eyes right now onto this page of my diary, making it so that I can't see what I'm writing—

⁓

Late last night C. came to see me and found me with eyes swollen from crying. He stared at me and then asked in a frightened voice, "What happened?"

"Nothing."

"What do you mean nothing? You were crying, dearest!"

I realized that I hadn't even pictured him at my funeral. I felt like laughing. But I didn't laugh, I just smiled sadly. I wondered how he was interpreting my crying, what he thought caused it and how he'd try to silence those causes.

"Why were you crying?" he asked gently, trying to get me to look him in the eye.

"Oh, who knows why people cry?"

"No, there must be a reason. Why won't you tell me?"

"There's nothing to tell."

"You're hiding something from me."

"I'm not hiding anything."

"I'm begging you. Tell me what's wrong."

"I'm cold."

"Should I heat the stove for you?"

"I don't need the stove."

"You don't have any coal. Doesn't the German lady know that you need to be warm? It's like she's deaf for seeing and blind for hearing. But she'll take your money for the room, and what else does she need, the old bitch? And you don't complain. You sit here in the cold and cry. Look, your eyes are heavy with tears."

We heard squeaks and tiny footsteps coming from the wardrobe. "Mice!" he shrieked. "Aren't you afraid of them? All women are afraid of mice. But you're a brave girl. You're not scared of them. There's only one thing you're afraid of."

"What's that?"

"Love. Free love. Isn't that right?"

"That's right."

"And do you know why you're so scared?"

"Why?"

"Because you've never tried it. It's always hard to try something for the first time."

"It's better not to start."

"Then what would be the end?"

"The end is the same for everyone—death."

"Death? Why did you bring that up? You haven't even begun to live yet, you don't even know what life is! Take now, for example. Here you are, just sitting here and shivering from cold. You could be lying in bed, covered in a warm quilt, sleeping in the arms of a man who loves you. But what's the point of talking about it when you don't even know what good is?" He gestured helplessly and paced between the oilcloth and the carpet. He scowled at the gaslight and then turned to me and whispered, "Don't be a child."

I wanted to tell him not to be a fool, but that wouldn't help anything. I just looked at him, and he continued, "Madam, I give you my word of honor that I will be a gentleman. I will just sit next to you and talk to you until you fall asleep. And as soon as you're asleep I'll leave and close the door behind me."

"Then the door will be unlocked all night."

"Then I won't leave at all. I'll stay until morning."

"You'll be a gentlemen until morning?"

Instead of answering my question he turned down the gas so that we found ourselves in the dark.

"Why did you do that?" I cried, pushing him away with both hands so he wouldn't get too close.

"Don't ask, my dear. You don't want the light to shine in the German lady's eyes, do you? There's no need to struggle like that. Let me make you comfortable. I'll—"

"You'll do no such thing!"

"Calm down and be careful. You're going to break my eyeglasses."

He took off his eyeglasses like someone preparing for a fight, and then he lunged toward me. "My dearest!" He held out his arms and reached out for me. He tripped over a corner of the carpet and fell. "Oh, hell!" he shouted. "What's with this awful oilcloth and disgusting carpet? You could get killed tripping over this trash. Now, where are you? Come!"

It was as though he was inviting me to get killed with him! I wanted to laugh out loud but I just smirked to myself in the darkness and kept quiet.

He asked why I was so quiet, why I didn't go to him to make sure he was alright. He'd torn up his whole leg. Did I have some peroxide? You should always have a bottle of peroxide. You never know when you'll need it. You could even get blood poisoning from the prick of a needle. What intellectual person doesn't know this? Couldn't I at least give him a washcloth dipped in cold water?

I saw that he was acting like it hurt when he tried to stand up so that I would come and put my arms around him and try to heal his "serious" injury. But I pretended not to notice. Let him make himself sick, as long as he doesn't make me sick trying to preserve myself from his advances.

"Here's a washcloth."

"You're so kind!"

He didn't mean it, but by saying so he was hoping he would make me want to "be good" to him. Feeling a little guilty for laughing at him, I asked, "Does it hurt a lot?"

Trying to show how brave he was, how heroically he could withstand pain, he restricted his answer to a few words and replied in a soft voice, "It's alright, darling. It will pass. It's a miracle that I didn't lose an eye!"

"Yes, isn't it a miracle that there wasn't an eye in your leg in the first place!" I couldn't keep myself from laughing anymore.

"How can you laugh at a time like this?" he sighed. "I could've fallen off the chair and onto the rug and lost my eye! I was just lucky that I was already standing on the rug when I fell."

"You lost your mind instead."

"It's all because of you. In trying to keep yourself from falling, you made me fall down."

"Better you than me."

"It's harder to get up."

"It depends on who you're talking about."

"It's the same for everyone. It takes some people longer than others, but sooner or later everyone comes around to it. And once they come to it, they don't want to stop. Unless they're going to come right back to it. It's just human nature. You can't go against it. My, how cold it is here! If only I were King David." He began to tell me the story of King David in his old age, and how good he had it. When C. was finished with King David's old age he started thinking out loud about himself and how bad he had it, right now, in the bloom of his youth.

"*He* was made happy in his old age . . . I hear those mice again. They must be having a party. Maybe a wedding?"

"Or free love?"

"Maybe." C. meant this comment seriously and began to demonstrate how mice are more forward thinking than humans in that regard. At least more forward thinking than those miserable people who follow outmoded laws and rotten ceremonies created by people who want to keep them in the dark. Mice are free from these burdens. They can do what they please.

From there, C. began to lecture me about cats, and then dogs, and so forth. As he lectured me he patted his leg with the washcloth to keep it from getting warm, so it wouldn't swell. His hands were kept busy with his leg, and I wished that it was always this way so that he wouldn't be able to make advances or bother me so much.

47

His Free, Wild Path

C. says that he won't take any more lopsided wagons down windy roads that delay him. He will openly and forthrightly pursue his goals. "If you like it, then good! If you don't, I don't need your approval!" It won't take long, he claims, for me to change my mind and realize that I can't live alone with only my mind for company. The body is more than just the head. The heart also has needs. In the meantime, I can act as respectably as I want. And he won't call me darling anymore. Not even in the dark. It's better not to use such words with someone like me. He knows that sooner or later I'll act on my own accord. I won't be able to sit and wait for someone else to do it. Sooner or later, just like everyone else, I'll get tired of it. I'll realize that no one's going to give me a medal for my restraint; I won't get any awards from society for acting honorably. Future generations won't even recite psalms in my memory. Maybe, if I'm lucky, a few old *yakhnes* will pray to have children like me.

He laughs at me while he says all this. But I only listen with a complacent smile that makes his blood boil. It's my refusal to speak that makes him talk like this, he complains, forgetting his resolve to say not even one more word on the subject. "Now I won't say anything else, not one word more. It'll be as though I've gone mute. All that I want to say before I stop talking is this: even if the world turns upside down, I won't be moved from my principles. I'll stand by them with my dying breath. Whoever wants to tread the narrow path of our forefathers can go right ahead! I will forge my free, wide path through life. I won't beg you anymore. That's all! *Basta!*"

I enjoy listening to him talk like this. But I'm nervous that the landlady might hear. Last night when he left my room late in the evening her door opened and closed. I didn't know if I should be glad that she knew that he wasn't in my room anymore or worried that she saw how late he'd stayed.

~

Two rainy days passed and C. only came to see me once, to tell me that he barely had time to come and tell me that he had no time for me. He's too busy with his future. His college professors are showering praise on him. He says that they've told him that they see him as someone who is already on his way to having a professor's mind. When he graduates, he'll begin his path and make broad strides toward higher rungs on the ladder of success.

He told me this, and much more, and then hurried away because he didn't want to be late to the event this evening at a professor's house that was practically being held in his honor. He asked me to excuse him for having no time to spend with me.

He left and now I'm alone. I believe in his future. I can picture him climbing the ladder of success while I'm left behind on the lowest rung. I imagine how it will be when he's already achieved his life's fortune, and I'm just a fool, a rejected leftover woman with no hope for the future, with no goal to look forward to. Yes, with the help of my imagination his glistening future has already darkened my present and my whole life. I think to myself, "What are you, after all? You aren't poor, or ugly, or even very old, but some might say that you're not rich, or pretty, or even very young. You're clever. That's what they say about you, you're smart. Maybe that's true, but what good is that? What has it taught you about life? It didn't even help you to win the man who you thought was your one and only true love!" I turn my thoughts toward my love, A., and I find myself blaming him for how I'm envisioning C.'s great future. I would look at other people differently if I didn't have this love fantasy with A. They'd seem more important to me, and better. A. ruined my taste for good things.

"You're so educated," I say to myself, "you're so full of books that you're like the largest library, and yet you can't manage to do anything that your heroines do! All you know how to do is think sophisticated thoughts! In the end you'll die without ever having lived. You'll regret all the things you didn't do . . ."

Now that C. isn't with me, I've taken over his role, arguing to myself that I should try living, for once.

 ∽

I saw Rae, who brought greetings from B. and a few words about A. and others who were living life. I was filled with protests against myself: How dare I swear off life? I can't stop thinking about what B. said to Rae about me today: "What's she up to, that strange girl? Is she raising her prices higher? Or maybe she's entered a convent by now? She's no fool, but she doesn't know how to live."

 ∽

I was just reading yesterday that Schiller says life is slumber, and the best way to live is to have sweet dreams.

"Life is as short as the blink of an eye between two eternities," as Plato says. So I ask myself why I spend my time worrying so much about something as insignificant as blinking. What's the use? Whatever will be will be. Imagine I was someone else, looking at myself from the outside. Would I care what happened to me? Not for a minute! I made up my mind to care as little about myself as I would care about a stranger.

Gorky recommended "indifference toward everything, not spoiling your life with philosophy." He said, "In the end your life will be judged like a fable, not by how you got there but by what you did." I must try to do more with my life.

Because I hadn't seen C. in a whole week, he'd grown in my estimation. His absence gave me the chance to imagine him as better than he really is. If he'd known what effect it was having on me, he'd have been very smart to stay away a few more weeks. Or not to come back at all! Then I'd certainly have developed a better opinion of him! But he was here yesterday, seven days after I'd last seen him. He came to my room in the evening and looked at me knowingly. He asked whether I'd been thinking about him.

He said that he was sure that I must have been thinking of him. You always think of people who love you.

I thought of A. Does he ever think about me?

"It was very hard for me to force myself not to come see you, and I couldn't keep myself from you any longer," C. said. "I felt that I had to see you. And were you pining after me? Tell me the truth, didn't you miss me?"

"I was pining."

"Just pining, in general?"

"Yes."

"Not for me, specifically? You weren't pining for my love?"

"I was longing for life."

"Oh, for *living*! Well, that certainly has something to do with me. *Living* and I go hand in hand. If you want to *live*, I'm your man."

He didn't wait for my response. Straightaway he turned down the gaslights like a punctilious janitor noticing that it was ten o'clock. He called me "darling," took me in his arms, and cursed my corset. What's the purpose of this torture device, anyway? The most beautiful thing is to just be as you are, as nature made you. Why should you stifle yourself?

I stopped dreaming as I realized what was happening, and I took control of myself. C. couldn't tolerate this, since in his mind this was the appropriate moment for *living*. Right now.

"No, no. Not now—"

"Why not now?"

"Don't ask."

"I understand."

"You understand as much as a corpse," I wanted to say. Instead I was silent. If only he understood enough to leave me alone.

❧

I couldn't sleep for a long time after C. left. I lay with my eyes open listening to a clock tick behind the wall. Time passed. It was almost as though it dragged along, like it had lost the strength to keep going with its eternal momentum.

It had been easy enough to shake C. off this time. I was left thinking how hard it was going to be for me next time, when he wouldn't be so understanding. Although my life has little value to me, still it seems a shame for it to end in such a way. And I can see the end of my life so clearly if I were to begin *living* as he wants. I won't let him come see me, so I won't have to beg him to leave! It's like lighting your house on fire and then trying to put it out.

But something in me spurs me to provoke him and myself. Maybe I want to reject someone else's desire because my own love is unrequited?

48

Amusement

As soon as C. entered my room he looked me in the eye and asked how I was feeling.

"Alright."

"Alright? Alright?" he repeated with a smile, gently stroking my cheek.

He was very pleased to hear my "alright." He was so happy he didn't know what to do. And, as though he wanted to reward me for it, he asked me if I wanted to go out for a little amusement.

"Amusement? Yes, why not?" I had nothing to say against it. It's better this way, I thought to myself. But then his fine spirits made me think about how hard it would be later to get him to leave my room when we got back late at night.

Digging in his pockets, he said that he forgot his wallet. He emptied out his pockets and laid his change on the table. What a damned bad habit it was to forget it! He begged my pardon.

He knew there was no need to apologize. It wasn't the first time that he'd forgotten it and I'd forgiven him. I gave him some money. Of course I wasn't going to pay for him. I had to give him the money so that he could play the cavalier and pay for me in public. He accepted the loan, as usual, with another apology, this time for forgetting to repay the money he already owed me. Of course I didn't ask for the money back. It's only natural for a future professor to already be forgetting such insignificant details. In his defense, I must say that he didn't borrow any more money than he needed. And he was very frugal—almost as careful with my money as he would be with his own.

"Money is a necessity," he said. "You need one dollar to save another. It's always easier to spend than to make money. It's a delicate thing."

I showed C. my pocketbook so he could take the "delicate thing" out and went to the mirror to put on my hat. When he was done with the pocketbook he approached me. "You're beautiful," he said joyfully, "Today you look sweet and soft and—accommodating. Isn't that right?"

"Is it?" I asked, not knowing how to respond.

"Yes!" he avowed. "A hundred times, yes! A thousand times, yes! Your eyes say, 'Do you see? I see now what living is! Life is stronger than everything and I give myself over to it!' Your silence today says that you are ready to love. Today you will finally get to know what living is. Today you are 'alright'! See, I've taken two dollars from your pocketbook. Two is enough. After we go out we can stop at a restaurant for something to eat. I missed supper because I was in a hurry to see you. Where do you want to go? To the theater, or a movie? Or vaudeville?"

"I'd rather see a drama."

"But vaudeville is easier. We don't want to take in anything heavy today. We don't want to cry. Tell me, don't we want to laugh? We want to see the happy side of life. If you want to, you can also learn a lot from that. Don't you want to learn something today?"

"It never hurts to learn something."

"You know what? Why don't we go to a lecture?"

"A lecture about what?"

"How about a lecture on free love? Let's go! The head of the anarchist group today is speaking at Backwards Hall. Come, you can hear him talk and you'll have a lot to think about. Maybe today you'll finally understand. Come on, you won't regret it. Maybe you'll come away with an impression of me as someone who's not out to fool you. I'm not trying to get you to surrender to me against your will. I want your consent every step of the way. Do you understand? So, let's set off on the right foot!" He energetically gave these orders, and we set out into the street.

"It's so nice in the street!" I called out, in spite of myself.

"Yes, it is!" he exclaimed, as though he was responsible for it. "Everything will seem good to you today, because everything will change for you. You've had plenty of time to think it over, haven't you?"

"Yes."

"And you really do want to be like other women."

"Which other women?"

"Those who think about only today and spit on their tomorrows."

"Oh, those women. I'd love to meet someone like that and hear what they have to say."

"Listen to what I have to say. I'm like them. I'm one of the—"

"I don't want to hear from just any someone—I want to hear from a woman."

"What's the difference? A man, a woman—as far as relationships go, they are completely equal. Both of them must never forget to think about people as free, without any obligations, who are bound together just for as long as they love each other. When the love ends, so does the relationship. Do you see what I mean?"

"I see, I see. Tell me more."

He continued, "The trouble with most people is that they're inexperienced. It's no good dealing with inexperienced people. They heap on too many expectations and then they claim that they were fooled. They let themselves believe in eternal love, and then they're disappointed. Because there's no such thing. Nothing is eternal except eternity. When you set out to love, you should know that no one loves forever. Everything is temporary. Isn't that so?"

"Yes."

"Well, my dear," he continued, pleased with my "yes," caressing my hand, "that's what life is all about. You can't make plans for years and years. You have to keep your eyes open. You know, a lot of men won't be interested in a girl who's inexperienced. They don't want to waste their time enlightening you. The real problem is very young girls. They throw themselves into your arms and then they place the blame on someone else. They were forced! They're still innocent!"

"What a dirty trick!"

"Yes, it's a nasty business," C. said, blaming the nastiness on the girls, of course. "There's no such thing as being forced. But they say so, and people believe them. A friend of mine was thrown in jail because of a girl like that. I told him to take it easy with the young ones. If you want to get intimate, you should do it with an older, independent woman, who agrees to everything, so that no one has anything to complain about. Isn't that so?"

"Sure!"

"You understand me so well!" he cried, pulling my arms around him.

It's true. I understood him so well. As they say, I saw him clearly. I knew that he was trying to prepare me for everything. He wanted to protect himself now from anything I might later accuse him of being responsible for. I let him talk. He liked to hear himself talk, and to think that he was being heard.

His talk didn't convince me to *live* as he wanted me to, but the opposite. Sure that his talk wouldn't convince me of anything, I was able to walk with him and look proudly and openly in the eyes of passers-by.

C. didn't like the way I was looking at people. "You shouldn't look that man in the eye, it's not nice."

"Not nice? Why not?"

"He might think that you mean something by it."

"Oh, I see. Then why does he look at me that way?"

"He's a man."

"I see. But what's the difference?"

"What do you mean, what's the difference?"

"I mean—didn't you say that men and women are equal? Don't both have a right to be free and to look where they please?"

"Oh, so when you're walking with me you want to look at other men?"

"Truth be told, yes!"

"Well, that's an uncomfortable truth."

"Most truths are."

"That's also true."

∽

Sitting at a table at a dairy restaurant, C. opined in a serious tone, "It's remarkable that girls can be so modest, even if you don't tell them they have to be. Once they grow to be women they start to be disappointed and they lose their innocence. They lose their inhibitions and start looking you right in the eye, like they're about to order something. Men aren't like that."

"Men have nothing to lose."

"They certainly *do* have something to lose. There are men who are even more modest than women. They're really ashamed."

"They probably have something to be ashamed of."

"No, it's nothing like that. A while ago, when I was . . ."

" . . . a laughingstock?"

"For someone who has a big mouth."

C. looked at me for a while like he was trying to decide whether to chastise me for laughing at his seriousness or let me laugh so I'd stay happy. Taking away my pleasure might make me change my mind about the decision that he approved so heartily. He decided to educate me indirectly.

He declaimed, "Some girls, even when they become women, are able to preserve their girlish charm. The key to this charm is in not noticing the men who admire them. They don't pay them any heed at all. When a girl goes out with someone, she should give him her full attention. No one else should exist for her except for him."

"And what about him?"

"The same goes for him. For example, if I appeared to be interested in someone else while I was with you, that would be a personal insult to you. That would be wrong! Isn't that right?"

"I don't know. I'd only be insulted or disturbed by that behavior if I was jealous, and I'd only be jealous if I was with someone I loved."

"I'm jealous of others when I'm with you. Isn't that good?"

"It's not good."

"Why not? If it's a sign of love—don't you want me to love you?"

"Not like that. Not if it interferes with my freedom."

"What do you need freedom for?" He laughed dryly.

"To love whoever I want."

"Oh, maybe you want to love more than one man at a time?"

"Maybe!"

"I think there's no need for you to go to the lecture. You're already more open-minded than you should be to carry out a love affair. With you it's all or nothing."

"That's how it is with me."

The waiter served our latkes, and C. gobbled them down with an angry appetite. My remarkably quick self-development upset him. Now he was afraid that I wouldn't *stop* loving, even before I'd ever started.

As though he could read my mind, he explained, "I'm afraid that you'll exhaust your love too soon."

"Me too."

"Can't you see the beauty in it, or are you only capable of cynicism?"

"I don't know what I see. All I know is that if a man ever succeeds in besmirching my innocence, he won't ever succeed in making me forget his sin."

"Well," he responded, "even so, it's interesting to see how the innocent take to sin. Maybe by sinning you'll become more seductive and exciting. Virtue, however pure, is pale and boring. But sin, that's the stuff of life. Those who don't sin, they're the real sinners. In order to sin well, though, you must have elegance, tact, consistency and—"

"Anything else?" asked the waiter as he returned to our table, "Tea or coffee?"

C. stared at him for a moment as though confused, and then asked me what I wanted. What I wanted was a glass of water, but it's not nice to order something free, so I asked for a celery soda.

C. waited until the waiter went to a different table before telling me that he hated him. He always hates waiters. All they care about is their tips, and he's against them on principle. And, meanwhile, he forgot what he was saying before the waiter had interrupted.

I prompted him: "Elegance, tact, consistency, and—"

"—a good disposition!" he added.

"That's exactly what I don't have."

"Never mind. You'll get one," he reassured me. "The more you eat the hungrier you get. Do you want to order some more latkes?" he asked, scooping up the last latke. "Or are you in the mood for blintzes? Blintzes are more expensive."

"It depends how long we'll have to wait for them."

"Are we in a hurry? It's only a quarter to eight. The lecture won't start before eight thirty. Anyway," he said, conspiratorially, "if we have to leave the waiter a tip, let him work a little more for it. You really don't want anything else?"

"Nope."

"You know, you'd be a bargain to have as a wife," he said, laughing. "You hardly eat anything at all. Who are you looking at? Who did you see?"

I saw Rae with someone. They were standing in front of the door to the restaurant, trying to decide whether to come in. She saw us and started to come closer. Whoever it was who was with her followed.

"Who wants them here?" C. complained. "I didn't want to see anyone today. Absolutely no one. Only you. You and no one else. My dear, sweet darling—" He snuck in his endearments before the intruders arrived at our table.

Rae greeted us and introduced us to her escort, who turned out to be the young engineer. She had gone with him to see a birth control lecture. He carried a gray checked coat, soft gray hat, and a gray muff. Rae was dressed almost entirely in black, but her face looked gray and pale. His face was white and flushed, and the contrast made an impression.

They sat down at our table and waited for the waiter. Rae told us, "We want to go out somewhere, but don't know where to go. Mr. Davis," she said, gesturing toward the engineer, "wanted to go hear Emma Goldman talk about birth control, but I would rather see *Where Are My Children?* They say it's a very good movie, right?"

～

Rae asked C. the question about the movie directly because, she said, he knows everything. There's nothing he doesn't know!

C. thanked her for the compliment and gladly gave his opinion: *"Where Are My Children?* is plain old propaganda for having children! It's—"

"It's only propaganda for those who can afford to have them," Davis interrupted. "It's only for the rich. It's not concerned with the poor. The man in the film wants to have children and his wife doesn't."

"Why would the man want to have children?" C. laughed, bemused. "What kind of a man wants such a thing? Children are just a burden. In our times, in these circumstances, you can barely get by on your own. Even women are too preoccupied to want to burden themselves with children."

"Women think they can tie themselves to men by having children," Davis said. "There's truth to that, but woe to the woman whose husband stays with her only for the sake of the children!"

"What do you mean?" C. said, "It's certainly good for them. When a woman has children, a man has to support her. That's what all women are really after. They don't want to be independent. And without children, it's no good to be dependent. So children become an excuse for demanding regular wages from the man who had the misfortune to become a father."

Our knights in shining armor were so engrossed in conversation that they barely glanced at the steaming latkes they swallowed without noticing. Rae winked at me, telling me to pay attention to C.'s words. His heartfelt attitude toward birth control did not impress her. But she decided not to say anything. Her silence said enough. It was plain to see that she had made up her mind. She wouldn't consummate the affair, and she wouldn't wait either. If he would marry her now, then fine. If not, as she put it, "He can go to hell!"

"And where are you two going today?" Rae asked me.

"Wherever we feel like going," C. answered, cutting into our conversation. I knew that he didn't want to tell her where we were going so that they wouldn't come along.

"Come with us! Or we'll go wherever you're going!" Rae offered. I quickly agreed. I was hoping someone would keep us from our plans. I wanted C. to be annoyed with me so that he wouldn't want to come to my room after our evening out. I laughed to myself imagining the scene: he'd be so annoyed to find me indifferent after my earlier "alright." Still, I wanted to prevent that comedy, or at least to postpone it.

"So where are we going?" Rae asked again.

"Wait," I responded. "We'll walk out to the street and see what strikes our fancy."

As we waited by the door for our knights to pay the bill, Rae asked me to have a chat with her *yold*, that nitwit—maybe I'll have better luck finding out what he's after. I took a while to consider whether to agree to this. She asked, "Are you afraid your beau will be jealous? Or are you jealous of me? Do you think I'll steal him away from you if you leave me alone with him?"

I assured her that I wasn't worried about either of these things. By all means, she can certainly talk to him. I'd be glad of it.

"Talk to him. Whatever he says will be better than my not knowing anything, right?"

"I guess."

Our escorts made their way to us.

49

Our Knights

Let's go this way!" C. urged me, gesturing that he wanted to part ways with Rae and Davis.

"Where are we going?" asked Rae. "Why don't we all go to see *Where Are My Children?*"

We stood for a while arguing about where to go until we agreed not to decide on a destination, but to wander a little and stroll over the Brooklyn Bridge.

"We're better off this way," C. whispered to me. "After a long walk, it's so pleasant to return to your room . . ."

In order to free me up so I could sleuth about Davis, Rae took C. to the side. She simply *had* to ask him a question. She took his arm and walked ahead with him. I was left to walk with Davis.

"May I take your arm?" he asked, looking at Rae and C. "Allow me."

"If it's hard for you to walk on your own. Do you need someone's arm to support you?"

"I mean it might be more pleasant for you."

"It's all the same to me."

"I've heard that you're the kind of girl who likes to keep her distance. Rae told me so."

"If Rae says it, it's the truth. Rae doesn't lie. She also told me something about you."

"Oh, yes? What? I'm dying to know. Tell me, what did she say?"

I paused, considering what I should tell him from all that Rae had told me. "She said that you're a very nice young man."

"Is that all?"

"She told me a lot about you."

"What else?"

"Good things. You're working to make yourself a career, to be successful, to make a name for yourself and make a lot of money."

"That's not interesting. I meant what did she tell you about how I am at love? She must have told you all about it."

"When girls talk to each other they tell each other everything. It's almost a point of pride. It must be the same way with men."

We chuckled and C. pulled away from Rae to ask what I was laughing about. He wanted to laugh too. He pressed me to hurry home. He said he wanted to take me home soon because he had somewhere else to go later.

I knew what he meant. I told him that if he was in such a hurry we'd walk with him to the foot of the bridge and let him go his way. As for me, I'd just keep walking with our friends.

He was not at all pleased. He didn't know what to do. No matter how much Rae urged him to keep walking he didn't want to go. He sat down on a bench in angry silence.

"Sit with him," Rae laughed, "can't you see how pained he looks?"

"If you can't bear his pain, why don't *you* sit with him?" I retorted. "You interrupted me. I was in the middle of a conversation with Mr. Davis."

Rae sat with C. for a while. I walked on with Davis until we decided it was time to go home. C. refused to speak to me. Rae was eager to find out what Davis had to say about her. I looked at C.'s face and then invited Rae to spend the night in my room so that we could talk alone. Rae glanced at Davis and agreed.

I hope the curses that C. heaped upon Rae when she told him she was spending the night with me never come true. Davis also scowled at me when he heard the news. As Rae put it, both of our knights just stood there humiliated while we left them behind, like they'd been turned to stone.

☙

Rae wanted to know what I thought of Dave, as she called him. I told her, "He's far from ugly and not a fool, but he's not—logical.

He doesn't even know what he wants. Maybe it's because he's so young."

"He's not all that young," Rae insisted. "I'm not much older than him."

"I was only guessing based on his looks."

"Does he look much younger than me?"

"It's hard to answer a question like that. It depends who you ask."

"What if I told you that you don't look any younger than Mr. Cheek. Wouldn't that bother you at all?"

"Why should it? But the comparison isn't a good one. We're not about to get married."

"You aren't even talking about it?"

"No."

"He's only after an affair?"

"That's all!"

"And what about you? What do you want?"

"Nothing."

"That's not true."

"You're right. It's not true," I admitted. "What I want is to learn how he plans to convince me with his vaunted ideals and heartfelt principles. I want test my willpower against his desire. I want to see how strong I can be in standing up to each new argument. When I'm with him I can study myself and understand myself better. I can—"

"These are nothing but empty words!" Rae interrupted impatiently. "The truth is that you like him but you won't admit it because you doubt that he is capable of loving you as long as you want him to."

"If that's what you want to think about me, go ahead. I don't care."

Rae paused. "What I really think is that neither of us is suited for the sort of life that they want. We take life seriously. We think about the consequences of things. They only want to live for the present. They shut out any thought of the past or the future and think only of right now. Maybe if we were in their shoes we'd be no different."

"Maybe."

"Do you really think I look too old?"

"No, I think he looks too young."

"What's the difference? But I feel so young! What does it mean to be young, if it isn't to feel young?" Rae cried exasperatedly.

"Being young is looking young. A woman's only as young as she looks. A man's as young as he feels."

"I'll have to figure out how to look younger. The way I dress makes me look older than I am. That's what Mr. Cheek told me today. He knows what he's talking about. What do you think?"

"The same as I said before."

"Today he asked me what my landlords are like. He wanted to know how they act when people come to visit me and when I stay in. He asked if I wanted him to come visit me. What do you think I should've said?"

"What did you say?"

"Well, I asked him how he would find the time to visit me, when he has to go to see you?"

"What did he say?"

"He says he can find the time to do whatever he wants. The question is whether I want it. Should he come to see me? I told him to ask you first. If you don't care if he comes to see me, then let him! The only thing that will come of it is that my engineer might get jealous and—well, maybe not. He would probably just start seeing you instead. You certainly captured his attention."

"Really?"

"Really. It hardly takes anything to grab their attention. One word, one smile, one walk, and that's it! Their love bursts into flame like newly lit kindling. It doesn't hurt that you look younger than me. As you say, the only thing that matters is how we look." Rae forced a laugh. "You know what? Why don't we switch?"

She talked about them like a horse trader.

50

Begging Forgiveness

C. came to see me to give me a chance to apologize! "Apologize? For what?" I stared at him in disbelief.

"For—you know what. It isn't nice to play with someone's nerves like that—to give hope, awaken desire, and then walk around in the street like a fool with some *idiot* and go back to your room with a silly girl. Why do you spend time with her? What do you need a friend like that for? She's so *prost*. She really has no manners at all! And what about her boyfriend, that engineer-to-be, with his birth control and her *Where Are My Children?* How could you stand to walk arm in arm with him? I saw how close he was holding you! And you just laughed along with it. What were you laughing about?"

"I just felt like laughing," I said, and laughed.

"Yesterday you wanted to laugh with him, tomorrow it will be with some other man. How could any man ever trust you enough to think of something like marrying you? When a girl is so free with herself before marriage, you can't expect any better from her after the wedding."

"Is that so?"

"That's how it is." He wanted me to apologize and swear to him that it would never happen again. I would have done it, but I have some self-respect.

He grew angrier and stormed to the door with his hat in his hand. He flung it open and started closing it behind him slowly. Then, before it was closed, he turned back toward me to give me another chance to apologize! I was so outraged at his audacity that I stood there, speechless.

"Apologize, before it's too late," he demanded.

I wanted to laugh in his face. But I held myself back, though a smile quivered on my lips.

"I'll say it one last time. Apologize!"

I couldn't hold myself back and I guffawed.

"Don't laugh!"

"Don't make such a fool of yourself!"

"You're driving me wild!"

"There's no reason for that."

"No, you'll see. You'll regret this. You'll miss me. You'll fall on your feet and beg for forgiveness, but it'll be too late. I'll be totally indifferent to you. You'll be a victim of your own stubbornness. You'll sit alone in your room, heartbroken. You'll wander the earth with your arms reaching out for me, but you'll never get me back!" he warned.

"What a clever tongue you have!"

"Be quiet! This is no time for your ironic tone!" he chided.

"This is no time for you to be here!" I rebuked.

"I have a right to be here whenever I want."

"Go!" I cried, showing him the door.

"My God!" he interjected, staring at me in surprise. "You look so beautiful in that pose! Oh, I beg you, hold your arm like that just a little longer. Please don't put it down! If only I had a camera. Why didn't you take to the stage? You were made for the stage. Who knows what great talent you've wasted. Give me your hand. I long to kiss it!"

This is a new trick, I thought to myself. I didn't give him my hand. I didn't want him to think he could change my mind so easily.

He stepped closer to me and fell to his knees, grasping for my hand. When he didn't get it, he bent his head and grabbed my legs with his hands so that I had to hold onto the edge of the rocking chair to keep from falling down.

Since I wouldn't beg him for forgiveness, he decided to beg me for it instead.

"Please, you must forgive me! I didn't treat you well. I was wild with jealousy. I didn't sleep all night. I talked out loud to you. I loved you and hated you because I loved you so much."

"Let go of my legs!"

"You see? I'm kissing your legs. They aren't your legs, they are *my* legs. They've crept their way deep into my heart. They've sauntered into my soul. It kills me to know that these legs were walking with another man last night! And with such an *idiot!* Can it be, that you would consider exchanging me for him?"

"It's hard for me to stand like this."

"Take a seat. I'll lie here by your feet like a loyal dog after a long hunt."

I didn't like the idea of carrying on this way until dawn. As soon as he let go of my legs so that I could sit down I went to my window and looked out on the street, wondering what I was going to do with him. The street, full of people paying attention to their own business, pushed me away from the cold window. I looked over at C. He held his head in his hands like a true martyr, prostrate on his knees before the empty rocking chair.

⁓

I contemplated this romantic pose, trying to decide whether to help him to his feet or wait for his knees to start hurting so that he would get up on his own.

The light in the hallway was already extinguished. The old, sick, deaf and blind German lady must already be asleep. The gas lamp in my room threw pale shadows at the wall. The alarm clock, with its monotonous ticking, announced that time was passing.

If only it wasn't C., but A., who was here in my room at this hour to take my hand and drive away the rosy brown shadows from my wall. Cloaked in darkness, I'd sit next to him on the footstool, gazing at him and burying my face in his arms. Wordlessly, I'd tell him everything that I feel. But it wasn't A., it was C. I didn't go to him. I regretted playing at love with him so much, even though I used to enjoy it. I don't want to lose myself to someone like that. I only want to love if I can find someone who deserves it.

He got up and sat in the rocking chair. He stared at the bent tops of his unpolished shoes, and from time to time he looked away from them to steal a glance at me. He thought for a while, then he stood up and made his way to the door tiredly.

"Good bye!" he whispered in a quivering voice, not looking at me.

"Good bye!" I responded sympathetically to his dejectedness.

"I'm going now."

I nodded in response to this pronouncement.

"Yes, I'm going away," he sighed, gazing at the wall. But he still didn't leave. He still stood there.

"I can't humiliate myself like this anymore."

"Of course not," I wanted to agree with him. But seeing that it might be better not to say anything at all, I kept my mouth shut.

"It would've been better if I'd never come. I was too democratic in my taste. A man should know where he belongs. Don't you think so?"

"Yes—"

"And I forgot myself. I've learned my lesson. Next time, when someone deserves my apology I won't fall at their feet. No matter how developed my aesthetic sensibilities are, I'll suppress my passion for such a pose, which seems to me so attractive."

He waited for a while, hoping I'd say something. When I didn't respond, he continued. "The ancient Greeks represented love in the form of a woman with a torch. Modern women carry torches too, but not to light the way toward love. They use it to see the men and find out if the men can support them, if they'll be able to get steady jobs.

"Oh, yes," he remembered suddenly, "I borrowed two dollars from you yesterday. Don't worry, I'll pay you back. What a waste, to spend them on an evening with your tactless friend. And today? How are we spending our time?"

"Standing in one place."

I was hoping to remind him that he was supposed to be leaving. But he took it differently. He moved away from the door and made himself comfortable.

51

Ishkabibble

It's foolish to waste the best minutes of our life being jealous. You don't have to forgive me; I don't have to forgive you. We both have a right to behave however we want," he proclaimed.

Without giving me the time to say that I had the right to give him no right to be in my room and to behave however he wanted, he asserted his right to behave exactly the way I was hoping he wouldn't.

He turned down the gas, made it dark, and began his overtures. "My darling!" he cried enthusiastically. "I love you so! Molière had it right when he said that the love of a jealous man is like hatred. How I hated you yesterday! Why? Because I was jealous. Of whom? Of that nobody, that birth control lover! Next to me, he's nothing but a *karlik*. He has no more in his head than I have in my heel. And who knows, he might even be married! Is he married?"

"I don't know if he's married, or even if he's against the institution entirely, and I don't care."

"Then I don't want to hear any more about it. As long as you aren't interested in him, that's good enough for me. I beg you a thousand times over, don't revive my jealousy. Ask what you will of me; your wish is my command!"

I responded, "I don't want to drive you away. I enjoy your company because you're so educated. But it would be better if you left. If I had a nicer, more comfortable room, maybe it would be more pleasant for you to stay longer."

"That's childish," he scolded me. "You want to put off an opportunity for love because of the way your room looks. The things you come up with! *Amor*, the god of love, will transform this simple room into paradise. You'll forget where you are entirely."

I didn't want to forget where I was. I reminded him that he'd promised not to take his holy ideal by force. So he shouldn't pull at my blouse like that!

"Well, fine," he said. "I won't pull at it." Instead he suggested that I take it off myself. You can't see anything in the dark, so what is there to be ashamed of? What do I have to hide from him anyway? Doesn't he know all about me already? He knows me much better than I do myself. And one more thing, if I really want him to stay calm, I shouldn't protest, because resisting love is like throwing oil on a flame. Is that what I mean to do? Throw oil on a flame?

No, I didn't want to throw oil on a flame. I didn't want him to want me at all. I wanted him to let me sit by myself, and for him to sit by himself too. If the German lady saw how he trampled her ancient quilt with his muddy shoes—

"Then I'll take off my shoes," he said. "It's very uncomfortable to sleep in all this."

"Do you mean to say—"

"Yes, my dear. That's what I mean to say, and what I mean to do. I mean that this night was especially made for—"

I didn't want to hear what the night was especially made for. Before he could stow his shoes under my bed I wrapped myself in a long coat and stole out of my room.

ᔆᕽ

I ran into the street as though evil spirits were chasing me. I went several blocks, my thoughts awhirl, and then stood still in front of a path to a little park with a few bare trees. The dry, thin branches bent toward and away from me like the whips of angry horsemen. Passers-by stared at me. It was already almost midnight. What could they be thinking about a woman out alone, walking in a side street next to a secluded park?

The thought that C. might come looking for me here sent me back to my home. I paced back and forth on the sidewalk outside my window like a watchman. "A fine situation I'll be in," I thought to myself, "if C. falls asleep in my room!"

Now my running away started to seem foolish to me. Now he'll think I was really scared of him. Well, let him think so! Who cares what he thinks?

"In love, as in war, it's very nice to win," I said to myself in his voice. But I answered myself, "Sometimes it's better to retreat."

The old door of my building disgorged a manly figure. It was—not C. I couldn't even smile to myself at the impression my night wanderings in front of the building must be making. The policeman standing at the corner had already begun to take notice of me. I thought of the Tenement House Act and pictures from the news flashed before my eyes. I already felt like I'd been arrested and carted away.

Suddenly, there was C.! He emerged from the front door into the street and looked around. I thought of hiding from him and then going back inside once he went away. But he'd already spotted me. He started to cross the street.

"Why did you run away?" he asked.

I gave no answer. I wanted to walk right past him, but he didn't let me.

"There's no reason to run away from here. The street is not a bedroom."

"Let me go!"

"And if I don't?"

"If you don't?" I gestured toward a policeman.

"Oh, so you want to be famous, do you? You want your name in all the newspapers?" He laughed out loud. "Or maybe you want to spend the night in a police station?"

I didn't want any of those things. I didn't answer his questions.

"Come closer," he coaxed, taking my hand. "Let's take a walk together. Let's try to understand each other better. I'm not talking about grabbing and fondling. We'll talk about certain things that can happen between two grown people who have a right to do whatever they want."

∽

After we walked for a while, C. began to complain that his legs hurt and he wanted to sit down and rest. I led him to the little park and showed him a bench.

"In such a cold park?"

"It's not so cold, and it's not such a park. But if your legs are bothering you so much, we can sit here awhile."

"But what were you so afraid of about just staying in your room?" he cried. "You know what? If you're so afraid of your own room, why don't you come to mine? Come, I'll take you there."

"You'll *take* me."

"*Take* you?" He chuckled callously. "As though you were a fifteen year old girl, so naïve, so innocent!"

"You can still be innocent, even if you are two times fifteen."

"How can you prove that you're innocent? You can't prove it with any facts. There's no way you could convince me. You want me to take you at your word? If I want to, I'll believe you. If I don't, I won't. What can you do about it?"

"Maybe I could explain it to you if you would just yell a little quieter."

He sat down on the bench and looked me in the eyes, demanding, "Do you love me?"

"Well . . ." I hesitated.

"Do you want to marry me?"

"Well . . ."

"And I don't," he stated flatly.

"You don't? Fine, so be it."

"So be it?!" he yelled, enraged at my indifference.

"Fine, if that's how it is," I repeated.

"Oh, shut up!" he cried.

"How dare you? You didn't marry me, and you have no right to yell at me like that," I scolded coolly.

"I didn't marry you and I never will!"

I pooh-poohed his exclamation, saying, "*Ishkabibble!* Why should I care?"

Now he was really angry. He looked for a way to shake my composure. I waited for him to come up with more and more insults that I could respond to with my "*ishkabibble.*" There's nothing worse you can do to someone who's seeing red and wants to get a rise out of someone else than to respond with indifference and trite phrases. But, as always, when he saw that his bad behavior wasn't accomplishing anything, he changed tacks.

I shouldn't be so hard on him, he said. I should understand that when I don't show him any affection it makes him sick, he gets so upset that he hardly knows what he's saying. He's never loved someone so much in his whole life. He's even afraid he won't pass this year and will have to repeat his college classes, all because of me. It's like Tolstoy said: "It's hard to love a woman and do anything."

He spewed aphorisms, cited great men, excused himself with the words of others, and then asked me to forgive him. But I was certain that even as he was trying to be good to me he was hatching another plan against me. Good! The more he schemed against me, the less I would feel about him. And in a battle like this one, the less you feel the more you win.

Angry with me and the whole world, C. left me at the front door without so much as a "good night." I tiptoed into my own room like a thief.

When I came back to my room I heard quiet footsteps from the German lady's room, and I was grateful that I was alone. I undressed in the dark and lay down in bed. I felt a gush of relief that I had no one to run from anymore.

I could still hear her footsteps behind the door. They were heavy steps, and the floorboards creaked under them.

From behind my wardrobe, in the rodents' clubroom, there was a mass meeting. One member yelled something and the others protested. Things got out of hand and to quiet them down the German lady, or perhaps her son, pounded on their side of the closet. The pounding worked for a while. But soon the noise started up again. I tucked myself tightly in my quilt, hoping that when their meeting disbanded they wouldn't come to visit me in bed.

I couldn't sleep. I lay with my eyes half-open and thought, "There's no end to it with him! One minute he's terrible, the next he's good, and then he's back to being bad again. If he can't go over, he goes under. He believes in getting there any way he can."

I drove him out of my thoughts and thought about A. instead. In my imagination I gazed into A.'s eyes and waited to hear what he had to say to me. I waited for him to tell me to leave C. once and for all, to run away from my room so that no one except for A. would know my address. But he didn't say anything. He didn't care what happened to me. My eyelids grew heavy with tears, and I closed my eyes painfully. I fell into a fitful sleep plagued by a gnawing deep in my heart.

～

I was awakened by the loud ruckus of wheels driving over the brick streets. I felt like my head was filled with clay. When I opened my eyes my heart sunk. The blood froze in my veins. A pair of sharp, burning eyes stared at me through the curtained window over which the German lady had strung paper baskets of hats.

When the German lady came in to water her plant, I told her that she could put the room up for rent the next week. She was silent for a while, and then she said, "Alright." She left, and then came back, was silent again for a while and then said "Alright" again and left the room.

Now I'll need to find another room.

52

I Can't Get Unstuck

Finally!

Finally I am free of that *nudnik* and the German lady and her room, and the patchwork quilt, and the icons, and the horrible feeling that I was going to fall into a net with my soul chained to "enlightenment"!

Now I feel like things are looking up—up to the fifth floor! I'm in a small but clean room in the home of a good, simple, poor Jewish family. My new landlady, Mrs. Kotik, is an old woman with a kind, motherly face and soft, youthful eyes. She views me with pride. I'm just the sort of girl she wanted to have stay with her. So quiet and composed—like an angel!

That's how I am now. I can feel it. My whole self is filled with longing to be quiet and composed, to hardly be anything at all. From my room I look down at the street and the people seem so small. I look up and I wish I were even higher. I hardly understood my landlady as she said, "It's hard to climb up here, but once you're up it's nice. No one to bother you. No dirty water to fall on your head from the clothesline above. There's plenty of air here. It's bright too. Such a pleasure!"

The noise of the street barely reaches here. I feel disconnected from the world. I'll be able to read here, and think, and dream . . .

Now that I'm here I'm going to write more often to my relatives who are far away. I'll go to lectures, I'll attend night school. I won't waste my time anymore.

No, once something gets stuck on me, I can't get unstuck!

It happened when I ran into my landlady one day. I was coming home from work one evening and Mrs. Kotik greeted me with a motherly smile, telling me that she had something to say to me. She would come see me in my room. She came in. "What'll you give me if I tell you something?" she asked with a playful smile.

"It depends on what you have to say," I answered, returning her smile.

"It's something good. Guess!"

"I can't guess."

"Can't you? The long and short of it is that I met your fiancé here today!"

"My what?!"

"Yes! He wants to make up with you. He told me everything. Absolutely everything. You argued over something or other and won't talk to him anymore. He's happy to do whatever you want, he says, as long as things can be as they were. There's no need to hurry with the wedding. You can wait until he finishes school. He says that you should wait a little. He says it's for your sake—things will be better for you that way. He seems like a fine young man. Educated, modern, and he even speaks Yiddish. How is it that you've been staying with me for two weeks now and you never once told me that you're engaged? Young men are not like girls, you know, they don't hold back."

She was so eager to talk about my young man that she practically accosted me for—not being like a man. I didn't know how to respond, so I pretended to rummage around for something that I didn't really need. She continued, "In my foolish opinion, a girl shouldn't let herself get so angry. You should make up with him. Of course, it's always better when more people know that you're a couple. If one person wants to split up and the other doesn't, it can be useful, legally speaking—I'd be the first to act as a witness to vouch that you're engaged to him, that he told me himself that he's your fiancé.

"I'll tell you, just like a mother would, that it's better to have the wedding over and done with and to take yourself off the market. If you end up waiting awhile too bad! What can you do? But you shouldn't be a fool, and you should know how to behave until that lucky hour. Surely, you must know what I mean, that waiting is—waiting. Other girls sit alone with their fiancés until late at night. That's no good. First, it's not healthy when you have to get up early and you didn't get a good night's rest. Second, you'll get bored of one another. There's nothing new to find out about each other. Everything is good in moderation. I can talk with you more about that later. Now I have to go serve supper."

⟡

My "fiancé" came to see me.

Actually, he didn't come to see me directly—he came to visit Mrs. Kotik.

Mrs. Kotik came to me and asked if I wanted to go out to see him or whether he could come into my room. Because he told her that he's happy with either: I can come to him or he can come to me. Although, of course, *I* am the guilty party, but since he's such a gentleman, he'll give the lady some deference. He'll be the first one to try to set things right.

"Good evening," he began, speaking in English. Unable to wait until Mrs. Kotik brought him an answer from me, he spoke to me from outside my room, where I'd left the door somewhat ajar. I closed the door tightly.

"What are you doing?" my landlady scolded, as though insulted on his behalf. "How can you slam the door in a man's face like that? Whatever you have to say, you should at least say *something* to him! Give him a chance to speak."

She ran after him to excuse my behavior, begging him to have a seat. She told him I wasn't dressed yet, and that I'd come down to see him when I was ready. He had completely won her over.

They say that "the world loves a man in love." And so it is. The world loves him, and especially women love him. Mrs. Kotik, seeing how in love he was with me, the poor sweet man, told me that I must give him a chance to speak his heart. She was afraid he wouldn't survive his heartache. "Only one of two things can come of this," she argued, "and whether it goes one way or the other, the least you can do is talk to him!" Eventually, she prevailed upon me to go out and speak to him. She left us in the front room and retreated to the kitchen.

C. stood up from the rocking chair. "Good evening," he began in English again, bowing slightly. "I see that you're still mad at me . . ."

"What do you want from me?" I asked tersely.

"Forgive me!"

"Will that make you go away? If you'll go away after I forgive you and you won't come back again, then I'll gladly forgive you."

"Is that an ultimatum?"

"It is what it is."

"I understand it differently. Your current behavior is obviously an expression of your love for me. Yes, your love. The more you try to drive me away from you, the more you show me that you aren't indifferent to me after all!"

"Fine. Our conversation is closed. I need to go now."

"I'll come along."

"Not with me."

"Then I'll follow you."

"Goodbye!" I called, returning to my room and closing the door behind me.

"So, did you make up?" Mrs. Kotik asked, returning from the kitchen to the front room.

"Yes!" he said. "But I can't stay any longer today. I have to go, but I'll be back tomorrow. Goodnight, Madame, and thank you very much."

"Oh, you're very welcome," answered Mrs. Kotik, moved by his gratitude. "You can thank me by dancing with me at your wedding, God willing."

∽

My landlady thanks her lucky stars that she has me. She's never seen such a lovely girl in her life. So well-behaved, so reliable. And with a fiancé, to boot!

"He's crazy about you!" she teases. "Just one smile from you makes an ordinary day into a holiday for him. You'll make it so that he won't be able to wait until he graduates. He'll soon be begging you to marry him right away." She advises me, "Just keep on doing what you're doing. Make him keep his distance. Don't sit together in the dark. Never mind about the cost of gas. We're talking about something far more important here. You know what I mean."

I know what she means. I like to listen to her talk and see how proud she was that I follow all of her advice. "These days, a child doesn't follow her own mother's advice so closely as she follows mine. It's because she is a dear girl, so dependable and good. You should have such good fortune!"

53

A Fiancé's Rights

Rae came to see me. She loyally nodded her head as she listened to my landlady rattle off my good qualities. When the landlady left, Rae angrily asked, "How did you end up with such a busybody?"

"She's a good woman," I protested.

"Good?! Just your luck!"

"She means well."

"Let her mean whatever she wants, as long as she keeps quiet. How did she come to get involved between you and him? How is it any of her business?"

"From a business standpoint, it's nobody's business."

"Maybe it's none of my business either. But it's funny. What does Mr. Cheek think of all this? Out of nowhere, there's a mother-in-law to deal with!"

I told Rae that I didn't care what Mr. Cheek thought about it. He can think whatever he wants. His presenting himself to the landlady as my fiancé hadn't brought us any closer. I make a strict bride-to-be.

Rae laughed. I might put the wedding on the line by being so strict. A fiancé who's such a radical might jilt a reactionary bride-to-be. She, Rae, knows what kind of specimen he is. He visited her during the few weeks when he wasn't coming to see me, and "My God!" she exclaimed, I'd be shocked if I heard everything she could tell about him.

❧

Mrs. Kotik is always singing C.'s praises: he's such a well-educated young man, but his behavior with her is so simple and straightforward. He knows how to act around a *mishteyns gezogt* simple *yidene* like

267

herself. A few times, she invited him to her table and he didn't refuse. He ate and even praised her cooking! She asked him to listen to how well her children speak English and he listened and promised to bring them some books that they needed. "Not that I begrudge you anything, but I wish a man like that were engaged to my own daughter!"

He didn't visit me at home. Instead, he came to see Mrs. Kotik. He read her the latest news from the paper, told her this and that, lectured her a little about children and economics. He tried to curry favor with the simple, well-meaning woman.

I came in from the street and quietly went straight to my room. They were in the front room, talking to each other. "Do you think that I'd ever try to force her?" C. asked. "What is she? If I wanted to, I could get ten more like her."

"Of course you could," agreed Mrs. Kotik. "But why would you need so many? Have a wedding, get married, and get yourself off the market!"

"Did she tell you that she wants to get married?"

"She? She doesn't say anything. She only listens to what I say. Just as if I were her own mother! She's such a godsend, that girl. If I were a young man, I'd marry her as soon as I could. I'd be afraid that some other man might snatch her first!"

"No one snatches girls away so quickly these days."

"That's true. But when a girl sees a man hesitating, waiting, not saying anything, if she sees that he's namby-pamby, *ni be ni me*, not willing to commit, sooner or later she'll find someone else who'll take her up faster."

"She doesn't have anyone else, though. Does she?"

"Maybe she does. Neither you nor I can be sure. How do we know who she meets outside the house? She's not home today. Maybe she met a young man and went for a walk with him."

"What kind of behavior is that? Tell me, what do you think? Is it acceptable for her to go on a walk with another man when she already has a fiancé?"

"A fiancé today, a fiancé tomorrow. What good is a fiancé who keeps putting everything off for later?"

"Why is she in such a hurry?"

"You said yourself that she's not such a young woman anymore."

"Yes, she might even be older than I am."

"Older, younger, it doesn't matter. After the wedding, it doesn't make a difference. She is, for all her faults, just like a child to me. Listen, I made a borscht and *teygekhts* so good that it's fit for a president! Try it! It'll make your mouth water."

He went off to taste my landlady's food and I left my room as stealthily as I'd entered it. I stayed out for a while. I bought a few things and went to see a moving picture.

When I came back C. wasn't there anymore. Mrs. Kotik told me that he waited for me a long time. She thought he'd die from waiting! He couldn't even enjoy his food.

"Sometimes it's good to give your fiancé a hard time," she advised with a diplomatic smile. "Let him know that he's not the only man in the world. But everything in moderation. This time it was probably for the best that he felt bad, but pulling such a clever trick next time might be foolish."

Mrs. Kotik made it her business to manage our affairs.

"I'm your fiancé!" C. proclaimed. "And I have a fiancé's rights! Everyone should know that."

He said that it was embarrassing that his bride-to-be is so cold to him. Who would have thought that in taking the title "fiancé" he'd become like a stranger to me? After all, he chided, he was taking a risk on me. Now, if he left me, I could bring him up on a "breach of promise" charge, with Mrs. Kotik as my witness.

I assured him that I wouldn't press such charges. He said that he knew I wouldn't. I'm too intelligent for that. I'm not the kind of girl who would force him to marry, and that's why he loves me so much. That's why he believes that free love is the best thing for us.

I told him that I believe it would be the worst thing—for me.

He got very angry. He said that I am narrow-minded, with bourgeois values, and that he wouldn't talk to me about it anymore. Let his tongue be cut out of his mouth if he does!

I agreed.

I started to sew something and he read the newspaper.

"Feh!" he spat. "To pay so much money for a meaningless ceremony!"

I looked up from my handiwork and looked at him questioningly.

"It's a scandal!" he said, showing me the newspaper. "This man takes a poor, fallen girl—a *fallen* girl, mind you—and has a legal wedding with her. Then he gets rich. Very, very rich. He mingles in high society. He meets a pretty, young, respectable girl and falls in love with her. The law gets hold of it and they bring him before a court and charge him, and make him pay the legal wife a large sum of money each week in support, and on top of that she gets half of the revenue from his estate. Isn't it a scandal?"

"No."

"No? Why does *she* deserve the money?"

"Why do you think he was right to leave her? He probably broke her heart."

"And the money will fix it?!"

"Of course not. But without the money, things would be a lot worse for her."

"Yes, worse! But marriage didn't stop him from leaving her and falling in love with someone else! So what good is it?" C. cried triumphantly.

"Yes, but he didn't marry the other woman. He's forced to have a free love affair with the other woman."

He argued for a while longer about the injustice of the justice system. It doesn't let a free man hold his head up. It gets mixed up in his private affairs! He is definitely going to give a lecture on this topic, he told me. He tore out the article from the newspaper and stuffed it in his pocket.

Once and for all, I *must* get rid of C.!

Today, Rae came to see me when C. was here. He teasingly asked after her birth control advocate.

Rae answered, "Mr. Davis is alright."

"And what about his birth control? And your *Where Are My Children?*"

"They're much better than your free love affairs."

"Don't talk like that in front of my bride-to-be! For shame!"

"Oh? Since when?"

"You don't need to know."

"Yes, I certainly do. If you've been engaged for a while, I have to complain to her for not telling me, her good friend, about it. And if it just happened then I have to congratulate you."

"Congratulate us."

"I wish you all the—" Rae began, but I didn't let her finish, explaining that it was all in fun. "We're *nothing*," I told her. He laughed.

"Oy, you're laughing about this? This is no laughing matter!" Rae warned with an affected sigh. "I know another young man who laughed like that and he died laughing," Rae added, laughing along with him.

C. told her that she shouldn't express herself in a way that is as simple and vulgar as she is. Rae ignored him and turned toward me, saying, "Should I clam up, or should I give him what's coming to him?"

"Whatever you want."

"So you really aren't engaged?"

"No, and I don't want to be."

"If that's so, then Mr. Cheek," she said, turning toward him, "now that I know I have no risk of breaking apart the *shidukh*, I can tell you that I think you're a fool!"

"*Shut*—"

"Never mind your 'shut up.' After all, it's not a very elevated word to use, especially for someone who is going to graduate college soon. If you get fresh with me, I'll tell your bride-to-be what you said to me when you were visiting me at home the other day."

"Never kiss an ugly girl! Everyone says that, and now you've proven them right!" C. laughed. "Fine, go ahead and say what I said to you the other day. I've told her plenty about other encounters with women and nothing you can say will surprise her."

Who knows what their argument would have led to if I hadn't asked him to leave, and if Davis hadn't arrived at the same time. I suggested that we all take a walk together. Davis supported my plan. C. was against it. Rae was neutral.

When we got to the street, C. and Rae kept on arguing. Both of them were upset that Davis was walking with me.

❧

For a while I was amazed that Rae is so opposed to C. But after hearing what Davis had to say, there was nothing to wonder at. C. insulted her in Davis's presence, telling him that girls like Rae are only useful for telling about your interest in other girls.

Davis thinks that he was talking about me. Because Rae told him that she had mostly talked with him about me.

Davis says that he believes her. Because I'm the kind of person that people could have a lot to say about. Precisely because I'm so good at not talking. I keep quiet with a silence that seems to speak for itself.

He said that he could never get tired of talking about my silence. And when I say something, it's always worth listening to. And I have a smile that goes straight to his heart. And I carry myself like someone lost in thought. And I'm proud, and don't bother with the ordinary people that I meet along my way.

After he said all of that to me, we were quiet for a while. I could hear C. saying to Rae, "You keep talking when there's no need for it. Your laughter tries my patience. To you, all people are equal, and there's no difference between them."

Rae said to him, "You always have something to say about other people, but you have no self-awareness. The way you look at women makes them feel like you're spitting at them. Your cynical smile never leaves your lips. You only have one thing on your mind."

Catching up to Rae, I took her arm and we left the "gentlemen" behind. I didn't want her to feel jealous that I was walking with Davis.

"You're walking with me but you're still thinking about one of those men," she accused.

"When I was walking with them, with one of them, I was thinking about *you!*" I responded.

"You were thinking about how unnecessary I am."

"I was thinking about what a martyr you are. Why would you even consider going for a walk with someone you despise so much?"

"And you went for a walk with someone that you—"

"Do not like."

"You don't like anyone."

"Unfortunately, that's true."

She thought for a while, then added, "If you'd like to pretend to be interested in Mr. Davis to annoy your cynical man, I can help you with that. As they say, 'Sometimes it's worth putting out your own eye, if it takes out two of his.'"

Without waiting for an answer, she turned toward Davis, feigning jealousy, and told him that I'd certainly be happier talking with him than with her.

"Isn't it remarkable?" Davis said, taking her place next to me. "I just knew somehow that you two were talking about me. What did you ask Rae about me?"

"I wanted to know about your *yikhes*."

He started to tell me about his family background. Meanwhile, Rae played the part of an insulted girlfriend, trying to make C. more jealous. It worked.

Later on, C. needled me, "It's good that we haven't gotten married yet. Can you imagine how horrible it would be if you fell in love with that engineer after the wedding? What would we do then?"

"I don't think loving someone is horrible, even after the wedding."

"Oh, of course, it's all the more cozy."

"What else is a divorce for?"

"Would you divorce me for an idiot like that? Very nice! And you're already planning on a divorce, from the get-go! You can go ahead and have an affair with him. I won't interfere!"

"Thanks."

"Oh, there's no need for thanks. You're free to do whatever you want."

"Yes, of course."

"Do you really love him?"

"I like him well enough."

C. glared at me with his teeth clenched. He didn't want to talk about it anymore.

54

Regret

Today, C. came to me proposing that if he wasn't willing to go entirely against his principles, he might be willing to bend them a little bit.

"Alright," he said, "I'll give in. As soon as I graduate, we'll be husband and wife, for all the world to see. In the meantime, we can get a marriage license. We'll go to a court or a rabbi later. For now, you'll support yourself, as you have been doing. We'll live separately. And we won't have any children."

I understood what he meant. I didn't invite him into my room, I didn't throw him out, and I didn't scream or curse. I just stood there for a while silently, and then I said, "It's too late."

"Too late? What do you mean, too late? Too late at night? Or too late in life?"

"Too late in life," I answered. "I'm in love with someone else."

He looked at me with confusion and angst, and then asked again, as though he didn't believe what he'd heard, "You love someone else?"

"Yes."

"So—you love someone else. And does he love you back?"

"I think so."

"Does he want to marry you?"

"Oh, I don't care what he wants!"

"Would you have a free love affair with him?"

"Yes," I answered in a hushed voice, like I was admitting to a sin.

"But not with me?"

"No."

"Why would you have one with him, but not with me?"

"Because I'm in love with him."

"How long have you loved him? Tell me! How long?"

"You don't measure love in how long. Only how much."

"Do you love him so much?"

"Very!"

He was quiet for some time and then he asked, glowering, what made me love "him" so much. I responded to his question truthfully.

"It's hard to answer that question."

"Did you tell him that you love him?"

"Such a thing need not be said."

He interrogated me further. "Honestly," I told him, it was thanks to him, to C., that I was able to love this man so much. He opened my eyes to life. C. showed me how not to be so calculating and controlled when it comes to love. C. was the first one to teach me that you only live once, and that you should take all that you can from life, because you're living today and tomorrow you may die. In short, I gave him a long explanation using his own explications. My voice was full of obedience to this inevitable truth. I told him that I had decided to give in to life itself, which is stronger than I am.

"Do you mean to say that I awakened you to life, just so you could give yours to someone else?" he asked incredulously, like a man who was buried alive, looking up at me desperately as I walked by. "Why did I do it?"

I told him that yes, I was giving it to someone else. I'll never forget all he's done for me. I'll be forever grateful.

Humiliated, he and his principles walked away.

There's nothing worse in the world than regret. It's like a sickness without a cure.

C. is full of regrets that he had not made me his one once and for all.

"There was a time," he told me today, "that you wanted, with all your heart, to have me as yours forever. Didn't you want to go with me from the intellectuals' home to city hall to take out a marriage license?"

"Yes, I did," I agreed, to make matters worse.

"And there were moments when you would have given yourself to me without a license too. Why didn't I take the opportunity when I had it?"

"Really, why didn't you?"

"Are you saying that just to upset me? Or do you mean it?"

"Why shouldn't I mean it?"

"I was an ass."

"Yes."

Unhappy with my response, he retorted, "Anyway, if I offered today to marry you, you would agree to it."

"It's too late!"

"It's never too late!" he cried. After all, *he's* the one who woke me from my lethargic sleep! He doesn't want to hear about the other man. Where was that he before, that *yold*, while C. was working so hard to prepare me for living? No, he's not going to walk away from me with his hat in his hand like he did yesterday. He'll demand what he deserves!

I laughed at him and showed him the door.

"What was your fiancé yelling about today?" asked my landlady. "Did you quarrel about something?"

"Yes, we quarreled."

"What does he want?"

"He doesn't know what he wants."

"Maybe he's having second thoughts?"

"Let him regret it if he wants."

"That's right! Why should you care? So what if he finds another bride? There are plenty of *holodriges* who'd be happy to take him, who don't have anything else. Don't fool yourself. Why should you wait until he graduates? That'll only give you misery. You should find yourself a plain man, not someone who's so full of himself. Find yourself a man who'd follow you anywhere, who'd give you everything he had. Do you think that's a small thing? You should look for a horse doctor or a butcher. He might bring you thousands. He'd lay his grandmother's inheritance at your feet. Why do you need to crawl, with a healthy head on your shoulders, into a sickbed of a marriage? Just because he's studying to be a doctor, does that give him a right to make you sick? Let him be the one to suffer."

My landlady spoke to me like this for a long time. The past few weeks, C. had lost all of his good graces with her. Who knows if it's because he didn't taste or eat her food, or because he didn't follow her advice and try to get married as soon as possible and get off the market, or because he didn't bring the books he'd promised for her children, or because he gave them candy and ruined their books with it, or maybe for all of those things together. Whatever it was, now she thought as badly of him as she used to think well, and warned me away from him.

I said yes to everything she said, and she wished me luck.

Today, on a Sunday morning, I came in to see my landlady and asked her, now that I've split with my fiancé once and for all, if he calls on me would she please tell him that I'm not at home?

"It's good that you told me," she responded with righteous anger. "When he sees me I'll be as loyal as your left eye. You've done very well. It's one way or the other. There's no use in drawing things out. We don't need him coming in here waiting for you and burning up our gas. He used to sneak in here like a man who'd been married to you ten years. What did he want from you? What a fool! Listen, as sure as my name is Mrs. Kotik, I'll drop him, right before your very eyes." With tears in her eyes, she added, "How dare he come to see you! He should wash your feet and drink the water. And I am such a cow for ever being so enamored with him."

An older sister of Mrs. Kotik's who had come to visit from Browns-ville smiled at me good-naturedly as I went into my room and looked me over with approval. Her sister must have told her already what a rare, dear, kosher child I was.

"*Nishkoshe*," she added, "you'll land on your feet. A girl like you, with God's help, will never be lost. Don't worry. *Nishkoshe*. There's a good God in heaven who watches over young people and makes *shidukhim* from among them. As they say, 'The long and short of it is that right man will come along.'"

I thought that would be the long and short of what she had to say, and that I'd be able to go. But she kept on talking, and out of politeness I kept on listening.

"I have a boarder, a wonderful young man. In the old days, they would have kept a young man like that on *kest* for a whole year and showered him with gold and wood. But we're in America, so he has to make a living for himself. What does he do, you ask? What doesn't he do? He does everything you can imagine. He tutors, he sings to accompany cantors, he can engrave names onto tin badges—by hand, no less! He can transcribe letters in English, in Christian German, in Polish and in Hebrew. And Yiddish too, but that goes without saying. He says that there was never a need for him to learn to write in Yiddish, he just knew it from the start."

"What's the point of telling us all his good qualities?" Mrs. Kotik interrupted. "Bring him here and let us see for ourselves!"

"Of course, you're right. I'll bring him here. What was your former fiancé? He must have been a socialist, right?"

"Yes, so what? He thought the whole world should be his," complained Mrs. Kotik.

"Was that his profession? Talking to socialists?"

"Sure, he talked to them!"

"Speaking about socialism! That's hardly a profession for a Jew. What kind of a life could he build from that? I tell you, if she'd come to me for advice—there are so many backward thinkers among those socialists! It's important to, as they say in English, 'Be careful.' There aren't very many of them who deserve 'respect.' They talk a fine talk, but they believe the opposite of what they say. If you talk to my boarder about them, he'll tell you what they really are. They wouldn't let him into any union he tried to join. They demanded that he give them money first! Socialists asking for money, imagine that. What would the capitalists say? That's America for you."

When I finally returned to my room I could still hear the sisters talking about me. Not so much about me as about the wonderful boarder that the older sister promised the younger sister she'd bring for me.

◦◦

Gorky says, "Everything comes to an end. That's one of the best things about life." I've been thinking about this for a while. For those whose life is a joy, the passing of things hardly brings pleasure. But for me, whose life is gray, workaday, pale, and bleak, knowing that there will be an end is a consolation.

◦◦

I gaze up at the full moon in the starry night sky and the faith that I'll be happy someday settles inside of me. It's like a ladder of hope that my spirit climbs up to knock on my shuttered heart.

I believe and I doubt. I hope and I wait. I imagine things that I'm almost sure will never happen in my lifetime. But I can't take away from myself the possibility of imagining and thinking about them, even though they're far removed from reality.

With a strange, almost religious sadness, I think of A. My lips mouth his name like a prayer and it makes me feel so painfully good and weak. I love him for the suffering that my love for him causes me. It brings me to a holy feeling. It elevates my soul. It disinfects the impure thoughts that C. caused me while he was mounting his campaign for me.

C.'s battle to convince me to *live* had the opposite effect on me. He didn't arouse sinful desires in me, as he wanted to, but instead he strengthened my desire to have a soulful, beautiful, eternal devotion to one person.

55

Not for Anyone

I found a few words from C. scrawled on a paper slipped under my door: "I must see you. I have to speak to you. I came to see you but you weren't here. Try to be at home. It's very important."

Very important!

There's nothing else we can say to each other. I am amazed at my iron patience up until now. If I am going to die, let it be an easy death. I don't want to allow myself to be bored to death.

❧

I wasn't at home. This was safer than staying at home and having Mrs. Kotik make excuses and tell him that I wasn't there. If he asked her, she wouldn't be able to refuse his request. She would start to believe that he might finally marry me, after all, and her good soul would be moved to tears by the thought that by letting him in she was doing the *mitzve* of *shadkhones*.

I know how C. is. He won't let me have the last word. He thinks that there was a time when I was under the power of his influence, and he regrets that he didn't seize that brief moment when I loved him and use it for *living*. Now he can see how impractically he handled the whole matter. He was the sculptor and he'd had the clay in his hands, but rather than kneading me into the figure he desired, he made a *golem* of himself.

❧

Davis came to see me with two tickets to the opera and invited me to accompany him. I didn't like this at all. Why was he interested in me all of a sudden? What happened to Rae? I excused myself, saying something about an appointment, and he took Rae to the opera.

∽

Rae told me that she hadn't had such a lovely evening in a long time. They had good seats, and he sat there quietly all evening, like a man in love. Poor Rae! How differently she would feel if she knew that she had gone to the opera with my ticket!

"It's better to have a seat at the table than a vague dream in your head," she offered with a friendly smile.

"What makes you say that?" I asked.

"I'm thinking about the moon!" she said laughing, and then explained that she wasn't really talking about the moon, but about me. Davis told her that he had come to visit me and ask if I wanted to join them at the opera, but I had been tactful enough to refuse the invitation because, as he understood it, I didn't want to get in the way. "So," she explained, "if one of your beaus ever invites me to join you, I'll return the favor with similar tact."

I told her not to. I'm not seeing anyone that she would get in the way of. She peered at me with a furrowed brow, and then asked, "What's the story with Mr. Cheek?"

"Nothing."

"Nothing at all?"

"Absolutely nothing."

"That can't be!"

"That's how it is."

After a while, Rae remarked, "What a shame, after you wasted so much time on him."

"It wasn't wasted. I learned a lot."

"What did you learn?"

"I learned that I, and women like me, were created for more choices, for more freedom than free love offers."

"You can speak for yourself," Rae said dismissively. "As for me, I would be happy to have a free love affair, as long as the man and I had some kind of understanding."

"The more you understand, the less self-respect you'll have."

"Why? What does one thing have to do with the other? I've seen others who have made the choice to live like that, and they seem very happy. And if she has a child, there's nothing more to be said. He feels bound to it, just like a real father."

"Yes? And what about birth control?"

"Well, you have me there. It's no good. It's very sad. I think it's a sin to take away a woman's right to become a mother!"

"Is that so? But what if the woman just wants to rob a man of his manhood by tying him down with a child?"

"That's what Mr. Davis says. He says that he loves children, but he loves his freedom more."

"He loves *himself* more."

"Everyone loves themselves best of all." Rae smiled bitterly, with tears in her eyes. "Everyone is only looking out for themselves. You can waste your whole life that way and end up with nothing to show for it."

⌒

"I have news for you!" my landlady greeted me in a singsong voice as I returned home from work to my room this evening. "Something that will make you very happy!"

"What kind of news is it?"

"It's about your fiancé!"

"I've heard enough about him."

"He was here, and—"

"I don't want to hear any news about him. I've had enough."

"But just listen!"

"Please, Mrs. Kotik, tell me something else. How is your cat? Has she scratched someone lately?"

"Never mind about the cat. Let me at least tell you what he said." She went on without allowing me to interrupt. "I promised him that I'd tell you everything he said."

"How long did he spend here?"

"A few hours."

"Good night! I'm already running late for the place I'm heading this evening!"

"You won't be late. I'll make it quick. In short, he's ready to marry you now, with a *khupe*, a rabbi, and the *sheva brokhes*, right here in this house! There's just one thing. We have to keep it a secret until he graduates. And he doesn't want to rent a room with you. He wants each of you to keep living as you have been, for the time being. I told him that's no way to live, even for a dog! So he agreed for you to live together, in one bedroom, right here in this house. He says he's going to pay me his portion of the rent, and everything will be fine and dandy! So, can you guess how I answered him?"

"That you would not agree to have him live in your house?" I guessed.

"No! I told him: 'You're getting ahead of yourself! She's already seeing another man.'"

"Good."

"But he told me that you have no other man, and that he feels sorry for you that you're pining for him like a candle without a flame. He can't sleep at night, knowing he's broken his word to an orphan, such a lonely girl. He's sure you cry your eyes out every night because he left you. And he doesn't want you to cry."

"Alright. I won't cry. Is that all?"

"That's only the beginning of the story. He'll be here later."

"When?" I asked, so I could know when to make sure not to be at home.

"Tomorrow, Sunday, early in the morning, when he's sure to find you at home."

"Alright," I said, and asked my landlady not to let him in, or to tell him that I wasn't at home. I would spend the night with Rae. She refused. She wasn't going to cover for me anymore. A *khupe* is a *khupe*. A girl shouldn't throw that away. If I say that I don't want it, that's my business. She doesn't want to get mixed up in it anymore.

"Anyway, my sister from Brownsville will be here tomorrow with her boarder. He's very interested in meeting you. Surely you'll be home to see him?"

"I won't be here for him either. I won't be here for anyone."

"What a pity," the landlady sighed. "I always keep my promises. I don't like to mislead anyone. And you never know who is going to be the right man for you. Maybe it's my sister's boarder, who's coming to see you tomorrow!"

56

Nutcracker

M y God! What a zoo!" I cried as soon as Mrs. Kotik's sister's boarder left.

Since Mrs. Kotik has been so good to me and protected my reputation from C., not letting him in to see me, I couldn't refuse to visit with her guest. Yes, she's been very stern this time in standing up to C. She hasn't even let him near my door.

He came to see me at eleven in the morning. "She's not at home," I heard her telling him as I hid in my room.

"Alright," answered C. "Then I'll wait for her in her room until she comes back."

"*No, sir*, you may not go in her room."

"Why not?"

"That's just how it is."

"Is that how it is? But why?"

"It goes without saying."

"It seems a little strange, doesn't it?" C. forced a laugh. "It's really rather funny."

"That's how it is, and that's how it's going to be," she retorted. "And no matter how much you beg or argue there's nothing you can do about it."

"Did you tell her what I told you?"

"Yes, I told her everything."

"So what did she say?"

"Nothing."

"She didn't say anything?"

"What did I tell you? Not a thing!"

"Don't get so *excited*," he chided her in English.

"Who's getting excited? I have enough work to attend to without all this nonsense."

"Then get to work!"

"*Mister*," she addressed him in English, "this will not do. I won't be able to get my work done if you won't leave. Go away!"

"What a mood you're in today!"

"Alright, so I'm in a mood! Let my husband deal with it. My mood isn't your problem. I hate getting pushed around."

"I'm not pushing you around."

"Then what? I'm pushing myself around? I know your tricks."

"You're nothing but a foolish old *yidene*."

"Get out of my house! How dare you speak to me that way in my house! What a nerve!"

"If you're throwing me out—"

"If you had any brains you'd know yourself when it was time to leave."

"Don't I have a right to see my bride-to-be?"

"She's as much your bride as she is my bride! How dare you latch yourself onto a girl like that! You've as much right to marry me as you do her."

"Didn't it ever even occur to you that it's the girl's fault? That she's the one who latched onto me?" he demanded. "What do you know about it?"

"*A nekhtiker tog!* She's not the kind of girl who just attaches herself to some man. She won't let herself be taken advantage of either."

"How do you know? I've known her longer than you. Even if she isn't now, she used to be engaged to me. Surely I know her better than you do."

"Longer, better, worse, who cares? It doesn't matter now."

"She wanted to marry me."

"If you had wanted to marry her when she wanted to marry you, you'd already be married. It's too late now. She's not interested."

"Yes, she is. She still wants a wedding."

"She doesn't."

"Let me talk to her."

"There's nothing for you to say to her."

"Then you ask her. Tell her that I'm here."

"How can I tell her that when she isn't here?" shouted the landlady, and then stole away into my room.

"What should I say to him?" she whispered to me.

"Tell him to go away."

"It won't do any good. You heard him! Maybe you should tell him yourself?"

"Tell him that I'm asleep."

"She's asleep," the landlady informed him.

"Alright, then I'll wait here until she wakes up." He sat down.

He waited for a long time, and I went on "sleeping." Eventually his pride was wounded enough that he got up in a huff and left, slamming the door behind him.

"*Barukh shepatarni*, thank God, and good riddance!" the landlady said, uttering a prayer, and I responded, "Amen."

And then the guests from Brownsville arrived!

The landlady's sister came dressed to the nines, like a future mother-in-law seeking a bride for her son, and the boarder was dressed like a prospective groom. He was wearing a full dress coat. His white necktie was knotted tightly around his white collar. He was clearly uncomfortable in this getup, as he kept leaning his head to one side and pulling at his collar to free his neck.

He was short and thin and entirely swamped by his full dress coat. His hair, which was thick, stiff, and pointy, refused to lie flat on his head. It gave the impression that he'd once met with a sudden fright that left his hair standing on edge ever since. He had gray-blue eyes that looked sharp and keen. His nose, which was a bit pronounced, seemed to tug at the trimmed hairs that hung on his upper lip like Charlie Chaplin's moustache. He had a dimple on his chin. All in all, he appeared to be a happy, comfortable sort of person, and at first glance

I couldn't help but smile. Then, when I heard his voice, and not just the voice but his words, his way of speaking—all I could do was laugh.

They introduced us. He stood as straight as a soldier and then bowed low with great aplomb. Then he corrected his landlady's pronunciation of his name: "Excuse me, but it isn't Eshkin, it's Ezshkin."

"What's new in Brownsville?" I asked my landlady's older sister, trying to start a casual conversation.

"Nothing much," she answered with exaggerated offhandedness. "Brownsville is full of goats. It's a lovely little world unto itself. I'm partial to it. But still, it's just yard after yard."

"If only I had a yard like yours!" my landlady sighed wistfully.

"What would *you* do? Hoe the ground? I'm partial to yards. I'd rather have a hundred yards in Brownsville than a whole tenement house in New York!"

"What do you think about *dieses*, Miss?" asked Mr. Eshkin.

"I think Brownsville is alright."

"It's not for single people. It's for married couples. Doesn't the lady think so?" he asked me.

"Aren't married couples people too?" his landlady responded, as though insulted. "He thinks that our souls are dried up like raisins. Even married people prefer to live among other people, and not with goats."

⌒⌒

My landlady invited her sister and the boarder to have something to eat and stop fighting like *goyim*. You can't exchange one world for another anyway, and sometimes people just disagree. That's a good thing. If not, everyone would want the same thing, and they would tear each other to pieces going after it. "Isn't that so, Mr. Eshkin?"

Mr. Eshkin agreed emphatically. "That's very diplomatic." With that, he took a nut, put it in his mouth, squeezed his eyes shut, and tried to crack it between his teeth.

"Here, use this nutcracker," my landlady offered. "Don't ruin your teeth."

But, no, he was insistent on demonstrating how he could crack the nut with his teeth!

"Did you see his teeth?" His landlady nudged her sister. "Look how healthy they are, every one of them."

No matter how hard he tried, or how much his landlady praised his teeth, the long and short of it was that he could not crack the nut with them. He took the nut out of his mouth, wiped it with a handkerchief, and remarked, "What a peculiar nut!" Holding it and remarking on its uniqueness, he continued, "It's hardly a nut at all! It's practically a stone!"

He returned the "stone" to its former place and took a different one. He was able to successfully crack open the next nut, and the third and fourth nuts besides, and he talked to me as he shelled them.

"May I ask, Miss, if the young lady has been in these United States for some time?"

"The young lady?"

"Pardon me, Fräulein, I was asking about yourself."

"Oh, about me! I've been here a few years."

"Do you often dream of returning to darkest Russia?"

"Yes," I answered hesitantly. "I often dream that I'm going home. And when I wake up there, I wish I was back here. Isn't that funny?" I asked, smiling, in order to give an excuse for my laughing.

"Excuse me, once again. I'm not speaking of dreaming, as one does at night. No, Miss. What I meant was, do you intend to return to the country from which you came?"

"Oh. No."

"Where are you from?"

"Minsk."

"Isn't it remarkable that everyone seems to come from Minsk? Lately every person with whom I have the honor to speak seems to be from Minsk. I was in Minsk once. Do you know someone by the name Reb Yaakov Meyer?"

"Of course! He was a fine man. He died."

"Did you go to him for a blessing before you made your journey to America?"

"I didn't quite do that."

"From what I've heard, everyone goes to him for a blessing. Were you raised, as I think you were, by Orthodox parents?"

"No, I come from freethinkers."

"Is that so? And what about yourself?"

"Me? I'm . . . Orthodox."

"How remarkable! How wonderful! This must be your grandfather's doing?"

"It is because of my grandmother, my *bobe*."

"I see. I would very much like to have the honor of knowing your family."

"How could you, unless you went back to Europe?"

"My apologies, Miss. I do not mean know them personally. Unfortunately, that would be impossible. I mean, I would like to see their photographs. I am able to learn a lot about who people truly are from their photographs."

My landlady asked me calmly, though her eyes were begging, to bring out my album so they could all have a look. I couldn't refuse her. I went to my room to retrieve it.

When I was a few steps away I heard him saying, "She is a fine *Mädchen*." My landlady replied heartily, "And how!" I believe that my landlady's sister nodded in agreement.

༄

Curious to hear how Mr. Eshkin would judge my relatives by their photographs, I brought my album into my landlady's dining room. She held the edge of the tablecloth in one hand and swept cookie crumbs and nutshells into it with the other, clearing a place for my album.

As soon as I started paging through the album, everyone watched with interest. As we were looking, the landlady's sister suggested that she didn't see why we shouldn't sit in the front room to look at the pictures. It's much nicer and lighter there. Once we were in the front room, she didn't show much interest. Instead of looking at the album she meaningfully locked eyes with her sister, and it wasn't long until I was left alone with Mr. Eshkin, staring at the pictures.

"I beg your apology," he said, seeing that we were alone. "May I please look at it from the beginning?"

I apologized. I didn't realize he'd be so eager to see the album over again from beginning to end. But I was interested in hearing his assessment. I asked him what he thought of the pictures.

"These are fine, extraordinary photographs! This girl here, she must be your sister?" he asked, pointing to a picture of me.

"No, that's me," I said.

"When you were quite young."

"Yes!"

"How old were you then?"

"When I was young?"

"Yes, Miss."

"How old can a person be when they're young? I was young!"

"Oh, excuse me—"

"And here's a picture that was taken of me when I was older."

"What a *vortrefliches* picture! It's terrific. But perhaps a bit too . . . melancholy. If I may be so bold as to ask, are you, at heart, a pessimist?"

"I was, and am, an optimist."

"How so?"

"I simply am."

"You speak Yiddish like a real *Litvashke*."

"And you speak it like a German."

"I was born outside of Riga, raised in Hamburg, studied in Lemberg. I graduated from school and learned a profession."

He was especially interested in the picture of my father. He stopped and contemplated it for a while, and then said with approval, "Your father does not look like a *khniak*!"

"What?"

"Don't you know what I mean? I mean, he doesn't look like a *schlemiel*, a good-for-nothing," he explained. "I'm surprised you've never heard this word before."

"Is it German?"

"God forbid! It's plain old Yiddish. Real, authentic Yiddish. Do you mean to say that you don't know German? That's a shame. It's necessary in high society. Everyone, in all the best establishments, respects the German language as the language of culture. You know, you really must learn that language if you want to be in high society or be able to express yourself!" he said, flipping through the album without really looking at the pictures.

I thought of asking jokingly if he wanted to be my teacher, but I didn't because I was afraid he'd take the joke seriously and use it as an excuse to come see me and bore me with his lectures.

He went on, "How, for example, would you express your most genteel, *ehrlich* feelings in high society if all that comes out is *zhargon*?"

"I honestly don't know how—"

"*Takeh*, that's it! Don't you see? *Takeh*. Take the word *takeh*, for example. If you used that word in high society, German speakers wouldn't even believe that it was a word at all."

"Then how would you say it in German?" I asked, holding back my laughter.

"In German I can express everything I want instinctively. You can't express your instinctives in Yiddish. Certainly not. For example, what are your instinctives telling you right now?"

"My instincts?" I repeated back to him, delicately prompting him with the correct form of the word. But he did not take my instincts under advisement and kept saying "instinctives" until my landlady and her sister and some of their children came in from the street and entered the front room.

57

A Work of Art

A brand new love affair—a literary one!

We met at a literary and musical reception one evening and he told me right away that he thought I was *the one*. I am *the* girl he is looking for, the girl of his romantic dreams.

He's heard of me already. He's heard that I'm well read and interesting to talk to. He's wanted to meet me for a long time, but his literary preoccupations have prevented him. His muses tied him to his writing table and demanded that he keep writing.

He wants to carry on a love affair with me out of his love for art. I simply *must* have an affair with him, to give him inspiration for the new work he's writing, with me as the heroine.

"The only thing that I can give you is this smile," I said.

"That's not enough. There's no need for you to be that way. Be like the heroine of a modern romance: free and uninhibited."

"If free is what you want, don't force me."

"You're my model now. You're the material I'm using to create a work of art that will be the talk of the literary world. I will immortalize you; you'll live forever in my art. With my style, with my words, I'll create a work that will be the wonder of the twentieth century! Even my enemies, who won't want to acknowledge my triumph, will have to agree that I am original, modern, great!"

When he saw that I was looking at him skeptically, he asked, "What, you don't believe me? That's because you don't know me yet. If only you knew how everyone tries to imitate my work. I have a style all of my own, absolutely unique. You can only be born with a style like mine, it can't be learned. You might say that I was born with a pen in my hand."

"Did you start writing when you were a baby?"

"I was practically a child. Yes, it was *in* me from the start, before I was even—"

"Before you were even anything at all!"

"Perhaps. My soul was filled with poetry as soon as it arrived in the world. I had a precocious curiosity about writing, and I started writing from the first time I ever saw paper. I wrote in sand, on snow, even in water, I loved writing so much! And whenever I got my hands on a book I tore it to pieces. It was as though my heart was telling me that I could write better than anyone who had ever written before me. Doesn't that make me distinctive?"

"Quite!"

"If you were to read everything I've written," he continued, encouraged by my "quite," "you would see that I have never created a single piece of weak writing. Everything I write is strong and full of life. All those other *lapatsanes* bite their own fingers with envy because they can't write like I can. And do you know the reason they can't?"

"The reason they can't?"

"Yes. The reason is that they can't. And they can't because it is not *in* them to do it. You must have a great soul in order to accomplish great things."

"Where do you get it all from?" I asked, "Not your soul"—I added this joke so I could allow my face to relax into a smile—"but the material that you write about?"

"Life. Of course, life alone is not enough if you don't have an imagination. And I have a rich imagination and a very deep psychology."

❧

"Just last week I completed a story," continued my new literary acquaintance. "It's a gem! It's very good. This is the story—do you want me to tell you how it goes? It's very interesting."

"Well—"

He told me the story. "The name of the story is 'Feelings.' A talented writer falls head over heels for a young, picture-perfect girl and wants to immortalize her in writing. He sees in her the woman of his dreams and he wants to sing her praises and make her eternal. But she won't let him. She doesn't know what she's doing. Her naïve, inexperienced soul shies away in fear from the artist and she begs him not to bother her. But eventually she realizes that she is too weak to withstand his advances and she lets him immortalize her. She becomes as pliant as wax. She is good, soft, accommodating. He makes her eternal.

"The girl has some money. Just a few hundred dollars. She gives it to him so that he can publish the work that he wrote about her. He finds a publisher and both of them are in seventh heaven because the book is the talk of the town. She sits with him in the literary café and is proud of him. All those other *lapatsanes* who don't even know how to hold a pen in their hands see her and are jealous of him. With a muse like her by his side, they say, they'd be able to create something as magnificent as he did. She sees how they are devouring her with their eyes and is embarrassed.

"And so it goes, until we come to the material side of things. Finances are the nail in the coffin. The printer turns out to be a fraud. He decides for personal reasons to stop publishing the author and bring someone else's work to market instead. The critics, who do not wish our author well, insult and ignore his work. He would rather they tore it to shreds than not notice it at all. But who cares what he thinks? He loses his head over his misfortune, and she falls into a depression because she can't stand to see him suffering.

"The more she can't stand to see him suffer, the more he suffers from her sadness. He grows wild with sadness and contemplates suicide, but she won't let him do it. He watches her descent—she fades, withers, grows old before her time. Inspired by her suffering, he comes up with an idea for a tragedy. 'Art's Martyr,' he'll call it. He'll show the world how she was the victim of art. And to make sure it has a happy ending he'll change her fortunes in the fourth act and make sure she lives happily ever after. But man plans and the devil laughs. She dies before the curtain falls. The funeral director lays her down into the earth. Prose overtakes poetry, death wins over life. The writer lays his hot forehead on her cold breast and looks with pessimism into the future. He looks, but he sees nothing.

"Isn't it a wonderful story?" he asked me excitedly. Without waiting for my answer, he said himself that it was a rare, remarkable, tremendous accomplishment! From now on, it will be known as one of the greatest works that has ever been written in Yiddish literature, in all the literature in the world, even! It's true art. It's how people were meant to write. He hates to praise himself overmuch, but the truth is the truth, and he can't help saying so.

To give myself a rest from his rich imagination, deep psychology, elevated soul, tremendous insight and colossal talent, I remarked on his unusual appearance. "Why are you so pale?" I asked.

"I'm a poet. A Yiddish poet," he responded pointedly. "I am an *intellectual.*"

"You have such deep wrinkles in your brow."

"It's from thinking, pondering, cogitating."

"Why do you have a cut on your cheek?"

"It's from the barber."

"Where did you get that scratch on your neck?"

"From the barber!"

"You have such a strange way of pressing your lips together."

"Really? It's because I have so many words in me that want to express themselves. There are things that you have to hold inside, to save for later. For instance, I wish I could tell you right now how much I love you, but I feel that it isn't time to say so yet. You'll be upset that I spoke too soon. For someone like you, love comes much more gradually, it's long and drawn out. You torment a man before he can declare himself to you. You're afraid that I'll come to such feelings too fast, because it makes you believe that I'll stop loving you as quickly as I began. But artists like me are people who live in the moment. We give ourselves over to the present. Our creative energy comes from expressing ourselves. 'Mr. Finkin,' a girl said to me the other day, 'you are the greatest psychologist I have ever met in my life. You can see what's in our very souls. You really understand women.' And the girl who said that had met many psychologists in her life, both great and humble, profound and superficial."

"Who was the girl? I'd like to meet her."

"No, you can't meet her. She's not here. What a shame. I'd like to introduce you to her. She could tell you what it's like to be loved by a writer. It's not like being loved by another man, a man of ordinary flesh and blood. Of course, there are all kinds of love, just like there are all kinds of writers. One man's love comes out like a *shundroman*, another's is beautiful, poetic, literary."

The love he feels for me, he claims, is a literary one. But just because it's literary doesn't mean that it can't also happen in real life. In the name of literature, he said, I simply *must* love him too.

"Tell me, Mr. F.," I asked, redirecting him from his demand that I love him, "how you write. It must be very interesting."

"Oh, yes, it's very interesting. I think it's the most interesting thing in the world. You create something and everyone is delighted by it. You can see with your own eyes how everyone laps up the literary delicacy that you've served them, and it makes you think that there's a reason for your existence in the world. Often when I'm in an elevator, a streetcar, or the subway, I see someone reading something I wrote and I feel—oh! It's such a wonderful feeling! I read their faces, and I see how each one of them feels exactly what I wanted to make them feel when I wrote the piece. When I create something, I'm not just a writer—I'm a reader too!"

58

The World Isn't Ending Yet

E. had a proposal to offer me. Earlier he had asked me what my instinctives told me. Seeing that my instinctives were silent, he told me what his instinctives had to say:

"My instinctives tell me that you are the right person for me in every aspect. Taking into account all of your behavior, you appear to be a fine *fräulein* who comes from a good family. Something about you is very attractive. I want to make you *glücklich*, you would be very happy. I would give you my name, introduce you to my friends, and take you on a *Lustreise* to Germany after the war is over."

"Mr. Eshkin—"

"I beg your pardon, but let me speak. You must know that I have thought long and hard about this and I have decided that I must speak to you. What does my landlady say? She is a plain woman but a clever one. She says, 'Making a match is not eating a bagel.' That's true, but—"

"But—"

"I beg your pardon, but I'm the one who's talking. When I've finished you may say what you want. When you interrupt me I forget what it is that I am saying, and I might forget to say what is very important for both of us. What I want to ask you now is this: Would you help me to go into business? Not help me with the work, that is, but with the *Geld*. Let me assure you, I'm not only interested in money. I am looking for the right person. You are a gracious, upstanding person in the full sense of the word. But don't you know that it wouldn't take anything away from how wonderful a person you are if you have something more? In these times—"

"Mr. Eshkin, I beg you!"

"Wait, I haven't finished. In these times, when you have no *Geld* then you are poor, and a poor man might as well be dead man. He's as good as *tot*."

I corrected his pronunciation of the word *toyt*, dead. He took this as an admission that I too was poor, and dead.

"Well, *liebes Fräulein*," he said with regret, "I am very sorry for you, but it hardly matters. You are a good person. But you have no *Geld*! Money is spent, but the person remains. I am a gentleman and my word is my word. I promised my landlady, as she lives and breathes to tell you all this, and I'm telling you just what I told her I'd say. So what do you think? You may speak now."

"You truly are a gentleman," I said, "and, therefore, I regret to inform you that I am no longer available. I have already promised myself to someone else."

"What? You're already engaged? Impossible!" he cried.

"Why is it impossible?"

"Ach, how can this be? My landlady told me that your landlady told her that you weren't engaged. You must know. You really must have known."

"Know what?"

"You must have known that I was coming to see you because I was interested in you as a potential bride. But all along you were engaged to someone else! It's unbelievable. Then who is your fiancé?"

"He's not here right now. He is—traveling."

"Why did he go away?"

"For—business."

"What kind of business does he have?"

"It's none of your business."

"Is he coming back? Or are you going to him?"

"We have to write to each other to figure that out."

"And I made you a proposal! How can such a thing have happened! Why didn't you say something?"

"I wanted to say something, but you wouldn't let me speak."

"I see, I see . . ."

∽

My landlady's sister from Brownsville made a special trip to New York to talk about me.

"What's wrong? What didn't you like about him?" she demanded of my landlady. "What was wrong with him? He seems like a wonderful man, a good man, without any pretentions. He's educated, he comes from fine parents, he speaks German, he understands business, there's so much to recommend him. Right now, he sings! Come the holidays, he makes good money singing *khazones*. How can you not like him? Where's the logic in that?"

I was very curious to hear how my landlady would answer. She responded, "The logic is that the question itself is foolish. Anyone with a head on her shoulders could see what a crooked deal it was and would try to peddle that *shliumper* as a match somewhere else! How could you even think of speaking to a girl with a figure as straight as a pine tree, a beautiful girl, about a man who could go for a walk under a table wearing a top hat and still have room to spare?"

"Pfui!" spat her sister. "Do you see what problem she has with the man? She thinks the bride is too pretty for him! Pity the girl who looks for a husband prettier than she is. These days an older girl who finds herself among strangers should open both hands wide to the heavens and thank God above that a man with so many advantages is interested in her. There aren't many men interested in marrying at all these days, and if she waits a while longer there'll be even fewer. The shortage is getting bigger every day. Soon the war will be over, and there will be even more women falling over themselves to find such a man! I swear, you mustn't be so picky or overthink it. Just close your eyes and take what you can get, because soon it won't be there at all."

My landlady replied, "Never mind what you say, there will still be something. The world isn't ending yet, and it's ten times better to think anything over before you do it once and for all. God is a Father who sends every spinner his wool, every weaver his flax, or every wool her spinner, every flax her weaver, as the case may be. And you can't put a peacock in the same wagon as a billy goat. It's very hard to find an equal, fitting match. But there's no need to just snatch up whatever you can find. We're not talking about hot noodles here. God will send a better match for a better girl. And the man won't go to waste. He'll find a different girl too."

That's how my landlady sided with me against her sister and the "groom." It was very interesting to hear, but I had to leave them in the middle of their conversation and hurry to my room because Mr. Finkin had come to call on me.

59

A New Beginning

Rae came to see me one evening, cursing the whole world. She spoke about her sorry life. She lost her job because she spent too much time going out with Davis. Her head wasn't in her work. She couldn't follow the instructions they gave her precisely, so they replaced her. And Davis? Now that she can give him all of her time, he's nowhere to be found. He's taken up with someone else: Katya. Only now has Rae found out that they knew each other before; they'd gone out with each other for a while in the past and now they've taken a room together, to live together according to the laws of free love. Maybe they'll even get married someday.

She'd been to see B. but left him indignantly. He and his wife moved from their old rooms to a pretty apartment on the West Side. They had a maid living with them, and guess who else, Rae told me, is their boarder?

My heart plummeted, pounded against my chest like a frightened bird, and nearly stopped altogether. Feeling Rae's familiar penetrating glare as she stared at me with her furrowed brow, I was afraid to guess, but she soon supplied the answer I was expecting.

"A.! A. moved in with them! Yes, that's how it is! Can you believe it? But there's no need to gossip about *them*. What we need to worry about is keeping *ourselves* out of all the malicious gossip. There are those, believe me, who are blind to *their* trespasses but strict about ours."

Rae gave this moral about society as a bitter warning, and asked my advice about how to tear herself away from all of them once and for all, because she'd had it up to here with all of it. She needs to get away, she doesn't want to see any of them ever again!

"The best thing would be to leave," I said.

"Yes, leave," nodded Rae, sadly, "only to show up alone in a strange city . . ."

I thought to myself, "Why shouldn't I leave here too? What would I miss? Would I be at all sorry to leave behind all the A.'s, B.'s, C.'s, D.'s, E.'s, and F.'s? They'd meet other girls soon enough. And what of my love for A.? I can take that with me!"

When I told Rae that I'd go with her she grabbed me by both hands and almost cried with joy that she wouldn't need to leave by herself. She would *not be alone*! She was already imagining how good things will be for us in the other—not strange now but new—city. We'll live there together like sisters. We'll make new friends. We will start a new life and it will be so much better than our life is here.

"Who even cares if it's worse, as long as it's different," I said, and she liked that very much.

"Yes, even if it's worse, it'll be different. Let's not get our hopes up, imagining too much happiness for ourselves, because we don't want to be disappointed. Whatever happens to us we won't be here anymore, so that's already better. The heart aches less from a distance."

We've decided not to tell anyone where we're going. The only thing we'll tell them is this: we are leaving them. We won't be here in New York any longer. We've had enough. And there: who even cares if it's worse, as long as it's different!

The Agitator

∽

Glossary

The Agitator

BY MIRIAM KARPILOVE
Translated by Jessica Kirzane

ALTKA SAT, thinking to herself that if she could only find someone she could make it with, she'd like to be married already. She's fed up with loneliness, with living among strangers. She wants a real home.

She realizes that she lacks some quality that would help her get closer to people. She makes no effort to please the people she doesn't like, and when she meets someone she does like she hides her feelings from him and from others like it's something to be ashamed of. Instead of smiling at him she looks away, instead of offering kind words she snaps at him or says nothing at all.

There are men who are very interested in her, and she likes them too. They're married men. But she isn't interested in being a homewrecker. She feels sorry for their wives. And there's no point in having an affair with one of them. Nothing could come of it.

There are others who say they'd like to marry her if only they had the means. They tell her that in order to marry her a man would have to be well off. A girl as lovely as she deserves a home with every comfort, and they'd never be able to give her that kind of a home with what they earn.

Some want to have a "free love" affair with her. She thinks "free love" ought to be called "unprofitable love" and she isn't interested. No one from her family (she comes from a respectable family) has ever carried on a "free love" affair, so why should she get caught up in one? No matter that they

Originally appeared in *Di tsukunft*, January 1915.

live across an ocean from her. She can't, and doesn't ever want to, write lies to them. And telling them the truth about such an affair would cause them pain. She is very dear to them.

Her friends see her as a decent, honorable, clever, innocent girl. Some say that she is a bit too innocent.

She's given up on the grand kind of love that she once dreamt of. Now what she wants is sympathy, affection, friendship. Perhaps, like so many other poor girls stuck in sweatshops, she should attach herself to some man so that she can have a steady job as a wife waiting on a person who is no better than a beggar himself? No, she's not that desperate, she has a good job as a designer. She even has something put away for a rainy day. She doesn't live in poverty, she doesn't cut corners, and she's even able to help others. Marrying just so she can take someone else's name or shorten her years is something she doesn't want and won't do.

Altka went over all this in her mind for the hundredth time and her heart was so heavy that she felt on the verge of tears.

It was the first spring evening. Her book fell from her hands and she knew that soon she wouldn't be able to find a spot in her house to sit comfortably. She readied herself and walked down to the street. It was still early, around eight in the evening. She didn't want to wander alone for long, so when she saw an advertisement for a concert and literary evening featuring countless clever people whose names she knew, she purchased a ticket and entered the hall.

After the first number in the program she felt she already wanted to leave. That's how good it was. The second was a little better and after the third she thought she could get used to it. By the fourth she'd decided that she would leave before the beginning of the fifth act. As she neared the door a young man stood in her way and asked, "Are you the girl I've been looking for? Your name is Alta, right?"

She looked him up and down. He was tall, a little taller than she, blond, with skin dark enough that it looked as though he hadn't washed himself recently. His squinty eyes were hidden behind a pince-nez. His long nose jutted out from his face and bent toward his upper lip. His bottom lip bulged and this gave an impression of nobility or stubbornness. There was dirt under the fingernails of the hand he used to adjust his pince-nez.

"Who are you?" she asked him.

"I am Mr. Mars. Dr. Mars, if you please! So are you the girl I'm looking for? They described you to me as tall and graceful with black hair, red lips, pretty eyes, a very attractive girl!"

"Since you know all about her, you can keep on looking for her."

"But I've already found her."

"So?"

"I want to speak with her, that is to say, with you. Why are you leaving so early? Where are you going? If I may ask—"

"To the street."

"Will you permit me to join you?"

She paused a moment and then nodded, thinking to herself, "He can walk with me, I suppose. He isn't bothering anyone."

"Let's go to the park," he suggested as they left.

"Which park? The one on Hester Street?"

"What's wrong with the park on Hester Street? Or if you don't like it, then let's just walk wherever our feet take us."

So they went off. The air smelled of May, a warm breeze cooled her flushed face. She sensed his penetrating gaze. She felt lighthearted and sure-footed and smiled at the people walking by, all of whom seemed to stare at her with curiosity. It seemed to her that love-seeking personal ads shined out of most of their eyes. A mob of lonely souls, revived by the onset of spring, crawled out of their caskets, the tenement houses, looking for life and greeting nature's reawakening.

The eyes of the women and girls were more earnest and deliberate than the eyes of the men. The women were looking for three men in one: a lover, a husband, and a father. But the men were only looking for one thing: a lover.

Newspaper salesmen called out the headlines of tomorrow's freshly printed newspaper and ran with them as though in panic among the crowd mulling around the various places for amusement on the street. Many bought newspapers from the boys, others were indifferent to their cries and hubbub. What did they care how many thousand people died over there in Europe?

Dr. Mars laughed that since he came from Poland, from a town that's now under German control, that must mean that he's a German and she's a Russian, and they're from enemy territories.

"Tell me," she asked him, paying little notice to his joking, "who sent you to ask if I was me?"

"My heart did."

"Seriously, who was it?"

"It's a secret."

"Then tell me the secret. Who was it?"

"Well—do I have to say? Alright, if I have to. It was someone who's in love with you. He's seen you often from a distance. He's head over heels for you! He wants to meet you, to talk to you, but he doesn't dare. So I did it for him. And I'm very glad I did because to tell you the truth I like you very much myself. I like you so much that I won't tell you who he is because I'm jealous of his feelings for you."

"What's his name?"

"Isn't that just fine? Here I am speaking of my feelings, and you just want to know about him!"

"Is he good-looking?"

"Do you like good-looking men?"

"Yes."

"Well, excuse me—"

"What's the problem?"

"Are you saying that I'm not good-looking?"

She didn't deny it. After a pause she asked, "Are you really a doctor?"

"Yes, I'm in my third year of medical school."

"Oh, so you aren't a doctor yet."

He explained that he already has the title "doctor" from before he started studying medicine, from his time in Switzerland where he earned a doctorate in chemistry. He also has diplomas and medals of distinction in art, music, and agriculture. He'll graduate in a year and then he plans to travel the world. Would she like to go with him? She should know that he has a grand future ahead of him. He wants to share it with someone, and why shouldn't it be her? He likes her. One more thing: she's a little too cold, without enough spirit. Or maybe that's just a pretense? He'll soon find out. He asked if she wanted to sit awhile and rest from their walk.

They were next to a park and free benches beckoned to them. They sat down. He put his arm around her waist.

"There's no need for that," she said, removing his arm. He circled her waist another time and she pulled his arm off again. This happened again and again until they both laughed and his arm remained where he wanted it.

"Now I want to kiss you," he declared.

"You may not."

"You can't do this and you can't do that, what's with all these rules? Look," he said, gesturing in front of them, "it's so pretty here. Trees, birds, couples in love. It's spring. The air is filled with love."

"Then kiss the air."

∽

It was late when they arrived at the house where she lived. He insisted that she agree to allow him to come the next day to see her in her room. He promised that she'd really get to know him them.

After he left she vigorously rubbed the remains of his goodbye from her lips and her neck.

∽

The next evening he came to see her. Every inch of him was scrubbed over, his collar was turned to its clean side, and he wore a different suit. But he still had the same dirt under his nails.

"A doctor!" she thought to herself. "Are those the nails of a doctor?"

"Have a seat," she said to him, gesturing toward a chair near the table. The table was covered in books that had never quite made it to the bookshelf.

He sat, never taking his eyes off her, and put down the package he was carrying.

"What's that?"

"Dates and raisins. They're good for the digestion. Do you ever eat them? Would you like one?"

"No, thanks. I don't like to get my hands dirty and don't want sticky fingers."

He opened the package and started eating as he looked around her room. "How much do you pay for this?"

"Ten dollars a month."

"It's expensive. And what kind of people are your landlords? 'Intellectuals?'" He hated "intellectuals."

"'Intellectuals,'" she smiled. "Or at least that's how they advertised themselves. They sell phonographs. One of the sons, the oldest, is studying to be a dentist, and the second one walks with crutches. One of his legs is shorter than the other. They have a daughter who works as a telephone girl. She's pretty and stylish, she looks like she came right out of a fashion book. She plays piano. She's full of noise. The parents are proud of their Russianness. The children are proud to be Americans." She, their boarder, tries to be the neutral territory, and often comes between the embattled nations to make peace.

"Do you mean to say that you spend time with them?"

"Oh, yes, she has to. She has a key to the kitchen door and whenever she needs to use the washbasin she opens it. And sometimes when she forgets to lock it, she unchains the door to the front room and goes through the rooms."

"So those are the so-called improvements they advertise! That hardly sounds comfortable. And what if someone comes to visit you? For instance, if they have sticky fingers from raisins and dates and want to wash them?"

"Hardly anyone ever comes to see me."

"Do you mean to say I'm the first one? Really? I'm glad to hear it. I hardly believe it. You know, I dreamed about you all night. I woke up several times, sat up in bed, stretched out my arms and called out begging you to come. Why are you so far away? Sit closer to me, like when we were at the park. Will your landlords care if I'm sitting next to you? Do you know how beautiful you are? Take off your corset. What do you need it for? Make yourself comfortable! You must have long hair. Why do you bundle it up? It's true, you aren't very friendly. I can tell that you read a lot. I can give you some good books to read, books that you can't get from the library. Very interesting and scholarly. They will make you competent in the matter of love. Do you know that the greatest people are sometimes as ignorant as little children when it comes to love? Take some of the literati—George Sand, George Eliot, and so forth. Yes, under the skin all men are brothers and all women are sisters. Do you want me to go already?"

"It's getting late. Eleven o'clock."

"Happy people don't count the hours. You're afraid of what your intellectuals will say? Why should we care? But it's not good that your room has no water. I'd like to wash my hands. A room should come with its own improvements, with a little plumbing."

He stood up, stretched, and paced, considering the room and then unwillingly said his goodbyes, promising to return tomorrow. He left quickly.

The same thing happened for the next five or six evenings. He came bearing raisins, dates, or figs. He told her about his dreams, he spoke and agitated for free love, tried to illustrate for her, to persuade her. He stayed until late, sitting, pacing, looking around the room, spitting frustratedly in the floral patterned spittoon, and then he left.

⌒

One evening he arrived with a smile as wide as if it were a holiday and told her to wish him a happy birthday. She hadn't been expecting him to come, and she was dressed a long Japanese kimono with her hair in a long braid. She was in a sour mood. She was reading as usual and thinking about the emptiness of her life. Why should she be feeling this way when she'd met a man who was a doctor, an agriculturalist, and so much else? Why don't her heart and soul leap at his words? Because, she answered herself, they are only words and she doesn't believe he is what he says he is, although another girl in her position would convince herself that he was telling the truth. She would play the role of lover and then rope him into marrying her, and then whatever would be, would be. Leave those details for later. Every beginning is difficult, but you have to live while you can.

But she wasn't able to fool herself. She felt hatred rising up in her—hatred for him and for herself too—and it caused her pain. She knows she behaves and speaks in a way that just puts more and more stones blocking the path toward living her life.

She wasn't expecting his sudden knock on the door and it gave her a fright. When she saw him he seemed fresh and vivacious, like he'd just come from a shave and a stroll. He clasped her hands, looked her over, and remarked, "This is exactly how I hoped I'd find you! You're stunning! Just as I saw you in a dream. What a splendid kimono you're wearing. You only need a few flowers in your hair." He grabbed a few flowers from the table and stuck them in her hair. "Geisha, my geisha!"

He caught her looking at the huge windows in the front-room door, through which she could see shadows.

"What's that?" he asked.

"Windows like that are in fashion."

"You could hang a curtain over it from your room. Hang a thick curtain from ceiling to floor," he said, pulling her toward him for a kiss. She gently pushed him away.

"Don't be so cruel to me, especially today. It's the day I was born, and how can you be so cruel to a baby? Don't you have a heart? Do you have any pity? You should be gentle with me," he said, taking her hand and placing it on his face. She smiled. He was cheered by this and cooed, thinking she was asking for more of the baby talk. He took off his jacket and hung it on the back of a chair. She tore herself from him and cried, "Do you want someone to see us?"

Annoyed, he responded, "Let them look in and see. There's nothing to see here."

"But what if something happens?"

"Nothing will."

They looked at each other like brooding hens. "Go away," she urged, showing him the door. He settled in more comfortably and started snacking on his raisins.

"Go away."

"Like fun I will!" he teased. They heard whispers from the other side of the door.

"Alright!" she hissed, and bit her lips as she stood by the window looking out to the street. For a while neither of them said anything. He stood up and paced impatiently. She was happy to see this. She thought to herself, "Now he'll do the same thing he's done every evening he's been here. After he gets his 'exercise,' he'll glare at me in exasperation and leave."

"Goodbye!" he said and the shadows behind the door seemed to move a little.

"Goodbye!" she answered him, already feeling less angry, and smiled sweetly, promising herself that once he'd left she'd let herself laugh out loud at him. He strode toward the door, opened it, stomped away a few steps, and then turned around, came back, and slammed the door closed with himself inside. He turned down the lights.

Before she knew what he was doing he grabbed her and held her in his arms, held her so tight he was choking her, and kissed her so hard she felt he might smash her to pieces. She thrust herself against him, biting him and pounding him with her fists and then escaping his grasp stood by the window angrily in bitter silence.

"You'll fall out!"

"Shut up."

In the front room a window opened. She could tell that her landlords were checking to see if he had left yet.

He grabbed her again but this time instead of fighting him as she had before, she calmly requested, "Let me go for a moment."

"Why?"

"I have to go."

"Alright."

When she was on the other side of the door she said, "I'm finished," and hid in the dark hall. He went to look for her with feigned indifference. He saw something moving on the stairs. It was she. He crept after her as quiet as a thief and hurriedly stretched his arms out to grab her. A frightened cat darted in front of him. Not knowing where to run it blundered under his feet and he stumbled, trying not to step on it. He stepped on his own untied shoelaces and slid down to the first step, grasping for something that would keep him from falling. He rolled down the whole flight of stairs.

Glossary

Unless otherwise noted, these terms come from Yiddish.

Aferist: Swindler, racketeer.

Afn pripetshik: In the hearth, the title of a popular Yiddish song by M. M. Warshawsky.

Akh du sheyne meydele: Oh, you pretty girl, the title of a popular Yiddish folk song.

A nekhtiker tog: Nonsense! (literally "[you should have] a day dark as night!").

Backwards Hall: An ironic reference to the Forward Building at 175 East Broadway, the home of the Yiddish newspaper *Forverts* (a competitor of *Di varhayt*, the publisher of Karpilove's *Diary*), where political lectures were often held.

Barukh shepatarni: The blessing a father traditionally recites when his son becomes a bar mitzvah, thanking God for allowing his son to reach the age of adulthood and releasing the father from responsibility for actions committed by his son, now an independent adult.

Basta: That's enough, stop! Borrowed from Italian, it was used popularly as slang in Polish and in English.

Billiardnye: Billiard hall (Russian).

Bobe: Grandmother.

Buyan: Gangster, lout, loafer (Russian).

Desiat'ia liubila, deviat' razliubila: Russian song lyric ("I loved ten men and fell out of love with nine of them") from the Russian folk song *Vse govoriat chto ia vetrena byvaiu* ("Everyone Says I Can Be Flighty").

Dieses: That (German).

Ehrlich: Honorable, genteel (German).

Es ist wahr: That's true (German).

Frechheit: Effrontery, brashness (German).

Gan eydn: Garden of Eden, Heaven.

Gehenem: Hell.

Geld: Money (German).

Glücklich: Happy (German).

Golem: In Jewish folklore, an animated anthropomorphic being magically created from inanimate clay or mud.

Goles: Exile, a condition in Jewish history and theology of being uprooted from homeland and thrust into uncertain times.

Got fun Avrom: A prayer in Yiddish recited by women on Saturday night as the Sabbath ends, separating the Sabbath from the week.

Goyish: Non-Jewish, alien.

Gymnasium: Secular high school (German).

Hamavdil: (literally: He who makes a distinction) a passage sung as part of the *havdole* ceremony. The *Got fun Avrom* prayer, related to *havdole*, is an extended Yiddish reflection of the *hamavdil*. According to Jewish mystical traditions, during *shabes*, souls are elevated to experience a taste of *gan eyden*, and by heralding the end of *shabes*, the *hamavdil* also marks the return of souls to earthly matters.

Havdole: A Jewish ritual ceremony marking the end of the Sabbath.

Holodriges: Ragamuffins, paupers.

Ishkabibble: An American slang term meaning "Why should I worry?" popularized in the 1913 novelty song of the same name by George W. Meyer and Sam Lewis. In 1915 the phrase appeared in Harry Hershfield's cartoon strip *Abie the Agent* and it was also circulated in popular postcards; the expression is said to have roots in the Yiddish phrase "*nisht gefidlt.*"

Karlik: Dwarf.

Kest: In a traditional East European Jewish marriage arrangement, the obligation of the bride or groom's parents to support the new couple for a specified period.

Khazones: Liturgical, cantorial music.

Khniak: Clumsy, incompetent person.

Khupe: Wedding canopy.

King David: Significant Biblical figure. In the passage in which he appears in Karpilove's narrative, C. references a moment in 1 Kings 1 in which, in his old age, King David is warmed in his bed by a young woman.

Kosher: Suitable according to Jewish ritual law (often but not exclusively applied to food).

Kruzhok: An often revolutionary-oriented reading circle common among the Russian intelligentsia (Russian).

Lapatsanes: Scoundrels, hooligans.

Liebes Fräulein: Dear lady (German).

Litvashke: A woman from the territory of historical (or "greater") Lithuania, which includes large swaths of northeastern Poland, northern and western Belarus, Minsk, Slutsk, Pinks, Brisk, Shklov, Mogilev, Gomel, and Vitebsk, southern Latvia, and northeastern Prussia. In Yiddish culture certain distinctive characteristics tend to be attributed to Litvaks—they are portrayed as cold, rational, cerebral, and skeptical, the polar opposite of Galitsianers (Galician Jews). Litvaks also are identifiable through a distinctive dialect with divergent vowel pronunciations. Karpilove, born outside of Minsk, would have fallen into this category.

Lomir zikh iberbetn: Let's make up, the title of a popular Yiddish folk song.

Lustreise: Honeymoon (German).

Mädchen: Girl or young woman (German).

Mishteyns gezogt: In a manner of speaking, so-called.

Mitzve: Religious obligation or meritorious deed.

Nicht wahr?: Isn't that so? (German).

Nishkoshe: Never mind.

Nudnik: Pest, irritating person, bore.

Obrazovanie: Education (Russian).

Paklanitsa: Devotée (Russian).

Povedenie: Behavior, conduct (Russian).

Prost: Simple, crude.

Razocharovaniye: Disappointment (Russian).

Samovar: A heated metal container traditionally used to heat and boil water for tea (Russian).

Schlemiel: Stupid, awkward person.

Shabes night: Saturday night, the evening that the Sabbath ends.

Shadkhn: A marriage broker, matchmaker.

Shadkhones: The system or process of arranging marriages, matchmaking.

Sheva brokhes: The seven blessings traditionally recited for a bride and groom at a Jewish wedding.

Shidukh: A marriage match, most often referring to an arranged marriage (plural: *shidukhim*).

Shliumper: Unkempt person, slob, loser.

Sholem Aleichem's "Advice": Reference to the Yiddish writer Sholem Aleichem's monologue *An eytse.*

Sholem aleykhem: A traditional song sung by Jews on Friday night, on the Sabbath eve, upon returning home from synagogue prayer. It welcomes the angels who accompany a person home on the eve of the Sabbath.

Shul: Synagogue, house of prayer.

Shundroman: Serialized popular fiction, often melodramatic.

Simkhes toyre: A Jewish holiday that celebrates finishing the annual cycle of public Torah readings and inaugurating a new cycle.

Skatina: Literally a cow, used pejoratively to mean scoundrel, bastard (Russian).

Strastna: Passionate (Russian).

Takeh: Truly, really, indeed (Yiddish, of Slavic origin).

Tenement House Act: One of the reforms of the Progressive Era, the New York State Tenement House Act of 1901 banned the construction of dark, poorly ventilated tenement buildings in the State of New York. The legislation included penalties for prostitution in tenement houses (see introduction).

Teygekhts: Also known as *kugel*, potato casserole.

The Tombs: The colloquial name for City Prison, built in 1902. It had an eight-story façade with conical towers along Centre Street, bounded by Centre Street, White Street, Elm Street (today's Lafayette), and Leonard Street. It was replaced in 1941 by the Manhattan House of Detention (also colloquially known as the Tombs).

Tot: Death (German).

Toyt: Death.

Toyre: A scroll containing the first five books of the Hebrew Scriptures.

Um Gottes willen!: For God's sake! (German).

Vielleicht: Perhaps (German).

Vortrefliches: Sublime, superb (German).

Where Are My Children?: A 1916 silent film, directed by Philips Smalley and Lois Weber (see introduction).

White slave trader: The term "white slavery" was used in the beginning of the twentieth century to refer to forced prostitution and sexual slavery.

Wunderbar: Wonderful (German).

Yakhnes: Informally, female meddlers or busybodies.

Yener velt: The hereafter.

Yenta: Gossip, busybody.

Yidene: Older Jewish woman, often used pejoratively.

Yikhes: Pedigree, prestigious lineage, or marriage-based family connections based on scholarly merit, wealth, or political status.

Yold: Fool, sucker.

Zeyde: Grandfather.

Zhargon: Jargon; a derogatory term for Yiddish.

Miriam Karpilove (1888–1956) was a prolific author of Yiddish prose and one of a very small number of women who made their living as Yiddish writers. Born in a small town outside of Minsk, she immigrated to the United States in 1905 and resided in New York City and in Bridgeport, Connecticut. Her work, including dramas, criticism, sketches, short stories, novellas, and feuilletons, appeared in many Yiddish periodicals, and she was particularly known for her serialized novels.

Jessica Kirzane is an assistant instruction professor in Yiddish at the University of Chicago and the editor in chief of *In geveb: A Journal of Yiddish Studies*. She was a 2017 Translation Fellow at the Yiddish Book Center.

Select titles in Judaic Traditions in Literature, Music, and Art

Classic Yiddish Stories of S. Y. Abramovitsh, Sholem Aleichem, and I. L. Peretz
Ken Frieden, ed. and trans.; Ted Gorelick and Michael Wex, trans.

The Odyssey of an Apple Thief
Moishe Rozenbaumas; Isabelle Rozenbaumas, ed.; Jonathan Layton, trans.

Paul Celan: The Romanian Dimension
Petre Solomon; Emanuela Tegla, trans.

The People of Godlbozhits
Leyb Rashkin; Jordan Finkin, trans.

Petty Business
Yirmi Pinkus; Evan Fallenberg and Yardenne Greenspan, trans.

Pioneers: The First Breach
S. An-sky; Rose Waldman, trans.

Red Shoes for Rachel: Three Novellas
Boris Sandler; Barnett Zumoff, trans.

Vilna My Vilna: Stories by Abraham Karpinowitz
Helen Mintz, trans.

For a full list of titles in this series, visit:
https://press.syr.edu/supressbook-series
/judaic-traditions-in-literature-music-and-art/.

2/1/22

1